Déjeuner au
Rat-Mort

(Luncheon at the Dead Rat)

Byron Grush

Published in the United States by Broadhorn Publishing, Delavan, WI

ISBN-10: 0-9985454-2-2
ISBN-13: 978-0-9985454-2-4

At the Café Gerbois by Édouard Manet, 1869, National Gallery of Art

Author's Preface

This is a work of fiction and history married in fact and imagination, based in part on *Dame Impétueux, la Mémoire de Émilie-Claire Lebeau-Richelieu*, in the English translation, published by Charles W. Karr & Co., Chicago, 1897, and upon Mm. Lebeau-Richelieu's journals and notebooks, which surfaced only recently…but that is another story for another time. I have endeavored to piece together a believable narrative about this impetuous lady.

Some of what is presented in the memoir is suspect: for instance, her friendships with Alfred Jarry *and* Charles Baudelaire, two important figures who later influenced the Surrealist literary movement. Like odd bookends, they were unique icons of different eras. And her account of posing for the sculptor, Auguste Rodin, and falling from the model platform in a faint, seems far-fetched. The journals are less guarded with respect to her true emotional responses and, to my interest and fascination with Paris in the nineteenth century, more attune to the flavor of the environment and daily life.

Émilie-Claire had been born in 1839 in France but immigrated with her parents to New Orleans when she was four. Her memories of early childhood in France seem seeped in fantasy and longing, and her rendition of the family's situation in the Crescent City of the Deep South of the United States is incomplete, dwelling on the niceties of what she must have thought a privileged existence. Records of the time in New Orleans reveal the following:

They lived in a modest house on Dauphine Street in the Old French Quarter. Henri Robert Lebeau was not a wealthy man, but he managed to send his only daughter to a private school. Dance and music lessons and tutoring in French grammar further augmented Émilie-Claire's education. The Lebeaus spoke both French and English at home. Lebeau invested heavily in cotton, buying the raw product from plantations in Mississippi and shipping it to England, where cotton had become an important import. Monsieur Lebeau made a substantial fortune in cotton and later in tobacco.

In 1848 the family moved to Prytania Street in nearby Lafayette. The City of Lafayette would be incorporated into the City of New Orleans four years later and eventually become known as the

"Garden District." Filled with the Greek Revival mansions of the well-to-do, the area was fertile ground for an idyllic childhood. As she writes in her memoir, her home seemed a castle, and she, a princess. But in 1853 a yellow-fever epidemic decimated New Orleans, killing over 11,000 people, including her mother, her father, and her only sibling, a younger brother named Luc.

Émilie-Claire was sent to live with her aunt and uncle in Cincinnati. Her inheritance, which was considerable after the sale of the house in New Orleans and some bonds left to her by her father, came under the control of her uncle, Alfred Abel, who was her mother's half-brother and now her only relative in America. Abel, an unstable and devious man, soon caught gold fever and rushed to the Sacramento Valley of California, leaving behind his wife, Marie, and fifteen year-old Émilie-Claire. He took with him money he had stolen from the girl's trust fund.

Alfred Abel later wrote Marie that he was broke—an unscrupulous miner had sold him a played-out claim. More than likely he had gambled his money away. He needed more cash. Marie, suspicious, decided to travel to California bringing Émilie-Claire with her. They traveled first by steamboat to St. Louis, then by train and coach, reaching Sacramento in November of 1855. Émilie-Claire was sixteen. Alfred Abel was nowhere to be found. Émilie-Claire was fond of her aunt, but the woman proved to be out of sorts in the rough and tumble environment of the Gold Rush West. Émilie-Claire:

"With no man and no money and no prospects—well, there was no role model for me there. I broke loose for the first time in my life. I fled to San Francisco. As the French say, 'Ce que femme veut, Dieu le veut.' There were men, of course. Many who would have treated me well—given me anything I wanted. But I found more comfort in the company of other women…"

Here we find a partial insight into the impetuous lady's development intellectually, emotionally and romantically. She obviously was savvy, worldly wise and independent at a time when few women desired to be more than wives and mothers. Émilie-Claire:

"…the 'gentle sex' as they call us, can be as hard-boiled about life as any man. They advance their own cause without compromise or regret. Ils n'ont pas besoin de l'homme! They have no need for men!

And they are compassionate—they have an understanding of each other's needs."

Émilie-Claire's distrust of men is understandable. Her memoir outlines several episodes of encounters with men of questionable character: the "dastardly Robert Delany" who took her innocence and left her alone on the Barbary Coast, the "handsome but devious Eli Wilson" who set her up in a small apartment to keep her existence a secret from his wife, and others.

Yet we know she adopted a young boy she had rescued during a voyage around the horn from San Francisco to New Orleans in 1860 as she returned to that city to claim her inheritance. Émilie-Claire:

"His name was Teodor. He was born in Haiti. That country had a rebellion of its slave population in 1804! His people had been free for half a century, but eight years ago when he was a small child, pirates captured him along with many others and he was sold at the slave market in Rio de Janeiro. He worked on a sugar plantation until a Cuban bought him and the others."

The story of how Émilie-Claire and Teodor, who she called Teo, were first united is told in the historical novel, *Once Upon A Gold Rush*. We need not go into the details here. She traveled with the boy to France shortly thereafter. Another companion who accompanied her and Teo to Europe, Phoebe Stapleton, figured in a shipboard drama: on that trip around the horn there was a death—perhaps a murder. Her story and her connection to Émilie-Claire are related in that same novel about the gold rush era in America. Phoebe was a shy girl, an only child, the then eighteen year-old daughter of the Reverend Joshua Billings, a widower, who had brought his congregation, and Phoebe, overland by wagon from Massachusetts. She had married Willard Stapleton in Nevada City but the marriage was not a happy one.

The voyage of Mm. Lebeau and the others across the Atlantic was uneventful according to the memoir. We pick up the story of Émilie-Claire Lebeau shortly after she and her companions arrived in Paris at the beginning of that decade which would see an end to the decadence of the Second Empire and the reign of Napoleon III, a terrible war, a rebellion, and the rechristening of Paris by blood.

1

Le Café Tortoni de Paris

Mademoiselle Émilie-Claire Lebeau was seated at a small round table on the sidewalk in front of the Café Tortoni. On the table in front of her was a glass of claret, a notebook bound in green leather and a fountain pen. The blue and white striped awning above was worn and ripped in two places. It harkened back to the era of the café's greater popularity and fame.

Now Baron Georges-Eugène Haussmann's vast redesign of the city threatened the Boulevard des Italiens and its institutions. Café Tortoni, Café Riche, Café Anglais, Café de Paris, La Maison Dorée, and others might become only memories for the artists and writers who frequented them. The number of morning coffee seekers was dwindling and the evening throng of theater-goers stopping for M. Tortoni's famous ice cream desserts was considerably less intense. The afternoon, however, still saw a café filled with absinthe drinkers, cigar smokers, and card players. Ladies in crinolines preferred the outdoor tables, away from the smoke.

Thus Émilie-Claire sat pondering the casual drift of people in the street, the carriages of the wealthy, the wagons of the vendors, the strutting, smartly dressed waiters balancing trays on one raised hand while delivering late lunch morsels from La Maison Dorée to cloistered stock brokers in nearby offices, the au pairs pushing perambulators, their charges peeking from pink or blue blankets. She opened the notebook and unscrewed the cap from the pen. She turned through pages emblazoned with her own elegant cursive until she found the next blank page. She touched nib to paper, a dot of purple ink emerged. She wrote:

May 15, 1862

    Waiting patiently for M. Delamain's shipment of the final volumes of M. Hugo's Les Misérables to arrive at his bookstore. Today is to be the day! I was so taken with the character of Cosette. I hope her wretched life will be redeemed, that she will grow to be the beautiful woman she has vowed to be and find the love of her life. But I am such a hopeless romantic! Didn't the beautiful Esmeralda die at the end of that previous tome about the hunchback? Perhaps Hugo's exile was warranted…but now, even with the general amnesty, he still refuses to return to France. Curious.

    Only two years since we arrived here in Paris yet it seems like decades. That brave new country from which I expatriated—(how can I be an expatriate…I was born <u>here</u>!)—from which we sailed away so swiftly, leaving a lifetime of bittersweet memories behind—it is at war with itself! Brother fights brother in bloody and pointless battles that rip apart a nation founded upon liberty. The French have also wrestled with those ideas: liberté, égalité, fraternité. But now they…we…have little interest in the American Civil War. We send soldiers to Mexico instead!

    I am so glad I brought Teo with me to France. No one knows what the outcome of that war will be. Certainly the Southern States will never give up their belief in white supremacy. The boy, his dark skin…so beautiful but so much a beacon for hatred…would be at risk. He might be thrown back into the life of slavery he only just escaped. Or worse.

    Someday I may turn these scribbles into a proper mémoire. But I ramble so. And there is always the specter of the blank page which mocks and jeers as if to say, "You are unworthy of my endless possibilities." Better for me to dabble with the trifles of my days on these more forgiving pages. And yet…

The clatter of horses' hooves and the creaking of wheels wanting grease caused Émilie-Claire to look up from her notebook. An impériale omnibus was passing, unusual for the Boulevard des Italiens as this was not an official route of the Compagnie Impériale des voitures de Paris. The Parisian transport was a double-decker bus drawn by two dappled grey horses. There was seating on the open upper deck, restricted to men only, as ladies could catch their crinolines climbing the steep stairs and potential falls were feared. The driver was perched on a small seat on top, silver buttons shining against his dark blue uniform, a black straw hat at a rakish angle on his head. Several of the gentlemen on the top deck held umbrellas against the sun.

"Isn't that the tram for Boulevard Haussmann?" someone at another table asked. Another spoke, answering: "Something's happened to make them reroute that omnibus." Then opinions arose all over the café's sidewalk seating area: "A fire!" "A parade!" "A labor strike!" "The driver is lost!" "The horses have rebelled!" "Someone important is being given a special ride home. Your wife, Marcel?" "The Emperor's mistress?" "The Empress's lover!"

In fact, the omnibus route along the Boulevard des Italiens had been added that very day in anticipation of the need for transport to the new opera house which was being constructed at its terminus. The irony of this hurried addition was that only recently had the corner stone of the Opéra Garnier been placed—it would not be finished until 1875.

At this juncture, Émilie-Claire lost interest in the musing of the patrons of the crowded café. She turned her attention back to her writing. Just as her nib touched the page a bit of purple ink leaked from the fountain pen, staining her white gloves. "Merde!" she said loudly.

"Oh, that's a shame," said a man: a strange man who hovered, or at least that was her estimate of the situation. "Do you think that will wash out?" he asked.

He seemed to her to be a bit of a flâneur, a street-stroller masquerading as a gentleman, as over confident as he was over dressed. Would he claim to be a stock merchant, an art dealer, a publisher of renown? His smile was smirk, he had pose, not poise. He carried his gloves as if to say, "I do not need to wear them, but as you see, I own one of the finest pair." She was about to turn her glance away from him when she realized suddenly that the man had spoken to her in English. And not British English. He was Américain!

"You're an American. How did you know to speak to me in English?" she asked, forgetting her intention to totally ignore this brazen man.

"My French is not yet so very good. I instinctively start out a conversation in English because, you know, many Parisians speak it."

"But will not speak it if they do not speak it well. They are too proud. And you…you have an accent of somewhere in the South, do you not? Lousiana? Alabama? I can't quite place it."

"Tennessee, Ma'am. Born and reared in Chattanooga."

"And why aren't you at home, fighting in your civil war to protect your right to own slaves?" Émilie-Claire squinted her eyes as she delivered this would-be insult.

"I am not one to sacrifice for the ideals…and the enrichment…of the wealthy few as many are wont to do. The army of Lee is made up of poor men who have never owned a slave. They are fools. And I have more to offer the world than to become cannon fodder."

"You interest me, Sir. And how will you contribute to the betterment of the world, may I ask?"

"I am an artist. I have come to Paris to apply for the École des Beaux-Arts. I hope to study with the great Alexandre Cabanel who I learned has been asked to join the faculty there."

"Ah," said Émilie-Claire, "the favorite portrait painter of Napoleon III. His style is that of l'art pompier of the academy. This is how you wish to paint? All idealism and classicism?"

Ignoring her pointed comment: "You must think me rude and uncivilized! I have failed to introduce myself. My name is Jeffrey Dolan Flaherty…the Third. May I have the honor of knowing your name?"

"I am Émilie-Claire Lebeau…the First. And yes, I do think you are somewhat rude. But you are forgiven."

"May I join you at your table? Perhaps order some more refreshments?"

"I must be off to the Librairie Delamain on Rue Saint Honoré to pick up a book I have on order."

"But that is many blocks from here. May I escort you? I will hail a carriage."

This man, he was all pomp and no circumstance. Not established as an artist…not even applied to the academy yet. He was arrogant, audacious, presumptuous, and probably something of a fool. She noticed the ragged cuffs of his trousers and the stain on his cravat which spoke of better days and little money for cleaning and repair of what was probably his only suit and tie. She should walk away from him now before he was encouraged to pursue her.

Then she had a thought: she could afford the carriage but perhaps he could not. "I've already a carriage on order," she told him. "Wait here while I check with the head waiter." She disappeared into the café, asked the head waiter to please order a carriage for her, then leisurely returned to the table where sat the artless poseur, Jeffrey Dolan Flaherty…the Third.

"It has been delayed by the closing of some avenues but it will be here shortly. If you still wish to escort me…"

"The honor, lovely lady, would be all mine."

She thought she may have noticed a faint blush to his checks.

The bookstore was a labyrinth of dusty shelves which stretched from floor to ceiling. Patrons explored the narrow caverns, glancing at gilded bindings on books far older than the Hôtel du Louvre which housed the Librairie Delamain. M. Delamain ushered Émilie-Claire through a section of shelving with more modern tomes. He pointed out works by Honoré de Balzac, translations of stories by Edgar Allen Poe and of *Confessions of an English Opium Eater* by Thomas De Quincey—these translations were by Charles Baudelaire. Recently published works by Jules Verne sat next to copies of Gustave Flaubert's scandalous *Madame Bovary*. On display were the 1861 editions of Baudelaire's *Les Fleurs du mal*, the one without the six suppressed poems.

"If you are interested," Delamain told Émilie-Claire, "I have original copies of *Les Fleurs du mal* directly received from Auguste Malassis, the publisher in 1857. We don't put them on display, of course."

"Merci, but I have my own personalized copy of that."

"You've met Baudelaire?"

"When I first got to Paris I met him at a salon. We had a few drinks and talked several times after that. He is a most extraordinary man. A genius, I think. But all that is a story for another time"

"As you wish. Ah…" Delamain reached for a thick volume bound in blue leather. "Here is volume three of *Les Misérables* which you ordered. I will be receiving volumes four and five in a few days. This should hold you until then."

"I am an avid reader, Monsieur Delamain. We shall see."

Jeffrey Flaherty had waited outside while Émilie-Claire fetched her book. Now he strolled absent-mindedly down the Rue de Rivoli toward Musée du Louvre, the Quai des Tuileries, and the River Seine. Eventually he found himself standing on the Pont des Arts, staring at the Île de la Cité where the Seine divided into separate channels. The afternoon was so delightful with the scent of spring in the moist air, that he had forgotten his charge of galanterie…and the woman. When he returned to the street where he had left the carriage waiting, it was gone. And she was gone. He had neglected to inquire for her address. The day was now a ruine colossale!

He returned to the Café Tortoni the next day to look for her but she was not there. Nor was she present the following day nor the next. He asked around if anyone knew her, knew where to find her. No one seemed to know anything about her. Finally, he resigned himself to the fact that theirs had been one of those chance meetings which occur once and only once…especially in Paris. He had work to do: he needed to ready his portfolio for the interview at the École des Beaux-Arts. Perhaps, he thought, I might render a likeness of her from memory. Those dark eyes, the upturned nose, the hair that fell in silken strands across her face as she tossed her head. Was he that good of an artist? Probably not.

At 98 Rue de la Victoire, where the narrow street formed an angular junction with the Rue Joubert, stood a neoclassical townhouse designed by the famous architect, François-Joseph Bélanger. Émilie-Claire occupied the third floor apartment with its three sets of French windows overlooking the street. Her center window was framed by an arch and flanked by two caryatids: classical Greek sculptures of women acting as pillars to support the arch. She loved to swing wide the tall double windows and stand at the narrow balcony between the caryatids to study their draped figures. The folds of cloth might be carved from stone, but in them she could fantasize the cascading of waterfalls or the waving manes of wild horses—or the folds of flesh found in secret places. Ladies of her era, of course, dressed in layers of fabric which in no way resembled the garb of these classical maidens. Except possibly the ladies of the Folies Bergére—although that would not be opened until the end of the decade.

The architect, François-Joseph Bélanger, had died in 1818. He had been sent to prison at Saint-Lazare during the French Revolution but afterward managed to build many hôtels particuliers for aristocratic Parisians and to design buildings in the Paris Bourse including the cupola of the Halle au blé, one of the first uses of iron and glass to create large interior spaces.,

Further up the Rue de la Victoire was the Grand Synagogue of Paris, a gargantuan building that dominated the area. Close by was the Hôtel Beauharnais, where Napoleon Bonaparte, as First Consul of France, orchestrated the famous coup d'état of 18 Brumaire which had brought him to power. The street exhaled the bitter-sweet perfume of history. It hadn't been called Victoire until Napoleon was victorious in Italy in 1797; at first it had the dubious name of Rue Chantereine after the singing frogs that dwelt in the then swampy quarter.

Émilie-Claire shared the apartment with her companion, Phoebe Stapleton, and her ward, the Haitian boy Teodor Presume, whom she called Teo. Teo was off to school these days. Émilie-Claire had originally thought to arrange for a tutor for the boy but decided at last that the social aspects of a boarding school would benefit him more than a concentration on works of classicism, geometry…and refined arrogance?…taught diligently by some spectacled popinjay of a tutor. Would his race be an obstacle in an environment of immature children from a spectrum of backgrounds? Possibly. But the challenge to overcome the prejudice of others…the opportunity to rise above ignorance and intolerance…this might provide a strengthening of character for Teo that could not evolve in the confines of the tutorial chamber. He would be made stronger…if it didn't kill him.

Her relationship with Phoebe Stapleton was complicated. She had taken Phoebe under her wing during a sea voyage around the horn. Phoebe's husband had been a domineering brute; Émilie-Claire encouraged and even enabled Phoebe's affair with another male passenger—a man who was killed in an accident which looked suspiciously not like an accident. Whether or not Phoebe's husband had murdered her lover, it was obvious that Phoebe needed to leave him.

Émilie-Claire had at first shocked, then intrigued Phoebe with stories of her early life in San Francisco and with her philosophy of the natural and necessary independence of women—in all things. Phoebe became drawn to the free-spirited and out-spoken Émilie-Claire. Never before had she felt quite so close to another woman. It didn't seem unnatural…only joyous.

But Émilie-Claire had not pursued an affair of the heart or of the body. She identified with Phoebe in terms of her youth, her sheltered life as the daughter of a clergyman, her mistreatment at the hands of a self-centered man…that was all. Her empathy and her regard for Phoebe led her to suggest they travel together to Paris, where Phoebe's liberation might be completed. Now she again encouraged Phoebe to seek out male companionship, but to be guarded in her affairs. Phoebe was troubled by the apparent rejection and what seemed to be a denial of passion truly felt by herself…and she suspected by Émilie-Claire…but unfulfilled in deed.

The two young women took many a stroll along the Seine, sat on the Point of the Île de la Cité, climbed the many steep stairs of Montmarte, visited the Parc Monceau, always with Émilie-Claire trying to assure Phoebe of her deep respect and, yes, even her love. But Phoebe was hurt and angry and spiteful. She decided to follow Émilie-Claire's advice and find a man…or many men. This, not to satisfy her sexual urges, but to inflict punishment upon Émilie-Claire.

When Émilie-Claire returned to the apartment on Rue de la Victoire she found Phoebe was absent. Gone too were her clothes. She had left only a short note:

Dearest Em:

It is with some sadness that I now leave you for a new adventure. And it is not without the profoundest gratitude I have for all that you have done for me. You know how I feel. But I have met someone…a man. His name is François Arnaud Gardinier and besides being outrageously handsome, he is wealthy. He has an estate in Neuilly-sur-Seine and I am going to live there. He has invited me to act as au pair for his two young children, a boy of 8 and a girl of 10. His poor wife is an invalid and is bed-ridden. I know what you are probably thinking…I am naïve and will become his paramour. Indeed, that would not be so terrible. But, yes, I remember your warnings about men. I will not give him my heart…although it may be that I will steal his! Kiss Teo goodbye for me. I will keep in touch.

Yours faithfully,
Phoebe

Émilie-Claire sank heavily into the over-stuffed cushions of the divan which was positioned facing the windows. Phoebe's leaving so suddenly jolted her, created an ache which surprised her. She had encouraged the woman to seek out just such an adventure…and just such a man…but this! She felt alone, empty, purposeless. She stared out at the mansard roof across the street. There was a cat sitting in a window on at the top of the building. Staring at her. The cat abruptly backed away just as a knock sounded at her own door. Émilie-Claire jumped.

It was only a messenger with a letter. She saw the return address on the light blue envelope and a premonition of something ominous took hold of her. It was from Madame Noëlle Boucher's boarding school, where Teo was studying. Quickly she ripped open the letter. She read:

There has been an incident involving your ward, Teodor Presume. It is imperative you arrive here without delay to collect him.

2

Château des Ternes

Outside of Paris, in a hilly wooded area of countryside, the Abbey of Saint Denis established a farm and hunting estate. The year was 1320. This farm changed hands in 1356, and in 1540 passed yet again to a new owner, this time one Pierre Habert, a writer and the valet of Henry III. Habert constructed a castle complete with turrets and drawbridge, acquired adjacent property, and added fields and orchards. The castle was bought in 1715 by an advisor to King Louis XIV, Mirey Pomponne, who removed the moat and drawbridge and created a sumptuous park with an ornate dovecote and a greenhouse filled with orange trees. By then, the hamlet had acquired five houses and came to be known as Ternes.

More alterations took place after 1778, when the property came under the ownership of an architect and speculator with the somewhat excessive name of Charles-Nicolas Rolland Samson-Nicolas Lenoir. He divided the estate into four parcels, erecting a wall. He then opened a passageway through the main building, creating a lane which he called Rue de l'Arcade. This fragmentation of the Château gave it an unseemly character; pierced and wounded, yet still a proud edifice.

In 1802, Lenoir experienced financial declines which forced him to sell off the property. The real estate speculator, Edmond Mathias Gardinier, acquired Château Ternes for a modest sum. Edmond Gardinier was the grandfather of the François Arnaud Gardinier who will be the subject of our story. Edmond never lived at the Château and had purchased it for a quick turn around and handsome profit.

But Paris proper was the new destination for the upper classes, not the suburbs. Although Ternes was on the Seine and close enough to Paris for a buggy ride, Edmond failed to find a buyer. When he passed on, his son, Herbert, inherited the castle and its lands, gardens, orchards and tenants. And its problems.

It looked for a time as if the castle would fall into disrepair, that it might even suffer the fate of the nearby Château de Neuilly which had been burned and looted during the Revolution of 1848. Herbert Gardinier held on to it however, making small improvements whenever his financial status allowed it, for he had an eye to selling it for a great deal of money. Herbert Gardinier was privy to a well-kept secret plan to extend and widen the streets and avenues of Paris. Those holding real estate along those streets to be widened stood to gain an excellent profit.

By 1852, Napoleon III had confiscated the ruined Château de Neuilly, divided it into parcels and created wide boulevards and streets there. Over 700 lots were auctioned off. But Herbert Gardinier did not find that the new development of the former Port Neuilly was reaching close enough to Ternes to suggest that Château des Ternes would be gobbled up in the immediate future. He began to buy properties in central Paris, along those routes he had learned were to be gutted and broadened to become main arteries of the city. His strategy paid off. His fortune tripled, then tripled again.

He had brought his son, François, into the real estate business with him. François had married Solange Florianne Desrosiers, the daughter of a wealthy official in the new government, Jacques Jérémie Desrosiers. Desrosiers, in fact, had been a principle investor and conspirator in Herbert Gardinier's sometimes unethical business dealings, and had used his position to learn the names of the doomed streets in Baron Haussmann's plan to slice up older neighborhoods in the name of progress…and commerce. He was also in a position to approve building contracts.

For his own part, François Arnaud Gardinier had contributed an needed element to his father's business. He was the contact between the Gardiniers and the contractors who would seek work in demolition or road building. For a kickback, François would assure those contractors that their bids would be accepted; Jacques Desrosiers would see to that. It was a nice, cozy, elite, and highly unethical game they played. And it was making them rich.

By 1860, the city of Paris began annexing neighboring suburbs. Ternes was absorbed into Neuilly-sur-Seine and the area became part of the 17th arrondissement. François Arnaud Gardinier had moved into the Château des Ternes with his wife, Solange, and their two young children, Geoffroy and Jeanne-Alice. What should have been an idyllic existence in the glorious countryside turned tragic.

Solange had been riding in the Parc du Bois one afternoon when her horse was spooked by the sudden appearance of a stag bounding from the woods along the bridle path. The horse bolted in a furious gallop. Solange was thrown to the ground where she lay unconscious for nearly an hour before another rider came along and found her. Her hip was broken and there was some injury to her spine which the doctors were unable to treat. She had been bedridden since that fateful day.

Solange spent her days and her nights in an antique four-poster in a dim and dusty attic room with a single window which poked out from the mansard roof on the main building. She had memorized every vine and faded blossom on the wall paper and had counted the ceiling tiles so often that she thought she would go mad. Geoffroy and Jeanne-Alice visited the poor woman nearly every afternoon, which kept her spirits up at least for the short duration that the children could stand being in that depressing chamber. François was often in town on business but when he managed to be home at supper time he would bring a tray up to Solange and sit with her while she ate. They discussed hiring someone to look after the children.

Phoebe, following her new plan: the pursuance of gentlemen (in all the right places), desperately wanted to explore the new café that had just opened in the Grand-Hôtel de la Paix, that magnificent edifice which stood on the corner of the Boulevard des Capucines and what would soon be called the Place de l'Opéra. She had spent the exorbitant amount of 2 francs to ride in a four-passenger fiacre, relaxing in its boxy interior of dark blue velvet as it rumbled through the streets of Paris. When she descended from the fiacre in front of the Café de la Paix she was dismayed to find that plaster dust and dirt from the construction site of the nearby Garnier Opéra had closed the sidewalk area of the café.

As a single, unescorted young woman she would not be allowed inside—unless she wished to be taken for a prostitute. She stood aimlessly for several moments considering what to do. It would be depressing to walk back to the Rue de la Victoire where, no doubt, Émilie-Claire would be waiting to interrogate her concerning her ill-fated adventure. "Why the fancy gown, mon chérie?" she would ask. Phoebe had hoped to throw in her friend's face a delicious tale of debauchery and romantic revelry.

Now she turned to begin her retreat but found that a few paces away from her a young man stood, apparently also contemplating the exterior of the Café de la Paix. Or was it herself that commanded his attention? He was fine looking, she decided, and dressed well in double-breasted frock coat, long trousers which covered the tops of his black leather shoes, fresh linen shirt with up-turned collar, striped waistcoat, and a necktie fastened by a jewel which flashed as he stepped forward from shadow to a sunny patch of sidewalk. He was approaching!

He introduced himself as François Arnaud Gardinier. Was she in need of some assistance? It seemed she was disoriented or puzzled or lost. Why no, Monsieur, not at all. He apologized for his impertinence. She smiled demurely. He commented on the mess being made of the streets by the new destruction/construction. The new opera. The new boulevards. But that was progress, wasn't it? Paris would become the center of Europe because of entrepreneurs (like himself). She told him her name. Now that they had been introduced, would the gentleman wish to escort her into the café? It is said to be magnificent! He offered his arm.

This once sheltered and shy clergyman's daughter now boldly flashed her lashes at the handsome François Arnaud Gardinier as he led her into a cavern of opulence. Gilded classical moldings framed recessed ceiling motifs and medallions amid a forest of Corinthian columns. Gas-lit chandeliers cast flames of crimson and gold against etched crystal goblets; tongues of the stuff danced on the silver dinnerware. Chairs and divans were upholstered in red leather and surrounded round tables draped in white linen. A long bar of polished walnut edged in brass ran the length of one section of the interior; large windows on the street side gave a view of the terrace: nearly 40 feet of outdoor seating, sadly filled with dust and dirt: the drifting debris of progress.

François nodded to a person here and a person there as they followed the maître d'hôtel to their table. Phoebe was charmed, elated. She absorbed the ambience of blatant wealth with relish. She also relished the appetizer François ordered to accompany their flutes of champagne: foie gras de canard with a compote de fruits and lightly toasted brioche. He talked nonchalantly of the great futures to be made in real estate. She listened attentively. He mentioned that he knew influential men at the Hôtel de Ville. She nodded and smiled sweetly in a way that suggested her indifference and masked the truth of her enthusiasm for the acquisition of money, no matter how ill might be the gains. He asked to see her again. Tomorrow? The day after. In the afternoon for apéritifs at Café Riche. She hesitated for just the proper amount of time before agreeing.

It was at their third meeting, this also at Café Riche, that François broached the subject of wife, children and the need for an au pair. Would she consider the position? The dame de comptoir had seated them too close to the bar; the Loysel's Patent Hydrostatic Percolator was producing clouds of coffee-scented steam—the great silver-plated urn seemed about to blow its top. Phoebe pleaded to move to a table near the windows. François would have to wait for her answer.

Once they had shuffled across the sawdust covered floor and taken seats at a small round table with a view of the Boulevard des Italiens, Phoebe shook her head and frowned.

"But I have no experience," she complained. "I would not know the first thing about raising children."

"You would be wonderful at it. I've sensed in you a gentleness and an eagerness to please. Besides, the children are of an age when they virtually take care of themselves."

"You wife…is she…?"

"My wife suffered a riding accident which left her partially paralyzed. She cannot leave her bed. I would hope that you could, as well as supervising the children, look in on her from time to time."

Again Phoebe allowed a proper interval to elapse before answering. It would not do to let this man know how dreadfully happy she was made by this turn of events. Her fore finger found her pursed lips, lingered a moment, then descended. She smiled. She answered:

"Let me come to meet the children at the first possible time. We'll let them decide."

"Absurdité! Those rascals have nothing to say about it. You'll accept my offer?"

"Oui."

Geoffroy and Jeanne-Alice were in the orangerie. The trees had suffered years of neglect; it was doubtful there would be many oranges this year. Before her accident, their mother had ordered several dozen exotic plants placed in and around the building. The more hardy of these still thrived: broad green fronds of cyclanthus nuzzled against date palms; purple-veined elephant ear caladium (thriving only indoors) brushed against windows of frosted glass; spiky dracaena and bamboo provided a sharp linear décor while flowering vines of clematis, clumps of hibiscus, begonia, and gloxinia struggled to put forth their delicate blooms. The maiden-hair ferns had died, as had some shrubs that could no longer be identified.

The children played inside the greenhouse. It was a private place of fantasy where they alone were in command. Jeanne-Alice was two years older than her brother. She was wise for a ten year-old, and took no guff nor grief from Geoffroy. Geoffroy had learned from schoolmates of the superiority of the male to the female and therefore felt obligated to act out this role with his sister, but failed miserably at his attempts to be domineering. He therefore acted Sir Galahad to avoid the embarrassment he felt. Still, he entertained the illusion that as soon as he stopped being gallant, she would come to understand his superior status in the family. This was not likely.

The orangerie's floor-to-ceiling windows were arched at the top in imitation of the big bays on the main house. They were frosted, but here and there, since the glass had not been etched but painted, the frosting had worn off so that the children could peek through these apertures to spy out at the long drive when a carriage could be heard scuttling across the pea gravel. This was such a time. Phoebe Stapleton had left a note for Émilie-Claire, packed a steamer trunk with clothes, books, and a few mementos, and dragged the heavy trunk down the stairs to wait for the carriage François was sending. Now this conveyance and its eager occupant plunged through the odd opening that had been punched through the main house, trundled down the path, and stopped right at the edge of the garden.

"Oh look," said Jeanne-Alice as Phoebe climbed from the carriage. "She's very pretty!"

"Who cares!" exclaimed Geoffroy. "Does she know any good stories?"

Phoebe's steamer trunk had been taken to her room on the second floor of the main house. Phoebe lingered in the salon, just off the main entrance, while the housekeeper, Mme. Popelin, fetched the children. She strolled across a large Aubusson rug which nearly filled the room from wall to wall. In its center was a richly woven medallion featuring twisting rose vines; its colors were muted pinks and pale turquoise. Against one wall was a console table in the style…or perhaps it was authentic…of eighteenth century German Rococo, heavily gilded with a violet-veined marble top and hand-carved legs with scrolls at the top and bottom. Sitting on the console table was an elegant Barbedienne bronze of a nude sleeping maiden, perhaps Persephone or Psyche.

A Régence armchair with slim cabriole legs and a caned seat supporting a fringed velvet cushion joined a Bergère chair upholstered in needlepoint (more entangled roses) to flank an appealing Louis XVI chaise longue in walnut with ormolu embellishments depicting florets and bows. Phoebe wished she could stretch out on the long chair but didn't want to appear unladylike. She was fatigued and apprehensive about meeting the children. She felt as if the forest of floral brambles on rug and furniture was threatening to reach out to grab her, wrap her in thorny tendrils, strangle her. Presently Mme. Popelin appeared with Geoffroy and Jeanne-Alice following, but stopping sheepishly at the doorway.

"The Monsieur is in the city and will be back late," said Mme. Popelin. "Here I turn over to you these petits enfants. Jeanne-Alice…Geoffroy…come meet your new au pair, Maîtresse Stapleton."

Jeanne-Alice came boldly forward until she was an arm's length from her new au pair. She curtsied sweetly and said "Bonjour, Mademoiselle Stapleton." Geoffroy, however, hung back, allowing only half of his face to appear around the edge of the door jam, like a gargoyle perched on a cathedral's parapet. Phoebe smiled at him: "Don't be afraid. I won't bite you." Mme. Popelin placed her hands on her hips in the manner of a sailor about to weather a gale.

"Geoffroy! Venez ici…tout de suite!"

"Oh…the boy is obviously shy. Please don't yell at him, Mme. Popelin," said Phoebe.

"Oh, shy is he? He can be comme un éléphant dans un magasin du porcelaine. Têtu comme une mule! He is le vieux renard! He…"

"Assez! He sounds like the entire menagerie! I'm sure he is very sweet. Come here, mon petit homme."

Consider the mind of an eight year-old boy. It considers practicalities only of the moment. The bug that crawls on the new linen table cloth must be squashed. The puppy must be turned loose from its cage, leaving the outer gate open. Sister's curls call out to be dyed crimson with paint from the coloring set. There are no consequences in the moment. No instinctive tendency toward reasoning will lead the way to obvious conclusions. The memory of punishment contributes nothing to deter a purely wild, tantalizingly novel, obliquely irreverent act. The pursuit of amusement trumps logic and deportment.

"Come here, mon petit homme," said Phoebe.

Slowly the boy inched forward, a deviant grin which might be mistaken for a pleasant countenance on his face, his hands hidden behind his back.

"Closer now. Let me see your handsome face."

Closer still with grin widening into a smile came the lad. Phoebe was charmed. She held out her hands waiting to enclose the boy's in a tender grip. Perhaps an embrace would not be too daring. This was a time to instigate a loving relationship with her charges. These first impressions were so important!

Geoffroy brought his hands from behind his back and thrust them forward. In each squirmed a loathsome creature from the garden: in one, a frog, slime-coated skin glistening in the gas light; in the other, a tiny snake…a baby…coiling and uncoiling in a frenzy.

The reaction, however, was not what the boy had expected:

"Oh how sweet…you've brought me a present. But I must choose, mustn't I? Well, let me see…I choose the little frog. I think I'll name him…Geoffroy."

Geoffroy blanched, dropped the frog and the snake and bolted from the room.

3

École des Beaux-Arts

The École Nationale Supérieure des Beaux-Arts, the most prestigious art school in all of France, was situated on the left bank between the Rue Bonaparte and the Quai Malaquais, across the Seine from the Louvre. In its present form it dated back to 1819 when the Academie Royal de Peinture et Scuplture and the Academie Royale d'Architecture had merged. The primary building had been a monastery, the Couvent des Petits-Augustins. It was seized by the government of the revolution of 1789, and then became the Musée des Monument Français before being turned over to the École.

Extensions to the École followed in the early part of the nineteen century. The Batiment des Loges, a dormitory for the students was added. Then came the Palais d'Etudes which contained a library and amphitheater. The Cour Mûrier was constructed with exhibition spaces for the now defunct museum's collection of ancient sculpture and for student work: the Salle Melpoméne and the Salle Foch. The beautifully designed campus with its courtyards and sculptural installations attracted aspiring artists, sculptors and architects from all over France…and from the United States.

The American, Jeffrey Dolan Flaherty…the Third, stood at the open gate. He studied its iron scrollwork and its flanking pedestals supporting the busts of the sculptor Pierre Puget and the painter Nicolas Poussin. Beyond was a deep courtyard leading to the Palais d'Etudes. Standing like a sentinel in front of the building was the free-standing, two-tiered Arc de Gaillon. This had been assembled from elements of the portico and façade of the Château de Gaillon, principally its Genoa Gate, by architect Alexandre Lenoir as an entrance gate to the garden of the Couvent des Petits-Augustin. Now it enticed the visitor toward the Palais d'Etudes.

As he passed through the premiére cour, to his right was the Cour Mûrier, the cloister of the old convent. In its arched bays classical sculptures watched the young artist advance, portfolio under arm. These and other architectural elements were among fragments of the Renaissance castle of Anet, vandalized and demolished during the revolution. These salvaged bits created a rich classical environment in which young art students could absorb tradition. They would contribute little, however, to the artistic evolution that would take place in the years to come.

He passed through the Arc de Gaillon and climbed the steps to the door of the Palace of Studies with its bronze wreaths. It seemed that there was some piece of sculpture from antiquity in every nook which looked down on him critically, as to say, "Who do you think you are?" He stood for a moment, hesitant to take that fundamental step forward into his future, a future fraught with the possibility of failure. Then he recaptured his resolve and entered.

Up a flight of stairs so classical in design he felt himself in a perspective drawing. The second floor gallery also exhibited lines of a forced perspective reminiscent of Italian Renaissance illusion. The ceiling was painted with faux coffers of pretended depth greatly increasing the feeling of a vast space. The floors were of black and white marble. Columns of red-veined marble held up a roof of glass over the enclosed courtyard which the galleries surrounded. A staircase of wooden steps with bronze railings stuck out incongruently at one end of the gallery; an afterthought, a utilitarian addition, a necessary scar within the romanticized, Romanesque environment. The stairway led to the bibliothéque, the student library, where he was to meet the man who would review his portfolio—and determine his fate.

Behind a table stacked with musty volumes the man sat, the look of boredom on his face giving no clue as to possible outcomes. Immaculately dressed with a neatly trimmed bread in which streaks of gray reinforced an aura of authority, Charles Gleyre was 52 years old and had been in his position at the École des Beaux-Arts since 1843. Flaherty knew very little about him. He knew Gleyre had traveled in Egypt and the Middle East, producing drawings of architectural sites. His paintings were influenced by his teacher, Jean-Auguste-Dominique Ingres, and tended toward a similar neo-classical realism and yet exuded a subtle sense of symbolism and allegory.

Jeffrey Flaherty was overwhelmed by the singular profusion of antiquity surrounding him and by the standard of excellence for which the school stood and of which this man was an example. He was beginning to wish he were back in Tennessee, perhaps teaching art in a local grade school to snot-nosed urchins who would never draw another picture—something for which he was qualified. With nervous hands he opened his portfolio and displayed its contents for the Professor. Nothing ventured…

"You're an American, I see. I have a very gifted student now from America…a Mr. James Whistler. I don't suppose you know him? No? Well, someday you will. These studies here…they are not worth showing. Poorly realized and trite. This head of a woman…it has some promise, but I fear you need more practice in observation. I have to tell you now that you are not yet ready for the École des Beaux-Arts. Not yet, but maybe in time you should apply again."

Flaherty was stunned. He thought he had prepared himself for rejection. But this! It had always been his dream to attend this particular school of art. His dream to study under the masters. What now could he possibly do? Live in a ghetto like a bohemian and starve for his art? Return to the United States in failure? But no. This would not do. He would raise an objection. He began to say something but the words hung on his pallet like a rat caught in a trap. His expression must have betrayed him because the Professor then said:

"Do not be so disheartened my son. You merely need, as I have said, more practice. To draw from life. To work along side of others who are also struggling…and learning. And there is hope for you. You do not think so? Let me explain.

"When I came to the Academy I took over the position of Paul Delaroche. You know his work? No? I also acquired his studio which was called La République 5. I have opened there a workshop, a minor academy if you will, for just such as yourself. It is at 69 Rue Vaugirard in the Sixth. If you would wish to come there I would charge you only for a small amount of rent and, of course, for the models."

"Monsieur Gleyre, I don't know what to say. You are saving my life! Of course I will come."

"There are some very promising students who frequent the workshop and take advantage of the models and still life setups I provide. I do very little actual teaching, preferring to allow the personality of the artist to emerge on its own…something difficult to achieve here at the École. You will soon meet the young painters that work within my atelier. You will find them most stimulating."

"Again, Monsieur Gleyre, I can't thank you enough."

"This head of a woman…you must draw her again, but this time from life! You have idealized her too much. And now, I have some students waiting for me so…Monsieur Flaherty, I wish you luck. Au revoir."

The studio was near the apex of the triangular block formed by the intersection of Rue de Vaugirard and Rue de Rennes, south and west but within walking distance of the Saint Germain des Prés district and its cafés, and just a stone's throw due west of Le Jardin du Luxenbourg. Gleyre had the entire top floor of number 69. Its enormous ceiling was a grid of square glass panes, dusty and sometimes cracked but functional, especially to let in the light from east and south; there were shades which could be pulled to focus this light or to block it off where needed.

Peeling wallpaper of a dark red hue with faded flowers covered the three windowless walls. The street-facing wall had floor to ceiling windows, ornate in design, with wooden shutters. High shelves ran along the tops of the other walls holding various plaster busts or models of arms, legs, horses' heads, and other objects intended for inspiration and study. At one end of the large apartment was a model platform covered by an old, moth-eaten bearskin rug. Behind it painted backdrops could be hung of any number of exterior vistas.

There was a small alcove in which a cast iron stove functioned for cooking and for heat in the winter. Hanging behind it from a beam on the ceiling were the implements of culinary necessity: an iron skillet, long handled spoons and two-pronged forks which could have doubled as lethal weapons. Next to the stove stood a wooden table and two chairs and upon this scarred and stained piece of furniture sat an empty wine bottle and the remains of a two-day old hunk of bread, as hard and inedible as one of the plaster casts on the shelf.

Flaherty knocked and heard a muffled, "Entrez!" He entered. On a long, purple, velvet-covered divan sat a man, his feet up on the cushions, a pipe clinched between his teeth from which a steady stream of white smoke issued, his cravat untied and his collar open, the beginnings of a still scruffy beard decorating his chin. He had piercing brown eyes and a cinnamon-colored cat on his lap. He jumped up, flinging the cat mercilessly to the floor.

"Bonjour!" said the man. Noticing that Flaherty held a paint box under his arm, he followed this with, "You are a new arrival, I perceive. It is, as we say, avoir le cul bordé de nouilles…you are very lucky that we have room, as one of our number has just left for England. Did you know George du Maurier by any chance? His eyesight is beginning to fail, poor fellow. Taking a job as a cartoonist of all things."

"I'm afraid I do not know the man. My name is Jeffery Flaherty. I've talked with Monsieur Gleyre about joining the workshop."

"Well, ça passe ou ça casse. Welcome, I guess. I am Pierre-Auguste Renoir. Could you spare a few francs until next week? I am a bit short of cadmium red."

"Oh…I…"

"We should be on our way at any rate. To the Café Guerbois. It is on Rue des Batignolles…you know it? No? The others will already be there, no doubt. It is approaching l'heure verte…the green hour, and the fairy with the green eyes will be waiting for us."

"The fairy…oh, you mean absinthe. Well I…"

"Oh course, mon bon ami. We will take a cab. You have a few centimes?"

The Café Guerbois had none of the decadence of the Garnier designed Café de la Paix, nor had it the tapestries and statues which gave the Café Riche its bourgeois ambience. Instead, the Café Guerbois was the epitome of Parisien vie de bohème. The small café was crowded with table after table of Haussmann project workers, placiers and chineur merchants, as well as artisans and craftsmen, clerks and pawn brokers, off-duty omnibus drivers and sailors on leave. But it was beginning to attract college professors, artists and writers, and those middle class and upper class idlers who rejoiced in slumming among the sometimes indigent, occasionally violent, and always colorful lower classes.

Prostitutes didn't troll the café for customers: no one could afford them. But some had discovered a new source of livelihood as artists' models. As the atmosphere of the down-and-out attracted the intellectuals and artists, so the abundance of would-be artists attracted the girls. One such fille was seated at a table by the window, where three young artists were examining her qualifications. She was dressed simply, in a cotton frock with a gypsy pattern and puffed sleeves. Her blouse was pulled down to expose her shoulders.

Flaherty and Renoir had just entered. Recognizing the three artists at the window, Renoir pulled Flaherty toward them. "There are my camarades, enjoying the fruits of their non-labors," he said. One of the fellows looked up to see Renoir approaching.

"Bonjour, Renoir. Come join us. Here is someone for you to meet. Cyrielle, say hello to Renoir," the man said.

"Cyrielle Isabelle Océane," the girl said sweetly, holding her hand out for Renoir to take.

"Ha!" exclaimed Renoir. "A girl with three first names! How chaming. Gentlemen," he said, addressing the others, "I want you to meet our new workshop mate, Jeffery Flaherty. Jeffery, these ruffians are Jean Frédéric Bazille, Alfred Sisley, and Claude Monet. Collectively we are the Atelier Gleyre."

Cyrielle had been modeling now for the atelier for nearly a week. She was posed, nude, on the model stand, leaning against a support which she had insisted upon being provided for she was not steady on her feet. She much preferred the poses where she could recline. Flaherty, Renoir, and Bazille had set up easels and were sketching her in charcoal. Sisley and Monet had taken off for the country to draw landscapes. Alfred Sisley was adamant about working en plein air and had even argued the point with Charles Gleyre. Monet had learned the technique years ago from Eugene Boudin, and eagerly accompanied Sisley whenever he ventured outdoors.

Flaherty had learned the following about his new comarades: Monet had been born in Paris in 1840, and as a young boy had lived in Normandy where he had met Boudin and become interested in painting. Upon coming to Paris he visited the Louvre like other young aspiring artists but instead of copying the old masters as the others did, he set up his easel by a window and painted what he observed happening outside. He was drafted in 1861 into the First Regiment of Chasseurs d'Afrique and sent to Algeria to serve a seven-year tour of duty. His father had refused to buy his son's way out of the army because Monet had refused to give up painting. He contracted typhoid fever, went AWOL, and finally his aunt agreed to get him out of military service if he agreed to attend art school. Disillusioned with the schools in Paris and their traditional approaches to teaching art, Monet joined Charles Gleyre's atelier in 1862.

Alfred Sisley was born in Paris in 1839 to a wealthy British couple. He was the only one of the atelier artists who had come from and now had access to financial means. His parents sent him to London to become a businessman but after four years he returned to Paris where he met Marc-Charles-Gabriel Gleyre, Frédéric Bazille, Claude Monet, and Pierre-Auguste Renoir, and began a career as a painter of landscapes. His father still sent the young man an allowance. He sported a neatly trimmed beard of jet black and liked to wear a long frock coat and checkered trousers with a matching vest, even while painting.

Pierre-Auguste Renoir was born in Limoges, Haute-Vienne, France, in 1841. His father, a tailor, moved the family to Paris to find better prospects. Their house was near the Louvre so Renoir, the boy, spent many happy hours wandering its hallways. He aspired to become a singer, but his family's dire financial circumstances brought his studies to an end. At thirteen he became an apprentice in a porcelain factory. Still he strolled the hallways of the Louvre. By 1862 he was studying art under Charles Gleyre. He was peaked and thin of face and paid little attention to the state of his clothing.

Frédéric Bazille was born in Montpellier, Hérault, Languedoc-Roussillon, France, in 1841, into a Protestant family. He discovered the works of Eugène Delacroix and became interested in pursuing a career in painting. His parents agreed, but only if he also studied medicine and became a physician. He began his medical studies in

1859 but by 1862 was also enrolled in the Gleyre atelier along with Monet, Renoir, and Sisley. He wouldn't be taking his final medical exams for two more years and it looked like his disinterest in that profession and his immersion into painting would affect his future path.

Cyrielle sneezed the sneeze of one afflicted by dust, cold, and fatigue. She sneezed again and again. She nearly fell from the platform. "Better take a break," said Bazille. She sat down hard, causing a belch to emerge from one end and flatulence from the other. She giggled. The model stand was covered with a bearskin rug which had lost more of its fur than it had retained. She pulled this up around herself.

"Ça me prend la tête," she exclaimed.

Yes, it makes me crazy too, thought Flaherty. Fou comme un jeune chien…for I am a young dog to be panting crazily over this petite fille. While she was posing Flaherty could suspend his belief that she was anything more than an object to be studied, observed, documented. Hadn't Gleyre told him observation was more important than idealization? Yet she was female flesh, and delectable as well. At least for a farm boy from Tennessee who had never seen a naked lady before…she was delicious looking. Flaherty was thankful for the bearskin rug although several apertures had opened in it which revealed bare skin—the skin he had been staring impassionedly at in toto was now revealed in bits and pieces of tantalizing pinkness.

It made him think of the other woman…*the* woman… Émilie-Claire Lebeau. He still had the portrait he had done of her from memory, the one Gleyre had criticized as too ideal. Would he ever see her again? He doubted it. He studied his charcoal drawing of Cyrielle. Not bad, he thought. Gleyre was right about practice and observation. If only he could paint Émilie-Claire once again…from life.

Three days later Charles Gleyre arrived at the studio for the bi-weekly critique. Flaherty was apprehensive although he felt he had improved greatly since Cyrielle had been modeling for the atelier. Gleyre began by critiquing a watercolor landscape by Sisley.

"You have all the colors and some of the textures, but where is the form? See this mountain in the background? It is a blob of dull brush work. Please, next time bring me something you have finished…not these splotches of random colors!"

Sisley stormed out of the studio. Gleyre next turned to Flaherty. He examined the charcoal sketch of Cyrielle for several minutes before voicing his opinion.

"You have the proportions correct. And the features are well delineated. But you still have a tendency to over-idealize the subject. Look for her defects…a pimple, a crease on the temple, a crooked nose. These things will give you a rendering of the person before you, not the idea of her in your mind. Forget what you know about the human form and observe, observe, observe! Otherwise, good work. Keep at it."

Flaherty was dumfounded. Was that a compliment or a criticism? He could take it either way, he supposed. Best to enjoy the encouragement and concede that he had a lot of work yet to do before he was ready…ready for what? Exhibition? A salon? That was his goal, but now he had to question his ability to produce work that would garner praise, advance him socially and financially. Gleyre's harsh words for Sisley remained in his mind. He had thought Sisley's watercolor was stunning. So what if it avoided details…it was an impression of nature that he had captured that was like nothing Flaherty had ever seen before. It was something new.

His thoughts turned again to Émilie-Claire. He didn't know where she was. He did know, however, where to find Cyrielle Océane.

4

Regarding Édouard Manet

Excerpt from: *Dame Impétueux, la Mémoire de Émilie-Claire Lebeau-Richelieu*, (English translation, published by Charles W. Karr & Co., Chicago, 1897)

It was the day after I finally placed Teo in a new boarding school after that disastrous incident at l'Internat de Madame Noëlle Boucher. That chienne Boucher had no empathy for poor Teo and claimed he had instigated the encounter. Teo said otherwise. He had been taunted, bullied, even physically abused by a few of the other children. He restrained himself as long as he could. The boy that ended up in hospital deserved what he got as far as I am concerned. Still, it is regrettable. No one is born with hate…it is learned. So we move on.

I was ready to sink into mindless oblivion after all that drama and so I sought out a new café where I wouldn't know anyone and I could just sit in the shadows and imbibe alone to my heart's content. Thus I found myself at the Café de Bade on the Boulevard des Italiens. But as soon as I had settled in, en un clin d'œil, through the entrance came Charles Baudelaire accompanied by two other men. These others (Charles lost no time in introducing me to his friends) were Jacques Offenbach, the composer, and a young painter named Édouard Manet.

Offenbach has his own theater on the Champs-Élysées and had just had great success with his opera, *Orphée aux Enfers* (which I hadn't seen), but I thought of him as an old man—he was balding and wore spectacles that pinched his nose. The other man, Manet, however was quite interesting to me…although at that time I was not seeking an affaire de coeur nor even un petit flirt.

He had dark, curly hair that sat upon a high forehead and a luxurious full beard which was neatly trimmed. High cheek bones and widely-spaced dark eyes gave him an absorbing mannerism from which one could not detach without feeling some amount of loss. He commanded attentiveness without effort or intention. He wore a long necktie decorated with polka dots which was unusual for the day's fashion of small cravats and high collars. A dark suit. He was hatless.

When his eyes met mine I knew that somehow we would become acquainted…intimately. I waited for Charles to invite me to join them at their table, a large, round table covered with a linen cloth situated dramatically in the center of the café. This was not forthcoming. The men sat, ordered wine and engaged in heated conversation. They seemed not to be concerned about…or maybe they enjoyed…the effect they produced as a mise en scène for the surrounding patrons. This was a café, I learned later, where the more conservative café-goers came to eavesdrop on the outrageous fringes of society—those dangerously unique artistic outsiders like Baudelaire and Offenbach.

I found myself to be among those eavesdroppers. The ideas that passed between Charles and this Édouard Manet were shocking, no doubt, to the crowd, but tantalizing to me. Sex and death have always been part and parcel of the arts…but disguised as allegory or the lessons of religious zeal. I was familiar with Baudelaire's explorations of profane love in his poetry. Now he seemed to be challenging Manet to paint in the manner in which the poet himself revealed the reality of the human condition, this through lurid images.

Manet replied that he indeed treated subject matter without regard for propriety. His critics accused him of having "an abominable lack of moral sense." His painting, *The Absinthe Drinker*, was an example. It had been rejected from the 1859 Salon for its realism in depicting a degenerate rag-picker, a subject which should have been scorned, not elevated to such a scale.

This put me in mind of Baudelaire's poem, "Le Vin de Chiffonniers," in which he describes the ragman coming, nodding his head (on voit un chiffonnier qui vient, hochant la tête), and those beautiful lines:

> Stand in front of them, solemn magic!
> And in the stunning and bright orgy
> Bugles, the sun, shouts and the drum,
> They bring glory to the people drunk with love!
> …
> To drown rancor and cradle indolence
> Of all those old cursed who die in silence,
> God, touched with remorse, had made sleep;
> Man added Wine, the sacred son of the Sun!

The discussion went on and on and eventually I left the café without saying goodbye to my friend Charles Baudelaire. I doubt he even noticed my withdrawal. I would return to Café Bade in the following weeks with the hope of seeing Manet. It was over a month before our paths crossed again. He was seated at a table in the corner, quite alone. He seemed distraught. Impetuous as always, I approached him unheralded and stood before him without speaking until he looked up from his glass of wine. That he didn't remember me was not a surprise. That he was not offended by my boldness was typical; I was to observe much of this tolerance for the inappropriate in times to come.

"Bonjour, Mademoiselle," he said to me. "Be apprised that I have left my purse at home. I cannot partake of your services today."

He had thought me a common street whore! The vieux bouc! I retorted:

"Monsieur, I assure you if I were marketing my most admirable attributes as you assume, it would not be yourself to whom I would apply."

He looked chagrinned. Good! I continued:

"We have a mutual friend, Monsieur Charles Baudelaire. I only wished to request that you relay my good wishes to him. And now, it is apparent you would have me gone. So…"

"But no, ma chère dame, I wish you to stay. I apologize for my rudeness. You must understand that under the circumstances…"

"A woman may not present herself without introduction by another. I believed you to be liberal in such matters. Any friend of Charles'…"

After this disastrous beginning, our relationship, if there were to be one, could only improve. But as Jules Verne said, when a journey begins badly it seldom ends well. Still I was hopeful. We saw each other off and on at the café and sometimes walked up the Champs-Élysées or in the Jarden des Tuileries. He took me to his studio at 81 Rue Guyot in the 17th arrondissement. This was near the Parc Monceau where we sometimes strolled from the rotunda to the colonnade, stopping to watch the puppets Guignol, Madelon, and Gnafron in their boisterous show.

The building was on a corner and included a café, a laundry and a series of apartments which were rented by merchants. There were two workshops on the second floor which were occupied by Manet and another artist named Johan-Jacob Bennetter (of whom I had heard nothing and of whom I still hear nothing). Manet's was a great open space with a high ceiling…two stories of the building…and had large floor-to-ceiling windows which looked to the northeast at the cross street.

In spite of the light from the windows the place seemed dark and somber to me. Canvases leaned against the walls, some empty, some partially finished, some completed. There stood the now infamous *Le Buveur d'absinthe*: *The Absinthe Drinker*. It was a full-length portrait of a rag-picker named Collardet who was often seen lurking about near the Louvre; the young artist had befriended him for some reason. The man stood unevenly against a ledge, wore a top hat (a dig by Manet at the bourgeois elite?) and a long overcoat. A bottle lay on the ground beside him. The painting was very dark in grays and browns…much like the studio itself.

Manet then showed me another painting he called *The Spanish Singer*, his first real success as it was accepted for exhibition in the Salon of 1861. This at least had some color. I commented that he had painted him playing the guitar left-handed and wondered if the model had been left-handed. He replied that he sometimes achieved proportions and perspective by painting while looking at his subject in a mirror. This amazed me.

Next to this romanticized portrait (in the style of Goya?) sat a wonderful painting of a nude woman. *La Nymphe Surprise*. Clothed only in a string of pearls, she sat in a wooded landscape, a look of surprise on her face as if she had just been discovered by the viewer. Manet told me the canvas had been cut down from a larger painting he had wished to destroy. He had saved only the nude. There was a reason for this.

I learned much later that the model was a woman named Suzanne Leenhoff. She was Dutch and had been Manet's piano teacher when he was in his teens. She was three years older than he but they started a secret love affair that lasted for ten years. In 1863, a year from my viewing of the nude in the landscape, they were married. Suzanne brought to the marriage a son, Léon, who may have been fathered by Manet's own father or by him...that is a mystery I have never been able to solve. Léon also appears as a model in several paintings.

At the time I did not know of this elicit relationship which would be resolved in marriage. I had no reason to believe I could not occupy a place in this man's heart...or his bed. I commented on the beauty of the woman in the painting and I said that I wondered how it felt to pose in the nude in that way. This was more than a dangerous flirtation on my part. I really envied the woman in the painting. I wanted to be her, to expose myself unashamed and natural.

Perhaps I hinted at this too strongly. Manet then led me to a large canvas covered with a cloth. He pulled at the cloth which fell to the floor revealing a woodland scene. Dark trees, of course, but in the background ran a little stream or river in which a woman bathed, clad only in a transparent chemise. Two men, dressed in the fashion of the middle class of the day, sat enjoying a picnic, a bowl of fruit and loaf of bread nearby. Another figure was blocked in next to the men. It was impossible to say much (yet) about this figure.

"I call it *Le Bain*, the bath," he said. (This, one of the most controversial of Manet's paintings...and that is saying a lot...would later be called *Le Dejeuner sur l'herbe—The Luncheon on the Grass*.) He continued:

"I was walking along the Seine with my friend Antonin Proust not long ago and we came upon a scene not unlike this one with a woman bathing while fully clothed men idled on the bank. It struck me as invoking Raphael's *Judgement of Paris* or *The Pastoral Concert* by Giorgione. I had started a copy of Giorgione's painting of the musicians and the women but it was awful. I painted over it and this is the result you see. I will finish this in a few weeks. All it needs is one more figure…"

"Will it be a woman?" I asked.

"It could be you, if you would pose for me."

"I would be delighted."

"It is to be a nude," he said.

There is nothing much to be said about posing nude for an extraordinary artist…or even for a mediocre one for that matter. It is hours of holding still until your muscles ache. It is days of hours of forced meditation; no conversation is allowed, no scratching of the head, no sneezing or coughing. Was it liberating? How can that be? Perhaps walking unclad down the Champs-Élysées would be liberating, but this? Pure boredom. And the image! Manet made me much too ample, especially around the hips and bust. It caused at least one critic to complain that I was ugly…but then, the critics were ruthless about the painting.

It was rejected by the committee for exhibition at the Salon of 1863—this was no surprise. The committee rejected two-thirds of all entries that year, including works by Pissarro, Courbet and the American, James Whistler. There were complaints. The Emperor, who was as conservative as the Academy and who could have cared less about the emerging avant-garde, still was sensitive to public opinion. And so he created the Salon des Refusés, an exhibition of those works refused by the jury. This was held simultaneously at the Palais de l'Industrie. Instead of the intended tipping of the hat to the artists in recognition of their efforts, the result was ridicule by both the critics and the public (who filled the galleries to overflowing to gawk at these great works of art, and laugh).

How did I feel? I did not go to the Palais de l'Industrie for fear of being recognized. I was heartened, however, by the defense of the painting by the writer, Émile Zola. He called it the greatest work of Édouard Manet's, one that "realizes the dream of all painters: to place figures of natural grandeur in a landscape." While he acknowledged the obvious scandal of a nude woman seated with two clothed male figures…something that perhaps represents an aspect of the social condition which is to be shunned, or at least denied: prostitution…Zola pointed out that there were at least 50 pictures in the Louvre showing combinations of clothed and unclothed figures, and that for Manet, the desire was only to portray the nude in an idyllic…and modern setting. Not to scandalize.

I am not so sure. There is that side of the man Manet that is akin to the satirist. In that painting I am…or I should say, she is…looking at the viewer with a gaze that possibly suggests she is oblivious. No one in the painting interacts. I think Manet is making a statement both about society and about himself. He is, although you would not think it, a shy being, so unsure of his own merit (although this is considerable). Do the critics somehow sense this and sharpen their criticism in order to deny the fact that we all have doubts about our own worth? Well, I am no art critic. I leave it for posterity to decide.

Now I must talk about the other woman. The surprised nymph. That Suzanne Leenhoff. As I have said, I didn't know of this long term romance between the nymph and Manet. I was to learn of it the hard way. There was a lot I didn't know about the future Mme. Manet. She had come to Paris from her home in Zaltbommel, Holland, in 1847, having been encouraged by the composer, Franz Liszt to further her music studies there. She found work in 1851 as a piano tutor with the family of Auguste Manet, where she taught Édouard and his brother Eugène. By 1852 she was pregnant. She gave birth out of wedlock to Léon Koella Leenhoff, the boy who appears in so many of Manet's paintings. Léon's birth certificate showed his father's name as Koella…but…? I later looked for some evidence of a man named Koella, but found none. Manet was made godfather at his baptism. Perhaps ironically.

The rumors were that Suzanne had been Auguste Manet's mistress and that he was Léon's father. At the time I was posing for Le Dejeuner sur l'herbe, in 1862, Auguste Manet died. One year later, Édouard traveled with her to Zaltbommel where they were married. Married his father's mistress? Does it not seem more likely that Édouard was Léon's father? Yet the boy was claimed by his mother to in fact be her brother! The newlywed Manets never did legitimize the boy. This is a question that may never be answered.

I met Suzanne one day near the end of that period when I was posing. She had brought Léon to the studio where he was to pose for Édouard who was finishing *Musique aux Tuileries* around that time and wished to insert a portrait of the boy into the crowd. I didn't recognize her from the *Nymphe Surprise* painting…*that* woman exuded a beauty that had struck me when I first saw it as celestial. *This* woman was stout, ordinary looking, and just shy of homely, with a prominent nose and eyes that seemed not to see you but to look past you. Well, that is just my opinion.

Victorine Meurent had also arrived. She was a model and a painter in her own right and Manet was working on a portrait of her. She would be the model for the nude *Olympia*, the next painting which was to scandalize Paris even more than *The Luncheon on the Grass*…but that is another story. We three woman, two coming and one going, were confronting Manet about this thing and that thing while Édouard was ignoring us and doting on Léon. He ran his hand through the boy's hair. This indifference seemed to infuriate Victorine which caused her to grab Édouard's arm in a manner that was definitely not casual. I noticed the inference of possession and so did Suzanne.

Now, I had no quarrel with Victorine. I knew that men of that era saw many women and I certainly had no claim upon Manet. Suzanne, who had seemed so passive and above making a scene however, did just that: she exploded with a temper that surprised me. (Édouard explained the reason to me later. That was when he told me of his plan to marry the woman.) Victorine had left in a huff and I retreated as well, saying goodbye to young Léon, who had witnessed the confrontation…and somehow had accepted it on face value as what adults did from time to time. He was a marvelous boy and I felt sorry for him. And for myself—for I now understood that any romance between myself and the painter was not to be.

You may be wondering whether the painter and I ever did become intimate. If I were a man I should be saying that gentlemen never tell tales. It might be obvious that under circumstances where a man and woman are alone…and much like the painting of *The Luncheon on the Grass*, where she is naked and he is clothed, that mischief could be afoot. Monsieur Manet was a professional. Never while we were working did he seem even to notice that I was a woman except for the purposes of rending the female form. I appreciated that restraint but still I desired that during nonworking hours we might pursue a more natural relationship. I could tell you that we did not. I could tell you that, but it might not be the truth.

So, a final word or two about Édouard Manet. He exhibited *Olympia* in 1865…the model was Victorine Meurent and all implications in the painting were that she was a prostitute. This by itself caused a lesser concern than the supposed vulgarity of the pose and the intense stare the model focused on the viewer. Again, I am not an art critic. I wished I could have posed for that one!

The scandal followed Manet everywhere. He traveled to Madrid, the source and inspiration for his self-proclaimed Spanish sensibilities. When he returned he abandoned his usual haunt at the Café Bebe for the Café Guerbois on the Rue Batignolles where he found, to his amazement, that the younger generation of artists (those we may speak of as the avant garde) admired his work...especially its radicalism. This group formed what we now know as the Impressionist movement, but Manet didn't join.

In 1870, after the Franco-Prussian War began and the Third Republic declared itself in Paris, Manet shuffled his family off to the Pyrenees and joined the Grande National. But I'm getting ahead of my story. Perhaps the day will come when the paintings of this unique and inspired artist will decorate the halls of our best museums. I hope so.

5

Le Boulevard du Crime

It was one of those unusual nights when François Arnaud Gardinier was present at the Château des Ternes for dinner. The occasion was not that he had made time to spend an evening with his children, but that he had invited some his prospective investors for entertainment and, if possible, to seal a few deals. Because Solange Gardinier was bedridden, François had enlisted Phoebe to act as hostess. The female touch added elegance to the event and kept the usual lewd and insensitive banter to a minimum. The children, Jeanne-Alice and Geoffroy, were dining with their mother and would be seen to afterwards by Mme. Popelin, the housekeeper, so the night belonged to Phoebe.

While the men finished up their aperitifs in the adjacent sitting room, Phoebe gave the dining room table one last inspection. The matched set of Sèrvres porcelain dinnerware gleamed in the gas light. Each plate shared a similar rich blue border with small cameo portraits of important personages, each from a different département of France; the center of each plate showed a topographical scene from that area…extravagant estates upon lush rolling hillsides, river or mountain scenes in a style that imitated the Italian Renaissance. A gilded edging ran around each plate and saucer, uniquely punctuating the non-style mélange which was "Style Napoléon III."

The porcelain and the silver dated from the Gardinier's acquisition of Château des Ternes. The linen tablecloth and napkins were new. Phoebe smoothed a wrinkle from the table cloth then suddenly gasped: there was chip on the rim of one of the crystal goblets! Just as the men entered the dining room she switched this goblet with the one that sat at her own place at the table. Disaster averted, she turned to smile demurely at the men.

They were: Bernard Lachapelle, an investor in real estate, Jonathan Blanchard, owner of an exclusive riding and shooting club on the outskirts of Paris, and Gauthier Lapointe, who dealt in stocks and bonds. François Gardinier was wining and dining them tonight to solicit their financial help for a grand scheme involving the latest Haussmann project. Phoebe had little interest in financial intrigue. In playing the part of hostess, however, she could immerse herself in the fantasy of being the next Mme. Gardinier. Thus she exhibited a somewhat spurious yet enthusiastic interest in the conversation.

"You've met Haussmann, of course," Lapointe was saying to Gardinier. "Do you find him intimidating?"

"Some do," François answered. "He is well over six feet tall and has quite the domineering attitude. Snaps orders at his people. But I know he is extremely intelligent, malin comme un singe. Around him one must be humble…avaler des couleuvres, so to speak. Then one listens and discovers certain beneficial facts."

"Facts such as the location of the next Rue de Rivoli, for example?" suggested Jonathan Blanchard.

"Perhaps nothing so grand as that first great scar of urban renewal. But perhaps something equally exciting…and potentially profitable."

"And no one else has a hint of this exciting project?" asked Bernard Lachapelle. "I myself have heard only about small widenings of streets here and there…the Avenue des Gobelins, for example. No great profits there."

"It is only a small square to be built. It will be called Place du Château-d'Eau," answered Gardinier.

"That seems inconsequential," replied Lachapelle.

"It is the location which is intriguing. Do you know the street, the Boulevard du Temple on the Right Bank?"

"Not the Boulevard du Crime? The theater row? Why, there is

the Théâtre Lyrique, the Cirque-Olympique, the Petit-Lazare…what else, Gauthier?"

"There must be ten or twelve theaters and as many cafés," answered Lapointe. "The Follies-Mayer, the Théâtre de la Gaîté. And the Théâtre des Pygmées! Scandaleux! Impensable! The public won't stand for it."

"Ah. That is what makes this scheme so delicious. No one will believe that Haussmann would demolish the Boulevard du Crime and rob the people of their weekly melodramas. Are you gentlemen with me on this? It must be done surreptitiously. There will be many buildings to acquire and their values to inflate."

Phoebe studied the three men as the servants took away the fruit compote dishes and began to pour the wine. Bernard Lachapelle was portly; in fact, pear-shaped with a head too small for the great girth that supported it. He was perhaps in his mid-forties and his graying hair was thinning at the apex of his skull, giving him the appearance of a medieval monk. Gauthier Lapointe's age she could not discern as the serious look frozen on his face betrayed the youthful aspect of his body language. He had no facial hair but sported long side whiskers which distorted the length of his countenance such that he appeared to have stepped out of a painting by El Greco. And then there was Jonathan Blanchard.

Jonathan Blanchard owned the exclusive riding and shooting club called "Le Adventure Extraordinaire" located on the outskirts of Paris. He was young, early thirties Phoebe guessed, and he radiated the energy of a stabled steed anxious to join a fox hunt. He was, she thought, extremely pleasant to look upon and his voice, musical in tonality, matched his good looks perfectly. She was charmed. And it seemed Blanchard had noticed Phoebe too as his gaze drifted in her direction whenever the conversation ebbed.

The Château-Margaux 1847 had been poured. The potage was served and taken away. A soufflés à la Reine and a spicey escalopes de turbot au gratin followed. Then came an entrée of poulet à la portugaise, asperges en branche, and rôtis of ortolans sur canapé (accompanied by a cru supérieur, Château Yquem 1847). By the time the sorbet au vin had been devoured and the Champagne Roederer frappé was poured into exquisitely slender flutes, the three guests were satiated both with the haute cuisine and the plan to purchase properties on the Boulevard du Temple. They had formed a coalition for intrigue and enterprise that promised wealth beyond imagining…or jail and abject suffering.

"We haven't time to purchase, sell, and repurchase many properties," said Gardinier. "We will have to inflate the values by showing that the tenants will suffer greater loses than perhaps is the actual case. Some concerns will be relocated by Haussmann and Associates, the Cirque-Olympique, for example. I've my eye on some vacant property along the Champs-Élysées. We can double our profits on that deal alone."

"I went to the circus once back in Massachusetts," said Phoebe. "They had elephants. My father, the Reverend Joshua Billings, disapproved and I wasn't allowed to go back. I wonder though, the circus I saw was all in tents. They could be folded up and moved quite easily. Why is the destruction of this Cirque-Olympique such a tragedy?"

"No, no, chéri, it is not a traveling circus as you have in America. It is a magnificent amphitheater constructed in…what do you say, Gauthier? Around the turn of the century?"

"It dates to 1782 but at the present location only since, oh…1826 or 7. Destroyed by fire then rebuilt." Gauthier swirled the Roederer in his flute after responding to Lachapelle.

"François," interrupted Phoebe, "I've a marvelous idea! Why don't I take the children to the Cirque-Olympique? They would love it, I am certain. Especially if you are going to tear it down…"

"Phoebe, I am not the one who will tear it down. I am hesitant to allow you to take the children there. For one thing, it is not proper for an unescorted woman…"

"I would be honored to escort the lady and her charges," said Jonathan Blanchard. "It would give me an opportunity to talk to Franconi, the director. My family and his have known each other for two generations now. Adolphe Franconi is an energetic businessman besides being a brilliant showman."

"D'accord," said Gardinier. "Just don't tip our hand. And Phoebe, keep a tight vigil where the children are concerned."

Phoebe rose and pecked Gardinier on the cheek. "Oh, thank you, François," she said. Blanchard was beaming. Gardinier had not failed to notice. Phoebe thought, "Is he a little jealous? I hope so!"

Le Boulevard du Crime! Phoebe was intrigued. She had never ventured here before…perhaps hesitant because of the ominous nickname. Jonathan Blanchard assured her, however, it was perfectly safe: "The name comes from the abundance of melodramas featuring crime," he explained. "The public does so love their murders, their robberies, their kidnappings."

Le Boulevard du Temple—so named because it intersected with the Paris priory of the Knights Templar—so seeped in history—so much part and parcel of the Parisian experience. Louis XIV in 1670 filled in a rancid ditch and planted trees; the walk attracted the people, the puppeteers and mimes, the shop keepers. The famous harlequin Nicolet performed there in 1760. Louis XV and Madame Dubarry attended the Théâtre des Grands Dancers du Roi. It was the street of Molière, Dumas, Martainville. It was the wax museum of M. Phillipe Curtius where it was said the figures changed costumes as often as France changed its government. It was the scene of the attempted assassination in 1835 of King Louis-Phillipe by Giuseppe Fiexchi which resulted in 18 dead and 23 injured. The writer Mario Proth in 1872 called it a "moving panorama of all pleasures, [a] synthesis of all fads of the big city." Concerts in the garden of the Café Turc, melodramas at the Folies-Dramatiques, the enactment of the capture of the Bastille at the National Circus, the shops, the gardens…and all to be swept away by the great hurricane of Haussmannism.

And the Cirque-Olympique—what history there! The building on this boulevard was its third incarnation. It had introduced Paris to its first elephant performer: Kiouny, who danced the gavotte e tutti quanti and gave flowers to the ladies in the audience; Coco the monkey who delighted children with his antics; the grotesque German acrobat Guertener who performed on roller skates; hippodramas which combined stage and arena where 36 horses were the main actors; the newest sensation, Le Course aux Trapèzes in which a daring young man swung on a flying trapeze.

Under the green-striped awning at the front of the Cirque-Olympique, Phoebe and her charges, Geoffroy and Jeanne-Alice, waited in the queue along with Jonathan Blanchard. The avenue was filled with people on promenade; strolling past the Théâtre Lyrique, the Théâtre de la Gaîté, the Théâtre Délassements-Comique. Vendors walked up and down the lines selling oranges, ice cream, and flowers.

Once inside the semi-circular arena Phoebe was dazzled by the huge interior space. The great dome above was supported by twelve metal columns; a proportionately large chandelier hung from the center of the dome with smaller ones positioned at its edges. Three floors of galleries provided seating for 2,250 spectators. Murals, lush drapery, and bas-reliefs of historical scenes added to the spender and gaieté of the room. The bustling and clamor of the people in the stalls gave energy to expectation as they waited for the show to begin.

"What wonderful seats," exclaimed Phoebe. They were in the first tier, near the stage where tableaux would be enacted. Their view of the arena was excellent.

"My old friend Franconi arranged to reserve these for us. It will be difficult convincing him to sell his circus," explained Blanchard.

"What a shame! I am beginning to hate your M. Haussmann for destroying all this."

"C'est vrai. This may be a most scandaleux act that will bring him down. However, think about what he has achieved. He clears away the slums…streets so narrow that wagons have difficulty traversing them. Too many families are thrown together in inadequate housing which breeds disease and starvation. He eliminates all that. He has installed water systems to keep waste away from fresh. He has installed gas lights everywhere…we are now the La ille Lumière!"

"And the widened streets are as soulless as the bland buildings he erects. And where will the poor go? Don't say 'Let them eat cake' or I will strike you!"

"They are provided for. Haussmann has created jobs with all the construction going on. Believe me, Paris will take her place as the world's premiere city. And besides, there are enormous profits to be made. Don't tell me you don't appreciate your employer's windfalls."

"Oh look," said Phoebe, "the show is beginning." Just in time, she thought…the conversation was getting tedious.

Ponies pranced around the circular arena kicking up dust from the dirt floor. They were costumed with ostrich plumes and sequined harnesses. A petit young woman in billowing bloomers controlled the procession from the center of the arena brandishing a long carriage whip which she cracked above the pony's heads. A harlequin ran around the circumference of the ring mimicking a horse's cantor.

The line of ponies exited and into the ring galloped an Arabian steed upon whose back stood an acrobatic rider; the crowd gasped as he twirled and somersaulted, ably dismounted and mounted again, all the while horse and rider circled the ring at a furious pace. Cheers rose up at each extraordinary feat. Now they were joined by a two horse-drawn chariot, its driver dressed as an ancient Roman soldier; his golden armor glinted under the crystal chandeliers.

Next entered Miss Lucy, the elephant, her trunk held high. A young woman in feathered headdress and tights sat upon the pachyderm, her legs wrapped around its massive neck. The horses were all gone and Lucy took to the center of the ring where large, brightly painted wooden boxes waited for her to mount. Her rider had dismounted and the girl now directed Lucy to stand on a box and lift first one front leg, then the other. Applause filled the room.

Now the woman lay on the arena floor, her face looking to one side as Miss Lucy gingerly lifted her enormous foot and lowered it down within inches of the woman's head. The crowd roared with an equal mixture of delight and alarm. Defying death was a main staple of circus performance; it was thrilling for spectators and brought them back again and again to the Cirque-Olympique.

Mimicking death was the lynch pin of the melodrama and one of these crime dramas was about to start on the stage. In the early days, fairytale tableaux or reenactments of Napoleon Bonaparte's famous battles would be presented. Extravaganzas of Greek myth were shown: Achilles dragged Hector behind his chariot. The pantomimes became more elaborate. An orchestra pit was installed between the stage and the arena. Scantily dressed woman danced the Rigolboche raising their skirts and kicking out their legs.

The melodrama unfolded revealing an obvious plot about a hen-pecked husband who ventured out into the night in search of release from his tortured existence. Under a street lamp he interviewed a woman of the night while thugs stole up behind him. Wham!—came down the bludgeon. Slowly the victim awoke. The next scene had him entering a sleazy establishment where men and women were raising glasses and singing. He pulled a small revolver from his vest pocket and sprayed the room with bullets just as the stage lights dimmed to plunge the scene into darkness. Applause.

"Mademoiselle, I want ice cream," Geoffroy shouted over the noise of the crowd.

"Geoffroy, say, 'May I have ice cream, s'il vous plaît?' "

"May I? I'm hungry."

"Might I purchase the boy some ice cream?" asked Blanchard. "There is a vender right next to the main entrance. It will only take a moment."

"I think not. Geoffroy can obtain his own refreshments. He is a big boy," answered Phoebe. She thrust a few francs into the boy's hands. "Jeanne-Alice, you go with your brother. And come right back…no idling."

An elaborate series of poles and wires had been erected in the center of the arena. Ascending a rope ladder to a platform on the top of one of the poles was a lean young man clad in a skin-tight one-piece uniform. His name was Jules Léotard. He was the son of a gymnastics instructor from Touloise. Like his circus predecessor, Antonio Diavolo, Léotard performed aerial acrobatics suspended from ropes high above the arena. Unlike other aerial acrobats, however, Léotard had a unique specialty: he had invented the trapeze act by adding bars and hoops to his equipment. He would leap from one swinging bar to the next, sometimes traversing five bars in a row to the delight of his audiences. He invented the tight-fitting suit he wore which allowed maximum body movement. It became as popular and famous as his trapeze act. The garment was named after him: the leotard.

Léotard performed a somersault between two swinging bars. He hung by his knees from the bar then dropped and caught the bar with his ankles. The crowd was mesmerized. They cheered, they gasped, they applauded with passion. It was yet early in the history of trapeze artists; Léotard did not employ a "catcher," another acrobat swinging from a bar who would capture him in midflight. He always aimed for the swinging trapeze bar…and always caught it just at the last possible moment, sending thrills and chills throughout the arena. He delighted ladies, gentlemen, and children of all ages. During one of his death-defying somersaults Phoebe clutched Blanchard's arm.

"Exciting, isn't it? He said, matter-of-factly. She withdrew her hand from his arm. This man…he wasn't the one. Too bad, she thought, he was handsome enough. Just a little bit too self-absorbed and crass.

Jeanne-Alice reappeared as the show evolved from the trapeze act to yet another equestrian display. She was slurping ice cream from a paper cup with a wooden spoon. Jeanne-Alice. Just Jeanne-Alice.

"Jeanne-Alice! Where is Geoffroy?" Phoebe demanded. "Weren't you with him?"

"I don't know," said the girl.

Now Phoebe clutched Blanchard's arm again. Now she was fearful. Now tears welled in her eyes.

"I'll go in search of the boy," he said.

"No, you wait here with Jeanne-Alice in case he comes back. I'll go. He is my responsibility. This is my fault."

Pushing aside spectators who crowded the gallery, Phoebe found her way to the entrance of the building where an ice cream vender was just packing up his wares.

"Have you seen a little boy?" she asked. "About this tall? He was with his sister but they became separated."

"Oui. But he went off with his parents. Down the street in that direction," he said, pointing.

"Parents? No…that can't be. You must be mistaken."

"Perhaps. I did think it a bit strange. Their appearance…they looked to me to be gypsies."

6

Les Catacombes de Paris

Auguste Renoir and Jeffrey Flaherty walked past alcoves stacked with femurs and skulls. Their hand-held lanterns illuminated the grisly remains of the long dead, casting deep shadows into empty eye sockets. As they moved and the shadows moved with them, the skeletons seemed animated in an overdue dance of death. What had the old sign above the entrance to the catacombs said? "Arrête, c'est ici l'empire de la mort!" (Stop! This is the empire of death!)

Some said the remains of six million dead were arrayed here in part of the miles of tunnels connecting the old mine shafts—the last transfer of bones having been made in 1859 as part of Haussmann's renovation of Paris. The earliest relocation of bodies had been in 1774 when the notoriously foul-smelling cemetery, the Saint's Innocents, suffered a wall collapse and necessitated the creation of an ossuary away from public spaces. Besides the disinterred from Saint's Innocents, remains were moved from Saint-Étienne-des-Grès, Madeleine Cemetery, Errancis Cemetery, and Notre-Dame-des-Blancs-Manteaux to the abandoned mining tunnels.

Stone mining during the twelfth century had left the Left Bank riddled with miles of tunnels. The catacombs now occupied a portion of these carrièrs de Paris starting from the city gate, the Barrière d'Enfer, and extending southward. Originally bodies were dumped unceremoniously into a shaft near the Rue de la Tombe-Issoire, but by 1810, the director of mine inspections, Louis-Étienne Héricart de Thury, had undertaken to stack femurs and skulls in an organized manner (one would say, perhaps, decorative) and to add to the resulting mausoleum some of the headstones, statuary, and tablets that could be procured from other cemeteries.

The two artists were less interested in these bizarre walls of bones than in the connecting tunnels that branched from the end of the catacombs. Renoir had learned from some of his more unsavory acquaintances that certain groups, sociétés secrètes, had hidden meeting places in the tunnels—groups that often trafficked in abducted children. Flaherty had enlisted Renoir's help in the search for the missing Geoffroy Gardinier. He had learned about the supposed kidnapping from Émilie-Claire, the woman he had been looking for since he had first seen her at the Café Tortoni.

At first Flaherty had had no luck locating Émilie-Claire, no matter how thorough his search. It was by accident that he finally learned her name and her whereabouts. The painters of the Gleyre atelier had paid a visit to the studio of one of the older artists they admired: Édouard Manet. There Flaherty had seen the as yet unfinished *Luncheon on the Grass*. The figure Émilie-Claire had posed for was complete enough that Flaherty recognized her immediately. He quizzed Manet as to her identity and subsequently was able to trace her to her apartment on the Rue de la Victoire.

Their reunion occurred just as Phoebe Stapleton had poured out her heart to Émilie-Claire concerning the missing child. Émilie-Claire related the sad story to Flaherty. Flaherty had decided that he would become a gallant knight in shining armor: he would find Geoffroy Gardinier and return him to his family. Whether this would impress Émilie-Claire or not was a matter to be determined.

"I will undertake to find the lad," he told Émilie-Claire. "I have a good, logical mind and I can follow clues."

"I fear for poor Geoffroy," Émilie-Claire replied. "There was talk of gypsies. They could be miles away…even in another country by now! I appreciate your desire to help but I believe he is lost to us. A sad thing. And devastating for Phoebe who feels it was her fault."

"Nonetheless I will persist."

Making their way through the darkened catacombs, Renoir and Flaherty were nearing the end of the main tunnel. Renoir spotted a round object on the floor before them and picked it up: a skull that must have become dislodged from its place against the wall. He held it up in the light of his lantern.

"Who do you suppose this was?" he asked. "A long dead Norman invader? A miner who perished in a mine collapse? A soldier of the Revolution? A victim of the plague?"

"Perhaps," answered Flaherty, "a woman…some flower seller or washer woman. Perhaps a lady in waiting from the court of Louis XV. Or a courtesan of some powerful political figure. A woman of the street from the Place Pigalle…"

"What is that against the far wall? Is that a door?"

"Maybe a barricade. It appears a passageway has been walled up."

Renoir moved to examine the rotting wood. He held his lantern close, ran his hands over the edges, pushed…

"Voilà! It is a door!"

The barricade pivoted open revealing a narrow passageway with a low ceiling and notches along the wall into which torches had been inserted. None of the torches were lit but the smell of burnt cloth permeated the tunnel.

"Someone has been here recently," said Renoir.

As they followed this new tunnel, the ceiling began to drop lower and lower until they needed to stoop. It seemed to them that it led only to some dead end. They were about to return to the main tunnel when a blast of fresh air signaled that further ahead, the tunnel connected with one of the vertical shafts of the old mines. They proceeded onward and soon saw light filtering down in a large chamber a few yards away. Entering this chamber they could stand erect once again.

"There are two new tunnels leading off from here…one to the right and one to the left," announced Renoir, stating the obvious.

"We could split up and each follow one."

"If we become separated we might lose one another. Let us take the turning to the right. Always turning right we can't become lost."

"As always, your wisdom amazes me!" Flaherty's tongue in cheek comment was lost on Renoir who seemed single-minded in his desire to forge ahead.

This next tunnel was not as demanding as had been the previous one. The two artists were understandably exhausted and, if pressed, would have admitted to a touch of claustrophobia. However, they could stand straight up and not sense the closeness of the walls as this tunnel was wide. Wide enough for a small cart or wagon. A few hundred feet up the tunnel they came to another branching.

"To the right," said Renoir.

"Of course," said Flaherty.

But moments later they were accosted from behind by a loud voice which said, "Well, well, well. What have we here?" Someone had approached them from the left turning.

The man who stood before them was unusually large; his bulk seemed to fill the tunnel, wide though it was. His clothes were ragged and filthy. In the dim light of their lanterns Flaherty smelled him before he saw him.

"We seek an audience with Le Société de la Rose Blanche," explained Renoir.

"Oh you do, do you? And who might you be?"

"My name is August Renoir and this is Jeffrey Flaherty. We have need of a discussion with your group which may prove beneficial to both you and to ourselves."

"I know not of your names. Why should I do anything other than expel you from this domain?"

"We are referred by Henri Gérôme, the chiffonnier who works on the Quai de l'Archêveché near the morgue, the one they call Le Chèvre.

"Henri Le Chèvre you say? If this be not true then it will be the last tale you will ever tell. I'll take you…however it will be at your own peril. Follow me."

The man held nothing to illuminate his way but seemed to know the turnings of the tunnel instinctively. He led Renoir and Flaherty back into the large chamber and then into the tunnel not taken…the one which had been to their left. Flaherty refrained from pointing out Renoir's initial mistake to him. The situation was tense enough with this giant of a man taking them to some unknown place to meet a group of men with the strange name of Le Société de la Rose Blanche—The Society of the White Rose.

"A secret society?" asked Émilie-Claire. She placed a cube of sugar on the slotted spoon that balanced across the top of her glass of absinthe. As she dripped ice water over the cube the drops began to cloud the green liquid, releasing the fragrances of anise, fennel and star anise.

"A clandestine society. Hidden because of course, just like the Blanquists, they would be considered revolutionary and conspiratorial by the government."

Jeffrey Flaherty had asked Émilie-Claire to meet him at the Café Guerbois so that he could report on his progress in locating the missing boy. He had an aversion to absinthe, primarily because of the over-powering flavor of anise, and so he had ordered a whiskey which he now sipped.

"They are related, somewhat distantly, to the old Order of Memphis through communication with the British-based Lodge of the Philadelphians," Flaherty continued, "but unlike that Freemason lodge, the Society of the White Rose is made up from the working classes. They are more in tune with the ideals of Karl Marx and Friedrich Engels—the organization of labor, the destructiveness of capitalism, the formation of an egalitarian society, etcetera."

"But they sound like thugs, thieves…akin almost to Hugo's Cour des Miracles, where the lame can walk, the blind can see, and pick-pockets rule…where they assault the citizens of Paris then scurry away to their hidey-holes, immune to arrest."

"That aspect of their behavior is merely a result of their political struggles. They stand in opposition to the emperor. They do what they have to do."

"And you and your friend, Renoir, just strolled into their hideout and asked for help?"

"We were more or less captured by this great hulk of a man who took us to the rest of the group. His name was Gaspard. He led us through a series of tunnels that crisscrossed and wound around such that I doubt we could have found our way back. We were at the mercy of Gaspard and his friends. The way was cold and dark, the walls seemed to close in on us, the ceiling to drop. If I didn't have claustrophobia before, I had it then.

"But imagine! The chamber we eventually reached was not dark, damp, nor dingy. One hundred feet beneath the streets of Paris was an elegant suite of large rooms: one was a sort of kitchen with cook stove and hanging meats; in another was a long table such as one might find in a hotel restaurant, set with glassware, mismatched yet which appeared to be crystal; the third room being a meeting room with chairs arrayed in a circle. Into this meeting area we were ushered by Gaspard. There were perhaps a dozen men who took to the chairs as we entered.

"We were placed in the center of the circle. I had expected some form of rough handling or abuse, and certainly the possibility of events turning against us was high, but these men showed only curiosity: first, how we had been able to locate them in this vast labyrinth of tunnels, and second, as to what it was that had drawn us to them…as it had not been by accident. We were questioned by…I wouldn't say the leader…a spokesman.

"Renoir gave the explanations, relating what we knew of the supposed kidnapping and mentioning the theory that gypsies were to blame. He withheld, for the moment, the child's name and address…a wise move I felt, but an omission the White Roses would not ignore. They pressed for the name. Their spokesman asked the obvious question: was there any money offered as reward or ransom? We replied that assuredly there would be funds for a rescue…the amount was unknown to us.

"We were taken by the giant into the dining area while the group conferred. This was when Gaspard gave us some insights into the Society of the White Rose and their aims. They were not, he told us, in league with those fellows who trafficked in stolen children, nor did they have any affiliates among the gypsy population of France. Their interest, in our case, would be the money, for funds were needed for future plans…plans which would for now remain secret. Of course, we would be required to keep the existence of the group and their location secret…under penalty of retribution. We agreed.

"We were called back into the meeting room. It was decided that Le Société de la Rose Blanche would assist us in rescuing the boy. We must reveal to them his name and the name of his parents, however. Upon this we agreed, although reluctantly, for there was always the possibility of a ransom being requested by the society without the actual return of the boy. Could we trust them? What choice did we have?"

Jeffrey downed the last few drops of his whiskey and waved to the waiter for another. He was exhausted in the telling of the tale and his anxiety over the risk they had taken was apparent. Émilie-Claire reached across the table and put her hand on top of his. Eagerly he looked into her eyes to discern any hint of a budding affection for him. Would his self-proclaimed gallantry have reversed her previous indifference toward him? His hopes were not as yet to be realized as she responded to his question ("What choice did we have?") with:

"You should have left it to the police. You may have created a circumstance which will bring harm to the boy. This group…if they were not the ones who kidnapped Geoffroy, then their interference may induce the real villains to hide their crime in some ugly way. Did I ever tell you that my ward, Teo, was kidnapped when we were in New Orleans?"

"And you let the police handle it alone?"

"Well…no. We searched and found the boy and rescued him with some great effort. But the danger! At any time Teo could have been killed…or worse."

"But you persevered to good effect. I don't trust the Paris police to do anything well accept the taking of bribes. And there is another chance to find him. You remember I told you about Gaspard? While he led us out of the labyrinth and back to the street level he told us of his own background. It seems his great size had been beneficial to him in finding employment in traveling circuses. He was billed as Gaspard Le Géant…Gaspard the Giant. He made many friends in that particular world. He vowed to make inquires on his own."

"That sounds as unlikely to produce results as does the presumed efforts by your White Rose people. You and your painter friends should stick to painting and leave the sleuthing to professionals. The boy's father, François Gardinier, has hired a detective, by the way. A man named Vidocq."

"Doesn't trust the police either, I see. Well, hopefully we will get some information soon with all these different people working on it. Meanwhile, may I call on you? I feel we could get to know each other better. We may have had some disagreements, but under the circumstances…"

"There has been a lot of tension and worry. We have been short with each other at times. I would be agreeable to seeing you…but…"

"But?"

"But understand that I am not in the least interested in beginning a romance with you or with any other person. Not at the present time. I have Teo to consider." Émilie-Claire was adamant, but wavering. She betrayed herself with a smile.

"Perhaps we could take the boy somewhere for entertainment," Jeffrey suggested.

"Hmm…just not to the circus!"

Another impulsive choice she would regret? Émilie-Claire tried to shake the self-doubt from her consciousness. She let her gaze travel through the crowded café, watching the diverse tangle of patrons as they drank and laughed together, or sat soberly alone as shadowy silhouettes. Here were the bourgeois in top hats from Montparnesse, craftsmen from Faubourg Saint-Antoine, factory workers from Batigolles, laborers from everywhere that Haussmann laid heavy hands, and women to match each category. They blended into one continuous gray mass in the dimly lit café. They emitted an incomprehensible din of bitter-sweet merriment.

Flaherty too looked around the room. Suddenly he stiffened and turned his back against something or someone he saw. Émilie-Claire could not help but notice. She quizzed the artist:

"What is it, Jeffrey? Did you see a ghost? Is it that woman who is now approaching? Someone you wish to avoid? My, but you're a man about town."

Flaherty ventured a glance over his shoulder. Too late. She had seen him and was coming over.

"She is a woman we have used for a model. I wished to avoid her because we were forced to let her go recently. She is just too fidgety and frankly, we were getting tired of drawing her."

"And paying her, most likely. Look…here she is."

Cyrielle Isabelle Océane, the woman with three first names, alleged former prostituée, sometime fidgety artist's model, and possibly scorned lover, stood patiently behind Jeffrey Flaherty, waiting to be acknowledged. At last, Flaherty turned.

"Bonjour, Cyrielle."

"Oh, Jeffy…I've been hoping to see you. Why have you not called upon me? I've been so lonesome!"

"Cyrielle, I'm with somebody here. Can't you see that? Can't you be polite and leave us alone?"

"Aren't you going to introduce me, Jeffy?" She extended her hand to Émilie-Claire who did not take it. "I'm Cyrielle, an old…friend…of Jeffy's."

"Émilie-Claire. An older friend of 'Jeffy's'. You are an artist's model I believe?"

"I was. I'm currently in between engagements. These artists are such cheap skates."

"Perhaps you should go back to you previous profession. I hear that pays well."

"What do you…? How do…? Oh! I've never been so insulted in my life! I'll not stay here another minute," Cyrielle said. But she remained standing where she was.

"Bonjour, Cyrielle," said Flaherty, turning his back on her. "We'll call you if we get desperate."

Now the woman did whirl around and walk swiftly away. Flaherty managed a forced smile for Émilie-Claire's benefit. It was not returned.

"That was cruel…of both of us," Émilie-Claire told him. "I'm sure the girl has a good heart. And needs a respectable job!" She laughed: "Jeffy!"

7

Vidocq Visits the Morgue

He wasn't *the* Vidocq, merely his son...or at least, that was what he claimed. Emile-Adolphe Vidocq was the son of the first wife of François Eugène Vidocq, the world's first private detective. When François Vidocq died Emile-Adolphe sought to be recognized as his alleged father's legitimate offspring but it turned out that the elder Vidocq had been in prison when the conception would have taken place. No inheritance for Emile-Adolphe.

Perhaps an obsession with the establishment of this paternity contributed to Emile-Adolphe's following in his famous father's footsteps. At any rate, Emile-Adolphe Vidocq now promoted himself as a detective for hire; the fame and popularity of the first Vidocq guaranteed clients and an adequate source of income. He had just been hired by François Gardinier to locate his missing son, Geoffroy. Where better to start than at the morgue?

The father, François Eugène Vidocq, had since the age of 13 been in and out of prison for various acts of thievery, battery, dueling to the death, forgery, escape, and other criminal acts. He escaped from prison several times, one time disguised as a sailor and another time as a nun. In 1809 when he was in La Force Prison in Paris he offered to act as an informant for the police, reporting on the other inmates. He was transferred to jail in Bicêtre and there began his career as a spy.

Once released in 1811 he continued his work as secret agent for the Paris police, making use of his knowledge of the criminal underground. He then organized the Brigade de la Sûreté. He hired ex-criminals like himself and encouraged his agents to "explore the various rendezvous in every part; to go to the theatres, the boulevards, the barriers, and all other public places, the haunts of thieves and pickpockets" including the local bars and brothels.

He resigned from the Sûreté twice, the final time in 1832 when he began to work full time as a private investigator. In 1833, Vidocq founded Le Bureau des Renseignements, a detective agency and private police force, again staffed by former criminal elements. It has been called the first detective agency in history.

Vidocq was responsible for a number of innovations in crime fighting, notably a criminal data base of index cards with personal descriptions, aliases, and modus operandi of known offenders. This had a great influence on a clerk working for the Sûreté named Alphonse Bertillon who extended the system by including actual measurements of the suspects. This anthropometric system called "bertillonage" predated fingerprint identification and was used around the world.

Vidocq refined crime scene investigation making the first plaster casts of footprints, measuring the ballistic properties of bullets, and using other techniques that would become part of modern forensics. He was a master of disguise and often took part in felonies in order to arrest criminals. It was said that he had a photographic memory and never forgot a criminal face. It was also said that Vidocq set up robberies himself to increase his arrest count.

Honoré de Balzac in his novel, *Le Père Goriot*, and in later works modeled the character of Vautrin (first an arch-criminal, then a police minister) after Vidocq. Victor Hugo, in *Les Misérables*, modeled both the main characters, Jean Valjean and Inspector Javert after Vidocq. Alexandre Dumas used attributes of the famous detective for his policeman character of Monsieur Jackal in *Les Mohicans de Paris*. Edgar Allan Poe referred to him in "The Murders in the Rue Morgue" and his own detective, C. Auguste Dupin, used deductive techniques such as Vidocq might have used to solve the murders. Eugène Sue wrote *Les Mystéries de Paris* with a Vidocq-like character named Rodolphe de Gerolstein. This work prompted Vidocq himself to write *Les Vrais Mystéries de Paris*, albeit using a ghost writer.

Like father, like son—Emile-Adolphe Vidocq had embarked upon a career as a private detective. While he lacked the first-hand knowledge of his father's criminal background and the experience of working as chief of police of the Sûreté, he had studied François Eugène Vidocq's memoires and other written works and had acquired an appreciation for the ratiocinative approach to solving crime He had few acquaintances among the criminal underground, but he knew which haunts to explore and which questions to ask. And he had a close associate who accompanied him on his cases: Henri Barbou.

Barbou and Vidocq had met at the Université de Rouen. Henri Barbou had studied mathematics and was finishing up an advanced degree when the younger Vidocq appeared on the scene. The two men shared rooms for the duration of Barbou's tenure as a student and became fast friends. They often strolled through the ancient town, exploring the botanical gardens at the Jardin des Plantes de Rouen or the Place du Vieux Marché, where Joan of Arc met her fiery death. Vidocq never finished his higher education. He moved to Paris when Barbou established a private tutoring service there, and again the two men shared an apartment.

Vidocq's detective business at first was slow and dull. His typical case was to follow a wife or husband suspected of infidelity. A big breakthrough came when he was hired to recover some rare jewels stolen from the estate of a prominent banker; the police had been stymied. Vidocq applied the principles of his father's investigative techniques, mainly, examining not only the obvious, but also the trivial. He observed that the window through which the thief or thieves had supposedly gained access had been broken from the inside. By following the wife he learned of her lover and the plans they had laid to leave Paris together, sustained by the sale of the jewelry. Vidocq proved that the wife was the guilty party. The notoriety of the banker and the degree of the scandal thus revealed was of great interest to the press and so the story stayed in newsprint for several days. Soon Vidocq, whose detecting prowess was glorified by the papers, was in demand.

Vidocq would routinely discuss his cases with his friend and soon found Barbou's insights beneficial. He began to invite Barbou to accompany him in matters of investigative difficulty. Barbou's fine mind for mathematical reasoning coupled with Vidocq's methodical approach and the ease with which the pair of sleuths could use each other as sounding boards proved to be a successful combination.

Today, they had hastened to the Île de la Cité to walk along the River Seine on the Quai de l'Archevêché, past men with wheeled hand carts pushing draped cargo shaped ominously like corpses, to the soiled stone façade of a low building over whose door appeared the familiar words, "Liberté! Egalité! Fraternité!"—the musée de la mort, the Paris Mortuary.

The morgue was conveniently located along the banks of the river (as a large number of the dead who found their way to its chambers were suicides fished from the Seine). These and others found in alleys or along the narrow streets of the city were often unidentified. The policy of the institution was to display the deceased to the public in the hopes of identification; the morgue was open to the curious, the thrill-seekers, the morbid and morose, and attracted artists and writers like Émile Zola and Charles Dickens who wrote in detail about the profundity of decay and the spectacle of mortality that elicited cheap emotions from the population: "…they express horror, they joke, they applaud or whistle, as at the theatre…" Zola wrote, describing the throngs of visitors who ogled at the "nudities, brutally exposed, bloodstained, and in places bored with holes."

In a long hallway the crowd gathered—pretty working girls from shops and rough-looking laborers and fashionably dressed women with their unruly children and old men carrying their lunches with them and the unemployed and those of independent means and even, now and then, the bereaved hoping to find a missing loved one—hoping against hope this battered body or that naked, purple-blotched and dripping semblance of a human being *wasn't* their missing loved one. The crowd, like the residents of the musée de morte, exemplified the Egalité of France in a bizarre and morbid way.

Along the hallway were large windows through which the corpses could be seen arrayed on slanted black marble slabs, not unlike the display of fruits and vegetables at the nearby market. They were stripped of clothing which hung on the wall behind them…the clothing sometimes gave a better indication of identity than did the decomposed state of the bodies. There was no refrigeration. If the putrefaction of the corpse had advanced too far, the body was replaced by a photograph or a wax sculpture of the face placed artistically on a manikin.

The crowd was centered at the far end of the hall where the most recent arrival had been deposited on its marble slab: the headless torso of a woman freshly fished from the Seine. Vidocq and Barbou skirted around the leering mob and shuttled through a doorway clearly marked "défense d'enter"—no admittance. Showing his special permit card to the guard, Vidocq led his friend into the musty, damp, and putrid smelling morgue proper, into the room where the theatrics of corpse preparation…the stripping, the cleaning, the arranging…were not part of the public circus.

"Look here, Barbou," said Vidocq, "these are the newest. The artifacts of their departure from this mortal coil are more apparent in this room. Observe the crust of dried mud on this one…it clearly indicates the body was pulled from the river, but sat somewhere for a time before its discovery. See, the bloating has given way to decomposition. Now why do you suppose someone retrieved the unfortunate from its watery grave only to abandon…or hide the body?"

"Perhaps the rescuer was also the instrument of destruction. See around the neck? There are indications of strangulation. A jilted lover kills in a fit of rage, pushes the evidence into the Seine in an effort to hide his crime, then, in a sudden pang of conscience, pulls her back out and conceals her in some alley."

"In that case there would not be time for the water to work its terrible effect. No, she had been in the river long enough to swell up…the body gases bringing her to the surface. She was spotted floating by some good Samaritan who fished her out, then panicked and left her high and dry where she lay undiscovered for at least a day."

"As you say, Vidocq. But we are looking for a young boy, are we not?"

"We are hoping to eliminate that possibility. Let us query the help. I say, good fellow," Vidocq called to the morgue attendant, "have you any young boys? About eight years old?"

The morgue attendant was a weary- and bedraggled-looking man in his late 50s carrying a mop and pail. More of a janitorial employee it seemed, as he appeared reluctant even to talk to the detectives. He simply pointed to a door, his arm, hand, extended finger, wavering slightly as if the weight of it was too much to sustain for long. Vidocq and Barbou made for the door.

Friends and admirers of Emile-Adolphe Vidocq kindly characterized him as "stout." Others, not so charitable in their estimate of the detective's physical attributes called him "obese." The truth was somewhere in between. He affected the thinnest of mustaches which he teased and twirled into an absurd curlicue. His appearance was accented by a severe and heartless stare, unblinking and inscrutable, which he had cultivated as a tool for the interrogation of suspects. Barbou, on the other hand, was as lanky as Vidocq was portly. His most notable feature was a hawk-like nose upon which balanced a pince-nez, often askew and never clean.

In this new chamber were the young: infants, children of various ages, adolescents. Victims of disease, exposure, starvation, or abuse. There was no particular order to the arrangement of the bodies; presumably it was first come, first to be laid out. As in the outer chamber, clothing was hung on the wall behind each victim. There was no window into this room. Parents searching for a lost child had to petition for entry.

"What a dreadful display, Vidocq! Tragic loss of the innocents, the helpless, the unloved and unwanted as well as the cherished."

"Ah, but how instructive, Barbou! See how the ravishes of disease have blackened the skin? Notice the effects of insects and vermin? This aids the determination of the time of death. And this one…a murder. You can see the marks of ligatures on the wrists and ankles."

"Where do we start? Sadly, there are so many."

"Eliminate the obvious. This one too young…that one too old…those putrefied beyond recognition. How many remain for our analysis? Not so many."

It was a ghastly chore, cataloging the dead. Barbou concentrated his mind upon statistics to quell his emotions; what percentage was of what age, what were the probabilities of misadventure; how long before each unknown person was carted away to an anonymous grave? He had pad and pencil at the ready as Vidocq examined each slab and related his findings; hash marks accumulated by each category as Barbou marked accordingly. He noted the identifying numbers of each corpse Vidocq included in the "not so many" that *might* be the object of their quest. When they were done, the number of possible victims that might be Geoffory Gardinier was four.

"More than I would have thought," commented Barbou.

Phoebe Stapleton was beside herself. Her young charge, Jeanne-Alice, had strayed from the au pair's sight during an afternoon rest period when the girl should have been in her room (allowing Phoebe a few moments to herself to indulge in her own devises). Checking on the girl, Phoebe was startled to find the bed empty and Jeanne-Alice no where to be found. Panic seized her.

She began a methodical search of the house looking even in closets and armoires and under beds but this did not avail her of the urchin. She searched the servant's wing: no Jeanne-Alice. She then extended her quest to the grounds. Remembering that the orangerie had been the favored haunt of Jeanne-Alice and Geoffroy, she entered the greenhouse calling periodically for the girl as she wound her way up and down the footpaths between the plants. Finally convinced that the girl was not present, she left the greenhouse and was about to return to the main house when she heard giggling.

The mirthful sounds came from the direction of the dovecote. Of course! The perfect place to hide from your au pair while sending shivers of fear through her thinking that you too had been kidnapped. This is all I need right now, Phoebe thought to herself: a belligerent child. She was furious.

The building was a round stone tower with a cone-shaped roof, about two stories tall and twenty feet in diameter. It had been built in an age when such structures were a symbol of wealth and status and it had served as an aviary for pigeons which, considered a delicacy, were harvested and eaten just as any food source on a farm would be. It had fallen out of use as such but had escaped the modernizing demolition that had eliminated the mote and drawbridge from the old castle.

Inside was a large empty space which was dark and musty smelling; the floor was covered with feathers and dried bird droppings. The walls were checkered with niches, each with a short platform upon which the pigeons could perch. The birds would enter from an opening at the top of the roof and settle into their very own bird condominium, sheltered from the weather and all predators—

except the human ones. Lately they had abandoned the dovecote. A tall ladder ran up to the top of the dovecote. Jeanne-Alice was perched at the top of the ladder.

"Jeanne-Alice! Come down here at once!" Phoebe screamed.

"I won't. You can't make me."

"I'll come up there and drag you down. I mean it. Right this instant. Venez ici!"

"You'd be too scared to climb up here. I won't come down until dinner."

"You won't get any dinner if you don't come down immediately!"

The battle of wills continued in this manner for many minutes while Phoebe became more and more concerned that the child would slip from her perch and plummet the two stories to the bird-soiled floor, leaving the family with two lost children. Frustrated and fearful, she tried one last threat:

"If you don't come down right now I'll tell your father."

"Tell me what?"

Phoebe turned to encounter the tall figure of M. François Arnaud Gardinier, silhouetted against the meager light that filtered in through the open door. All she could do was to point up toward the girl.

"Jeanne-Alice!" Gardinier said, his angry voice echoing in the dovecote. "Get down here immédiatement!"

"Yes, Papa."

Phoebe cringed at each placement of small foot upon rung as the girl scrambled down the ladder. How did small children escape death during such perilous activities, she wondered. Death? What was François doing home at this hour?

Once Jeanne-Alice was safely on the ground her father began to chastise her for her behavior. The girl looked up at him with tears in her eyes.

"When is Geoffroy coming home, Papa?" she asked.

"We'll talk about that later," he replied. "Now go back to the main house and tell Mme. Popelin to look after you for the remainder of the day. Mademoiselle Stapleton and I have something important to discuss."

Now Phoebe thought: "I'm to be fired for sure. Turned out into the cold. Well, I deserve it, don't I?" There in one instant would go all the dreams she had entertained about taking her place among the elite of Paris, not as the au pair of the master, but as his bride. She had yet to achieve even the status of mistress. And she was failing miserably as an au pair.

"Phoebe," Gardinier began, "something dreadful has come up. I have been contacted by M. Vidocq. It seems there is a real possibility that Geoffroy may be…I can't bring myself to say it! Vidocq wants me to identify a body…well, four bodies await our inspection at the morgue. It may not be he, but…"

"You said our…?"

"I need you to accompany me for this terrible task. I haven't the strength to do it alone if it turns out that…. I can't have Solange come, as you know. You are the only one I can count on for support. Come now, I've the carriage waiting."

8

Le Rat Mort

A light rain was falling when Phoebe Stapleton and François Gardinier reached the Île de la Cité. From the Pont Neuf they looked down onto the Seine where the wind blew a veil of raindrops across the tepid water. There barges were being poled by boatmen from Montereau-Fault-Yonne while other boats were docked along the quays offering vegetables or freshly butchered sheep for sale. The great cathedral of Nortre-Dame de Paris loomed high against the gray sky, its restoration by Eugène Viollet-le-Duc still incomplete; doves flew in and out of the flying buttresses or perched upon the heads of gargoyles.

As they approached the morgue Phoebe took François's arm. She was there to lend strength to him—equally, she needed his support if they were to survive the emotional ordeal to come. Emile-Adolphe Vidocq and Henri Barbou awaited them at the morgue's entrance. The dour looks on their faces were not encouraging. Thankfully the room of the young dead was not accessible for public viewing. No curious crowds would complicate the situation. Upon entering the room it seemed to Phoebe as if they had just arrived at the lowest circle of hell; only Satan was missing from the scene.

Vidocq led them to the first slab upon which lay the body of a young boy, his skin blackened in patches. François immediately rejected the notion that this was his son. "Too stout and too tall," he said. "I cannot be mistaken in this case…it is not Geoffroy."

Phoebe agreed. Barbou was quick to cross off the number of this corpse from his list. To the second grim display the four moved, slowly and reluctantly, but understanding it was imperative they do so. Here they examined another boy, an apparent drowning. The body had swelled and turned a purplish-blue. Identification here was nearly impossible, but again, François said, "No, this is not him. See, the hair is too dark and this foot…it is what they call a club foot, is it not?"

"Bien," said Vidocq. "We have eliminated two of the four. That is very good. Please attend to the next if your stamina is holding steady."

Phoebe staggered as they came to the slab with the next candidate for identification. It—she couldn't quite think of it as a human form—was clearly unrecognizable. Swollen, covered with blotches and sores, the face nearly fallen in upon itself, it was past the time it should be displayed, having putrefied to an insufferable degree. Yet, because of morgue inefficiency, it was still here.

"Is there anyway we can eliminate this one?" asked Barbou.

"It is unlikely this is the boy," answered Vidocq. "You see, the degree of decomposition indicates that the time of death precedes the disappearance of the boy."

Phoebe felt she was about to faint…in fact, she wished to faint, to remove herself from the scene in any way available to her. François held her up. She swallowed back the phlegm that had arisen in her throat and told herself to be brave. François was himself unsteady and turned abruptly from the body before them. "Can we move on?" he demanded.

The last body lay on its slab in innocent but explicit exposure. No creeping corruption marred its mortality; there were those, not anyone present, of course, who would have said it had an eternal beauty: pale skin like alabaster, a serene posture which suggested peaceful rest. Only a few details spoiled the purity of this death: the ligature marks on the wrists and ankles, the rough red abrasions at the throat, and the two long gashes from forehead to chin—a bloody "X" that canceled the features as if to say, "This person no longer exists." But exist, in horrible repose, this horrible specter of a former living, breathing, happy boy did.

"I don't know...I can't be sure," said François Gardinier." It could be him...but I don't believe it is. He is the right size and build...but that face! This is too horrible." He turned away, hiding his own face with his hands so that no one would see the tears that swiftly came.

"And therefore, no way to eliminate this one," said Vidocq.

"Oh no!" Phoebe said suddenly. "It *is* Geoffroy. Look at the clothes."

There, hanging on the wall behind the corpse, was the very suit of clothing that Phoebe had laid out for Geoffroy on the day they were to leave for the circus. She remembered the pearl buttons on the little jacket, the piping on the sleeves. There was now no doubt in her mind. She threw her arms around François and together they began to cry.

Barbou looked questioningly at Vidocq. What now, his glance seemed to ask. Vidocq shook his head. "Now we ask the morgue attendant for the pieces of rope that were found on the body." He said.

"But why?" asked Barbou. "We've found the boy."

"They are a clue that may lead us to the perpetrators. This case isn't over yet...not by a long shot."

Later, as the two detectives walked away from the morgue, out of hearing range, Vidocq added this:

"There is something strange, don't you think, about the way the face was carved with an 'X' or cross. This makes me question even whether this really is the boy or not. It is all too much like...a work of art. A dastardly art, but one of near perfection if indeed the intent was to confuse, distract, obliterate."

"And the rope?"

"There are several different types of rope, and several sources for procuring them. I am hopeful we can track these accoutrements of evil to the devils that used them."

"That's brilliant!"

"Of course! I am...Vidocq!"

Excerpt from Émilie-Claire Lebeau's daily journals

August 31, 1862

Spent the weekend consoling Phoebe. I suggested a trip to the country where there would be nothing to trigger remorseful or grievous thoughts. Normandy suggested itself to my wistful imaginings and, as it promised to be cooler there than it was in Paris, we boarded a train at the Gare de l'Oest and enjoyed a comfortable ride through the countryside. An hour later we arrived at Vernon, and there I hired a carriage to take us the six or seven kilometers to the charming village of Giverny.

Jeffrey Flaherty, bless his nouveau-bohemian heart, had made me aware of an establishment in Giverny run by a Madame Angélina Baudy: a quaint store to which is attached a bar and café and at which, Jeffrey informed me, one could get a room for the night or nights as needed. Some of his artist acquaintances, those "Americans in Paris" as they are called, had begun to explore the French country side, particularly Normandy, for subject matter and had discovered Giverny and the Baudy establishment.

It was a small brick structure along the main road with tables set outdoors under a trellis dripping with wisteria in a yard filled with rose bushes. Madame Baudy and her husband, Gaston, made us feel most welcome. When we inquired as to sight-seeing opportunities, Madame Baud suggested some walking paths along the River Epte. After a delicious déjeuner of cold cuts, cheeses and wine, we headed off toward the river.

Willows dipped delicate branches into L'Epte along its banks. Water fowl drifted lazily, dunking their heads into the water periodically. For me this was a serene respite from the hustle and bustle of "Le Vie Parisienne." Phoebe, however, remained dispirited, melancholy, preoccupied and conscience-stricken. I tried to distract her with some mundane conversation.

"This trickle of a river flows into the Seine not far from here," I said.

"Good," Phoebe replied, "let's walk down there so I can throw myself into it."

"Phoebe, mon amour, you aren't to blame for Geoffroy's death. It was tragic but you could not have prevented it."

"I shouldn't have allowed him to go for ice cream. Jonathan…M. Blanchard offered to go. I stopped him."

"The girl was with the boy. She is more to blame than you."

"Did I tell you? No…I don't think I did. About a week after the funeral some man came to the château. He claimed he represented the kidnappers and wanted François to pay a ransom for Geoffroy. We had just buried him!"

"That must have been awful! A false hope…or was there any truth to the matter?"

"François didn't think the body at the morgue was Geoffroy at first. I pointed out the clothing…it was definitely Geoffroy's. It was like I killed him twice!"

And here she broke down in tears and sobs. It was all I could do to try to calm her. "What did François do?" I asked.

"He told the man he needed some sort of proof that they really had the boy. The man brought out a shirt that looked a great deal like the one Geoffroy had been wearing."

"But?"

"But we had recovered the clothing. François sent the man packing. The man called back at us that they would probably kill the boy if they didn't get their ransom money. Kill the boy who was already dead!"

I thought to myself: what if Phoebe had been mistaken about the clothing. What if the boy they buried had been some other sad victim? But I refrained from mentioning my concerns. If this hadn't occurred to her as yet…I didn't want to be the one who put the thought into her head. Then she added this:

"François sent a message to the police about this man. They investigated. A few days later we were asked by the prefect at the Sûreté du Paris to identify a suspect they had apprehended. It was, in fact, our man. Apparently, he was known to the police as a confidence man who had used similar schemes before to extort money from unsuspecting victims. He was, they told us, working alone."

"But how did he know about the clothing that Geoffroy wore?"

"Remember the notice we placed in the newspapers? That described what he was wearing."

A logical explanation, yet I wondered…was this man by any chance a member of the Society of the White Rose? My mind was swimming with conspiracy theories.

At the foot of Montmarte Butte at Place Pigalle, a fountain had just this year been installed by Haussmann's favorite fountain architect, Gabriel Davioud. It had a broad circular base in which a pedestal with a fluted column stood supporting a cast iron basin from which water flowed in veils. It attracted the many dogs in the neighborhood who were routinely bathed in the fountain by their owners, and lately it had been used as a depository for discarded rubbish, including fish scraps and other disgusting organic items. It had a distinctly evil smell. Across from the fountain, on the Boulevard de Clichy, at the corner of Rue Frochot, was Le Grand Café Pigalle. It was the lair of literary types and artists. Perhaps because of the odor emanating from the nearby fountain, or perhaps, as a legend describes, when an illicit activity in a back room was interrupted by a large rat (immediately dispatched), the café was rechristened as "Le Rat Mort."

No beautification by fountains or trees could repair the lurid reputation of the district. Its brothels and street walkers made Pigalle notorious and brought many adventurers into the bohemian realm to sample its exotic and often forbidden fruits. Unlike these voyagers from more conservative realms, many artists and poets took up residence in Montmarte and practically lived in its cafés.

Another café, the New Athens, which early on had been the favorite of aspiring playwrights and poets and which was located just across the plaza from the Rat, soon saw an exodus of these patrons following a row they had with the owner. Alfred Delvau, Castagnary and Alphonse Duchesne instead started frequenting Le Rat Mort and soon were followed by Henri Murger, Eugene Ceyras, Catulle Mendès, and the poet Fernand Desnoyers, the avant garde of their day. Café de le Rat Mort was now the place to see and be seen, to drink and to expound upon the politics of the day.

Behind its windows of stained glass, at tables of polished wood, sat poets scribbling fresh verse on soiled napkins. Someday these heartfelt lines might inspire…or repulse the reading public. Was it here that Baudelaire would write these words…a tribute to Paris as seen from Monmartre?

Je t'aime, ô ma très belle ô ma charmante… Que de fois…
Tes débauches sans soif et tes aurores sans âme, Ton goût de l'infini,
Qui partout dans le mal lui-même se proclame,
Et tes feux d'artifice, éruptions de joie,
Qui font rire le ciel, muet et ténébreux.
O vous soyez témoins que j'ai fait mon devoir,
Comme un parfait chimiste et comme une âme sainte.
Car j'ai de chaque chose extrait la quintessence :
Tu m'a donné ta boue et j'en ai fait de l'or.

I love you, O my very beautiful O my charming ... How many times ...
Your debauchery without thirst and your dawn without soul, Your taste of the
infinite,
Who everywhere the evil itself proclaims itself,
and your fireworks, joy eruptions
Who are laughing at the sky, silent and dark.
O you are witnesses that I have done my duty,
as a perfect chemist and a holy soul.
for I have of everything extracted the quintessence:
You gave me your mud and I made some gold.

And here sat the young painter, Jeffrey Flaherty, sipping his whiskey slowly while he waited to be joined by an unlikely visitor to the now popular café. There was music from a trio of guitar, violin, and accordion. More than one couple arose from booth or table to dance, holding tightly to their partners in what Americans called "the French style." Waiters carried trays of oysters and champagne. No where could there be seen a dead rat (to the disappointment of those customers who were slumming).

Suddenly there was a stir of soft exclamation from those patrons whose proximity to the front door afforded them a view of the colossal form that now lumbered into the Rat. They stared, nonplused, at the voluminous and gorilla-like Gaspard Le Géant. He stood for a moment in the doorway surveying the café. Seeing Flaherty seated near the back of the café he began to weave his way through the tables toward the painter. Abruptly, he was confronted by a nervous looking serveur. This man he pushed aside (gently) and continued over to Flaherty's table. To the consternation of the waiter, Flaherty rose and motioned for Gaspard to sit, then ordered the waiter to bring his friend whatever he wanted. Gaspard asked for a beer.

Flaherty had not overcome his nervousness in the company of the giant. This even though Gaspard had never been aggressive nor even the slightest bit impolite. Was it the thick hair on the back of Gaspard's hands or the scar which traced a light pink across the ruddy forehead? Or the missing teeth? Or the odor which other patrons of Le Rat Mort were beginning to notice? Flaherty forced a smile to his lips.

"When you asked to meet me here I hadn't known at the time

that the boy was found…and dead and buried. Else I would have foregone the meeting."

"Dead and buried?" asked Gaspard. "Well, perhaps it is best that they think it so."

"What do you mean? You doubt it was the right boy?"

"Just listen for a moment to my story and then you make your own conclusions. I wanted to talk to my friends who knew things. I went first to…what do they call it? The scene of the crime. But the Cirque Olympique was gone! Just a hole in the ground and men covered in white dust all around digging and hauling away stones and the sort. Haussmann is a devil! He is removing the theaters and bars that give pleasure and putting in their place…what? Roads. As if we needed more roads.

"So I went down the boulevard to the other circus which still stood…Le Cirque Napoléon. Lady Luck smiled on this one for the new street will stop just short of it. There I looked for old friends but there only very few were known to me or I to them. I prowled around behind the area where the animals were kept. I found a familiar face tending to a very large elephant…with age his skin now nearly resembled that of his charge, but I recognized him easily.

"His full name is Viktor Milan Maksimov but we called him 'l'Ours Russe,' the Russian Bear, when he performed as a weight lifter at the traveling circus where we both worked so many yeas ago. Later he worked as a clown and an acrobat, then became a jumper of horses. Why, at one time he could vault over fourteen horses…can you imagine? He would leap from a batteau gaining twenty feet into the air, turn a somersault and land on his feet as if there were no effort involved in the feat at all. But I see he has now declined into the washing down of pachyderms and the feeding of monkeys.

"Anyway I ask the Bear, 'cause he knows everybody and everything that goes on in the circus, has he heard about the kidnapping at the Olympique? He says sure and it doesn't surprise him as it's happened before. So I ask, 'is it gypsies that done it?' He tells me he can't talk here and to meet me later. We agreed to reconnoiter at Place du Château d'Eau by the fountain.

"There I ask him again about the missing boy. He tells me there is a trafficking in young children who are sold to highest bidders seeking to expand their family for whatever reason there may be…maybe we don't ask about the reason. This one, he felt sure, was taken to a wealthy businessman in Germany. So he was not in the morgue, I think."

"But what about the clothing that was found on the dead boy? There was no mistaking it, I am told."

"Perhaps it was removed and discarded. After all, the transaction would not allow for any identification of the boy's origin. Someone picked up the clothes to give to the other boy who they later dispatched. There is a theory for you, n'est-ce pas?"

9

Regarding Jules Verne, the Emperor, and M. Richelieu

Excerpt from: *Dame Impétueux, la Mémoire de Émilie-Claire Lebeau-Richelieu*, (English translation, published by Charles W. Karr & Co., Chicago, 1897)

The manuscript was entitled, *Paris au XXe Siècle (Paris in the Twentieth Century)*. Pierre-Jules Hetzel, the publisher of Jules Verne's first adventure novel, *Cinq Semaines en ballon (Five Weeks in a Balloon)*, hated it, claiming it to be "mere science fiction" and therefore beneath his dignity as a publisher of quality literature. It was too unbelievable, he said. He would not touch it. This was in 1863. Verne took the manuscript to my good friend, M. Delamain at his bookstore, the Librairie Delamain, to see if he could do something with it. Not accustomed to publishing anything more ambitious that pamphlets or guide books, Delamain was dubious. He too was wary of the extreme fantasy represented by the setting of the story. He wanted the opinion of an expert reader, one versed in the nuances of literary experimentation. Enter myself.

The story is set in the Paris of 1960. It concerns a young man, Michel Dufrénoy, who writes a poem in Latin and wins an award for his effort, a circumstance that dumbfounds his family and amuses the public who are ordinarily concerned only with issues relating to the technologies of the day. These (unbelievable?) technologies are the true subjects of the novel. Verne paints a picture of the future that is a dream-like Eden supported through ingenious inventions but at the same time a frightening, soul-draining degeneration of the human condition. And, at the time of its writing, it certainly seemed to me a preposterous view of the future.

Take, for example, the method of transportation the people of twentieth century Paris use to move about their great, overgrown metropolis. There are no horse-drawn vehicles; instead, there are "gas-cabs." These are propelled by engines that burn hydrogen gas that can be obtained at the many fueling stations that are scattered around the city. And they can travel through tunnels under the streets. There are also trains driven by compressed air and magnetic fields which travel without the necessity of an engineer. I thought it ridiculous in 1863.

He writes of an electric lighthouse 500 feet high and electric lights which illuminate the streets to near daylight in the dead of night. Electricity is used to produce music by connecting together 200 pianos so they can be played by a single musician. There is photographic telegraphy where pictures are transmitted over wires from house to house. There is execution by electric charge…no more the guillotine! There are sophisticated mechanical calculators that are networked together to share information over distances that are unimaginable. And a weapon so awesome and devastating it makes warfare obsolete.

And the culture? It is all about science and money. Few people read. The Academic Credit Union is in control of things and it only encourages literature in "perfect harmony with the age's industrial aims." Popular entertainment consists of attending shows of live sex…can you imagine? The main character, Michel Dufrénoy, aspires to become a poet but is unable to interest anyone in his work. We see the struggling artist against this backdrop of cold, uniformly low-brow, academically sterile, state-prescribed blandness. And here is where the novel becomes melodramatic, depressing, and…well, I wouldn't say artless, but commonplace.

When I returned the manuscript to M. Delamain I told him that the author had some promise but that he should shy away from this particular effort by Verne. Science fiction wasn't ever going to be popular the way romance novels were. Of course, one year later, Jules Verne's *Voyage au centre de la Terre (Journey to the Center of the Earth)* became an instant best seller, and the next year, *De la Terre à la Lune (From the Earth to the Moon)* duplicated its success. What did I know?

That year, 1863, was filled with monumental occurrences. In the United States, President Abraham Lincoln issued his Emancipation Proclamation, freeing all slaves. Of course, the South rejected it and the war went on. I wondered if Jeffrey Flaherty ever regretted his decision not to fight in that war. His home town of Chattanooga came under siege by Union forces in September of that year and fell to them a month later. His family and friends? He didn't talk about them and I didn't press him. He would only talk generally about the futility of war.

We French laid siege to the Mexican city of Puebla and took it in May. We entered Mexico City in June. By October, Napoleon III had offered Archduke Ferdinand Maximilian of Austria the Imperial Crown of Mexico and he had accepted. He was installed in May of 1864 but his rule was to be short-lived. President Benito Juárez refused to recognize his authority and although the new Emperor and the Empress Carlota acted with liberal vigor to correct some of the instabilities and inequities of the realm (raising money for the poor houses, restricting working hours and abolishing child labor, canceling debts among the peasantry and ending corporal punishment, enacting land reforms and extending voting rights to the non-landholding classes), he was at odds with the mostly conservative officials in his government and a hearty resistance to his rule was forming.

After the Civil War ended in the United States, its government pressured Napoleon III to end support of Maximilian and to withdrawn French troops from Mexico. The US began supplying Benito Juárez and Porfirio Diaz, Maximilian's opposition, with arms. The handwriting was on the wall. Maximilian invited ex-Confederates to move to Mexico, further perturbing relations with the US. Maximilian issued his so-called Black Decree on October of 1865 which made the existence of any armed band of men illegal and subject to military action. Ultimately, he executed more than eleven thousand supporters of Juárez and the Resistance.

In 1866 Napoleon III did finally withdraw his troops. In June of 1867, Maximilian and his generals were executed by a firing squad. It was another great failure for our Emperor…one of the many blunders he would make as he became an aging, bitter old man. But, once again, my narrative is tending to jump ahead of itself. I was writing of that tumultuous year of 1863. And so…

It was the year of the Salon des Refusés where Manet showed the painting I posed for. I've written about this already and needn't elaborate. I didn't go to see it, instead, I went to the opera. The young composer, Georges Bizet, premiered his opera, *Les pâcheurs de perles* at the Théâtre-Lyrique which had been rebuilt on the Place du Châtelet after its destruction at the Boulevard du Temple the year before. The audience liked it…the critics did not. This was the occasion upon which I got my first glimpse of two men I would later meet: my future husband, Jean-Léon Richelieu and the Emperor, Louis-Napoleon Bonaparte.

The Théâtre-Lyrique was a palace of decadence; sumptuous in its decoration and voluminous like a cathedral built, not for God, but for the muses. François Gardinier had a box on the second of the three tiers, overlooking the stage. He had invited Phoebe to accompany him to the premiere and suggested she bring me along to forestall any appearance of impropriety (a man whose wife was an invalid consorting with his young, attractive female employee might raise eyebrows). I asked if I could bring Teo as I felt the boy needed exposure to the arts and this was an opportunity that would not present itself very often. It was Teo, in fact, who spotted the Emperor and Empress sitting in semi-darkness in a box positioned nearly at the foot of the stage.

"Oh look, Mademoiselle," he blurted, "the King and Queen!"

"Emperor and Empress," I corrected him.

I looked over at François. If he felt any pain of loss of his child, perhaps awakened by the presence of Teo, he didn't show it. Stoical, I thought. Certainly not unfeeling. He saw me looking at him and he smiled. I turned my attention back to the box where the royal couple sat. Another man leaned forward from the shadows. A distinguished-looking, handsome, elegantly dressed man with slightly (attractively) graying hair and an eye patch over his right eye. I may have let out a little gasp at the sight.

"Who is that man in the Emperor's box?" I asked.

François answered, "That is Jean-Léon Richelieu, one of the Emperor's advisers."

My interest in this intriguing man must have been obvious to François. But not so obvious was the nature of that interest (slightly scandalous?). With an emphasis, therefore, on the political, he began to expand upon Jean-Léon's résumé:

"He attempted to steer the Emperor toward moderation during the Italian unification question, aware that a division of opinion pulled him in two directions—the devout Catholicism of the Empress Eugénie which favored protection of the authority of the Pope verses the imperialism of Piedmont as championed by the Prince."

I had no idea what he was talking about, having little interest in politics or current events, but I let him ramble on.

"Of course Napoleon set up the ill-fated federation, giving the presidency to the Pope which suited no one. Against Richelieu's advice, the Emperor sent troops thinking to force peace on the region and you know the result of that."

I didn't but I nodded. He continued:

"The German Confederation came to the assistance of Austria. Prussia mobilized along the Rhine. Napoleon suddenly lost interest in waging war and the armistice came as an insult to the Italians. What else could go wrong?"

Quite a bit, I figured, and François was certain to enlighten me.

"Richelieu rightly realized that the tragic flaw in the Emperor's modus operandi was his failure to hear, much less to take into consideration, the opinion of the public in these adventures of empire building. A Catholic opposition sprang up in France because of the capitulation in Italy. A treaty with England brought foreign competition to France through a free trade agreement which angered industrialists. All this was because of the short-sightedness of the Emperor.

"Richelieu argued that the suppression of opinion which so isolated Napoleon should be lifted. At last, the Emperor acted in accordance with Richelieu's insights. He granted Chambers the right to vote an address in answer to his annual speech from the throne. He allowed the press to report parliamentary debates. He granted the right of voting on the budget. And now he is allowing labor unions to form. But there are some who feel Richelieu's advice has only given fuel to the fire of the liberal movement toward a parliamentary empire. It may be the empire's ultimate downfall."

"Well, that's all very interesting,' I said, "but what about the man himself?"

"Richelieu? Well, he is unmarried. Probably in his late thirties. He is related, although through very distant cousins, to the famous…or infamous…Cardinal Richelieu. He comes from a small village in the Loire Valley…not Chinon…I think I remember it as Champigny-sur-Veude or something like that. Yes…it is near the Town of Richelieu, the one constructed by the old Cardinal and where he built the château of his mistress. Our Richelieu comes from inherited wealth, much of which has evaporated in recent times. He is dependant upon the good graces of the Emperor from what I understand."

François had me at "he is unmarried."

I'd been waiting and hoping for an invitation to one of the Empress Eugénie's soirées or to one of the grand balls which were held at the Tuileries Palace. There were of course the Bal Mabilles (outdoors) on the Avenue Montaigne on the weekends and these were attended by various members of the aristocracy, but anyone suitably dressed could get in for under 2 francs so where was the prestige in that?

I worked on my friend Manet who had at least some contact with persons of influence and eventually my diligence paid off. An invitation to the New Year Ball came by hand delivery one evening when an unusually heavy early winter snow was falling. Carriages and wagons left deep tracks in the snow-covered street below my window but I delighted in the sight which seemed to have christened the world with a new and cleansing hope.

I entered the ballroom in the Salle de Maréchaux on the arm of M. Manet; he in spotless evening dress and I in a newly purchased ball gown of silk and lace. The room occupied the space of two entire floors of the central Pavillon de L'Horloge of the Tuileries Palace and was crowded with men, a goodly percentage of whom were in gaudily decorated uniforms, and women in every kind of elegant costume from bulging crinolines to the newer, form-fitting "style Anglais." Regarding the crinoline style, as a well-know clergyman once said of women's clothing, "They have used so much material on the skirts that they have run out of any with which to cover their shoulders."

(And their breasts.) I for one was happy to see the new, more slender styles coming in.

And what a grand setting for a royal ball! Along one wall four columns of caryatids held up a second floor balcony that ran around the perimeter of the large space. Behind the balcony were arched windows draped in luscious satin. From the ceiling hung two great chandeliers; crystal pendants decked with what seemed like hundreds of candles as if they were enormous wedding cakes. Along the other walls were large portraits; of course, the Emperor and Empress were duly represented in brilliant oils. Although there was no dirt circle with galloping steeds, the room did remind me somewhat of the old Cirque Olympique…albeit a few notches higher in quality. I wondered what the hero of Verne's futuristic novel would have thought of the tableau…to my mind it was anachronistically *First* Empire, not Second.

We waited in the receiving line while the Emperor and Empress greeted the minions of the dance floor. As they approached my thoughts went to the discrepancy between the grand and regal portrait of the Emperor and himself in reality. I thought him quite short, old, and fat. He seemed like an overdressed maître-chiffonier, a dealer in old clothes, or a wagon driver. The Empress was, to a large extent, his complement, but age showed on her face and bare upper arms. Was she thinking about the uncomfortable proximity of the Comtesse de Castiglione, the dazzling mistress of Napoleon III who was just across the room?

The Emperor took my hand (which was unusual because he hadn't touched any of the other guests). The image of a wet dish towel came to my mind. Then he smiled…or leered, as it seemed, and bent forward to whisper something in my ear. It had to do with the directions to the sweeping staircase which led up to his private quarters. Should I have felt complimented by his lewd advance? I did not. I did force a smile to appear on my lips but I'm sure this was betrayed by the fierce glare in my eyes.

Manet and I danced one or two dances, then split up to wander among the gentry. I searched for the man with the eye patch. There were hundreds of people in the ballroom, so this was no easy task. When finally I spotted him I had to wait until the group surrounding him dissipated and he stood momentarily alone. I approached. I wanted to say, "You are a very good-looking man, won't you come home with me?" but fearing an abrupt rejection at that kind of boldness I settled on, "Would you like to dance?"

Women didn't ask men to dance, especially before they had been introduced. My future husband looked at me with a surprise equal to seeing charging rhino suddenly appearing on the dance floor…then he smiled. With that smile I knew I had hooked him. And I would always remind him in the years to come, that *I* had found *him*.

The orchestra began playing a valse à deux temps. Jean-Léon led me unto the dance floor where couples were executing glissades, gliding against the waltz-time rhythm and turning, stepping back toward each other in a chasse. We faced each other and he took my hand in his, touching me gently at the waist with his other hand. We turned, he did a glissade and I a chasse. It was a smooth, elegant dance but not intimate. What had I expected? Later we climbed to the balcony overlooking the ballroom and paused at the window to watch the snow falling by the light of a full moon.

Down below they'd started a polka. Jean-Léon shook his head. "Not my cup of tea," he said. "Good," I said. "I'd like to just talk." And so we talked for the rest of the evening, strolling around on the balcony or descending again to the ballroom to hide in the shadows and be alone and together as if both of us were inexperienced adolescents stealing away from the adults to flirt.

I didn't bare my soul to him, not at first. I didn't narrate the story of my life, even with omissions. I gave him a general idea of who I was, where I was from and how I spent my time. But I was guarded, not wishing to spoil the fantasy of first encounters. I think he sensed I was holding back. Did he think me a coquette? Evasive in order to entrap? I began to loosen up and all at once it came bubbling out like a fountain. In short time he knew all about New Orleans, California, and even about *Le déjeuner sur l'herbe*.

Did I ask him about losing the use of his eye? I did not. I could imagine: an accident while practicing with epees, a tragic turn of events during a battle in some distant arena of war, childhood play gone wrong such as a pretend knife fight or arrows shot too close, a projectile fallen from the ramparts of a decaying edifice—don't look up! It was more romantic not to know.

It was not le coup de foudre [editor's note: "love at first sight"] between Jean-Léon and myself. There was a mutual physical attraction, of course, but true unconditional regard came much later.

One obstacle was the difference in station between this illustrious confidant of the Emperor and me as an ordinary, albeit *nouveau riche*, *femme du monde*. We saw each other when we were able and made the most of the fleeting moments. Gradually friendship emerged in tandem with affection. When we realized that we would suffer terribly to ever be apart we decided to make our relationship legitimate and marry. Surprisingly, Louis-Napoleon did not oppose the merger…in fact he viewed it as a minor function of state and suggested that the ceremony take place at Notre Dame Cathedral where he had married Eugénie, the Countess of Teba, but that is a story for another chapter.

Byron Grush

10

Le Bon Marché Rive Gauche

Émilie-Claire had taken Teo to the fabulous department store to buy clothes; the boy seemed to outgrow his things more rapidly than a caterpillar shed its cocoon. True, no butterfly had emerged, but Teo was beautiful in his own way. She loved the boy as if he was her own and in a sense, he was. He could scarcely remember his own mother. She had considered motherhood, in other words…giving birth…in its physical reality as the inevitable, painful payback for picking the Eden's apple. It was an ordeal she preferred to avoid as long as possible. And she had the boy. And so they thought of each other, if not as mother and son, at least as parent and child.

Wandering through the Bon Marché was always a pleasure for both the woman and her ward. The entrepreneur, Aristide Boucicaut, had created a wonderland of merchandise to appeal to the tastes of Parisian ladies of all classes and particularly, the well-moneyed upper crust of society, whom he lured with displays of the finest gowns and accessories. Intricate lace from Chantilly, Eau de Cologne from Jean Marie Farina's perfumery, high-topped silk faille shoes from Gartell, the most ostentatious (but fashionable) millinery from the Jean Beraud workshop (piled high with feathers from exotic and endangered species of bird life). Each item uniquely displayed in its own area, an innovation in merchandising.

In the years to come, Boucicaut would build an even larger store with the help of architect Louis-Auguste Boileau and the firm of Gustave Eiffel. Its extravagance and innovation, particularly the employment of an army of live-in women, would inspire Émile Zola to write *Au Bonheur des Dames* about the lives and loves of the establishment's employees. And this women's paradise that thrilled for profit would inspire Field in Chicago and Selfridge in London. But today, in 1865, it seemed impossible to imagine a more dramatic place for shopping; it was a prime form of entertainment for those with disposable income.

Often the Bon Marché offered entertainment for children. Today there was a puppet show—not the traditional Guignol and Polichinelle, but a gentler rendition of daily life featuring farm animals as the main characters. Émilie-Claire sat Teo down among the small audience of children while she went to shop for a pair of gloves she needed. Teo watched but soon was bored and left to find the mam'selle. He lingered awhile at the toy counter, inspecting tin drums and curious clockwork animals before realizing he had no idea which way she had gone.

Meanwhile Émilie-Claire had located the department where women's gloves were displayed on the amputated hands and arms of manikins that reached up from the countertop as a forest of disembodied limbs. She admired a pair of green satin gloves with embroidered flower petals, then turned her attention to a pair of elbow length opera gloves. Neither seemed practical. Beneath the glass she spotted a simple pair of kid gloves in tan. The salesgirl's back was turned so she rapped on the counter to gain her attention. When the girl turned around she was surprised to see a familiar face.

"Phoebe! What on earth on you doing here?" she exclaimed.

"I'm a working girl, you know. This is my job now."

"But I thought…"

"You don't know…of course not. François's wife, Solange, she…passed away. It was very sad. François fell into a deep depression. He had to escape all the grief somehow and so he took the girl, Jeanne-Alice, on a tour…of the Middle East of all places! There was nothing for me to do but to look for employment elsewhere."

"But Phoebe, you could have come to me…"

"Listen, I can't stand here and talk to you while I'm working. My supervisor will see and I'll be fired. Meet me later? I'm off at six."

"Of course. Where are you living? I'll call for you after six."

"Why, I live upstairs with the rest of the girls. It's part of our compensation, but the accommodations…well, I'll tell you all about it later."

When Émilie-Claire returned to the puppet theater to collect Teo she found him gone. Attendants recalled seeing a dark-skinned boy wandering through the toy department. She hurried through the aisles of counters and racks of clothing until she reached the room with a sign that read, "Les Jouets d'Enfants," but Teo wasn't present. Desperate, she cast about for some inkling of where the boy might have disappeared to, then she saw the zig-zagging metal stairs that led up to the second floor of the building. She was in an area that had a high atrium; its ceiling of stained glass arched above three floors with balustered balconies that fronted onto the open space. What boy wouldn't want to climb the metal-framed stairway to the top where a view of the great canyon of merchandise filled with its shopper denizens presented itself?

There was an elevator: a gilded cage of lacey metal with a scissoring gate that was open. She entered. A female operator in a plain brown smock greeted her with a cheery, "Bonjour," and closed the gate. The controls consisted of a round dial with a wooden handle, ornate with its decoration of metallic curlicues. Émilie-Claire might have imagined it had come from one of Jules Verne's futuristic airships, but she had no time to fantasize. Reaching the top floor of the atrium, she rushed to circumnavigate the surrounding balconies, calling for Teo. He was not there.

Gingerly she peered over the balcony; for her the height was dizzying. Below was a sea of women's large hats, swimming like so many feathered and flowered sting rays; a perspective quite unusual—a giddy spectacle for one used only to street-level crowds. She felt herself teetering. The swarm slowly came into focus and she could discern the arms and legs of people among the humongous hats. There…was that the dark brown head of a small boy skittering across the floor, dodging those arms and legs? "Teo! Teo!" she called from her great height, but the boy could not hear her.

She lifted her skirts and descended the stairs—this was much faster than taking the clinking clanging elevator and the action countered her anxiety. When she reached the main floor she was awash in that ocean of humanity that had seemed so unreal from her previous vantage point. Now she had no map of the area, no notion of where the boy was in the press of the crowd. She could only push her way through it going this way and that. Frantically seeking her ward.

She was jostled and bumped. Women scowled at her, yet she persisted, calling out his name as she went. A few people realized her plight; one woman asked whom she had lost. "A small boy...dark skinned," she replied. "That way, I think," the woman answered. She pointed in the direction of the street entrance. The area of Émilie-Claire's search was now to be broadened. He could be anywhere!

Teo had snaked through the crowd on the lower level looking in vain for his mam'selle. He was worried. Had she left the store without him? He worked his way toward the entrance. If he stood right outside the door she would be sure to see him when she did leave, and if she were already on the street he would find her. Fresh air took the edge off of his apprehension after the stale environment of dusty merchandise and pungent human body odor inside Le Bon Marché. He scanned the street for her finding nothing but the usual cluster of walkers, carriages, and push-cart operators.

His plan was to stay put and wait. But then he saw a short, rotund man with a thin mustache who was beckoning him. There was something in the man's manner which reassured Teo—a kindly smile, a suggestion of advocacy, deliverance. His early years in Haiti surfaced in his memory: the spirits they called the loa, protectors and guides of children, loa like Papa Legba and Erzulie Freda. Of course, he might be Baron Samedi, waiting to drag him into the underworld, but no...he wasn't wearing his top hat. No, he must be Boli Shah, the guardian of families. Teo found himself swept along the avenue toward Boli Shah like a leaf blowing in the wind.

Émilie-Claire now stood at the entrance of Le Bon Marché, looking up and down the narrow sidewalk. Strollers blocked her view—a parade of shop girls, laborers, sailors, porters, chambermaids, stock brokers; drab woolen frock coats, brightly printed calicos, shiny billowing silks, tattered and soiled uniforms of blue, white and red. A mélange of flesh and fabric: humankind at its best and worse hurrying along with an occasional "bonjour" or "bonsoir," or drifting in somnambulate indifference, or stopping to window gaze, or dodging horse manure, or scurrying after evasive children, or heading for the Bourse, the bank, the boutique, or the Tuileries.

And the boy from Haiti stood before the figure of the man he was sure must be Boli Shah. And Boli Shah looked down at the boy and said, "Bonjour, Teodor Presume." He knows my name, Teo thought to himself. Surely he must be loa, of the Ghede or of the Petro or of the Rada! The man smiled a smile that seemed to say, "I know many things." A smile that put the boy at ease.

"Bonjour, Boli Shah," Teo said.

The man was laughing when Émilie-Claire appeared. Finding her ward seemingly transfixed by a laughing fat man on the streets of Paris gave her no sense of relief. Indeed, her anxiety rose to a level that inhibited the language she was about to hurl at both boy and man. She simply stood and trembled with anger and frustration.

"Mademoiselle Lebeau," said the man, "as you can see, I have found Teodor for you."

Dumbfounded, Émilie-Claire could only stammer, "But how…"

"Mademoiselle," he said at once, "I am…Vidocq!"

The newsstand on the corner of the Rue de l'Ancienne-Comédie and the Boulevard Saint-Germain featured all the current dailies: L'Opinion Nationale, Le Temps, Le Siècle, and L'Époque. Their pages had stories about the outdoor fires lit to burn infected clothing to control the raging cholera epidemic, with drawings of a crazed crowd appearing to dance around the flames, and of the quarantines along the France-Italy border. There was a notice for the premiere of Giacomo Meyerbeer's opera, "L'Africaine," and an article describing the horrible disaster on the Mississippi River in the United States where the steamboat SS Sultana had exploded killing 1,800 passengers, many of whom were paroled Union POWs returning home.

There was an opinion column berating the Emperor for invading Algeria. There were incidental news stories about the P. T. Barnum Museum in New York City having burned to the ground and about the arrival of the elephant, Jumbo, at the London Zoo. Wild Bill Hickok had killed Davis Tutt on the streets of Springfield, Missouri, in a quick-draw shootout. L'Époque included a review of Lewis Carroll's new children's book, *Alice's Adventures in Wonderland* (French edition). But the biggest piece of international news (accompanied by a grisly photograph of the condemned on the gallows) was the group execution of four prisoners:

The four conspirators in the assassination of the American President, Abraham Lincoln, were today hanged together on the gallows in a penitentiary yard in Washington, D.C. They were David Herold, George Atzerodt, Lewis Payne, and Mary Surratt, the first woman to be executed by the federal government. They were marched in irons past the open graves they would soon occupy and climbed the steps to the platform where cotton hoods were placed over their heads and rope nooses were tied around their necks. Onlookers remained silent after the trapdoors fell open and the four conspirators plunged through, their necks snapping in unison.

President Lincoln died from a gunshot wound on the morning of April 15. He and the First Lady had been in attendance at a performance of Our American Cousin *at Ford's Theatre in Washington, D.C. the evening before when a Confederate sympathizer and former actor named John Wilkes Booth appeared in his private box and fired a bullet into Lincoln's head. The conspirators also attacked and nearly killed the Secretary of State, William H. Seward in his home that same night. Booth was eventually traced to a hiding place in a barn in Virginia where cavalryman Boston Corbett shot and killed him.*

Only last month Lincoln had been sworn in for his second term as President. The War Between the States is effectively over, as Confederate States General Robert E. Lee surrendered to Union Army General Ulysses S. Grant on April 9. It is a sad note that the American President, who devoted his life to the preservation of his country and the eradication of slavery there, will not be present to officiate at his country's reconstruction.

The newspaper containing this article had found its way to a table in the Café Procope where it was being discussed in loud voices by a trio of (Émilie-Claire, seated with Phoebe at a nearby table, could only think of them as) flâneurs…over-dressed and posturing idlers.

"How utterly barbarian," spouted the first. "Dangling the poor woman by a rope until she choked!"

"They say," said the second, "that they soil themselves. And they kick their feet until they expire."

"Not civilized like ourselves. The guillotine, you know, is painless."

"Messieurs, messieurs…please!" said the third. "The guillotine is painless? I've heard it said that the severed head remains conscious for many minutes after the blade falls. Can you imagine being aware that you are resting in a blood-soaked basket among other bodiless craniums while the rest of you is pouring out its life's fluid above on the scaffold?"

Émilie-Claire and Phoebe did their best to ignore the rant that continued until a waiter, mercifully, brought tankards of ale to the trio.

"Why is it always so noisy in restaurants?" asked Phoebe. "The space isn't small. Look at the high ceiling."

The Café Procope was indeed spacious. It dated to the late seventeenth century and was, perhaps, the oldest such establishment in Paris. It had served coffee to the likes of Voltaire and to Benjamin Franklin during his visits to Paris, as well as Thomas Jefferson and John Paul Jones. Robespierre, Danton and Marat met at the café and waived the symbolic Phrygian Cap of the Revolution there in celebration. It was a Mecca for literary giants such as George Sand, Anatole France, and Gustave Planche. Coffee, philosophy, and intense chatter were the way of life at the Café Procope—not to mention some of the best cuisine in France.

"I was playing with Jeanne-Alice in the nursery when I heard Solange calling," Phoebe told Émilie-Claire. "She had been fussing a lot lately so I was reluctant to check on her. An invalid can be a frustrating responsibility as they get so bored they demand attention any way they can. Solange was not above faking pain or hunger or fear. Suddenly, her fussing stopped and I heard a noise as if someone had tipped over or thrown a chair. I ran to Solange's room and found her lying on the floor unconscious."

Just then a loud crash came from the direction of the kitchen followed by the sound of breaking dishes and a few choice swear words. "I hope that wasn't our order," Émilie-Claire said.

"I rushed to summon Maurice, the footman," Phoebe continued, "and told him to fetch Doctor Roussel and then to find François and bring him back. It was already too late, of course. I had the sad task of telling poor Jeanne-Alice. But you know, it was funny, the girl seemed unaffected by the news. It was as if her mother had always been dead to her, and now that it was official she had no energy left to grieve."

"Horrible. You must have had mixed emotions yourself."

"That's so. I had hopes, as I have hinted before, that once

François was free…"

"Of course it was too soon. But had he shown the kind of interest in you that gave you the hope?"

"François was always a model of decorum around me. I felt he was fighting his own desires. He was conflicted and maintained an emotional distance between us, at least for his own part. I…I didn't press the matter for fear that he would turn me away."

"And now *he* has gone away. Was he running from you, do you think? And when he returns…"

The waiter interrupted, bringing their orders of ravioles du Daupiné, salade de haricots verts frais, and foie gras de canard mi-cuit avec pain toasté. From the carafe on their table he refilled their glasses with the Blaye Côtes de Bordeaux they had been sipping.

"Quite a spread for a mere shop girl," said Phoebe. "I have to thank you. But you said you had something to tell me, and here I am blabbing about my own problems."

"This will interest you. Today I took Teo shopping at the Bon Marché and he slipped away from me. When I finally located him he was outside talking to a fat man with whom you may be familiar. This man introduced himself as Emile-Adolphe Vidocq."

"The detective! The one that found poor Geoffroy. What a coincidence."

"Ce n'est pas vrai! As you will see, it was no coincidence. He told me that he was never convinced that the boy in the morgue was Geoffroy."

"I know. François wasn't sure either."

"He told me he had continued to work on the case and had reasons now to believe that the kidnapping ring was centered in London. He was close to exposing them but he needed what he called…bait."

"Bait? I don't think I like that notion."

"He had the audacity to suggest…oh, I can hardly bring myself to say it! He had a contact in England who told him that this gang of kidnappers had a request from a client for a boy of Teo's race…a Negro lad they wanted for some nefarious purpose!"

"I hope you told him to go to hell!'

"In no uncertain terms. I threatened him with the police if he ever came near Teo again. The pompous ass! Why can't he leave well enough alone? You've grieved, François has grieved and now he has more grieving to do. If Vidocq finds the boy alive he will certainly be in peril. He might die or be dead and then you would have to go through that realization all over again."

"But if there was a chance…"

"Not with my Teo there isn't."

Back in the apartment on Rue de la Victoire, the boy Teo sat on his small bed, thinking about Haiti and the spirits called the loa. He fingered edges of the card he held which gave, in embossed inked lettering, the name and address of the detective, Emile-Adolphe Vidocq, and the little engraving of a sinister-looking eye.

Byron Grush

11

Teodore Visits London

The carriage ride from Paris had taken them through Amiens where they had stopped for the night at a small inn on the outskirts of that town. The following morning, after a petit déjeuner of a variety of cheeses and meats, and some eggs, they continued on to Boulogne-sur-Mer where they caught the ferry across the Strait of Dover to Folkestone. Now Teo stood at the rail looking out toward a turbid horizon where greensand cliffs were pounded by angry waves. The channel was turbulent and offered the boy some entertainment, but it was nothing compared to those ocean voyages of his past.

Teo felt some remorse at having left Mam'selle with only a vague and hastily scribbled note of explanation. Gone to help Boli Shah, he had told her. Coming back soon. Don't worry. She *would* worry. Mam'selle…Teo had called her "Missy Em" when he was younger…Émilie-Claire would be frantic. He hadn't wished to cause her any pain but he also knew she would never have let him go with the loa who was appearing in human form as a detective. A detective who would rescue a lost boy just as Émilie-Claire had rescued him when he had been taken by a Vodou cult in New Orleans. Had Boli Shah been there to help Missy Em back then?

Now he was almost a man and it was his duty to repay the good loa. He had also lied to Boli Shah when the loa had asked if he had permission from his guardian to accompany him on a great adventure. He tried to shake off his shame at all the lies. As the ferry approached the harbor Teo could just make out the sharp outline of a tower on a cliff beyond the beach. It was called Martello Tower and although it seemed to welcome the travelers, it had been built in 1802 as a defense against Napoleon. Teo might have appreciated the irony of this if he had known more about history.

Emile-Adolphe Vidocq stood next to the boy as the ferry maneuvered closer to the pier. He should have talked to the boy's guardian, he thought to himself. Only…she was so caustic, so vehemently opposed to his very presence. He had asked Henri Barbou to contact her once they had left. Barbou had remained in Paris and would join Vidocq later in London once the trail was warm that would lead them to the kidnappers. He had given Barbou the thankless job of handling the irate woman. Well, somebody had to do it. Better him than Vidocq!

The boy and the detective/Vodou-spirit boarded the Southeastern Railway Folkestone to London boat train at 2:30 PM with only minutes to spare before its departure. They found no empty seats in the second class carriage and so walked through the connecting door through the train's first class carriages. Vidocq was perturbed. Now he would have to pay for two first class tickets. They entered a compartment with a vacant bench seat covered in green velvet. Already seated in the compartment on the bench opposite were three other travelers.

Teo, being uncharacteristically impolite, looked at their fellow passengers with a studying stare. Here was an older man, perhaps nearly 60, with a receding hair line accented by tuffs of hair he had combed forward above his ears. He had a luxurious beard and moustache but no sideburns, giving him, Teo decided, the appearance of an aging circus clown. His eyes, however, seemed deep with secret knowledge no clown could claim. He was dressed elegantly in a day coat with leather trimmed lapels.

Next to the man sat a young woman. She was, Teo thought, very pretty…too pretty to be this man's daughter, although she was the right age. She had light brown hair pinned back in a bun and wore a conservative traveling costume that called no attention to her equally lovely form (Teo, at 15, was just becoming interested in the female form). She could be an actress from the stage, Teo concluded. Next to her was an older woman dressed in black. The mother? Was this a man and his wife and their daughter returning from a tour of the continent?

"Monsieur," said Vidocq as the train pulled away from the station, "please forgive my impolitesse, but I seem to know you. May I ask your name?"

The man snorted. "Of course you know me," he replied. "I am Charles Dickens. *The* Charles Dickens. And you sir, how might your impertinent self be called?"

"Why, I am Vidocq! The detective."

"Vidocq! Impossible. Vidocq is dead."

"That was my father. I follow, as you say, in his footpads. Are you traveling with your family? Do you come from Paris? There was some fine weather there of late."

"Not that it is any of your business, Mr. Detective Vidocq, but yes, these ladies are in my party. This is Ellen Ternan and her mother, Frances Eleanor Jarman, who is our chaperon. They have both garnered acclaim as actresses in their day. I've convinced Ellen to retire from that profession at an early age. I add somewhat to their support."

I wonder what Madam Dickens thinks of that arrangement, Vidocq thought to himself.

"And you, young man, what is your name?" Dickens asked Teo.

"He speaks very little English," said Vidocq. "His name is Teodor Presume. He was originally from the island of Haiti but came, through many dire circumstances, finally to the safety of France. A story that might interest you."

"Perhaps it might. Perhaps it might not. But we have some time before we reach London. You may proceed to bore me with his tale."

Teo, although he had little occasion to use it these days, did in fact know the English language. Enough to follow with great interest the story of his life according to Vidocq. It amused him to hear how the detective embellished the tale of his capture by pirates…this most likely to garner prestige with the famous author. Teo had learned to remain silent and keep his facial expression as bland as possible when adults were engaged in conversation, even when it concerned himself, so he didn't react. That was how you learned things.

Dickens listened half-heartedly as Vidocq rambled on about Teo and the train rambled on through the shire of Kent, through Ashford and Headcorn. In this modern era of transportation the train was capable of over fifty miles per hour and it reached fifty-five miles per hour on a downgrade just outside of Stapleton. As it approached the

River Beult the engineer noticed a red flag being waved furiously at the train.

The flagman was only 500 yards away from the viaduct over the Beult where repairs to the track were taking place; he was supposed to be at least 1000 yards from the site. The foreman in charge of construction had consulted a timetable to insure no trains would be approaching—but he had picked up the wrong timetable. At the bridge, two rails had been removed leaving a gap in the tracks. Too late the brakes were engaged and the train struck the missing section of track and derailed.

The viaduct stood ten or fifteen feet above the dry river bed. Into this plunged the locomotive, dragging behind it the tender, a brake van, and a second class carriage. This part of the train managed to cross the river bed but the next seven cars remained stuck in the mud, tipped and buckled, the passengers thrown about. The accident would result in many injuries and at least ten deaths. The carriage in which Vidocq, Teo, and the Dickens party were sitting, hung precariously over the edge of the viaduct.

It was tipped both side to side and front to back so that the occupants of the compartment ended piled together uncomfortably in a corner. They struggled to untangled themselves. "Is anyone hurt?" asked Dickens.

Vidocq had a gash on his forehead which was bleeding. He ran a hand across this and stared in disbelief at his own blood. "I'm all right," he replied, "but we have to get out of this carriage before the whole thing plunges into the ravine."

"Sadly," said Dickens, "the door to the compartment is jammed. We'll have to go out the window."

"No…look…it is way too far to leap. Are the women all right?"

Dickens had been examining Ellen and her mother. "Shook up, but hopefully not in shock."

"I'm fine, sweetheart," replied Ellen Ternan. "Mother is stunned but I think she is uninjured. What do we do now?"

As if in answer to her question, Teo crawled up the slanted bench and stopped for just a moment at the window. "I'll get help," he said, and then out the window he went. The agile youth clung to the side of the railcar like a spider and worked his way up until he reached the edge of the viaduct. A short jump and he was on level ground.

"We won't be able to do that," moaned Ellen.

"Maybe he can find a rope and some strong men," said Vidocq.

"There are many below in the riverbed that need succor more than we," said Dickens. "You can hear their screams for help."

Moments later they heard: "Boli Shah! Boli Shah! I'm back. Look what I brought."

Teo had returned dragging two long wooden planks which he maneuvered into position as a bridge between the embankment and the train carriage. Dickens suggested to Vidocq that he go across first so that between the two of them, they could help the women negotiate the planks. He agreed and scrambled along the shaky makeshift bridge.

Dickens urged Mrs. Jarman to cross but the woman bulked at the idea. "I'll fall," she said. Her daughter climbed out the window, stopped half way across the planks, and motioned for her mother to come. At last Frances Jarman inched her way toward her daughter's outstretched arms. The girl backed her way to safety. Her mother followed, but not without looking down into the precipice and whining her distress loudly.

Once everyone was safely on the embankment they were able to survey the horrific scene below in the riverbed. Some of the carriages were merely piles of splintered wood. Bodies lay on the ground. Some writhing or attempting to crawl, some still. Dickens gasped. "Stay here," he said to the women.

Dickens crawled back across the planks and entered the teetering carriage, emerging minutes later carrying his top hat and a pocket flask filled with brandy. He found a construction cart along the side of the tracks upon which sat a water jug, there for the benefit of the workers. From this he filled his top hat with fresh water. He then climbed down the embankment and went to tend to the wounded.

"Come, Teo, we should help," said Vidocq.

When they reached the riverbed they saw Dickens administering to a man with a cut on his forehead from which blood came in short spurts. Dickens had the flask of brandy up to the man's lips, but they could tell at a glance that the man was gone. Leaning against a tree was a woman, ghostly white, clothing ripped and soiled with her own blood. Her head bobbed. Dickens came to her with the brandy. She took a few sips, looked up into the big man's whiskered face and said, "I am gone." And then she perished as had the other man.

There were people trapped under pieces of wood and twisted steel. Together, the detective and the author pulled several of the still living out from under the wreckage. By now there were half a dozen or so of the construction workers and those passengers who were not injured on the scene to help. Teo went around carrying the top hat and dribbling water into trembling mouths by cupping it in his hands.

Near the end of the rescue efforts, when all had been done that could be done, Dickens sat, exhausted and shaken. Suddenly a thought occurred to him that made him jump up. "My God!," he exclaimed. "I have left the manuscript of my novel in the carriage!" Back went the author, his energy renewed at the thought of losing the only copy of the latest installment of *Our Mutual Friend*, and into the still teetering carriage he climbed.

The Bunch of Grapes was a bar and restaurant. Dickens had modeled his Six Jolly Fellow Porters Public House after it in *Our Mutual Friend*. In the novel he had called it "a tavern of dropsical appearance...long settled down into a state of hale infirmity," and it was, indeed, an ancient landmark in the Limehouse Basin of London's East End. Situated on the aptly named Narrow Street, the current building dated to 1720 and occupied the site of a former pub that had originated there as long ago as 1583.

It hugged the channel that spilled into the basin from the Thames. A decrepit wooden veranda hung over the water with tables for the more fearless dockers and riggers and "Limeys" who frequented its roguish environment. From that vantage point one could spy the canal's narrow boats hauling lime from the kilns, and beyond, the masts of tall ships bringing tea from China which had been traded there for opium.

At a table on this self same veranda sat a robust man dressed in grubby sailor's togs who was attended by a young boy with glistening black skin dressed in despicable rags. The boy cowered at the man's side, watching his master as he drained a tankard of strong ale and dripped a good deal of it down his thickly bearded chin. The man ignored the boy, raising his tankard in a toast to the other swarthy inhabitants of the Bunch of Grapes.

One of these pub dwellers soon approached. He was of an ungainly Falstaff-like girth and as he walked reminded the seated man of a water buffalo wallowing through a swamp. Not asking for permission, the large man sat down.

"Be you from that Blackwall frigate lately docked on the Isle of Dog?" asked the Falstaff man.

"Aye…the Red Witch O' the Waves. Brought in some orange pekoe and some gunpowder tea for the swells, we did."

"I see you are an enterprising fellow. I would not be wrong in thinking you would like to make a quid or two, would I?"

"That's a healthy offer…but for what? I do not do violence or thievery. I am waiting to ship out in a fortnight and so I have little time to devote to any…enterprise."

"I'm referrin' to a purchase I'd like to make. Sell me the boy."

"What? In no way do I sell the boy. He has been with me since the Bahamas three year ago. He's like a son to me. No. I will not sell the boy!"

"You may wish to reconsider when you see this." The man drew a leather pouch from his pocket and spilled its contents out on the table. "That may be more than you'll make on the Red Witch, I'll bargain," he said.

The sailor swept the coins from the table top with his arm. As they clattered to the floor he rose, grabbed the boy by the arm and hurried him out of the pub. Once they gained the street, Vidocq removed his false beard and turned to Teo to whisper, "I think we have just made contact with the villains we seek. A good day's work! Now, not too fast. We mean for them to follow us."

"But Boli Shah," said Teo, "I am frightened. I don't want to play being the slave anymore. That man scared me."

"Don't worry, my fine fellow. It is nearly over. I have my good friend Henri Barbou also following us. If the miscreants attack we will prevail against them."

They continued walking up Narrow Street past Three Colts Street until they reached Gill Street. This they turned up and soon found themselves in the middle of Limehouse's China Town. Here they passed rambling wooden boarding houses for Cantonese sailors and a gambling house run by an English woman known as Chinese Emma. Chinese Emma had an opium den on the upper floor.

Crossing through a narrow alley between buildings brought them to the churchyard of Saint Anne's Limehouse, the local parish church. Ancient maples shaded a humble graveyard next to the old church. Teo and Vidocq found a bench there and sat to rest and admire the Baroque church with its square clock tower and golden ball-topped flag pole from which waved the Royal Navy's White Ensign. Teo studied the weathered grave markers, some dating to the early eighteenth century. Then he saw the pyramid.

"What is that, Boli Shah?" he asked.

Vidocq could just make out the inscription on the face of the pyramid: "The Widsdom of Solomon." There were some faint letters just below that in Hebrew and a coat of arms on which appeared the image of a unicorn. The four-sided monument, if that is what it was, stood nearly six feet tall with sharper angles than its counterparts in Egypt. Was it a grave marker? Or an architectural detail that had never been hauled up to grace the ramparts of the old church?

"May I go look, Boli Shah?"

"Go, but stay in my sight," said the detective.

Teo puzzled at the strange writing on the pyramid. The Hebrew inscription made the monument seem even more exotic and mysterious. Down by the base Teo noticed the trail of some small animal. He followed this around the perimeter and found a hole—the lodging of some rabbit or chipmunk that had burrowed under the base of the pyramid. He examined this, oblivious to the fact that he had strayed from the line of sight of the detective.

Vidocq sat cleaning his nails with a pipe damper when his companion in sleuthing, Henri Barbou stood suddenly before him. Barbou should have been trailing them from a distance, keeping watch for any suspicious people who might also have been following them. Vidocq tweaked his moustache, a habit he had when irritated, looked askance at Barbou and said, "So?"

"There is no one following you," Barbou reported. "I think it is a failure, this ploy to ferret out the villains."

"You are absolutely certain? You used stealth and careful observation? You know my methods, Barbou."

"Cetainement! I am the best jouer au chat et à la souris!"

"You are sure, are you, just who was the cat and who was the mouse?"

"Il n'y a pas de quoi fouetter un chat…it's not a big deal. We just have to try again."

Vidocq sighed. This was taking too long. And no one was offering to pay his expenses. He couldn't ask for compensation until, and if, he recovered the missing boy. Missing boy? Where was Teo?

"Where is Teodore, Barbou? Did you see him when you approached? He was supposed to stay by that monument over there."

"I came right by that thing. I didn't see him."

They searched the graveyard, calling for Teo, but the boy had disappeared. They looked inside the church and all around the grounds, then split up to search independently through the alleys and side streets surrounding St. Anne's Limehouse. But Teo was nowhere to be found.

Byron Grush

12

The Opium Eaters

When Teo regained consciousness he saw that he was slumped up against the leg of a brass bed on a grimy floor, his arms tied behind him. The room was filled with a rancid smell as if something small and furry had died there not so long ago. Weak rays of sunlight fell through a ripped window shade and set dust mites sparkling in the air of the darkened room. His head ached and there was an unpleasant odor in his mouth and nose.

His arms tingled; the unnatural position was cutting off his circulation. He brought his knees up against his chest and struggled to bring his bound hands under his body. Once he had his arms in front of him he could see that a soiled rag had been tied around his wrists. He began pulling at this with his teeth to undo the knot; the rag tasted as bad as it smelled.

His hands were free! Now he worked to untie the rags that bound his ankles. He did not know where he was. All he remembered was the sickeningly sweet smell of the ether-soaked cloth someone had held to his face in the cemetery. Free from his restraints, he got to his feet but still woozy and disoriented, he collapsed onto the bed. He must have slept for when he opened his eyes the room was no longer illuminated by light from the outside. It was dark as pitch.

There was a sliver of light marking the bottom of the door. Toward this he stumbled, slowly regaining his equilibrium, as if he were a toddler learning to walk for the first time. At the door he paused and listened. There were faint sounds, indistinguishable and probably distant. He turned the doorknob and was surprised to find the door unlocked.

Beyond was a long hallway, dimly lit by gas lights protruding at intervals from the walls. Which direction to go? The muffled sounds came from the right so Teo went to the left. There were several doors along the hall and a window at the end. He hoped to find a staircase where he could descend to the street. As he was about to pass the first door he noticed that it was ajar. He heard sounds coming from the room beyond—sounds like someone was beating a pig with a heavy stick. The smell of musk was prominent. He pushed the door open.

There on a bed lay an old man, pinkish-gray and fat, an ugly mountain of lard. He was making the pig noises. Straddling his middle section was a slim Chinese girl. She bounced up and down as if she were riding a horse. Teo froze in fascination and shock. It took him a moment to realize that he was witnessing sex. He knew about sex from the lurid discussions held after hours by the boys at his boarding school. But their fantasies about the sexual act were nothing like this.

It wasn't the first naked woman he had ever seen…that is, if you counted the times Mam'selle had bathed with him when he was much younger. She would enter the brass tub where he played in the soapy water to scrub him clean. He remembered her breasts. They were much bigger than the Chinese girl's. The man on the bed, an Englishman, gave out a long moan. The girl stopped bouncing and leaned down across the man's body. Her head turned toward the door and she saw Teo standing there. She began to scream at him in Cantonese. Teo pulled the door shut and continued down the hallway.

The next door down the hall posed a dilemma for Teo. It too was slightly ajar. The ambiance of the hall, its creaking wooden floor boards, its faded and peeling wall paper, its dust and clutter, and its reek of stale alcohol and fresh sex, combined to induce the youth to flee. But the partly open door seduced. A quick look. More deviate sex to tantalize? But no, as he pushed the door open he was greeted by a most bizarre and frightening scene. He knew at once what it was. It was an opium den!

Wooden pallets were scattered around on the floor. On these reclined Chinese men in traditional dress—some in ragged disarray, some in silken elegance. Bodies seemed twisted and distorted, with limbs in impossible juxtapositions. No heads turned toward the intruder; no eyes seemed capable of viewing anything real through the haze, yet the blank stares of the pleasure seekers were indeed focused on something…eternity?

There also were a few women present. These were clearly not Orientals but must have come from London's elite, judging by their costumes of stylish silk and satin. They too lay back on the rough wood and held the long thin opium pipes over lamps of open flame to heat the drug and suck its vapors into their lungs. They too gazed with glassy eyes at veiled mirages which they alone could sense and dwell within; imagined vistas of their dreamquest.

A tall man would strut though the maze of the possessed carrying a tray upon which was a dish in which was a dark substance. Each pipe ended in a knob-shaped bowl with a small opening. Once the pipe's contents had vaporized away, the smoker would shake or moan or writhe and the attendant would hurry to scoop more of the vile poison into the bowl.

There was little in the way of smoke in the room, such as one might find in the smoking area of a café. But the drug vapors filled the space. The one who stood near the door was not immune to its effects. Teo felt light-headed as he looked at the scene before him. He had inadvertently leaned against the door causing it to shut with a sharp click. The attendant saw the boy, knew instinctively the danger of allowing a child into that arena of pipe dreamers; moved toward him.

As he stared at the montage of bodies Teo felt disoriented. Perhaps it was the held-over effects of the ether or the heavy atmosphere of opium vapor in the room or a combination of both. Flames from the lamps colored the haze that hung low over the heads of the reclining smokers. It was like watching shimmering sunlight reflecting in a flowing stream, only the light was of a darker, blood-like hue. Limbs and torsos undulated within flickering shadows. Teo was reminded of giant snakes or the limbs of trees in a harsh wind.

He worried about his gros bon ange, his big good angel that kept him breathing and kept his heart pumping blood; his own body felt as if it had melted into the mass of the dead-alive before him. He called upon his ti bon ange, his little good angel, to guide his thoughts and spur him into action…the action of escape. Yet he was transfixed and immobile. Neither angel was helping.

 He saw something rise up and move toward him: Papa Legba? Or was it a hougan, a priest, carrying his asson and waving that gourd rattle to summon the loa who would come to take Teo away? He could not offer the blood of a chicken or a pig to the loa. He could not serve the loa in good faith, having spent so much of his life living with the Mam'selle, away from the sight of Bondye, the Supreme God. His ti bon ange would be judged inadequate and his gros bon ange would be forced to wander the earth endlessly.

The being, priest or loa or something unimaginable, took Teo by the arm. This must be a bokor, Teo thought, a sorcerer who dabbled in the darker side of magic. Would it cast a spell that would harm…or kill? The bokor, who was the opium den's attendant, pushed Teo out of the door and into the hallway. Teo landed in a heap on the dirty floor. He lay there, trying to collect his thoughts and clear his head of the drugs. Sleep beckoned. Blissful slumber to erase the dread.

How long he lay there in dreamless sleep he would not know. A distant pounding like drumsticks against wood roused him. Someone was coming down the hall; footsteps became louder and he could almost feel the floor shake. Teo struggled to his feet and ran as fast as he could. Reaching the end of the hallway he found a flight of stairs and leaped down them, entering a crowded bar room on the first floor of the building. He pushed his way through a cluster of men, both Asian and white, who bulked at his impolite passage and grabbed at him or pushed. It was a difficult flight through the barroom but at last he reached the outside door and plunged out into the crepuscular streets of Chinatown.

The word "scathing" had a certain appeal for Émilie-Claire. It aptly described the tongue lashing she had given Emile-Adolphe Vidocq when she had finally located him at the Langham Hotel in Marylebone near London's West End. It was enough that he had virtually spirited away Teo in a ploy to ferret out young Geoffroy Gardinier's kidnappers and had failed miserably to do so—he now had lost Teo! She threatened him with the police.

"Mademoiselle Lebeau, please listen. I am your best hope of reuniting with the boy. I am working diligently on the case. The police…they are incompetent."

"I think it is you who are incompetent. Your plan didn't work, did it? And how is it I find you in this plush hotel? I thought you would be slumming to be closer to those you seek."

"It is elegant, is it not? It has just been opened recently and the Prince of Wales was here to do it. It has water closets for every other room and those rising rooms…the elevators. I am here posing as a wealthy Frenchman who wishes to purchase a young boy."

"Oh, are you wealthy?"

"Alas, no. I am running up a monumental bill at this establishment. If you could see your way toward contributing to the effort…"

"Scandaleux! Quel nerf!"

"I may have to pay for the boy's return."

"What is the going rate for boys these days?"

"Fifty pounds in English money."

"Ridicule!"

Émilie-Claire fell silent for a moment and considered. This outrageous detective might have a slim chance with this new approach.

"If it is required to pay, I am good for the money," she said. "But no outlay in advance. I am going to search for him myself. So tell me all the details of this East End and the establishments where to look."

"But Mademoiselle! Really! It is not safe for a woman…especially one so beautiful as you."

"I have my companion, Phoebe Stapleton with me. She is waiting for me now in that decadent lobby downstairs. Together we will search and find Teo. And you will be stuck with your hotel bill."

Teo didn't know where he should go, he just knew he had to get as far away as possible from Chinatown. In the middle of the night the only souls at large were suspicious lowlifes, at least as far as the boy was concerned. He ducked into alleyways and around the stoops of houses to avoid the nefarious lurkers along the Limehouse Basin. Soon he saw a dustman with his wagon approaching. The wagon was piled high with debris and items collected from people's dustbins. It was destined for a nearby dust heap where the accumulation would be picked through by the poverty stricken. Teo didn't hesitate. He leaped up on the back of the wagon and hunkered down into the dirt and grime, the old shoes, broken bricks, and torn rags.

He almost slept despite the bumping of the wagon along cobblestone alleys. Up Whitehall Road to the Mile End Waste drove the dustman. At Sidney Street the dustman pulled up on the horse's reins and stopped the wagon in front of ancient pub called The Vine. Into The Vine he went; collecting rubbish was thirsty business.

Teo slid from the wagon and looked around. Across the narrow street was an old Quaker cemetery, now abandoned and turned into an ersatz fair ground. He could just make out the silhouette of a dilapidated merry-go-round in the darkness. Another structure resembled the kind of puppet theater where a Punch and Judy show might be performed. He walked toward this, seeking at least temporary shelter for the night. On the top of the rise in the little park sat a tent. A hand-lettered sign identified it as belonging to the Christian Mission. There was no one around, so into the tent Teo went.

Bramwell Booth was nine years of age. His brother Ballington would turn eight on the 28th of July. Their sister Kate was six going on seven. The three children played on the wooden swings at the deserted fair grounds at Mile End Waste. It was late morning and soon their mother and father, Catherine and William Booth, would be returning from the public market down on Whitehall Road where they handed out leaflets and prevailed upon the sinners they found there to follow them back to the small tent they called their Christian Mission. They would be singing, "Only a step, only a step! Why not take it now?"

Bramwell remembered his father bringing him into that bar, The Vine, across the street and saying to him, "These are the people I want you to live and labor for." It was a given fact that he, as the oldest, would be expected to follow his parents in the spreading of the Gospel to the poor, the drunkards and gamblers, and the fast-time girls. It didn't matter that William Booth, a Methodist Preacher, had been forced from the body of the church because of his propensity to preach to the indigent. It didn't matter that his parents, going out to minister on the streets of the worst parts of London, had been met with hostility, had clods of dirt thrown at them, had the police tell them to move along and stop creating a disturbance.

And it didn't matter that he, Bramwell, would rather be playing at marbles with the urchins down by the market or watching the cock fights that were held there when no police were patrolling. But he was watching his brother and sister now, keeping them from straying. Keeping them, and himself, from becoming so bored that getting into trouble might be a delicious alternative. As a last resort there was always the game of hide and seek. As long as they kept to the fair grounds. So Bramwell asked, "Okay, who wants to hide?"

Ballington and Kate had both insisted that they be the hiders and Bramwell be the seeker. He had covered his eyes and counted to one hundred…by tens. "Here I come, ready or not," he announced and started slowly and methodically to explore the nooks and crannies of the fair grounds. Slowly, because besides occupying and energizing the other children, the game gave him a brief reprieve from the rigors and responsibilities of caretaking. Hopefully nobody would fall down a well or walk out into the street in front of an omnibus.

After peering under the merry-go-round he headed for the Mission tent. An obvious place to hide and so he didn't expect to find anyone within. Except he did. Curled up in a corner with a rug pulled over him was a young black boy…snoring loudly.

"Hey there, buddy," yelled Bramwell, "you can't sleep here." But then he tried to think of what his father would do. Would the preacher chase the boy away or welcome him into growing army of the saved—those saved by the Blood of the Lamb—the army of salvation that marched to glory through repentance?

The Salvation Army, as it would come to be called, was Reverend Booth's horde of followers who, once saved by the Blood of the Lamb, would journey out to minister to other sinners all across the world. This tent was its birthplace. The young boy who had slept here was about to join an army although he did not know it yet.

Émilie-Claire and Phoebe Stapleton had attempted to inquire about the lost boy from the inhabitants of Ah Tack's lodging house on the causeway but were thwarted by the Chinese sailors' and dock workers' inability (or refusal) to speak English. They had fared no better at any of the pubs along Narrow Street where the Queen's English was spoken (although with heavy accents from all corners of the sea-faring world). No one knew anything about anything that was not related to ocean travel or fishing or rope making or which pub watered down the whiskey the least. Émilie-Claire expressed her frustration in her diary entry for the day:

What would I do if I were forced to return to France without Teo? I was getting desperate and although I hesitated to drag poor Phoebe into any of the notoriously seedy establishments in Limehouse, I could see no other path to take. We came to a rickety old building and found two Oriental women sitting on wicker chairs outside a doorway that had something written on it in chalky Chinese characters. Each wore a smock of decorated silk, one bright red and the other a luxurious green. Having learned from past experiences that women like these would feign ignorance of English, I immediately showed them a half crown coin and demanded in English to know what was this establishment we stood before. When they bulked at the question I added another half crown to my palm. This loosened their tongues enough that I garnered the following information:

We stood in front of a hotel which was a front for an opium den run by a Chinese man who called himself Johnstone or Johnson but whose real name was Ah Sing. The proprietor was not present, having recently opened another "hotel for the celestial pleasures" over on Victoria Street at the other end of London where his presence was required.

Would we two gentlewomen desire to partake of a pipe? We explained we only sought to locate a young boy who had disappeared and so described Teo for them. The Oriental is characterized in the popular literature as "inscrutable," meaning that their countenance will betray no clue as to their inner thoughts. I can testify this is inaccurate for the woman in green blinked and lowered her eyes in such a way that I could only interpret that her expressed ignorance of the boy was false. I added a full crown to the coins in my hand.

It was thus that we learned that Teo had been the victim of an entrapment and had been held at another location by miscreants who, of course, had no relationship to the kind landlord, the aforementioned Ah Sing. That Teo had escaped and was being sought by the criminals was apparently common knowledge around Chinatown. No one would talk about it for fear of the police as well as fear of this ruthless gang of thugs who seemed only to exist to give the community a bad name. We were then offered the free use of pipes…pipes having previously been used by royalty and the privileged elite of finance and culture; we declined.

No one was going to indentify the culprits…they were all afraid. In a way, it didn't matter because Teo had escaped. At least for the time being. If the criminal element found him before we did…

13

Dîner des Trois Empereurs

Two years had passed since Teo had disappeared into the squalid reaches of London's East End. Émilie-Claire had spent days at the Metropolitan Police headquarters on Whitehall Place and Great Scotland Yard pleading with the commissioners to intensify the search for the boy. The scores of murders and general mayhem in the East End meant Teo ranked low as a priority, but in order to relieve themselves of the badgering French woman, they agreed to place two of their best investigators on the case. They told her to go back to France and reluctantly, she finally did go.

Emile-Adolphe Vidocq and Henri Barbou, faltering in their own efforts to locate the boy, had run up a monumental bill at the Langham which they could not pay and so skipped town to avoid the inevitable arrest and imprisonment that would result. They fled first to Liverpool then across the Irish Sea to Dublin where they hid out in the Temple Bar district near the River Liffey, a bustling waterway that reminded them of their beloved River Seine. They would return to London in the spring of 1888 to investigate the vicious murders of prostitutes in Whitehall but would again fail to solve the crimes.

Teodore Presume had been adopted into the family of William and Catherine Booth, if not legally, by virtue of Reverend Booth's strong will and determination to save the boy from his heathen ways. Teo took to the kind couple and adapted to the teaching and the praying and the singing as well he could. The Haitian Vodou religion had adopted, because of the necessity of hiding their practices from their French conquerors, aspects of Catholicism; the Catholic Saints were strongly associated with various loa. But Booth's Protestant beliefs rejected the Saints and all the rituals that went along with them. Teo found this both shocking and intriguing. Booth preached that salvation was an individual accomplishment. No one could ordain it for you. This gave the boy a new outlook on life. Soon he was singing the hymns and helping with the day-to-day evangelism of the mission.

Back in France, Phoebe Stapleton had become Madame Phoebe Gardinier. One day François had appeared at her counter at the Bon Marché and expressed his love with a diamond bracelet worth a year of her own salary. The bracelet was not the deciding factor—however, it helped. Phoebe and François became engaged that afternoon. His daughter, Jeanne-Alice, now a teenager, carried a basket of jonquils up the aisle at her father's wedding. Although she missed her deceased mother, she had loved Phoebe as if she were a big sister. Now Phoebe would be her stepmother. The holes left by the loss of her brother and mother were being partially filled.

Émilie-Claire was now Émilie-Claire Lebeau-Richelieu. She had married Jean-Léon Richelieu at Notre Dame Cathedral in front of a crowd of onlookers that included many from the Royal Court and the government. The Emperor and Empress were not in attendance, however. Napoleon III had arranged for the marriage to be given at the famous cathedral where he and his own bride had been wed, but his involvement in the personal life of his favorite advisor stopped short of a public appearance.

It was the seventh of June, 1867. Émilie-Claire and Jean-Léon were busy preparing to spend the evening at the Café Anglais where a fabulous dinner was to be given by Chef Adolphe Dugléré. Kaiser Wilhelm I of Prussia had requested the dinner to honor his guests, Tsar Alexander II of Russia, his son the Tsarevitch who would later become Tsar Alexander III, and Prince Otto von Bismarck. It was to be a sixteen course meal served over the space of eight hours and Chef Dugléré and the café owner, Claudius Burdel, were to spare no expense. The expense for those attending the meal was 400 francs per person.

"Be a darling and help me fasten this necklace," said Émilie-Claire. "Will there be anyone I know at this dinner?"

"I doubt it at these prices," answered Jean-Léon, fumbling with the clasp on the emerald choker. "This matches your gown superbly. You are so beautiful!."

"And you are such a sweetheart for giving it to me."

"It was my mother's and her mother's before her. An heirloom."

"And this dinner…such extravagance!"

"It is merely duty, mon amour. The Emperor will expect a full report on these Germans…especially Bismarck. Trouble is brewing, mark my words."

The Café Anglais was on the corner of the Boulevard des Italiens and the Rue de Marivaux. It dated back to 1802 and was considered one of the very best restaurants in Paris. It was the haunt of those of privilege and importance, European royalty, famous actors, and the fabulously wealthy. The main restaurant and café occupied the first floor of the white masonry building. It was lined with gold-leafed mirrors and mahogany woodwork and featured chairs upholstered in red velvet. Upstairs were 22 private dining rooms; the largest of these, called Le Grand Seize, would be the setting for the dinner of the Three Emperors.

Chef Adolphe Dugléré had been a chef de cuisine to the Rothschild family, then manager at the restaurant Les Frères Provençaux at the Palais-Royal. He had come to the Café Anglais in 1866. He was considered one of the premier chefs in all of France, having created many unique dishes, some of which he named for the mistresses of famous clients, or those clients themselves. Potage Fontanges, for instance, was a purée of fresh peas diluted with consommé and an addition of a chiffonade of sorrel and sprigs of chervil. Dugléré named it after Marie Angelique de Scorailles, La Duchesse de Fontanges, a mistress of Louis XIV. Pommes de Anna, a layered dish of thin-sliced potatoes topped with clarified butter, was named after a famous street courtesan, Anna Deslions (la lionne des boulevards).

The composer Gioachino Rossini called Dugléré "le Mozart de la cuisine" and once asked the chef to prepare his favorite fillet of beef right at his dinner table in a chafing dish. Dugléré declined to do so and Rossini's harsh retort, "tournez-moi le dos…turn your back on me," gave birth to the dish called Tournedos Rossini. For the dîner des trois empereurs, the Mozart de la cuisine would not turn his back on his illustrious guests. They were in store for a meal fit for…well, for an emperor.

When Émilie-Claire and Jean-Léon entered the chambre separée, His Imperial Majesty the Emperor and Autocrat of All the Russias, Tsar Alexander Nikolayevich the Second, and a woman who was not the Tsarina Maria Alexandrovna (but Alexander's mistress) were already seated at the large round table. Their son, Tsarevitch Alexander III, heir to the throne, and his new bride, the former Princess Dagmar of Denmark stood just behind the royal couple. Jean-Léon bowed and Émilie-Claire curtsied. Jean-Léon had given Émilie-Claire a short dissertation on the backgrounds of these Russians during the carriage ride to the Café Anglais.

The Russian Emperor was known as Alexander the Liberator having established many reforms including the emancipation of all the serfs in his country. He had recently sold a remote bit of real estate to the United States of America because this territory, called Alaska, was coveted by Great Britain and anyway, it was barren and practically worthless. He had visited the Paris World's Fair, the Exposition Universelle d'art et d'industrie, four days ago. While riding in his carriage with two of his sons and the Emperor Napoleon III, a Polish immigrant, Antoni Berezowski, wanting to avenge the occupation of his country by Russia, fired a double-barreled pistol at the Tsar. The gun misfired and the only victim of the attempt was a wounded horse.

The son, Alexander III had not always been the heir apparent. His brother, Nicholas, had been the original Tsarevich but became fatally ill in 1865. It was Nicholas's wish on his death bed that his fiancée would marry his successor, his brother Alexander. And so Princess Dagmar was joined in marriage to Alexander III, converted to the Russian Orthodox Church, and took the name Maria Feodorovna. Unlike his father, Alexander III hadn't taken a mistress. He also stayed well out the way of politics.

There were introductions all around and they sat down to await the other guests. Claudius Burdel, acting as maître de cave, filled their glasses with the first of the wines they would sample: a Madère Retour de l'Inde 1810. It was said that the restaurant had a wine cellar of 200 thousand bottles of the best, most exotic, most expensive wines in Europe.

A Parisian couple came to the table. Thank God, thought Émilie-Claire, at last someone I can talk to! They introduced themselves as Armand Moulin and his wife, Amélie Frédérique. He was the owner of a bank and a powerful figure in the politics of Haussmann's redesign of Paris. Finally, the last two guests arrived: Kaiser Wilhelm I, King of Prussia, and Otto Eduard Leopold, Prince of Bismarck, Duke of Lauenburg, also known as Otto von Bismarck.

Musicians entered the room and began to play the String Quartet in E-flat Major by Édouard Lalo. Kaiser Wilhelm frowned—perhaps he wished for something by Bach or Beethoven. Now waiters brought a Potage Impératrice consisting of a chicken stock thickened with tapioca and finished with egg yolks and cream, to which was added poached rounds of chicken forcemeat, cockscombs, cocks' kidneys and green peas. Then came the expected Potage Fontanges, the rich soup with green peas and sorrel.

After the potages, Burdel came around to light cigars. Smoking was only allowed in between courses, never when guests were eating. The café supplied French cigars from Reuilly, made with the finest tobacco imported from Havana. While the men smoked, the women congregated near the windows which mercifully were opened just a crack. Émilie-Claire was the first to speak.

"Have you been to the Exposition Universelle?" she asked Amélie Frédérique Moulin.

"Of course. We loved the English lighthouse and the Egyptian temple and the Tunisian Bardo of the Bey. Oh, and the exhibition of Japanese art was so striking."

"Yes, I think my friend Manet will be interested in that. And you, Madam Feodorovna, have you been to the fair?"

"I did not go," answered the Tsarevich's wife, "but Alexander went with his father. They were very much taken with the display of machinery and especially the great cannon that could shoot 1000 pound shells. Imagine! Of course, there was that incident with the terrible man who tried to shoot Alexander."

The meal continued with a Soufflé à la Reine, a chicken soufflé made with truffles. A Xérès 1821 sherry was poured. The musicians began playing the String Quartet in F Major by Mikhail Glinka. Tsar Alexander seemed pleased at hearing a work by one of his countrymen. Kaiser Wilhelm continued to frown. One man seemed to have no reaction…seemed incapable of reaction. The stolid, stoical Otto von Bismarck, had said very little during the meal. Now he looked at Jean-Léon Richelieu and the faintest flicker of curiosity crept across his face.

"Your eye patch," Bismarck said, "it is the result of a duel, is it not?"

"Something like that," answered Jean-Léon. He never revealed the truth about his injury, especially to people like Bismarck, a possible political adversary to whom he should never show any weakness. In fact, he had lost the eye as a small child by running headlong into a sharp tree branch during a game of tag. His silence about the incident encouraged a host of theories from people willing to assume the manliest of answers to the mystery.

Jean-Léon was right to be suspicious of Bismarck. He had provoked a war with Austria and he was undertaking to abolish the old German Confederation to form what was to be the North German Confederation, essentially the first German National State. This aligned them with Prussia and suggested a certain danger to France. He had become the "Iron Chancellor" and he dominated his cabinet with the steadfast determination of conservative nationalism. Yet there were those who felt his strong leadership masked an irrational and unstable despot whose suppressed anxiety and anger would lead to disaster.

Burdel himself served the next course, Filets de Sole à la Vénitienne. The Vénitienne was a sauce of white wine, tarragon vinegar, shallots and chervil, mounted with butter and finished with chopped chervil and tarragon. The wine which accompanied the fish course was a Châteaux d'Yquem 1847. A second fish course followed with a Escalope de Turbot au gratin, and then Selle de Mouton purée Bretonne which was a saddle of mutton with a purée of broad beans bound with Breton sauce.

More cigars, a Chambertin 1846, then back to entrées of ambrosial elegance: Poulet à la Portugaise, a whole chicken roasted with a covering of adobo paste consisting of tomato, red bell pepper, garlic, origanum, paprika, cayenne pepper, brown sugar, lemon juice, white wine, chicken stock and olive oil, stuffed with tomato flavored rice; a Pâté Chaud de Cailles of warm quail; Homard à la Parisienne which was lobster cooked in court bouillon, cut into slices and glazed with aspic, with a garnish of tomatoes stuffed with a macédoine of vegetables, dressed with a mixture of mayonnaise and aspic and garnished with sliced truffle. And more wines: Châteaux Margaux 1847 and Château Latour 1847.

It was around one in the morning when Chef Adolphe Duglèrè appeared at the table to learn if the diners were pleased. There was applause and extolment. Tsar Alexander, however, had a complaint: where was the foie gras? Duglèrè answered:

"Sire, in Gastronomie Française it is not the custom to eat foie gras in the month of June. If you will but wait until October, you will have no cause for regret."

It seemed as though the meal itself would last until October. The musicians, who had taken a long break, had returned. They started playing the String Quartet Number 2 in A Minor by Felix Mendelssohn. Finally, thought Kaiser Wilhelm, a German composer! Châteaux Lafite 1848 was served. Ortolans sur Canapés and Aubergines à l'Espagnole (a dish of aubergine shells filled with chopped aubergine, tomato and ham, gratinéed with gruyère) appeared.

Wilhelm Friedrich Ludwig von Hohenzollern, the King of Prussia, had established Otto von Bismarck in his position as Minister President of the German Confederation and had left much of the governing to the Prince. Yet he had reservations about Bismarck because of his heavy-handedness and anti-Catholic stance. Jean-Léon sensed the tension between the two. Bismarck was hopeful that the Southern Germany States would soon join with the Northern German Confederation and lead to a unified Germany, a Deutsches Reich. This seemed unlikely without a common cause…like a war with a traditional enemy…like France.

Jean-Léon had tried to steer the conversation toward topics that might reveal the attitudes, if not the plans, of the two Germans. But the mention of Austria or of Italy, two nations where France's interactions had caused friction with the Confederation, failed to provoke Bismarck or the Kaiser. The intercourse seemed always to drift back to the food. Émilie-Claire could feel Jean-Léon's frustration. When Canetons à la rouennaise was brought in by Burdel and the waiters, she said:

"Cladius, you must stop bringing such heavenly delicacies to our German friends. They will develop such a fondness for French food that they may decide to invade Paris just for the cuisine."

There was a lull…a profound silence after this comment that betrayed the innocence of the occasion. But if Émilie-Claire had made a faux pas she did not show it. Her smile was disarming and soon spread to the rest of the company. Kaiser Wilhelm contributed a chuckle to smoothing over situation—although Bismarck broke from his usual inscrutable expression and scowled. Of course, there was always the food.

Canetons à la Rouennaise was a roast duckling stuffed with forcemeat with legs and breasts removed, the legs grilled and the breasts thinly sliced and arranged around the stuffing. Juices extracted through a poultry press and added to a Rouennaise sauce were poured over the sliced duck. The accompanying Cassolette Princesse was a cassolette with a border of duchesse potatoes and an asparagus filling in cream sauce. The only item more spectacular than this was the Champagne Roedere Frappé.

The champagne was twenty years old and served in a clear crystal bottle that had been custom made for the dîner des trois empereurs. The pale color and effervescent bubbles so delighted the Tsar that he ordered that a case of it be sent to him in Russia. "Make sure the bottles have a flat bottom," he added. Émilie-Claire looked at Jean-Léon, a question in her eyes.

"That's so no one can conceal a bomb in the curved glass of the bottles," he whispered to her.

But there was a bomb—an ice bomb. Dessert was a Bombe Glacée. Ice cream blended with blackberries had been pressed into a semi-spherical mold then filled with a custard of syrup, egg yolks, and crème frâiche before being refrozen. A dribbling of rich chocolate sauce graced the top of the "bomb" and a circle of surrounding berries finished the dish.

Home again. Émilie-Claire collapsed on the bed while Jean-Léon began undressing, removing his dinner jacket and reaching down to loosen his shoe laces. "I'll never have to eat again," she said.

"It would be difficult to top that meal," said Jean-Léon. "Political intrigue and the finest cuisine that money can buy."

"Did you learn anything tonight, mon amour?"

"Nothing substantial. They all were too guarded. We know they resent Napoleon's interference in Italy. The alliance between the German states and Prussia is suggestive. Don't mention that I ever said this, but Napoleon keeps making foolish mistakes. He is getting old."

"After I sleep for a few days I wouldn't mind it if we went to see the fair. That Moulin woman, Amélie, was talking about it."

"I think I can arrange some free time to do just that. After all, it is another of Napoleon's great enterprises. He was trying to one up the English and their world fair of five years ago. From what I hear, he has succeeded. We should be happy he has succeeded in something worth while."

"Ah, mon petit chou, you are so cynical. Perhaps that is why I love you so much."

"If you will get out of the clothes, I will give you a chance to prove that to me."

Byron Grush

14

Exposition Universelle

They had crossed from the Trocadero over the Pont d'Lena, past the pylons holding the heroic sculptures of ancient warriors, Greek, Roman, Gallic, and Arab, and stood in the queue with Parisians, Englishmen, Germans, Americans, Poles, Russians, and all manner of people foreign and domestic, waiting for tickets at the booths on the Quai d'Orsay. Once through the gate they had entered the vast park that surrounded the main exhibition building, the Palais du Champ de Mars.

Here, in sculpted nature, wound curved paths through flowering bushes that led to the overflow of exhibits, offerings too large to fit in the main structure, and to rows of peddlers' stalls, refreshment stands, restaurants, and bars. Here was a replica of a Tunsian king's palace, the Bardo of the Bey. Here was an underground grotto in an aquarium. Here was the Electric Tower built of British iron, perhaps predicting the future iconic construction by M. Eiffel which would one day stand as a monument to industrialism and French pride in more or less the same location.

Here was a full-sized Gothic cathedral designed by Charles Leveque. Here was an Egyptian temple, a school house, and an American bar serving mint juleps. An incongruous display perhaps, but a smattering of history and culture in an international carnival of one-upmanship. It was a taste of what was inside. All of it, too numerous and overwhelming to be experienced in one day.

Émilie-Claire had coaxed Jean-Léon into bringing her to the fair. Phoebe and François had come too, bringing Jeanne-Alice with them. It was a time to become inspired, to marvel at the achievements of humankind. To acknowledge France's place in the world as a leader in science and culture. Even Victor Hugo had returned briefly to Paris to attend the fair. He had written a preamble to the Paris Guide of 1867 in which he had said: "O my country; and as Athens became Greece, as Rome became Christianity, thou, France, become the world!" Of course, he had also added, "Down with war! Let there be alliance! Concord! Unity!"

The Champ de Mars had been the military parade grounds before preparations for the fair began. It consisted of nearly 120 aces of land, land now reconfigured with an immense exhibition hall and its surrounding park area. The building, the Palais du Champ de Mars, was a big rectangle with semi-circular ends and an open center where gardens surrounded a dome-shaped pavilion. It was 1608 feet long and 1247 feet wide. Big enough for 50,000 exhibits from 42 countries. Seven million people would wander through it by the time the fair closed.

Jeanne-Alice held a cup of hot cocoa she had gotten from a vender as they entered the elliptical building. Iron girders in a thick weave vaulted long corridors. At the side walls were crystal clear glass arches. The effect, to some critics, was "fatiguing to the eye," "in defiance of tradition," "dull and gray and irrational." Jeanne-Alice thought it was rather striking, like a fantasy building made with a toy building set like the one her brother had gotten for Christmas one year—only enlarged to a human scale. Her brother, Geoffroy…how he would have loved this new adventure!

And Émilie-Claire, did she wish Teo could be here to witness all of this? Or had she put the young boy out of her mind, so painful was his loss? The fair, at least, was a good distraction from her daily regrets. She would allow herself to become overwhelmed by its spectacle.

The great ellipse was organized into concentric rings. Each area was devoted to a category of human endeavor where similar products could be displayed by many nations, or where separate nations could represent themselves by spectacular inventions. According to the guide book, a system of classification divided the exhibition into ten major groups: "works of art, apparatus and application of the liberal arts; furniture and other objects for use in dwellings; clothing, including fabrics and other objects worn upon the person; livestock and specimens of agricultural buildings; live produce and specimens of horticultural works; articles whose special purpose was meant to improve the physical and moral conditions of the people."

The skeleton framework of an elevator display rose three stories to the underside of the vaulted roof; the cages were of lace-like iron through which could be seen the frightened women and men who rode up and down in them. Émilie-Claire remembered the elevators in the Langham Hotel in London and the one at the Bon Marché, but most Parisians had never seen one before. The largest machinery was in the outer ellipse; it was the biggest ring and had the most windows. There was a huge iron ingot and a gigantic cannon exhibited by the Krupp Company, a working model of the Suez Canal, a telegraphy exhibit by Samuel F. B. Morse, a model of Chicago's Lake Water Tunnel, C. H. McCormick's reaping machine, a display of war time ambulances, and a machine that turned rabbit skins into felt hats.

By the time they got to the fine arts exhibits, Émilie-Claire was exhausted. If she had expected to see art works by her friends, the future impressionists, she was disappointed. In the past, contemporary painters had been represented only by the most famous: Ingres and Delacroix had vied for the grand prize at the 1855 exposition. Ingres had died in January and some of his works were being shown. But this year, two officially recognized painters, Jean-Louis-Ernest Meissonier and Jean-Léon Gérôme were the favorites, and one of them would win the grand prize. Genre scenes and staged historical events dominated the canvases. Monet had submitted a large canvas called *Women in the Garden* but it was rejected. Gustave Courbet and Édouard Manet declined even to submit paintings realizing that they too would be rejected. They each set up independent galleries nearby.

Jeffrey Dolan Flaherty was standing before a painting by Frederic Church in the American art exhibit. It was a spectacular panorama of Niagara Falls—the water flowing over the edge of the falls seemed nearly to be in real motion; you could almost taste the rising mist. It would win a silver medal. Émilie-Claire came up behind Flaherty and tapped him on the shoulder.

"That is magnificent," she said.

"It's certainly not like any French landscapes," mused Flaherty.

"Come look at these canvases by Whistler. That one, *The Woman in White*, was rejected by the Paris Salon two different times. Finally it gets its showing…and to the entire world."

"You don't have…"

"No, I was rejected with the best of them. I'm seriously thinking of returning to the U.S.A. There is a horde of American artists coming to Paris now. And all this realism…I'm more and more intrigued with the work by the people in our studio…Renoir and Monet and the others. I am nowhere their equal, but I could bring a certain insight home with me, and perhaps achieve some recognition there."

"I would be sorry to see you go. I've missed our talks."

"I always thought maybe…you and I…"

"Your attentions were not unappreciated. I always liked you."

"Then why…?"

"One meets one's soul mate only once in a lifetime. When I met Jean-Léon, I knew I had met mine."

"It is the destiny of the artist always to be rejected, I suppose. Still, if I could see you again…just once…before I go back to America."

"Yes? That would be acceptable. Oh look, here come Jean-Léon and Phoebe and François and Jeanne-Alice."

"And the whole rest of Paris."

The last experience of the Exposition Universelle that Jeanne-Alice had that day was one she would always remember. The pioneer photographer, Nadar, whose real name was Gaspard-Félix Tournachon, had tethered his hot air balloon on the fair grounds, having risen above the Champ de Mars earlier to take aerial photographs. This was a precarious process since the technology of photography at that time involved wet glass plates which had to be prepared during the flight and protected from chemical influences. Finished with the day's pictorial endeavor, Nadar now offered to take people up in the balloon for a bird's eye view of Paris.

Jeanne-Alice pleaded and Phoebe agreed and so up they went into the cloudless blue sky in M. Nadar's flying balloon. They could see the extent of the park and the oval-shaped exhibition hall with its concentric roof tops. They could see out over the city, toward the widened avenues lined with gas lights that criss-crossed like the huge web of a deranged spider. It gave them a sense of the grand plan of

M. Haussmann and Napoleon III to remake Paris into the capitol of the world. The elegant geometry of the City of Lights, the parks, the monuments, the fountains…. Yet here and there were still pockets of the old Paris: narrow alley-like streets of cobblestone, chimneys smoking with the soot of eons past, wobbling windmills and ancient chestnut trees that hugged the odd conglomeration of buildings as if to say, "this is the real Paris which fostered me and which I love."

And Phoebe Stapleton Gardinier now loved this, her foster city, the old and the new of it.

*   *   *

Émilie-Claire met Jeffrey Flaherty on the Boulevard des Italiens outside of the Maison Dorée, also known as Restaurant of the Cité, and also known as the Gilded House. Jeffrey was uneasy; this was, perhaps, the most expensive restaurant in Paris—and one of the most notorious. He began to shake his head.

"Don't be absurd, Jeffrey. This is my treat. For once let the woman pay. And by the way, the food here is excellent."

The entrance from the Boulevard des Italiens was for ordinary people. Émilie-Claire led Flaherty around the corner to the entrance on the Rue Lafitte, where Maison Dorée's many private rooms were accessed—rooms often used for illicit encounters—some said orgies. True or not, private was private. Jeffrey looked up at the gilded balconies that graced the façade of the five-story building. There was a frieze across the first level representing a hunting scene. They entered and Émilie-Claire gestured to the maître d'hôtel whom she seemed to know. They were ushered up a flight of stairs with carved decorations by Gabriel-Joseph Garraud and into a private cabinet.

"The chef here is Casimir Moisson," Émilie-Claire told Jeffrey once they had been seated. "He studied under Adolphe Dugléré, so you can expect gastronomic delights."

"I am merely delighted to be with you. Alone for once. I care little for the food."

Besides the single round table there were comfortable chairs and a settee covered in velvet, which seemed to have seen much use. The room was hung with paintings and a gold-leafed framed floor-to-ceiling mirror which appeared to be covered with scratches. Émilie-Claire motioned to Jeffrey to take a closer look at the mirror. The scratches were writing, made by the diamond rings of female patrons. Some of the inscriptions were shocking, others mundane.

"Have you written anything here?" Jeffrey asked. But Émilie-Claire only smiled.

Later, after they had eaten a Bresse chicken which had been sliced, browned, and finished with a cream and egg yolk sauce, Jeffrey embarked upon a personal narrative—one that would make its way into Émilie-Claire's memoirs. She hadn't heard any of it before, and it seemed to answer some of the questions in her mind about the young American painter.

"You probably think," he began, "that I stayed in Paris to avoid the war back in the states. That is partially true, but there is more. It goes back...do you know much about Chattanooga, where I was born and raised? No? It is a river town. On the banks of the Tennessee River. Surrounded by mountains...well, we called them mountains. But very flat where the town is situated. Prone to flooding.

"The Cherokees were there before the settlers came. Chattanooga means something like 'pointed rock' in Cherokee...that's for the jagged peak on Lookout Mountain, I guess. I used to sit up there with...but I'm getting ahead of myself. Anyway, I was about 5 years of age when the army forced the Indians out. Forced them to march to Oklahoma, which was then called Indian Territory. The Cherokee called the march the Trail of Tears. The original town was called Ross Landing after their chief, Chief Ross. That all changed rapidly. The railroad came through about 1850.

"You may think it was an idyllic place in which to grow up. Certainly, the low hills surrounding the town, the high mountains, the rushing river gave a young boy a sense of adventure greater than any dime novel ever could. My father was the foreman at the steel mill. Highly regarded by his employers and hated by his underlings. Because of this, during my school days I was treated to verbal abuse and I was excluded from my schoolmate's social circles. I didn't mind all that much because I had a sense of my own importance...not based on my father's position, but stemming from my ability to render images. I had discovered art at an early age.

"I could wander the hills with sketch pad and charcoals and be happy as a lark. I did not need friendships and none were offered...except once. One day I was drawing a picture of a paddleboat that was moored at one of the wharfs and a girl came up to me. She sat down beside me and watched as I drew. It was a little unnerving, but I welcomed the attention…the first anyone had ever given to my ambitions as an artist. She had a sweet face and was dressed primly in a summer dress with flowers on it. I remember the flowers and remember thinking how incongruous they seemed in the dirty, wet environment of the docks.

"Her name was Sue Ellen Masters. Her father was a deacon at the Presbyterian Church. She was two years younger than me. During summers she came with me on my painting excursions. I would set up my easel on a hillside overlooking the river valley and she would spread a blanket on the ground next to me and relax with a book. We didn't talk much but we seemed to understand each other very well. In the spring the wild flowers were in bloom…a speckled carpet of yellows and blues. The girl lying on the blanket, her golden hair done in braids that coiled on top of her head, should have suggested to me a painting or two, but I never asked her to pose.

"As we got older and more familiar with each other a new sensation began to develop between us. The stirrings of adolescence, I suppose, but more. Sue Ellen read poetry books. Cheap, romantic poetry that would never grace the great library shelves of the world, but which sufficed to instill in her young mind the notion that love was inevitable between two such compatible beings as ourselves. For me it was an infatuation born of hormones I didn't quite understand. And we did not know what to do with the new feelings.

"Many times we went up to the point. This was a long granite outcropping shaped like the prow of a boat that stuck out over a sheer drop to the valley floor a thousand feet below. Sometimes we would sit and dangle our feet over the edge. Sometimes we played like fools at standing right at the edge and waving our arms as if we were losing balance and about to plummet down. Sometimes we spread Sue Ellen's blanket on the point and lay together looking up at clouds where we saw animal heads that ebbed and flowed together in a vast circus of vapors and sparkling sunlight.

"The first time I touched her we were standing on her front porch, she about to enter and I about to leave. I raised my hand to her face. We stood motionless for a few moments, and then I drew her face close to mine. The kiss never happened because just at that moment, while time stopped and a secret energy leaped between us, her father came through the door and caught us. I was ordered away and Sue Ellen was forbidden ever to see me again.

"I looked forward to the beginning of school that Autumn for I felt I would be able to see her then. But her father had sent her away, somewhere up north to stay with an aunt and attend an all-girls' school. I never found out exactly where it was or I might have tried to follow her, young though I was."

"Well," commented Emilie-Claire, "a pre-adolescent love affair doesn't sound all that tragic. Did you ever see her again?"

"In fact I did. I had graduated from high school and had spent the summer idling about, wondering about my future. I wanted to study art and I thought about going to New York or Chicago. My father, of course, wanted me to come to work with him as his assistant at the steel mill. I would have no part of that. But then I thought, I could save enough money to escape from Chattanooga…go to study art somewhere, so I said yes.

"For a time I sat behind a roll top desk and shuffled ledgers back and forth, bored and longing for the life of an artist. For over a year I suffered the fate of the drudge. But I was putting away my salary toward the time that would arrive when my destiny would be fulfilled. Then Sue Ellen came back.

"There was a coffee shop on the first floor of a hotel on Stuart Street, about a block from the river. We would meet there so that her father would not know of our affair. I say affair in the purist terms, as I often suggested that we get a room in the hotel…but she would say no. Yet we fantasized about how it would be. The two of us, naked skin touching beneath satin sheets, a bottle of champagne close by…we were still foolish children.

"It had been raining off and on for weeks. Sometimes slightly, sometimes furiously. The river already swelled and lapped its banks, especially along the great curve it took right at the town. One day we sat in the coffee shop, daydreaming as usual, when the rain began again. At first it seemed only an annoyance, as we hadn't thought to bring an umbrella. But it began to intensify. Soon you couldn't see individual drops. It came in a solid sheet of water, a deluge equal to the great flood in the Bible! Although we were far from the banks of the river, water began to seep under the door of the coffee shop.

"We mused that we would have to take a room here after all. Other people in the shop were not as flippant about the rising flood waters as we and they began to run to the windows and cry out in alarm. Finally some of us climbed the stairs to the upper stories while others ran out the door and sloshed through the knee deep water. And still the water rose.

"It was an angry river that swept through Chattanooga that day. The smaller houses were uprooted and carried far down stream. People climbed to the roof tops and hugged each other as heavy winds pushed up wave after wave of the terrible cascade, sometimes dislodging whole families from their perches to drown them mercilessly. We gained the roof of the hotel, some three stories above the street and we thought we were safe. The river peaked at 50 feet that day. 400 died.

"Later, someone came by in a row boat, rescuing those of us who had survived the storm. We clambered down the roof and dangled above the boat, afraid to release our grip on the edge. Finally I dropped and the small boat nearly upended, but stabilized and so I called to Sue Ellen to jump down. Just as she let go of the roof's metal gutter, a surge of water rolled into us and pushed the little boat forward. Sue Ellen fell into the maelstrom. She went under, flailing her arms and swallowing water from the grimy river.

"By now we were several yards away from the hotel and the boat was moving fast. I stood to jump into the fray but someone grabbed me. If not for this I surely would have joined Sue Ellen in a watery grave. For many days there after I wished I had."

"I understand now," said Émilie-Claire, "why you left. But why do you want to return? Surely there is nothing there for you now."

"I want to stay, but I fear there is nothing for me here either. I'm a failure as an artist, and as far as love is concerned…"

"Walk with me over to that mirror, Jeffrey. I want to write something."

They stood before the gilded frame and gazed into the mirror, its scratches reflecting the flickering gaslight. Individual words appeared when they looked at them from a certain angle. Love poems to long lost lovers, rants against abusive spouses, idle nothings, and political declarations. Émilie-Claire raised her hand and rotated the ring on her finger, its diamond sparkling. She pulled off the ring and attacked the mirror's surface, making a shrill sound like chalk stuttering on a blackboard. She wrote: "Jeffrey, please don't go."

She turned toward the young man and her hands went to his shoulders and up his neck. On tip toes she could just bring her face to his, her lips to softly touch his own.

"I can give you a reason to stay," she said.

15

Impetuous Lady

Excerpt from: *Dame Impétueux, la Mémoire de Émilie-Claire Lebeau-Richelieu*, (English translation, published by Charles W. Karr & Co., Chicago, 1897)

I could not write this chapter were my dear husband still alive. And well you may wonder, how could a woman, so completely in love with her soul mate, commit the brazen act of infidelity that commenced between me and the young artist, Jeffrey Flaherty, after that scrumptious (infamous?) night at the Maison Dorée. It is a well known fact that married men in the second half of the nineteenth century kept mistresses and that, while not a common subject to be discussed in polite society, there was little stigma attached to those affairs. While my own husband attended to his affairs of state, I was absorbed in a state of affairs…well, affair…which, if I were a man, would be as nothing in the scheme of such things. Do not judge me too harshly.

I have always been attracted to men of an artistic nature. It is often the case that their lives are tragic—is this part of their allure? My friend the poet, Charles Baudelaire, left Paris for Brussels where he hoped to overcome his perpetual poverty but fell into drinking and opium. He suffered a stroke and spent the last year of his life paralyzed and unable to work. He died in 1867 and only now is some of his poetry beginning to be recognized and republished. He had been a great friend to Édouard [Manet] and supported him in his own struggles for acceptance.

Well, we all have to die. Rossini, the composer, is gone just last November. Berlioz is also dead. It is as if Paris were on the cusp of a changing of the guard…the old styles and sensibilities eclipsed by new notions, new visions. Claude Monet, Jeffery's painter friend, has been painting scenes with boats and shimmering sunlight on the Seine. He is trying to capture the actual movement of the light. It is a new way of looking at things. And Jeffery is learning from Monet's and Renoir's approaches and beginning too to paint the light and the colors of scenes instead of just rendering those objects that reside there.

We could not keep meeting at the Maison Dorée, it was much too expensive. Although my husband, Jean-Léon, had a more than adequate salary from the Emperor and I still had my own money, it was foolish to squander funds (as Jean-Léon would say) with no return on the investment; Jeffery said the place made him nervous. Instead, we met at the Café Guerbois, the place where members of Jeffery's atelier gathered to drink absinth and talk of art and life.

They were all there at one time or another—Edgar Degas, Claude Monet, Pierre-Auguste Renoir, Alfred Sisley, Paul Cézanne, Camille Pissarro, Frédéric Bazille, Berthe Morisot, the art critic Louis Edmond Duranty (who Manet challenged to a dual in 1870), the writer Émile Zola, the photographer Nadar, and of course, Édouard Manet. I think it was Zola who called the group "the Batignolles Group," after the bohemian quarter where the café was located and where so many artists lived or had studios, bought their painting supplies, met with impetuous women, procured models, and lived la vie Parisienne.

Frédéric Bazille had a studio not far from the café on the Rue La Condamine. I mention Frédéric because he was one of those tragic characters whose life was cut short by circumstances he could not, or would not control. He was the only one of the Batignolles Group that had money. He would buy supplies and even pay the rent for his colleagues on those occasions when they became desperate for funds. I will write more about him later.

Jeffery and I would visit Brazille in his studio on occasion. Frédéric liked to make portraits of the other artists who visited him and, perhaps because of the Manet painting in which I appear, he suggested that I also pose for him, but I declined. My modeling days were long over…the last time I posed was for the sculptor, Rodin, and I fainted and fell off the modeling stand! I did let Jeffery sketch me, but very informally. He accomplished a very nice drawing of me sitting in the Café Guerbois listening to all the political ranting one afternoon in the late spring of 1869. I remember the approximate date because it was just before the riots of June 8 and 9.

Jean-Léon usually updated me on important political matters. It seemed the opposition was gaining strength and a poll showed that the Republicans, the Monarchists and the liberals…all of whom had only in common their hatred of the Emperor, were now 45 percent of the electorate. In the parliamentary elections in early June the Emperor's regime maintained control, but the opposition acquired many seats in the government. Opposition turnout was especially strong in the city. There were demonstrations and riots to follow.

The Marseillaise was sung by demonstrators on the Boulevard Montmartre—this had been banned during the Second Empire. In Belleville people attacked and tore down the gas street lights and broke windows in stores. They marched down Boulevard du Temple, overturned a police van, and assembled at the Place de la Bastille. There were arrests. Other crowds attempted to disrupt a soirée being held at the Tuileries Palace. It so happened that Jean-Léon and I were in attendance there, dancing and having a gay old time when an alarm was given that angry crowds were outside. The Emperor went to the musical director, Émil Waldteufel, and instructed him to continue playing as if nothing were happening to ruin the gala evening. So we danced while Paris sizzled in the heat of insurgency.

There were demonstrations in Bordeaux, Arles, and Nantes. The Bicêtre Fortress swelled with more than a thousand of those arrested by the police. The leader of the Monarchists was Adolphe Thiers, who I will have much to say about later. The Republican at the head of the opposition was Léon Gambetta. For what was to come, these men held much of the blame. The Emperor held the biggest part in his short-sightedness and his megalomania. Jean-Léon constantly tried to steer Louis Napoleon clear of the disasters that were to follow, but he could do little in the face of the foolishness that led France into the strife that threatened to end the Second Empire.

Meanwhile, back at the Café Guerbois, there was talk of a new venue that had just opened in Montmartre called the Folies Trévise [later the Folies-Bergère] where light operettas and comedy were mixed with acrobatics and dancers wearing scandalous costumes.

This music hall was undoubtedly the first of its kind in France, although in London there had been similar establishments such as the Alhambra. The Batignolles Group was quite interested in the possibilities of a place where the bourgeois met the bohemian, where decadence met debauchery. Manet, many years later, painted one of his most famous canvases called *The Bar at the Folies-Bergère*. One wondered how the Folies would evolve in the future—la musique la danse, leson, la lumiere!

Jeffery wanted to go and so did Frédéric [Bazille] and Pierre-Auguste [Renoir]. I didn't want to be the only woman in the group so I persuaded Berthe Morisot to come with us. Berthe was a very accomplished artist, having studied with Camille Corot and Aimé Millet. She had two landscapes in the Salon de Paris of 1864, but her forte was the figure. She and Édouard [Manet] became friends in a sort of on-again off-again relationship (Manet was too sensitive about criticism and this often affected his friendships). She later married Édouard's brother, Eugène. Personally, along with Mary Cassat, I think she was one of the best of the movement later to known as Impressionism.

We hopped on an omnibus going down the Boulevard Montmartre and got off at Rue Richer, walking the block or so to the Folies. We expected the usual café-concert style venue…singing had only been allowed in cafes since 1867…but this was all together different. First of all, it cost 2 francs to enter, so it was like a theater. But unlike a theater, there were no rows and rows of seats, reserved or otherwise. Instead, the enormous hall featured a bar, a promenade gallery, and scores of tables where one could view the stage. On the stage was an ever changing parade of entertainment that blended the opera with the circus.

We found a table and Jeffery, Pierre-Auguste, and Frédéric went off to the bar to buy drinks for our party. On stage, an act involving a boxing kangaroo was being led off as a team of acrobats took over, springing onto the stage with a series of hand stands and flips. It was very informal: a small orchestra provided dance music and couples, some not of the opposite sex, found room between the tables or danced off into the promenade gallery. People ate, talked, smoked, and engaged in amorous actions, daring for public places.

"Did you see," said Berthe, leaning close to me, "that in the promenade there were some unaccompanied young ladies?

Demimondaines, do you think?"

"Undoubtedly," I answered. "Our men are taking a great deal of time procuring those drinks. Let us hope that is all they procure."

The men returned with drinks and thankfully, without additional female companionship. We settled down to watch as the impresario of the Folies took the stage. He announced in a loud voice:

"Mesdames et messieurs, we at the Folies Trévise are proud to present…directly from a tour of Egypt…that great performer of commedia dell'arte, that elegant mime, the inheritor of the fame of Deburau, previously at the Funambulles, that embodiment of Gilles and Pierrot…the fabulous Paul Legrand!"

A short, plump man in "white face," dressed in the baggy white blouse with large buttons and the black skull cap of the traditional Pierrot character and sporting a ruffle around his neck strolled slowly onto the stage. A melancholy look, a slumping stance, presented to the audience the aspect of the sad clown they all knew and loved. A pantomime began involving Pierrot and another actor dressed as a policeman.

"I'm trying to convince Édouard to paint en plein air," Berthe said to me. "He only wants to work in that cramped studio on the Rue Guyot."

"It is not so cramped," I replied.

"Of course you would know that, wouldn't you? I'm just saying that painting from nature is so rewarding…the colors, the changing light, the gentle breezes…"

On the stage the silent drama unfolded as Pierrot and the policeman gestured in argument over a flower pot the clown had carried away from a window. Those in the audience who were actually watching the show laughed at the antics.

"I know you weren't Olympia," Berthe continued, "but were you the woman with the parrot?"

I couldn't help myself against the not-so-veiled insinuations. I countered:

"Édouard's portraits of you are so demure. Do you always slouch down on a divan as if you were inebriated?"

The pantomime was getting more energetic as the policeman and the clown pushed at each other, hilariously only connecting with thin air. Suddenly a figure emerged from stage right dressed in a military uniform hung with oversized ribbons and medals. The policeman snapped to attention. Pierrot gave a low bow and then thumbed his nose. From the audience someone yelled, "It's the Emperor! Show respect!"

This allusion to the actor as representing Louis Napoleon did not go unchallenged. Soon there were jeers and gibes from various sides of the room. The people of Paris were divided and not afraid of expressing opinion nor of deriding those who differed in their views. It appeared that a ruckus would take place any minute. Legrand and the other actors threw up their hands and exited the stage. Someone in the audience pushed someone else.

"These idiots," said Renoir, "will fight each other while the real vultures descend upon us. With no strength left to resist they...and therefore we...are doomed."

"What do you mean?" asked Bazille.

"I mean our friends the Germans are enjoying seeing the French at odds with one another. I am thinking of moving to the country. Taking the family for an extended vacation."

"Madame Richelieu," Bazille said to me, "what do you have to say to this? Surely your husband has his finger on the political pulse of Europe."

"He does," I answered, "and I can't give you an accounting that would make any sense. It is all too complicated." I couldn't say, even to my friends, what my husband's opinion of the Emperor's judgment really was.

The Folies' management had brought a string of dancers out onto the stage in order to quell the disturbance that was brewing in the audience. They were dressed...or undressed...in very little, but at least they were pretty. The height to which they could kick their legs was impressive. In spite of this new distraction the arguments among the crowded room continued. We decided to leave.

The following evening Jean-Léon had managed to escape his duties to the Emperor long enough to join me for dinner. We had a pleasant meal and then relaxed in our sitting room. I told him about the disturbance I had witnessed at the Folies Trévise. I didn't tell him, of course, about spending most of the evening afterwards with Jeffery. It is not that I meant to be dishonest; I simply would not have hurt Jean-Léon for all the money in the world.

The comments that Renoir had made about the growing

disenchantment with Louis Napoleon and the polarization of the Parisian people interested Jean-Léon greatly. He began talking about outside influences.

"There is this fellow Karl Marx," he told me. "A Russian who was living in London and writing about the labor movement…you know, the First International. He has a book out called *Das Kapital* which criticizes capitalism and points out that the worker in the world has no value which he can call his own. This has struck a chord with the workers of France, in spite of concessions the Emperor has made to labor.

"The Empire has been opposed to the Communists, calling them the 'Red Terror,' but this has only poured more fuel on the fire. You saw the strikes and the riots, easily quelled…for now…but in the future? There is much talk about replacing the form of government we have now with a parliamentary monarchy. A senatus-consulte has been called for. That could be the first step toward the overthrow of the Emperor."

"And if that happens," I asked, "what will happen to you? To us?"

"I don't believe we will see another revolution with the classes fighting in the streets. I think change will come, but gradually. Louis Napoleon is getting old and, as I have said before, careless or just plain incompetent. What worries me is the divisiveness of the public. All these different political views. And, of course, the Germans. If they don't declare war on us, I believe the Emperor will declare war on them! Either way France will suffer."

Very often Jean-Léon was half right in his predictions…this was one of those times. We dropped the politics for the rest of the evening and talked of the changes happening in Parisian life. The transformation of Paris by Haussmann with his underground plumbing and scores of gas lights, his wide avenues that connected all the proper places in the city and ignored the despicable ones. The public works had given jobs to many. And it did seem that the rest of the world was beginning to recognize Paris for its culture and importance to trade.

Then, ironically, Jean-Léon turned the topic to my artist friends. He praised them for entertaining me during his absences. Was he aware of just how much they entertained me? He gave no indication. And yet…

A few days later I was back at the Café Guerbois. Manet was there having an argument with Edgar Degas. Émile Zola was there persuading Felix Nadar to make a photo portrait of him. Jeffery was to meet me there presently. I have never been particularly fond of absinthe, but on this occasion I needed something to solidify my resolve. You see, I was about to break off the affair with Jeffery. He was a sweet man and devoted to me, but I couldn't continue to lead him up the chemin de jardin. It would hurt Jeffery more if we broke up later, and it might devastate Jean-Léon if he ever found out Jeffery and I had been intimate.

La fée verte sat in a decorative glass in front of me, a slotted silver spoon balanced across it which held a white alcohol-soaked sugar cube. I struck a lucifer and set fire to the sugar cube which flamed up nicely and gave off a sweet smell. This manner of preparing the drink was more interesting than merely dripping ice water onto the cube. I tipped the spoon and dropped the sugar cube into the green liquid which immediately turned a cloudy pale-green color. I sipped as I waited for Jeffery.

It may have been the wormwood in the liquor or some other element used in its manufacture that gave the drink its reputation for creating hallucinations. I had never experienced feelings of elation or of dread from drinking it before, but now I was slipping into a strange world where visual references seemed askew and inanimate objects took on personalities of their own. It was subtle, but somewhat disarming. I saw colors in the darkened café that only existed in, say, Monet's landscapes. Voices sharpened and I could hear conversations from the opposite reaches of the room as if they took place at my own table. I did not feel as if I were drunk—indeed, I felt elevated, my perceptions heightened, my spirits raised. Now I considered what I intended to say to Jeffery.

When he arrived and sat opposite me, I had a sense of not only the immediate present, but the possible future and its consequences. Images played across Jeffery's face like a magic lantern show—images of a man crushed and defeated. Did I think of myself as having that much effect on the man? I decided not to say anything, at least not under the influence of absinthe. But Jeffery spoke up as if he had read my thoughts.

"You have too much power over me," he said. "I can not go on unless it is mutual. But I know you will never leave your husband…you will never be totally mine. I think we should see less of each other for the time being."

I was now the one to be crushed. And yet, en un clin d'œil I saw the truth of the matter. It was la mort du petit cheval: the end of our story. Oui…sans l'ombre d'un doute it was over!

"Oh, Jeffery," I blubbered, "if you say we can still be friends I swear I'll hit you!"

I'd like to think it was the absinthe which caused my emotional outburst. Perhaps it was. Or perhaps I had a great deal more attachment to him than I had believed. We parted that day and saw each other very little in the months to come. And what turbulent months those were!

Byron Grush

16

A Tale of Two Cities

Berlin, Germany, January 1870

Geoffroy Pierre Gardinier, the boy who disappeared from the ice cream stand in front of the Cirque-Olympique in Paris eight years before, stood on the sidewalk along the Boulevard Unter den Linden, looking to the west toward the Brandenburg Gate. His eyes traced up the Doric columns to the Quadriga, a monumental sculpture perched on top of the classical style gate which depicted Victoria, the goddess of victory, in a four horse-drawn chariot. The boy, a Frenchman himself, was aware of the ironic history of the statue; Quadriga had been taken to Paris in 1806 by Napoleon Bonaparte after his defeat of Prussia, but it was returned to Berlin in 1814 after Napoleon's defeat and the subsequent Prussian occupation of Paris. The gate was originally called the Friendenstor (the Peace Gate), but Geoffery wasn't so sure that was an appropriate name.

Berlin was the capitol of Prussia, the seat of its government. The presidency was held by the hereditary House of Hohenzollern and there was a parliament of two houses, the Reichstag and the Bundesrat, but the real power, the official representative of the Kaiser, was His High-born, The Count of Bismarck-Schönhausen, Otto von Bismarck. Bismarck envisioned a united Germany, bringing together all the German states. But he feared, and was vocal about his fear, "that a Franco-German war must take place before the construction of a united Germany could be realized." If there were a war, Bismarck maintained, no one would come to France's aid and fighting alone, they would be lost to Prussia's superior forces.

Geoffroy understood the political situation. He agreed with Bismarck's philosophy, even to the point of rejecting his Catholic origins. Why? He was an unintentional French expatriate now, having been snatched at an early age and installed as a surrogate son to a German family. He had been lied to and told that his mother, his father and his sister, his only close relatives in Paris, were all dead. He had been raised with love and kindness and given the opportunity to grow into a responsible and able young man. He was sixteen now, and he wanted to join the army.

His new family lived in a spacious apartment in the borough of Charlottenberg, far from the dirt and pestilence of the city. Max and Felicie Meyerbeer, a retired couple, lived comfortably on Max's banker's pension. They had been childless during the forty-some years of their marriage and so when the opportunity to "adopt" a French orphan boy arose they jumped at it. They weren't aware that Geoffroy wasn't really an orphan, nor did they know that he had been abducted by criminals who profited from a virtual slave trade. By the time Geoffroy had learned enough German to explain his real circumstance, the old couple had endeared themselves to him through their kindness and so he went along with the charade.

You could walk from one end of Berlin to the other in under an hour, through the rectangular grid of streets with their rows and rows of identical houses and their stinking gutters filled with human and animal waste, to the edge of the town where swamp and marsh held sway against a receding forest where wild asparagus tangled around the rails of the new railroad—the vestiges of industrialization pushing Berlin forward toward revitalization.

The aging baroque buildings in the city were crowded with too many families living in single rooms. New construction was impressive; however it consisted only of government buildings, post offices and schools, museums and banks—all in the service of the Kaiser. The working classes lived above store fronts in the old quarters. The wealthy were abandoning the city for the suburbs. The Meyerbeers had been lucky in this regard.

Geoffroy returned to Charlottenberg after his walk along the Boulevard Unter den Linden. A cold wind had blown through the leafless branches of the linden trees, shaking the bulging nests of squirrels. The boy had pulled his scarf more tightly around his neck as he waved down a horse-drawn trolley. Seated in the vehicle with the boy had been a trio of soldiers, their uniforms pressed and newly laundered. They were joking and laughing and Geoffroy had felt attracted to their camaraderie. This helped determine for him the action he had contemplated. Once home he went immediately into his foster father's study where Max Meyerbeer sat behind an oak desk writing letters.

"Father," he said, "I have a wish...a very strong wish. And I hope you will grant me permission to pursue my career of choice."

"Oh? And what choice have you made?"

"I wish to become a soldier."

Max Meyerbeer thought for a moment. He himself had never served in the military, his position at the bank being more important to the economy than any sacrifice of flesh and blood he could make for his country. But he remembered the so-called Revolution of 1848 when Prussian soldiers—13,000 of them—had marched into Berlin to overthrow the parliament. He remembered the gaudy uniforms, the gleaming swords and muskets, the sharp step of the men as they paraded through the dusty streets. General Friedrich von Wrangel...what had happened to him after that short autocratic occupation? It was over within a year and now Berlin was the capital of Prussia and all the Northern German states. And the liberals were back in power.

"I understand how the glamour of the military inspires you," he told Geoffroy. "But, mein sohn, you are young. There is the university in Stuttgart. There is the world to see, but not following behind a caisson that might one day carry back your dead body draped with a flag. My advice is to wait."

"If you will not give me your permission I will go anyway. I will lie about my age. I am restless, Vater. The thought of university makes me ill. I'll be a good soldier. I won't be killed. You and Mutter will be proud of me."

"I guess you will do what you have to do. But it saddens my heart."

Geoffroy aspired to be an officer in the Prussian army. Therefore he applied to the Kriegsakademie, the officer's training academy instituted by General Helmuth von Moltke, the brilliant military planner. There was a major obstacle to this idea however, since

Geoffroy was of French descent. The instructors at the Kriegsakademie did consider using him as a spy, but ultimately rejected him for admission, unsure of his loyalty. For years Moltke had sent some of his General Staff to France dressed as civilians to observe the French garrisons and determine the strength of their supplies of ammunition and food. One officer, Major Alfred von Waldersee, even became a confidant of the mistress of a certain of Louis Napoleon's advisors.

Instead, Geoffroy was conscripted into the regular army and began his training with the Dreyse rifle, the so-called "needle gun." This was a breech-loading rifle, and had been used effectively against the Austrian army with their antiquated muzzle-loading weapons at the battle of Koniggratz. It was an old design yet its operation was smooth and its accuracy sufficient. Geoffroy mastered it well and scored a medal for marksmanship.

The lad wished to be a part of the Uhlan, the Prussian cavalry. He was so impressed by the sight of these mounted soldiers, splendid in their braid-decorated uniforms, their unique "mortar board" helmets, and the pistols they carried as side arms, as they paraded with their lances and sabers flashing in the sunlight. It was not to be, however. Young Geoffroy Gardinier was dispatched with his unit to the French-German border near the French town of Mertz. There they waited in anticipation of an attack by French troops, although, as yet, no state of war existed between the two countries.

*   *   *

London, England, March, 1870

Teodore Presume stopped next to the street locksmith's cart on Whitechapel Road to watch old Harley Mcleod opening a padlock for a customer. Mcleod sorted through his collection of keys, all hung neatly on a rack on the cart, trying one after another until he found the proper fit. "There!" said the locksmith, as the lock snapped open. He wiped his hands on the soiled leather apron he wore and pushed his peaked cap to the back of his head. Teo loved the old man and often stopped to chat with him as he made his rounds of the East End district.

Teo knew the regulars of the road intimately: the strawberry vendor with her cry of "All ripe! All ripe!," the bootblack with his box slung over his shoulder, the flying dustmen with their grubby wagon of discarded items and assorted filth, the boardman who trudged along the sidewalks wearing wooden advertisements like a cloak and who even had a sign on his top hat—who complained bitterly when the police forced him off the pavement and into the gutter. These were all people who had a means toward earning a living, meager though it might be. Teo's main concern, and that of his guardians, William and Catherine Booth, was the salvation of the poverty-stricken East-enders, the denizens of the gin palaces, the lost and lonely and directionless disbelievers.

"How are you today, my young friend?" asked Harley Mcleod once he saw Teo standing by his cart.

"I am very fine, Mr. Mcleod. I walk with the Man in White."

"Ho ho! It is hard to keep a white robe clean along this street!"

"The General will be holding an Experience Meeting at the East London Theater Hall this afternoon. It will be an open-air meeting in front of the old brewery. We hope to see you there."

"Ah, lad, I have my work to see to. There is many a lock needs fixin' and many scissors that need sharpenin'."

General William Booth had moved his Christian Mission from the old tent to an abandoned dance hall, then to the theater, and he now eyed a former warehouse on Whitechapel Road near the People's Market for a permanent venue. Too many meetings in discarded chapels and halls gave the Movement a haphazard aspect. It was time to settle in to a more practical space. Even his open-air meetings saw hundreds of attendees. Dozens would rise and give an account of their experiences: "Thank God I have been kept through the year," "I was a backslider before I met the Reverend," "My soul has been revived—the Lord has pardoned my sins," "What a miserable wretch I was till the Lord met with me!"

General Booth's Army of the Saved was growing. He could even compete favorably with the "Theater Preachings and Tea Meetings" held in the South of London at the Victoria Theater or at Astley's by ad hock preachers like William Carter. Instead of socially irrelevant tea meetings, Booth had opened the first of his "Food for the Millions" shops, basically a soup kitchen to feed the hungry. He was a model of self-sacrifice for the social programs liberal Londoners were now engaging in to combat serious housing and health problems. Booth's older children, Bramwell, Ballington, and Kate, as well as his ward, Teo, were soldiers in the army Booth was forming; spreading the good word in effective and humanitarian ways—the opposite, Booth thought, of how the established churches operated.

A chilling wind blew dust along the street in little whirl-winds as the meeting commenced. Reverend Booth was ministering to a crowd of nearly five hundred that afternoon. Rag-tag revelers comprised of the down-trodden, the hung-over, the depressed, the frightened, all gathered to hear the words of the Lord—his promise of salvation, of forgiveness, of hope. Booth stood on a raised platform which had been hastily put together from discarded boards found in the alleys. He read a passage to the crowd:

"Even the captives of the mighty shall be taken away, the prey of the terrible shall be delivered, for I will contend with them that contend with thee, and I will save thy children. And all flesh shall know that I, the Lord, am thy Savior, and thy Redeemer, the Mighty One of Jacob."

"Hallelujah!" someone called out and it was echoed all through the audience.

A man came forward and asked to testify. Booth helped him up onto the platform. He spoke with a voice that shook and stumbled at the onset but gained power and confidence as he progressed through his testimony.

"I was thirteen," he said, "when I began as a water-boy in a pub. It was only a few years before I learned to love the flavor of strong drink. This stayed with me even to my marriage and my work as an engine driver. And…how ashamed I am to say it…I have beaten my poor wife! Yes, it was the drink, but could I not have prevented her suffering, her blackened eyes, her blooded lips, if I had resisted the demon drink?

"Once I had beaten her so badly she ran down to her mother's with her face all bleeding and blackened. I got drunk and grabbed up a long kitchen knife which I stuck up my sleeve and went to the mother's house with the intention of murdering them both. But they saw the knife and the police were called. I was taken to the station house but with no one coming to press charges I got off.

"At work I was to stoke the engine but I had been drinking for a week steady and came to work as drunk as ever I can remember.

Without looking to see if there was any water in the boiler I began stoking up the fire. T'was risking an explosion and afterwards I was discharged but still the fright of this did not discourage me from the drink. Half my wages had gone to buy liquor. Now I had to borrow even for the price of a loaf of bread, and the Mrs. was threatening to leave me.

"Nothing could sway me from the evil road I was on. I even lay sick for thirteen weeks but returned to being bad as ever. Then one Sunday I happened to walk past a gathering of Reverend Booth's. I found God there and relinquished my sinning. Now I thank God for what He has done for me. He has changed my heart. He has filled me full of the love of Christ. My greatest desire is to tell sinners what a dear Savior I have found."

Teo listened from the edge of the crowd. He had heard many testimonies like this one before. It amazed him that people could sink so low and yet still be saved and become responsible citizens once again. It was one of the reasons he had stayed with the Booths for so long—witnessing the instance of revelation that turned people around. They credited God or Jesus or Reverend Booth, but it always came from within; a self-awareness that transformed and which inspired others. It had inspired Teo.

There was another reason Teo had stayed with the Booths. He had written letters to Mam'selle but had never received an answer. He was sure he had the address right and Reverend Booth had helped him with the stamps and had offered to post the letters. But no answer. He had no means to pay for passage back to France and he certainly couldn't ask the Booths for money. So he waited and became involved in converting sinners. Eventually he stopped writing.

Singing at these meetings usually consisted of a single verse of a well known song. This rang out:

> *Shall we meet beyond the river,*
> *Where the surges cease to roll?*

Again someone approached asking to testify. Reverend Booth helped a young woman up onto the platform. She began by saying that she had a heavy load of sin upon her shoulders. "Oh, please won't you point me toward Jesus?"

Teo noticed Kate Booth standing a few yards away from the edge of the crowd. She slowly walked toward the gathering. Kate and Teo had become close during the eight years Teo had been with the Booths. Of all the Booth children, she was the only one who did not seem to resent his presence in the family. The boys sometimes treated him cruelly and at best, they were cold and indifferent. Kate harbored a young girl's crush when it came to Teo…an admiration Teo welcomed, but being shy, never outwardly returned. He thought of the two of them as best friends. He moved toward her now.

The woman on the platform was telling her tale of a sinful life; how she was devious and lied to her husband about money she had taken for her own purposes. It was an emotional testimony. As Teo neared Kate he noticed that she stood stiff, her fists clinched, and that tears rolled down her cheeks. He touched her arm and she jumped, startled by his sudden appearance.

"Kate, what can be the matter?" he asked.

"Oh, Teo…it should be me up there confessing my sins."

"What? Impossible. You are a good person, Kate. You have no sin in you."

Kate looked at the boy, tears still streaking down her cheeks. She sobbed as she spoke: "Oh, Teo…don't you remember the letters you wrote to your Mam'selle?"

"Of course. The Reverend mailed them for me. But she never…"

"Teo, Father gave those letters to me to take to the post office. I knew what it meant…that you would be leaving, going home to your own family. I…"

"Kate!"

"I burned them. They were never sent. And that isn't the worst of it. I took down all the posters."

"Posters?"

"Reward for information leading to a young Black boy who had disappeared. One hundred pounds. They were all over the East End. It took me all day to tear them down."

"But Kate…why…why did you do that?"

"Because I love you, Teo. I don't want you to ever leave me."

Sudden revelation of salvation entered the hearts of many of the congregation of the New Christian Mission of the East End during the open-air services. Now Teo was about to be reborn—for the second or third time in his young life—the revelation struck him with a force that made him physically and mentally stagger. I am here falsely, he thought to himself. I am play-acting as God's servant and messenger. I have forgotten my true identity, my true heritage and the joy of life with my Mam'selle. I must return to Paris…but how?

The collection box sat next to the platform. Although the funds that found their way into it were sparse, Teo thought there might be just enough for the ferry across the channel. So at the end of the service he offered to carry the box as the Booths got ready to return to their residence in the West End of London. When the carriage that William and Catherine and their three children had hired to take them home arrived, there was no sign of Teo or of the collection box.

Byron Grush

17

Storm Clouds Gather

The Café de la Nouvelle-Athènes, June, 1870

The artists and writers of the Batignolles Group had moved their feast from the overcrowded Café Guerbois to the Café de la Nouvelle-Athènes, at 9 place Pigalle. Here, in the years to come, many sketches of the people and the atmosphere of the café would be translated into paintings, major works by Manet, Degas, and others who would follow. Now Émile Zola held court, taking over the role of officiator from the novelist, Louis Edmond Duranty, who had just been challenged to a duel by Manet.

Duranty, an avid supporter of Gustave Courbet and a good friend of Edgar Degas, was a promoter of Realism and had insulted Manet by writing a miniscule and therefore subtly derogatory commentary for two of his paintings in an exhibition. The duel was fought with swords in the forest of Saint-Germain with Zola acting as Manet's second and Paul Alexis acting as Durant's. Manet wounded Durant above the right breast and so the duel was stopped by the seconds, honor having been satisfied. Even among friends, tensions were rising.

"Dickens is dead," announced Zola to the group as they sipped their absinthes. "He has left an unfinished novel."

"This would never happen with you, Émile," commented Degas.

"You are too stubborn to die in the middle of one of your experiments."

"I am too much of a realist. I collect the observations of my characters and spin them into the plot. They lead where they will, and I cannot stop them before they arrive at their logical conclusions."

"And Dickens?"

"A sentimental humanist. The working classes were his fodder. His output was endless…it was inevitable he would die in the middle of something. Incidentally, it was a murder mystery. Now no one will be able to learn the solution. An elegant exit!"

The conversation quickly turned to politics. Back in January, Prince Pierre Napoléon Bonaparte had killed a popular French journalist, Victor Noir. Bonaparte was a nephew of Napoleon I and the son of Prince Lucien Bonaparte of Corsica. During a dispute between rival newspapers in Corsica, the Emperor, Louis Napoleon became the target of criticism by one of the papers, *La Revanche*. Incensed, Pierre Bonaparte wrote a letter to the editor of the other paper, the loyalist *L'Avenir*, calling *La Revanche* a bunch of cowards and traitors. Back in Paris, outraged by the exchange and siding with *La Revanche*, Grousset, the French newspaper editor of *La Marseillaise*, entered the battle of wits and demanded satisfaction.

Grousset sent his seconds, Victor Noir and Ulrich de Fonvielle to fix the terms of a duel with Bonaparte but instead of contacting Bonaparte's seconds as was the custom, they went directly to him carrying revolvers in their pockets. There was an argument and Prince Bonaparte slapped Noir in the face, then shot him. Public sentiment was aroused with Noir taking on the aspects of a martyr for many. Legend would have it that a statue of Noir became a fetish for infertile women who rubbed against it, seeking a sexual spell to aid them toward pregnancy.

Then, especially in Paris, the International Workers Alliance that was spreading its influence throughout Europe, appealed strongly to many French workers. The Emperor saw this as a threat. There had been a national plebiscite in May in which the Empire received a substantial vote of confidence but on the eve of the plebiscite, Louis Napoleon rounded up and arrested members of the Paris Federation of the IWA on grounds of conspiracy. Persecution of members of the International spread throughout France, causing further unrest.

At this particular meeting of the Batignolles Group at the Café de la Nouvelle-Athènes, Jeffrey Flaherty and Émilie-Claire Lebeau-Richelieu were not present. Émilie-Claire was involved with a ball at the Tuileries and Jeffrey was in his studio painting. Thus the discussion moved from politics to gossip—gossip relating to the former lovers. For such a worldly woman, it was pointed out by Jean Frédéric Bazille, Émilie-Claire was supremely naïve. She was unaware of her husband's infidelity even while being saddled with guilt about her own. Indeed, Jean-Léon Richelieu had a mistress and this was well known to everyone but Émilie-Claire. What was more ironic, the group agreed, was that Jean-Léon Richelieu's mistress was also being unfaithful to him! No one knew much about the mistress' lover, only that he was some kind of foreign diplomat. In fact, he was the Prussian military attaché at the Paris embassy, a spy named Alfred von Waldersee.

Clothilde Mailys Leon was remarkable for her intensely blue eyes and auburn hair (which she drew up into a bun). But beauty was her only asset. Trying to support her indigent mother and an infant son born out of wedlock was a nearly impossible task. She had earned less than three francs a day in a variety of jobs from factory work to garment making to rolling cigars. Returning home from work she would sew dresses for the fine china-headed dolls sold to the wealthy patrons of Madam Babineaux's doll factory—piece work. It was a hard life but she was not ready yet for the street where other young women practiced that ages-old profession that marked the end of struggle, the end of hope.

On her one day off she went to the zoo, the Ménagerie du Jardin des Plantes. There she could escape the drudgery and despair of her life. She would stroll through the botanical gardens of rare plants and stop at the cages of the small mammals to watch the antics of the spider monkeys or the slow, deliberate slinking of the Chinese leopards. There was a bear pit and an enclosure for two large elephants named Castor and Pollux. (We will hear more about these two later.) It was here, while watching the two pachyderms that she caught the eye of Alfred Ludwig Heinrich Karl Graf von Waldersee.

Major von Waldersee had been an artillery officer in the Prussian army. His outstanding performance of his duties and his particular knack for intelligence gathering had won him the position of attaché to the Prussian embassy in Paris. He would not have thought of himself as a spy but merely as an astute observer of his soon-to-be enemy's defenses and strengths. He had a small clandestine staff of plain clothes officers whose function it was to do the spying for him.

The girl with the blue eyes fascinated him. He was too dedicated to his professional life to risk a herzensangelegenheit, or in this case, an affaire du coeur, but...why not mix business with pleasure? And Clothilde found herself attracted to the Prussian officer who took up a conversation with her that day at the zoo. Before long, Clothilde was seeing von Waldersee regularly. She had succumbed to his advances sooner than she had expected and now, totally enamored, she was willing to do almost anything for him. After all, he was very generous; generous enough that she had quit her job and had stopped sewing doll dresses at night. Nighttime was for von Waldersee.

"You can be very seductive," he said to her one day. "You attract other men...I have noticed this. What would you say if I asked you to meet with another man for his pleasure? Not to forsake me, but to help me learn things that are important to my country? You would not be acting against your own country's interests...rather you would be helping to cement positive relationships between Prussia and France."

Von Waldersee explained what he had in mind. It didn't seem so awfully terrible to her; not as if he was selling her charms in Pigalle to the highest bidder. Certainly, helping her own country by aiding his...well, this concept somewhat eluded her...it brought the whole thing to another level (beyond the obvious one of sex for favors). A few days later, one of von Waldersee's undercover operatives arranged for her to meet her target: Jean-Léon Richelieu, the Emperor's trusted advisor. The rest would be up to her.

July, 1870: a Prelude to War

In an agreement with Napoleon III, Isabella II of Spain abdicated her throne in favor of her son. However, Baron von Bismarck, seeing an opportunity to sway the balance of power in Europe, manipulated Prince Leopold of Hohenzollen-Sigmaringen into proposing himself for the Spanish throne. A German on the Spanish throne! Angered, Louis Napoleon demanded that Kaiser Wilhelm I condemn the candidacy. Although miffed at the demand and expressing his objections publically, the King of Prussia secretly forced Hohenzollen to withdraw his candidacy. Not entirely satisfied, Napoleon III sent the Kaiser a missive asking for assurance that no Hohenzollen would ever aspire to such a position of power in the future and that the Kaiser would never support such a move.

The entire incident might have ended right there; however, Bismack was furious that his plans had been derailed and so he embarked upon a plot to anger and provoke both leaders—his ultimate aim was war between Prussia and France which would embroil the independent states of Germany, thus progressing toward his vision of a unified Germany. Ironically, the French Empress Eugénie also saw the positive side of such a war. "If there is no war," she said, "my son will never be emperor." Being of Spanish descent, the Empress would influence her husband greatly in the matter of the Spanish Crown.

Bismarck then published a belligerent dispatch about Napoleon III without the Kaiser's knowledge or agreement. The dispatch itself, which came to be called Dépêche d'Em, or the Ems Dispatch, was a report describing the meeting of the French ambassador to Prussia, Count Vincent Benedetti, with Wilhelm I in Ems, in which the ambassador had presented the Kaiser with the French demands (written by the duc de Gramont) never again to interfere with the Spanish government. Wilhelm I had of course rejected the demands and had told Benedetti he would no longer be received at court. He instructed that a report of the matter be sent to Bismarck for his own understanding of the situation. Bismarck carefully edited the dispatch, sent it to a newspaper, turning it into an insult to France.

Interlude at La Café Riche

On the corner of Rue le Peletier and the Boulevard des Italiens stood another Parisian institution of culinary excellence and discreet decadence: La Café Riche. The restaurant was famous for its exquisite cuisine, its extravagant décor. Décor despairingly described by the author, Goncourt as "ugly scoundrel…macabre frescoes of Forain (the decorator)…colored caryatids Raffaelli…mishmash of oriental architecture…." In its private rooms veiled ladies met bankers and politicians and government officials—but never their husbands.

After a sumptuous meal that began with oysters and ended with crème brulée romarin, Jean-Léon Richelieu relaxed on an overstuffed divan upholstered in purple velvet and lit a cigar. His dinner guest for the evening, Clothilde Mailys Leon, stood before him for a few moments in a pose resembling one of the caryatids. The private room on the second floor of the café was intimate enough for an orgy, although a view of the street could be had from the bank of bay windows now curtained in pale pink velour. Candlelight still flickered from the table. The gas lights were turned low. She sat, or rather, reclined next to him, positioning as much of her body as possible in contact with his.

"Why so glum?" she asked. "Affairs of state getting you down?"

"Can we talk about something else? Would you like to go shopping for a new gown?"

Richelieu clearly wanted to steer the topic away from current affairs. But Clothilde knew how to manipulate him. She ran her fingers across his neck dragging her nails lightly against the skin. "Oh, won't you tell me what worries you?" she responded.

"It's all because of this Hohenzollern thing. And Bismarck. That German has stirred up a hornets' nest where a little diplomacy might have settled the situation for everyone's benefit."

"I know you told me about the Spanish problem and Hohen…Hohenzollern withdrawing. You said it was a victory for the Emperor. What has happened?" she asked.

"You weren't at the Château de Saint-Cloud to hear the dialogue between the Council of Ministers. I was and unfortunately, my influence over the Emperor has been eclipsed by the outraged majority of that body. The Chamber of Deputes is also demanding a response to Prussia's meddling."

"Surely there can be peace with Prussia."

"Thiers thinks so. And so did Ollivier, who you know has been in opposition to Louis Napoleon for decades. And Léon Gambetta opposes war very strongly. But these men are being swayed. You know I tell you these things believing that you will not speak of them to anyone. They are strategic issues in terms of what may follow."

"You don't mean there may be war, do you? Surely the Council will not vote for a war with Prussia."

"They already have, mon cheri. 425 votes for and only 10 against. There will be an announcement in a few days. The Emperor will assemble his troops to attack at…well, I cannot tell you that. You might talk in your sleep!"

"If I did so, I would only be sleeping with you, mon amour. I'll breathe a word of it to no one."

Home Again, Home Again

"This isn't the same France that you left, Teo," Émilie-Claire was telling the boy as they sat at a sidewalk table at a small café on the Boulevard Haussmann. It was hot even for July. The wrens and sparrows that patrolled the sidewalk for crumbs beneath the tables stayed carefully in the shade. A feral cat was curled up along side of a water spout that still dripped from last night's rain. Tables not conveniently tucked under the café's awning were unoccupied.

Teo's journey from London to Paris hadn't been an easy one. He had to walk most of the way to Folkestone to catch the ferry, afraid to spend any of his money on food or transportation. The contents of the offering box that he had stolen were minimal: two shillings and a thruppence. He stole an egg from a farmer's hen house and pulled carrots from his garden, barely getting away when the farmer saw him lurking suspiciously and yelled abusive epithets at him.

He strayed off the road to gaze at Leed's Castle, a medieval dwelling rebuilt in Tudor style by its current owners. The original structure had been acquired by King Edward I. Centuries later it had been used by Richard II for one of his wives and then by King Henry VIII for Catherine of Aragon's home away from home. Teo was fascinated by the lake-like moat where swans circled lazily and the chirping of frogs could be heard. The reflection of the castle sitting on its island shimmered in the sparkling water. Again, however, he was chased away, this time by the grounds keeper. He decided he had had enough of England.

By the time he stepped off of the ferry at Calais, Teo was broke, hungry, and fatigued. He found an old shed in a back alley and slept there for most of the day and all of the night. In Calais he looked for any kind of work to earn a few francs and found a friendly butcher at a boucherie who hired him to carry goat and sheep carcasses into the shop from a delivery wagon. He had his few francs and a cured sausage to take with him when he thanked the butcher and started again down the road to Paris.

He learned to linger in the larger towns where he might find temporary employment. Odd jobs and the kindness shown him by the people he encountered on the road helped him make his slow but sure headway toward his goal: Paris. Paris in all her glamour and decadence, with her fountains and parks, her gas lights and broad avenues, her chestnut trees and her bustle of workmen and secretaries and ladies of the night—the Paris of his dreams! Now to find Mam'selle.

When Teo arrived at the townhouse at the juncture of Rue Joubert and Rue de la Victoire, he found to his dismay that Émilie-Claire no longer lived there. "She married some big shot in the Emperor's cabinet," he was told by the concierge. The Emperor? How was Teo going to walk into the Tuileries palace and ask for Mam'selle?

Teo went to the Jardin des Tuileries everyday in hopes of finding Émilie-Claire. Louis Napoleon had enlarged the garden surrounding his private residence. The grounds were open to the public. There were new pavilions, the Jeu de paume and the Orangerie, and Napoleon III had made a playground for the Prince Imperial along the Terrasse du bord-de-l'eau. Teo strolled the terrace along the edge of the blue-gray water of the Seine watching the ducks with their ducklings lined up behind, tails swishing; he watched children floating toy boats in the pond with their sails of blue, white, and red: the colors of France.

One day she appeared near the round pond in the Grand Carré, standing next to the statue of the *Nymphe* by Louis Auguste Lévêque. Two femmes: a naked woman of marble with a dog at her feet, up on a pedestal, surrounded by neatly trimmed and abundant nature—a human woman studying the other, herself neatly trimmed in silk and lace, perfumed and polished. The boy wondering, can this be the Mam'selle? She is too elegant, too royal, too removed from my memories of the worldly woman who reared me. But it must be she!

The reunion was not without tears; only the statue did not cry. Now they were sitting at a sidewalk table at a small café on the Boulevard Haussmann. Émilie-Claire was explaining to Teo that she would always support him, financially as well as emotionally and spiritually, but that it was time for his own independent transition into life (as if this had never happened to him before). For him to appear at court might elicit some dissonance in certain quarters and cause her husband, Jean-Léon Richelieu, problems politically. It was wrong, but it was l'état des lieux.

"I understand, Mam'selle," he said. "I can work and earn my own keep. But will I see you?"

"Always, mon amour. Always."

"I think…I may join the army. I enjoyed the camaraderie of the others in the Christian Army of Salvation I told you about…even though they betrayed me. I am not good for much else other than drudgery. The army…or maybe the navy."

"Oh, Teo, I have to dissuade you from the military. There will be a war and soon. I can't lose you again."

"You will never lose me. Never again."

And so Teodore Presume, the boy from Haiti, who had lived in America, France, and England, who had been kidnapped three times in his short life, determined to fight for his adopted country. There would be a war, she had said. France will fight with Prussia over trivial insults, veiled ambitions, the pursuit of power and wealth, and the preservation of empire. And of course, France would be victorious, wouldn't she?

Byron Grush

18

City of Light, City of Darkness

On July 19, 1870, France officially declared war on Prussia. Statesman Olivier Émile Ollivier, an avid opponent of Napoleon III, had nevertheless and "with a light heart" obtained a war vote of 500,000 francs to fund the war "that had been forced" upon the French people. Léon Gambetta still opposed the war and refused to vote for its funding, yet remained patriotic and agreed that the war had indeed been forced upon France by the Prussians. The truth, as usual, was more complicated.

Was France ready for war? She did have an advanced weapon, the Reffye Mitrailleuse, a sort of machine gun like the American Gatling with 25 barrels that could fire up to 125 rounds of 13mm bullets per minute. She had 190 of these but they weighed 1,750 pounds each and it required a team of six horses to move them. Additionally, with true French logic (read absurdity), the army insisted on keeping the weapon a secret, hence few French soldiers knew about it and even fewer could operate the gun.

French Chief of Staff, Maréchal Edmond Leboeuf felt they were ready "down to the last gaiter button." Field Marshals Bazaine, MacMahon and Canrobert were given command of various sectors. Napoleon III himself led the charge. On the Prussian side, Kaiser William I took the helm with Crown Prince Frederick commanding the Prussian 3rd Army and with Field-Marshal Helmuth von Moltke in charge of the General Staff. The Prussian army had the first general staff in the history of warfare, integrating it brilliantly within its military tactics.

The French used a modern rifle, the Chassepot, which could fire 8 to 15 rounds per minute. The Prussian's older style Dreyse needle rifles were limited to 4 or 5 rounds per minute, yet Prussian soldiers were better trained and more efficiently commanded than the French and this became evident almost immediately in the first battles. The Prussians also had a big gun: the breech-loading Krupp Cannon—the same model that had been featured at the Paris Exposition Universelle d'Art et d'Industrie in 1867. The Krupp shot 1,000 pound shells.

Prussia, Napoleon Bonaparte once said, had been hatched from a cannonball. She was ready and well practiced. Her troops were conscripted whereas France's were all voluntary. The Prussian military was decentralized; her commanders had much leeway in the field. The French army was disorganized and under equipped, short of medical supplies and had few strategic maps of the enemy's territory. French soldiers, in fact, were given money to purchase maps from local bookstores on their own. It was going to be a short war.

On July 28 Napoleon III took command at Metz where his Army of the Rhine was centralized. The French had 240,000 men at the ready. The Prussians brought up over 500,000. As the enemies assembled along the border, the French artists and writers assembled, some for the last time, in the cafés.

Only one month earlier, Claude Monet had married Camille Doncieux, his former model. Camille had become pregnant by Monet and had given birth to their son, Jean, in 1867. She had been *La Femme á la Robe Verte* and *La Femme dans le Jardin* and had posed for his *Sur les Rives de la Seine*. Now Monet announced that he and his family were moving to London, perhaps for the duration of the war. He would do so in September and would be greatly influenced by the paintings he would see there by Joseph Turner and John Constable. He would later visit Amsterdam and Zaandam in the Netherlands and not return to France until late 1871.

Édouard Manet also expressed his concern for the safety of his family, realizing that Paris could well come under attack. "I'm sending them to Oloron-SainteMarie in the Pyrenees," he told the others. "I will remain in Paris for the time being." He would close his studio on Rue Guyot and store his paintings at the home of the art collector, Théodore Duret. He would accept a commission as a lieutenant in the Garde National in November and serve on the General Staff under the command of a colonel, another painter, Ernest Meissonier. In February of 1871 he would rejoin his family in Oloron-SainteMarie and journey to Bordeaux and Arcachon, painting. He and his family would return to Paris in May.

Edgar Degas would also join the Garde National. It would be found, as he began training with rifles on the shooting range, that his eyesight was not normal. For a visual artist, of course, this was of grave concern. He would be haunted by the prospect of blindness for the rest of his life. It would not stop him, however, from producing some of the world's most stunning works of sculpture and painting.

Sisley was not interested in joining anything remotely related to the military and neither was Renoir. The two men took an antiwar position during discussions among the Batignolles Group. Zola, also antiwar, quoted Victor Hugo as often as possible when the subject of war arose. Frédéric Bazille, however, sided with Manet and Degas and could not help but voice his enthusiasm for the qualities of honor, duty, and bravery that military service offered.

"It's the Emperor's war," said Zola, "and so let him go fight the Kaiser one to one…if you want honor, duty, and bravery."

"I'll do more than just join the Garde to defend the city. I have a mind to volunteer for the infantry. The fiercest infantry regiment I can find," responded Bazille.

"That would be the Zouaves…if they'll have you. Berbers, Algerians, Arabs, Black North Africans…they're fierce enough for anyone's army! But Frédéric, give it some thought, won't you?"

"I already have. I'm leaving at the first of next month."

"We'll leave an empty chair here at the table for your return. God's speed," said Zola, shaking his head in frustration. Later, to the group once Bazille had departed, Zola said, "He is determined to faire le zouave (act the goat)…pun intended!"

And Jeffrey Flaherty? He wasn't French and hadn't returned to America to fight in its Civil War. Why would he be willing to risk his life for the Emperor's pride? Why would he put up his brushes and store his paintings like Manet did and run off to shoot bullets at the Prussians? Maybe because Émilie-Claire Lebeau-Richelieu, his former lover whom he still worshipped albeit from afar, had asked him to "take Teo under his wing and protect him." Maybe because he had failed to rescue his beloved Sue Ellen from the raging flood waters of the Tennessee River; this was a chance to redeem himself. Teo was off to join the army at the recruiting depot at Versailles. There was nothing for it but to follow young Teo and become a soldat de fortune. Perhaps he could keep both of them out of harm's way.

Versailles the town, not Versailles the château. Since the French Revolution, the Château de Vesailles was no longer the home of Kings nor was it anymore the capital of the Kingdom. The town, constructed by Louis XIV for support of his palace, now bulged with soldiers and recruits who were quartered in the town's garrisons and the château's annexes, waiting for orders. In the old quarter, Les Carrés Saint-Louis, near the cathedral, were rows of low houses used as market stalls during the rein of Louis XV. Now they were crammed with the sweaty bodies of farm boys from all over the Île-de-France region, and with eager francs-tireurs—"free-shooters" from shooting clubs with patriotic aspirations, and with grizzled veterans of the wars in Algeria or Italy, and with scared youths having second thoughts as the inevitable loomed and reality set in.

There was much drinking and whoring and little training since weapons to equip the troops had been sent on ahead by train to Metz. In a very short time Marshall Edmond Le Bœuf would order a mobilization of all French troops from garrison towns like Versaille and many other sites scattered across France. Until then it was Liberté, Egalité, Fraternité, and vin, femmes, et chanson. Into the pandemonium came Teo Presume and Jeffrey Flaherty, the former agog and animated, the latter apprehensive and ill at ease.

They hadn't had much time to see the town, much less the château. The home and playground of kings and the seat of the Revolution, Versailles was seeped in history and decadence and revolt. On the Rue du jeu de Paume was the old indoor tennis court where representatives of the Third Estate, the under-privileged classes, had gathered to take the Serment du Jeu de Paume, the so-called Tennis Court Oath, by which they swore to continue meeting until France was supplied with a constitution—seeds of the Revolution. The palace itself was the scene of a protest of bread prices (let them eat cake) in 1789 when a crowd of women and members of the Garde National invaded it and forced the royal family to move into Paris, where they lost their heads.

Jeffrey dearly wanted to explore the Galerie des Batailles, the Museum of the History of France, established by Louis-Philippe I for the royal collection of paintings and sculptures of the battles (and royal personages) of French history. There were displayed works by Eugène Delacroix, François Bouchot, Émile Jean-Horace Vernet, François-Édouard Picot, Charles-François Lebœuf, and other artists, perhaps a bit academic, but historically interesting to the young painter. The battles, the generals, the fighting men were glorified—entered into legend for the gratification of monarchs and the inspiration of today's soldiers—the future cannon fodder for future artists to depict. There was nothing more dramatic than an explosion rendered in cadmium red and chrome yellow, nor anything more magnificent than a uniform set down in cerulean blue and cobalt green. The colors of war.

A last minute sight-seeing for Jeffrey and Teo brought them to the Avenue de Berry in front of the city hall, the Hôtel de Ville. There was clock high up on the building's steeple which indicated that it was high noon, although it was early morning. A lone turkey vulture circled endlessly above them. There on the broad steps sat a familiar figure, although they hardly recognized him in his exotic dress: bright red baggy trousers tucked into brown leather boots which laced up the side, a short blue jacket trimmed in red and open in the front, a sash of yellow, and a tasseled cap of red felt, oriental in style. Frédéric Bazille looked as though he had just stepped out of one of the historical paintings in the Galerie des Batailles. Flaherty immediately sensed the humor and irony in Bazille's appearance.

"Ho, Frédéric," called Flaherty, "are you costumed to pose for one of Édouard's paintings? *The Spanish Troubador* or something like that?"

"Not Spanish, cerveaux d'âne! This is the uniform of the 3rd Zouave Regiment. I've joined the fiercest fighting group that France has ever put together. And don't let any of my comrades hear you disparage the uniform…you'll be carrying your head under your arm!"

"I apologize. You look very dapper."

"I didn't expect to see you here, Jeffrey. Your outlook on war would seem to suggest you are un poisson hors de l'eau. Surely you haven't enlisted."

"I am very much a fish in the water. Probaby hot water. But here I am, ready to do my duty for my adopted county."

"Just remember," added Bazille, "qui sème le vent récolte la tempête…who sows the wind, reaps the whirlwind."

Back in Paris, la vie went on as usual with little awareness or concern for the impending calamities that were certain to derail the population's well-oiled routines. Women shopped at Les Halles, that vast marketplace covered over with iron and glass. They arrived early, before the sun dropped shards of golden light to shimmer on the Seine. They scampered across the Pont Neuf with baskets hanging over their arms and confronted the fish vender demanding, "Fresh today? Or fresh yesterday?" Eels were suspect but the bass and mullet looked adequate. They scooped up armfuls of violets that lay in heaps on the pavement, yesterday's unsalables. A washing would revive the blooms and they could be sold on the street by hawkers.

The poultry stall featured geese hanging by their feet, blood still dripping from their slit throats. Slaughtered pigs were arranged at another stall, dismembered heads grimacing at the passing shoppers who might afford a foot or a haunch. Mixed meats were offered at a discount—bits and pieces of trim, fat and lard for cooking, and cans of fresh blood for sauces. Haggling was the order of the day; no set price ever achieved the turnover of a supposed bargain.

Fruits, vegetables, cheeses, and meats at Les Halles, then to the boulangerie for baguettes. Shopping completed as the early morning light snaked through the narrow streets and feral cats and pigeons stalked the alleyways for errant mice or other tidbits. Taverns had been open for hours; iron workers liked a nip before reporting to the factories—it eased headaches from last night's drunken revelry. Chiffoniers had begun their picking through the heaps of trash unceremoniously dumped in the streets. A discarded bone could be turned into a decorative button.

In the early afternoon children would be frolicking along the curved pathways of the Parc Monceau, playing hide and seek around the Rotunda or the miniature Egyptian pyramid, the Folly of the Duke of Chartres. Young lovers would stroll though the Parc des Buttes Chaumont, climbing the steep path up the craggy hill on the Île de la Belvédère to the Temple de la Sibylle where they would declare their love to one another. Or they would linger in the Jardin des Champs-Élysées perhaps sampling from a lunch basket the new champagne just created by Madame Pomeroy called "Brut."

Jeanne-Alice Gardinier had just turned 18. She proudly told her father, François Arnaud Gardinier, and her stepmother, Phoebe Stapleton Gardinier, that she planned to join the Croix-rouge Française, the French Red Cross. Then it was called the Société de Secours aux Blessés Militaires and had only been in existence since 1866 following an agreement reached that year at the International Geneva Convention to which both France and Germany adhered. All nations now recognized the flag and emblem of a red cross against a white field. There was a military hospital at Versailles where Jeanne-Alice hoped to learn nursing.

"And you should consider helping as well," she told Phoebe.

"Oh, Jeanne-Alice, I don't know. I'm a bit inept at certain things. And blood…it terrifies me."

"I am very proud of you for doing this," said her father. "But please, stay in Versailles or Paris. Don't go to the front!"

"But I might be of more use there. And I'll be careful."

In Paris, Jean-Léon Richelieu was getting ready to bid his wife a hasty farewell as his presence was required by the Emperor at the front. Émilie-Claire was never one to be weepy, nor did she figure that Jean-Léon would be in any particular danger. Surely Louis Napoleon would keep well to the back of the lines. Jean-Léon could not resist a bit of ranting about the incompetence of the Emperor however, and this did much to erode Émilie-Claire's confidence in the outcome of the battles to follow.

"War Minister Le Bœuf had planned to split the armies into three parts with troops at Metz, Strasbourg, and Chalons," Jean-Léon was saying. "We are spread all over the country with a battalion here, a battalion there, but little by little Le Bœuf was organizing the deployments. Then, the Emperor, who is bête à manger du foin, decided to amass the entire army at Metz. He thinks Austria will join us against Prussia. But if Austria enters the fray, Russia will side with the enemy. Besides that, the troops are being mobilized too quickly. There aren't enough supplies or ammunition at Metz and the train station there is too small to handle all the incoming men. Merde…ça ne tient pas debout…ça me prend la tête…ça me soûle!"

"Have courage, mon amour," said Émilie-Claire. "You will bring a voice of reason to the shambles."

"One only hopes."

Chief of Staff of the German Army, Helmuth von Molte, was no doubt laughing at the inept French who were mobilizing weeks before they were really ready. His own efforts were not without problems: the Prussian forces assembled more slowly than the French. But now the Southern German States were coming to Prussia's aid. Bismarck couldn't have been more delighted. The original plan Molte envisioned was to encircle Napoleon III's army after it invaded Germany. Instead, they amassed along the border where they presented a superior force against Louis Napoleon's Army of the Rhine.

By the time Jean-Léon reached Louis Napoleon's side, the Emperor had decided to launch a full scale attack before the German and Prussian troops could be fully mobilized. Jean-Léon saw that the Emperor was very ill, with an infected bladder and in constant pain. Jean-Léon advised doing more reconnaissance but by now only one Prussian division had been sighted; this one was guarding the border town of Saarbrücken. Napoleon III sent his Army of the Rhine across the Saar River to seize Saarbrücken on July 31. The war had begun.

19

Le Premier Sang

August 2, the German Border

The Second Corps under General Frossard and the Third Corps under Marshall Bazaine crossed into German territory early that morning. The 40th Regiment of the Prussian 16th Infantry was occupying the town of Saarbrüken. Marshall Bazaine led his troops across the Alte Brücke, an old stone bridge that dated to 1546. General Frossard set up his artillery on the opposite bank of the Saar.

The medieval town perhaps took its name from a large rock called the Saarbrocken on the edge of the river upon which the Castle of Sarabrucca had been erected. The spellings were similar. Saarbrüken had been captured in 1793 by French forces and ceded to France, but after 1815 it was absorbed into the Prussian Rhine Province. The denizens of the village therefore had mixed affiliations, being French, German, and even Swiss. They took no part in the battle and waited indifferently for the outcome.

The Prince Imperial, Napoléon Eugène Louis Jean Joseph Bonaparte, now 14 years of age, had accompanied his father, the Emperor, to the front. He had been tutored under the supervision of General Frossard and so he went to the commander asking that he be allowed to operate one of the big guns. Unable to refuse the boy, the General instructed him in the aiming and firing of one of the light cannons that was pointed at the Prussian garrison. His marksmanship proved to be excellent but Napoleon III, unhappy that his son was coming under fire from the retaliating Prussian troops, ordered the boy to be sent to Belgium. By September he would be in England.

The French used their Chassepot rifles to great advance, their range and firing rate far superior to that of the German Dreyse rifles that opposed them. The Prussians fought well, however, and suffered only 83 casualties to the French army's 86. At the end of the day the Prussian regiment had been driven from Saarbrüken and it seemed that the successful operation hailed eventual victories for the French in their invasion and that it was only a matter of time before they would be marching into Berlin.

August 4, Wissembourg

A French border town just a heartbeat or two from German territory, Wissembourg hosted a small garrison of French soldiers. The division stationed there was under the command of General Charles Abel Douay, a career officer and president of the military academy at Saint-Cyr. Recent additions to the fighting men at Wissembourg included a young Black man, Teodore Presume and his companion and would-be guardian, Jeffrey Flaherty.

Teo had recently made the acquaintance of a young Frenchman from Orléans named Émeric Linville. Linville was twenty, thin but muscular, and had joined the army under General Auguste-Alexandre Ducrot in Strasbourg after a two-day drunk that had left his better judgment impaired. Ducrot's troops had been sent to fortify Wissembourg and General Douay, but then all but one division had been withdrawn. There wasn't much to do in Wissembourg so Linville was teaching Teo how to hold his liquor, a feat he hadn't as yet mastered.

Except for Napoleon III's Army of the Rhine which was occupying Saarbrüken, the French army was strung out in too thin a line along the French-German border. Saarbrüken had proven to be a disappointing prize, having little access to the interior because of mountains and a semi-functional train line. Besides this, the Prussian and Bavarian forces were massing in the southeast and the north. The Prussian Second Army commanded by Crown Prince Friedrich Charles was 30 miles from Saarbrüken and advancing rapidly.

General Le Bœuf and Napoleon III decided to retreat to defensive positions. General Frossard, withdrew his elements of Army of the Rhine in Saarbrücken and sent them back to Spicheren and Forbach. Marshall MacMahon, although closest to Wissembourg, had been given no intelligence of the enemy's movements and was spread out over many miles due to a lack of supplies. Ducrot told Douay that he didn't believe there was any danger of an offensive by Prussia, and that the report of additional Bavarian forces was essentially a bluff. Hence the garrison at Wissembourg was tragically under supported.

Teo and Émeric Linville were sitting behind a caisson, finishing a bottle of brandy when Jeffrey Flaherty found them. A tongue-lashing followed. "Where is your patriotism that you would drink and let the enemy sneak up on you and your fellows?" he chided.

"Who would ever attack this miserable shithole in the middle of nowhere," was Linville's answer.

The miserable shithole had, in fact, been attacked once before in 1793 when the French Army of the Rhine had been beaten back by the Austrian-Allied Army during the War of First Coalition. The fortifications of the town had included the Lignes de Wissembourg, or Lines of Wissembourg, a series of earth works that extended for nine miles and afforded excellent cover; these were now gone, neglected and washed away—no help there. Still, it was quiet now; birdsong and the rustling of autumn leaves were the only sonic challenge to ears tempered by the merriment of the troops, their drinking songs, their chitchat and palaver. Perhaps if one had listened more closely one might have heard the footfalls of a deadly force approaching. But that would have spoiled the surprise.

About midmorning the alarm was raised. Soldiers scrambled for their rifles and manned the light artillery emplacements. The few cavalry soldiers that were present saddled their mounts. Flaherty grabbed Teo's arm and dragged him deeper into the fort where several multi-barreled Mitrailleuse guns were arrayed. The rapid fire guns, Flaherty reasoned, would be a good defense against the onslaught that was imminent. General Douay was issuing orders to load the guns so Flaherty and Teo set to the task. A plate with slots for 37 cartridges had to be loaded then slipped into position in front of the firing pins. A hand crank completed the operation and all the cartridges could be fired simultaneously.

A low stone wall surrounded the battlements. Teo's friend, Émeric Linville, hopped over it and crouched down, balancing his Chassepot rifle on the wall. "They're coming," he cried.

General Helmuth von Moltke had three massive forces along the border. General Karl von Steinmetz commanded the Prussian First Army near Saarlouis. Prince Friedrich Karl deployed his Prussian Second Army opposite Forbach-Spicheren, and the Prussian Third Army, commanded by Crown Prince Friedrich Wilhelm, moved on Wissembourg. The townspeople of Wissembourg were now being bombarded by cannon fire from the Prussian's Krupp guns. Although Marshall MacMahon, not far from the French garrison, could hear the rumble of the big guns he failed to come to the aid of the 2nd Division.

The Bavarians who Ducrot had thought were a bluff entered the town from one side; two Prussians infantry corps came from the other. The attack was ill coordinated and more of a show of brut force than of tactics, yet the French were outnumbered and not concentrated in one fortified area. Many Prussian causalities occurred as the French rifles with their greater range picked them off. But once they had infiltrated the town, it was the force with the superior numbers that held sway.

Horrified, Teo watched as Linville, firing from behind the low stone wall, suddenly stood up and let loose with a barrage of rifle fire which was returned in kind by the advancing enemy, and, with his body jerking and pitching, fell spurting blood from a multitude of bullet holes. Teo rushed to his side but there was nothing he could do.

"Keep down!" yelled Flaherty as he aimed the Mitrailleuse over the youth's head at the charging Prussian company and cranked off 37 shells into their midst. Most fell but three now jumped the wall and engaged the French company in hand-to-hand combat. Teo swung his saber wildly and only avoided a Prussian soldier's bayonet by inches as the man rushed at him. Flaherty's hand gun dispatched the enemy soldier as he turned for a second attempt.

But more came. Douay gave the order to retreat. Standing next to a caisson of Mitrailleuse ammunition, he waved his unit away. Suddenly an errant shell landed next to the caisson and the pile of munitions exploded sending Douay, now riddled with shrapnel, flying. He died instantly.

As the battle grew more bloody, the townspeople surrendered. Many of the French soldiers were captured or lay wounded. Those who had not been captured, among them, Jeffrey Flaherty and Teo

Presume, now escaped through the Prussian lines. The German cavalry, still disorganized, failed to pursue them. At least a thousand French lay dead or severely wounded. Another thousand were prisoners of war. The enemy had also captured the French artillery and ammunition. It was a decisive victory for Prussia. And it was just the beginning.

August 5-6, Spicheren

Geoffroy Pierre Gardinier, foster son of Max and Felicie Meyerbeer, had wished to be a part of the Uhlan, the Prussian cavalry. However, his superior marksmanship with the German needle gun had placed him in a position in the infantry, usually on the front line. So far he had been lucky. All around him soldiers had dropped, hit by bullets from the French Chassepots. It was a walking nightmare, one that forced false courage on the youth, rising from a sickened gut much as phlegm rose up through the throat into the mouth. Yet during the hand-to-hand combat he had just experienced at Wissembourg, he had felt in awe of the Uhlans, riding their chargers through the fray, their bright sashes streaming out behind them, their sabers flashing and dripping with blood.

He was now marching west from Saarbrücken toward the town of Spicheren, and the closest he got to the cavalry was avoiding the piles of horse manure that lined the road. To the east of the town ran the Saarbrübrucken ridge, heavily treed by the Stiftswald and the Giferts Forests. To the west lay the Forbach-Stiring Valley flanked by the Rotherberg spar. A seemingly adequate geography for the defense of the town. The Prussian forces approached cautiously.

General Frossard, commanding the French 2nd Corps, had abandoned the Spicheren Heights for a position between the town and neighboring Forbach. There were two French companies along the heights and on the Rotherberg spar, another division in Stiring in the Forbach Valley, and General Bataille held his division in reserve on the opposite side of the town. The French had 27,000 men and 90 big guns.

Prussian General Georg von Kameke and his 1st Army Advanced Guard, finding that the retreating French troops had failed to destroy the bridges leading into the Spicheren Plateau, realized that taking the high ground beyond the town would give him a great advantage and moved to do so. Prince Friedrich Karl of Prussia leading the 2nd Army also had spotted Frossard's armed forces along the distant plateau and, like Kameke, made the decision to attack in spite of a master plan put forth by General Molke which would have kept German forces beyond the Saar River until they were at full strength. Thus the rush to battle that characterized the operation at Wissembourg was repeated with neither the French nor the Prussians realizing the extent of each other's forces.

The French underestimated the size of the Prussian forces and treated each attack as a mere skirmish. Where they might have counter attacked for a sizable win, they continued in a defensive posture. The Prussians were taking heavy losses from the longer range French rifles, especially from the divisions on the hills. As the noonday sun reached its zenith, General Kameke began to understand that this was not just the rear guard of the retreating French army, but a very sizable threat. Consequently, he ordered General Bruno von François to take the 27th Brigade up the Rotherburg and destroy the French artillery battlements. Geoffroy Gardinier was part of the 27th Brigade.

Geoffroy stood at the ready as General François mounted his horse and waved his sword valiantly in the air as the bugler played the call for the charge. Geoffroy felt a rush of adrenalin as the excitement of the engagement reverberated among the men. While the Prussian artillery pelted the French with explosive shells, the cavalry began to climb the hill with the foot soldiers following. Unfortunately, although it looked as though there was a climbable path up the craggy hill, both men and horses found the passage nearly impossible to negotiate. Geoffroy lunged aside as a horse and rider tumbled down from above.

The French used their Mitrailleuse muli-fire guns as if they were artillery and positioned them to the rear instead of bringing them up front where they might have had a devastating effect against the enemy. It was up to the riflemen to repel the Prussians who, in spite of many casualties, were indeed scaling the steep cliffs and coming into range with their Dreyse needle guns. Many of the cavalry had abandoned their horses and clamored on foot along with Geoffroy and the infantry. Just as they reached the crest of the hill General François collapsed, bleeding from five bullet wounds. Geoffroy held the General's head up and tried to pour water between his lips as the man died.

Gunfire and the rattle of the Mitrailleuse. Brave men falling. Blood and bodies everywhere. Geoffroy held his Dreyse close to his chest and hurtled over a stone embankment that separated him and his comrades from the French battlements. Four of them rushed the artillery soldier manning the Mitrailleuse; he went down in an instant. Geoffroy and the others tugged and turned the gun around so that it now pointed at the French soldiers retreating down the other side of the hill. They cranked, fed the gun more shells, cranked again. More blood and bodies rolled into the valley below.

The Prussians, now in control of the Rotherburg, dragged four heavy cannons up the hill and began firing down at Spicheren. General Frossard had 58 cannons defending the town but the French muzzle-loaders were no match for the Prussian's breach-loading Krupps. Frossard was forced to pull his troops back toward Sarreguemines. In Forbach and Stiring the fighting went from house to house, even more brutal and retaliatory than the bloodbath in Wissembourg had been. By 9 o'clock that evening, the French had all but relinquished the entire Spicheren plateau to the Prussians.

French losses were 2,000 dead and another 2,000 wounded or captured. Prussian losses amounted to 4,400 dead or wounded. Meanwhile, 40 miles away in the Vosges Mountains, Crown Prince Federick had led the Prussian Third Army against Marshall MacMahon in what was the first major battle of the war and the third decisive victory for Prussia.

August 6, Wörth, Frœschwiller and Disaster

In the town of Frœschwiller near Wörth, only about ten miles distance from Wissembourg, the German 3rd Army, now reinforced to 140,000 strong, engaged Marshall MacMahon's much smaller force of 35,000. The French Chassepot rifles were keeping the Prussian cannon at bay and inflicting many casualties, but they were being slowly pushed back. Bavarian forces attacked and took the town of Frœschwiller, forcing a French retreat. In order to cover the retreat, General Michel's cavalry brigade was ordered to charge the enemy. The charge was not entirely successful and resulted in the death of horses and men which the French could not afford to loose.

At Morsbronn, 700 French cuirassiers were trapped and massacred. The cavalry now came under fire by the Prussian artillery. French reserves were rallied and temporarily drove the Prussians back, but soon the cost became too high, the troops were fatigued and discouraged and overwhelmed by the superior numbers they faced. MacMahon retreated to the west, heading for Metz. The Prussian cavalry had been held back from the battlefield and had no orders to pursue the fleeing French army. But Prussia was now in a position to invade and conquer France.

Prussia had put into play 75,000 infantry with Dreyse rifles and sabres, 6,000 cavalry, and 300 artillery guns. The French fought back with around 32,000 Chassepot rifles, a few thousand sabers and lances, and only about 100 artillery. German, Bavarian, and Prussian losses were 9,720 killed or wounded and 1,370 missing. About 8,000 French combatants were killed or wounded and some 12,000 were missing. Various French regiments lost up to 50 percent of their strength.

There were no ambulances, no mule liters to take away the wounded. Men were left where they fell, at the mercy of the enemy. All along the roads refugees dragged their weary bodies and sparse provisions past dying animals and dead riders. In the ditches where cadavers had been rolled the bottle flies and carrion birds were at work. First blood had been spilled. The first blood, but not the last.

20

Chestnuts in August

The lucky ones died instantly as musket shots took their heads apart like cracked chestnuts. Some lingered long enough to see shapes in the muddy ground as they pitched forward: a loved one's face, a favorite dog or horse or boat, the checkered stone floor of a cathedral. Others lay twisted and broken, the life flowing swiftly from a gash or a severed limb; they would not wait for rescue—it would never come. And some would be carried by others who limped and staggered until their bulk brought those merciful souls down as well. Then there were those who woke in hospital, or whatever served as hospital, and waited to be doctored but bled to death in the waiting. Then the half-dead, the battered and bloodied and maimed who lay screaming in some makeshift tent or back room: they wished for the darkness and emptiness of eternity, but that would not come; only suffering would come.

And the healthy, whose task it was to carry the dead and the dying, they would succumb to the pestilence that followed like a carrion bird or a conqueror worm. And those untouched by trauma of bullet or blade or shell or disease might struggle with memories that haunted until the horrors they had seen took their sanity and their souls. And those who waited for son or husband or brother or friend might never know what fate that loved one had met; would never walk behind the hearse or watch the casket lowered. War is not good for living things.

Great tear-drop leaves, their edges turning brown, dangled from branches overloaded with mature chestnuts. Squirrels gathered the few early fallen nuts to bury against winter. All along the Rue du Louvre by the Church of Saint-Germain l'Auxerrois and up the Rue de Rivoli to the Jardin des Tuileries the stately horse chestnuts or marroniers, rose above the avenues like sentinels guarding against…what? A war that would never, could never come to the Ville des Lumières?

Émilie-Claire and Phoebe walked through the Jardin des Tuileries, enjoying the crisp breeze that chased away summer's heat and pulled a fine mist from the Seine. They exited the park at the Place de La Concorde. Here they stopped to stare up at the obelisk and wonder at its journey to Paris some 40 years ago from Egypt where it had stood at the Luxor Temple for 3,300 years. It was covered with hieroglyphics which glorified Ramses II. And now it graced the public square where the Revolution's guillotine had separated the heads from the bodies of Louis XVI, Marie Antoinette, Madame du Barry, Robespierre and many others. Fountains and statues flanked the obelisk which rose 75 feet above their heads, a sparkling granite spire like…

"A giant penis," said Émilie-Claire. "Men! They glory in stupid wars and then erect monuments to their manhood."

"It's true," replied Phoebe. "What is the point of it all?"

"Perhaps it is God's way of keeping the planet from being over populated. But I think it has more to do with power and corruption and greed. Arrogance as well. If women ruled the word there would be no wars."

"I wonder…"

They had wandered next to the Fontaine de Commerce et de Navigation Fluviate. They leaned against the wall of the great stone basin. The allegorical figures, the dolphins and water sprites, the sea shell decorations on the large central pedestal from which rivulets of water poured all gave a neoclassical theme to the fountain. King Louis-Philippe had seen to its construction. The tradition of fountain building was now being overseen by Baron Haussmann.

"Dear Phoebe," said Émilie-Claire, "what news is there of Jeanne-Alice? Is she still at the hospital in Versailles?"

Phoebe brushed aside a lock of hair that had fallen over her forehead. "No, she is back in Paris," she responded. "There is such a need for volunteer medical assistance here. And a great many small hospitals…what they call ambulances. Flags with the Red Cross are waving from buildings as diverse as the Palais de Justice, the Odéon, and the Comédie-Française! Jeanne-Alice is volunteering at the Grand Hôtel. It is a dreadful place for a hospital, she tells me."

"Oh? It is a large building. It must have room for a great many beds."

"You see, that is just the problem. Too many patients all grouped together and bad ventilation. More die from germs passed among them than from wounds. We should be following the American model, she tells me. They use tents."

"And war casualties? Do they establish ambulances at the fronts?"

"Not so many as are needed. And it is difficult to transport the wounded. Again, the Americans have superior wagons. They learned much during the War Between the States. So some make it back to Paris but most do not."

"Tragic. Will Jeanne-Alice be sent to the front, do you think?"

"She wants to go…I and François do not wish to see her in danger. But you know what they say about duties during war: men to the combat and women to the ambulance."

"We can't vote and we can't fight but we can still dodge bullets for the good of the Emperor."

"Well, we are hoping she will be smart and stay put."

Maybe not so smart and definitely not staying put: Jeanne-Alice had been taken under the wing of a woman who would one day be heralded as a heroine of the war and receive the Legion of Honor (but not until much, much later), Coralie Cahen. Madame Cahen was 43 years of age, widowed, and a volunteer for the French Red Cross in Paris, where she was not always in the good graces of that organization, being critical of the unhygienic conditions of the Paris ambulances. Although her deceased husband had been a doctor, she had not had nurse's training as a Sister of Charity, being of the Jewish faith. If there was anti-Semitism at play it was not blatant, yet she was not regarded as being on equal footing with the other nurses. Nonetheless, Madame Cahen organized a small troop of like-minded angels-of-mercy to journey to Metz where Frenchmen and Germans alike were in dire need of medical attention. Jeanne-Alice followed along with her.

Jeanne-Alice's first glimpse of the medieval city of Metz was the thirteenth century bridge castle called the Porte des Allemands, or German's Gate. Straddling La Seille River, the bridge castle had fortified gates with twin towers on each side of the river and was a substantial element of the old town's defensive ramparts. The carriage in which Jeanne-Alice rode as part of Coralie Cahen's entourage rumbled across the bridge and along the Rue des Allemands. The medieval wall along the town side of the river featured a number of towers; Tour des Sorcières, Tour du Diable, and Tour des Corporations could be seen from the receding carriage even as they neared the Place Saint-Jacques—another square bloodied by action of the guillotine during the French Revolution.

They crossed the Centre Ancienne Ville past what once had been a chapel built by the Knights Templar in the twelfth century and at last arrived at the Saint-Pierre-aux-Nonnains. This ancient structure was believed to be the oldest church in France, dating back to the fourth century. It had been a Roman gymnasium and spa before being converted into a Christian church. When the French conquered Metz in 1556 they adapted the building for their main military headquarters, and now it was central to the current war effort.

What was it, thought Jeanne-Alice, about institutions…church, government, military, that the working minions could be relegated to shacks, tents, or worse, but the high officials always had elegant waiting rooms…large enough that they could have served to house whole families? Here they sat, waiting, outside the office of the newly appointed Commander-in-Chief, Marshall François Achille Bazaine, at his Saint-Pierre-aux-Nonnains headquarters. Lush carpets on the floors, paintings of French military battles on the walls, fresh flowers in a vase on the big oak desk where sat a hawk-nosed, eagle-eyed, old crane of a woman who had squawked at them to sit down—and wait.

Sitting across from Coralie Cahen, Jeanne-Alice, and another woman who had accompanied them from Paris, Arianne Mercier, was a tired and disheveled-looking woman in a ripped and dirty day dress. Her hair fell in unruly strings down face and neck. She introduced herself as Victorine Rouchy, an ambulance driver, just returned from the area around Wœrth, where there were more casualties than could be transported.

"I am here asking for more help," she said. "But I don't believe the Marshall is here in Metz. She…" here Madame Rouchy gestured toward the woman behind the desk, "won't say."

"But that is exactly why we are here. To help," said Madame Cahen.

"Good luck with that. There's not a wagon that can be had from this man's army."

"What about the townspeople? Couldn't they contribute wagons if not man power?"

"How do you convince them? They don't want to get anywhere near the fighting."

"I am a good organizer. I started the Maison Israélite de Refuge pour l'Enfance for homeless Jewish girls at Romainville in 1866. That involved a great deal of interaction with the public."

"I heard it was a home for prostitutes and their children."

"Anyone in need was always welcome."

Jeanne-Alice, sensing the tension, looked from the one scowling woman to the other, then back again. Then she looked at Arianne Mercier who simply shook her head gently. Mme. Rouchy seemed to be deliberating. Then she said:

"Well, I think that is admirable. It's all about helping needy people, isn't it? And those girls must be the neediest of all…or else they wouldn't be doing what they are doing."

Mme. Cahen accepted what was frankly a complément pour gaucher, but it was as good as she was going to receive from this hard-boiled woman. Even the woman roosting behind the desk seemed to nod in agreement. She cleared her throat and then sang out with:

"I should not have kept you waiting so long without an explanation. Marshall Bazaine is not here today, he is in the field. And perhaps you hadn't heard, but he was wounded by a shell burst only two days after he received his command status. Oh, he is fine. Didn't even accept any treatment. What a soldier!"

"Yes, but where does that leave us," asked Mme. Rouchy.

"You are right that there are no resources. You are better off following that plan to involve the town."

Suddenly the door burst open and a person, who at first Jeanne-Alice thought was a man because of the clothing she wore, but who was very much a woman, came bounding into the room as if she were being chased by the entire Prussian army.

"Where is he?" she demanded. "I have three messages. It was

difficult getting through enemy lines, but I did it. And I have some intelligence: the Prussians are using boats to build a bridge farther up the Moselle River."

"He is on a campaign. Better give your messages to the duty officer. He can get it to Marshall MacMahon."

"Ha! That idiot? I'll go to Bazaine. Where is he?"

After a hesitation that had the woman dressed as a man tapping her foot impatiently, the secretary or receptionist or aide or whatever she was leaned close and said in low voice, "He's at Borny."

"And the Emperor?"

"He has no doubt reached Chilons by now. They are pulling back, hoping we at Metz can forestall the inevitable attack on the Army of the Rhine. But I didn't tell you that."

"Merde! Well, I'm off. I'll probably meet Bazaine and his troops retreating back to Metz along the way!" And she was gone.

"Who was that woman who was dressed as a man?" asked Jeanne-Alice.

"What does it matter? She is known as the widow Imbert. Her name is Louis Nay Imbert. She has been most helpful in carrying messages across the enemy lines..."

"And spying?"

"Gathering information. She lives here in Metz. She might be of some help to you in organizing your civilian ambulances. She wears men's clothing in order to blend in with the masses. I think she likes it a bit too much sometimes."

On August 14 news came of the battle at Borny-Colombey. Marshall Bazaine had been ineffective in applying the superior numbers of his troops against General von Steinmetz's Prussian advanced guard. The battle had been indecisive but had allowed the French to retreat back to Metz. Thousands of the dead and wounded had been left on the battle field. By now Coralie Cahen had rallied the townspeople and acquired wagons for the journey to the Borny battlefield under the flag of the Red Cross.

There were no longer any French troops to the east of the Moselle River. German troops were now headed toward Metz where the siege of the city would begin within days. Mme. Cahen was challenged often as she and her caravan of makeshift ambulances entered the woods around the hills of the Borny plateau, but her determination, and the sight of women in civilian clothing doing the work of regrettably absent doctors and nurses swayed the enemy into allowing the removal of the wounded.

Nor were any Prussian medical personnel present to attend to the injured. So the French angels-of-mercy made no distinction as to the color of the uniforms on the men they lifted onto the wagons. The color of blood was identical for all. Jeanne-Alice now saw first hand the immediate results of war and she was mortified. She was unsure whether the mangled dead or the brutalized wounded presented a more gruesome sight. Seeing severed limbs or the twisted internal organs cascading from burst open bellies was the least of it; these were only details. The overall effect of a landscape littered with things that were unimaginably horrifying was a shock that she would be unable to chase from her memories in years to come. It was also, thank heaven, quite numbing.

Several trips with the wagons had brought over three thousand wounded and dying men back to Metz. Once the government buildings and churches which had been made over into ersatz hospitals had been filled to capacity, the townspeople opened their houses to receive the casualties of the battle. Jeanne-Alice found herself ministering to a room crowded with bloodied soldiers lying on blankets or old rugs on the floor of what was the banquet hall of a large mansion belonging to a wealthy family. She used the only vessel available to bring water to the trembling lips of the suffering men: a crystal goblet.

It seemed to her that there were more bandages visible than faces or limbs; it was a field of white lumps spotted with dark red, surrounded by the green-grey of the blankets and the dull brown of the parquet flooring. In the yellow gas light she could see the stirring and thrashing of a number of men and the ominous stillness of others. She could hear the moaning and sobbing and cries for mother or wife—and the death rattles. At least she was not alone among the gruesome company. Two other nurses or nurse volunteers like herself walked among the bodies checking—checking for life signs.

Was this one a boy from the communes of Paris? Was that one a youth conscripted in Berlin to do battle at the border? It was difficult to tell from what she could see of their faces. Blue-black bruises, dripping scars, missing teeth or worse—these were no indication of nationality. And what did it matter? They were together now in misery and pain, all deserving of sympathy and succor. She talked softly to them as she gave them water or adjusted a bandage. Some reacted to her soothing voice; some did not.

She came to the pallet upon which an injured boy was lying. He had bandages wrapped tightly around his forehead and one eye was swollen shut. Jeanne-Alice calculated that he must be a few years younger than she—how cruel to send so young a boy to war, she thought. He seemed barely aware of her closeness yet she felt compelled to soothe him as much as she could. "I'll sing you a song," she told him. "It's an old melody which my mother used to sing to me and my brother." She began:

> Il était un petit navire
> Il était un petit navire
> Qui n'avait ja-ja-jamais navigué
> Qui n'avait ja-ja-jamais navigué
> Ohé ! Ohé !
>
> Ohé ! Ohé ! Matelot,
> Matelot navigue sur les flots
> Ohé ! Ohé ! Matelot,
> Matelot navigue sur les flots
>
> There was once a little boat
> There was once a little boat
> That never on the sea had sailed
> That never on the sea had sailed
> Ahoy! Ahoy!
>
> Ahoy! Ahoy! Sailor,
> Sailor sailing on the high sea
> Ahoy! Ahoy! Sailor,
> Sailor sailing on the high sea

"Now it is a sad song in a way, but it has a happy ending," Jeanne-Alice said. "The ship is shipwrecked and the sailors have run out of food. They choose lots to see who they will eat and a boy is chosen. They then discuss what kind of sauce to eat the boy with. The boy prays to the Virgin Mary to save him. Suddenly…"

Des p'tits poissons dans le navire,
Des p'tits poissons dans le navire,
Sautèrent par-par-par et par milliers,
Sautèrent par-par-par et par milliers,
Ohé ! Ohé !

On les prit, on les mit à frire,
On les prit, on les mit à frire,
Le jeune mou-mou-mousse fut sauvé,
Le jeune mou-mou-mousse fut sauvé,
Ohé ! Ohé !

Small fishes upon the deck,
Small fishes upon the deck,
Leapt by the thousands,
Leapt by the thousands,
Ahoy! Ahoy!

Quickly they were grabbed and fried,
Quickly they were grabbed and fried,
And the ship's boy was saved,
And the ship's boy was saved,
Ahoy! Ahoy!

The youth to whom she sang stirred noticeably during the verses. After the final chorus he struggled to sit up. "It's you!" he managed to say in a voice that cracked and broke and was barely audible. Jeanne-Alice looked at him in wonder. It wasn't possible, but…

"What is your name, boy?" she said softly. "What do you mean by 'it's you?' " Then she looked more closely at his features, trying to look through the bruises and the bandages. And she saw who it was.

"Geoffroy Pierre!" she exclaimed. "My own dear brother lost so many years. You have come back! But you are dressed like a German. I don't understand."

But Geoffroy had lapsed back into unconsciousness. She would stay by his side now, until he either woke, or…

Byron Grush

21

Empire's End

Excerpt from: *Dame Impétueux, la Mémoire de Émilie-Claire Lebeau-Richelieu*, (English translation, published by Charles W. Karr & Co., Chicago, 1897)

This is a difficult chapter to write for in it I must tell of not only the end of the Empire, but of the loss of my beloved Jean-Léon Richelieu. I was not sad to see the last of the former, but I would pine eternally for the latter.

News from the front was always spotty. Eventually, as some of the wounded started pouring into Paris—and the numbers were small (which was encouraging until we found out what a tiny percentage of the injured it was)—we began to form a picture of the success or failure of our army. Only there wasn't much in the way of success. We learned that Metz was besieged by the Prussians. Jeanne-Alice, Phoebe's stepdaughter was there and had only managed to return to Paris by virtue of the fact that she was an ambulance assistant. She said that there will most likely be a reckoning with at least one of the generals for their incompetence. She told the story of discovering her long lost brother among the wounded—in a German uniform!

Patriotism! Already there were demonstrations going on against the Empire. Emille Ollivier's government fell and the Empress-regent instructed the Comte de Palikao, Charles Guillaume Cousin-

Montauban, to form a new government. He was the only general not in the field and so became president of the council. He was the one who formulated the plan to send Marshall MacMahon's Army of Châlons to secure Metz. Had those forces been more organized and capable, the disaster of Sedan might never have happened. But it did.

I was very worried about Teo and, of course, Jeffrey who were out there somewhere under fire from those big guns. Jean-Léon, being the Emperor's advisor, was with Louis Napoleon at Châlons-sur-Marne. That would be, I guessed, the largest of our forces and protected on all flanks by other divisions. But those other divisions were being gobbled up like so much sauerkraut.

I think it was General Auguste-Alexandre Ducrot who was quoted as saying, "Nous sommes dans un pot de chambre, et nous y serons emmerdes (We are in the chamber pot and about to be shat upon)." Marshall MacMahon had joined Napoleon III at Châlons and it was decided that they should march on Metz. Marshal François-Achille Bazaine had basically marched his troops into captivity and eventually would be sentenced to death as a traitor by the new Republic. The sentence would be commuted, which shows you that we French are not as barbaric as we used to be. But more about that later.

"Em," Phoebe said to me on a warm day in early September when pools of water left over from the last night's rain reflected a deep blue sky, "we've been through a lot together, haven't we?"

Of course we two women had met during that long voyage around the horn so many years ago. Her lover's death at sea—was it an accident?—had cemented a relationship between us that culminated in our venturing off to Paris together bringing Teo with us. Now she had regained her stepson from the long years of doubt and dread at his unknown fate. And I still yearned for reunion with my Teo. Even for news of him and, of course, of my beloved husband. What cruelties war heaps upon the women who must wait!

We walked as we often did, pouring out our hearts' concerns or, sometimes, joys, along the Seine on the lower walkway. Small boats still scurried seemingly unconcerned of war or threat of invasion. A couple of swans entwined their necks in a love ritual just below us as we passed by the Pont Royal. It could have been a peaceful day without strife or worry. But it was not.

We climbed up the stone stairs to the Quai Voltaire where the bookstalls lined the street. The bouquinistes were clustered around one of the stalls and cackling like a gaggle of geese. There was an element of concern bordering on hysteria in their raised voices. We moved closer to hear what the commotion was about. Somehow, we knew before any of the details were related, that the inevitable had occurred. This is what we gleaned from the frantic conversation among the booksellers:

Napoleon III was personally leading Marshall MacMahon's Army of Châlons in an effort to take Metz back and rescue Marshall Bazaine whose embittered forces were still holed up in the falling city. They were caught at Beaumont-en-Argonne by the Prussians and lost over 5,000 men and many cannons. They withdrew to Sedan where its castle was a formable fortress. They barricaded the streets and put up an admirable resistance to the invading Prussian and German forces, but the big artillery guns took a devastating toll on them. There was no hope of escape and seeing that the French losses were in the range of 17,000 killed and almost 6,000 wounded, Napoleon III called off his counterattacks and ran a white flag up upon the battlements. He surrendered the Army of Châlons and himself to the King of Prussia!

Now I knew that Jean-Léon was either dead or captured and would not be coming home any time soon. I was devastated. Phoebe tried to console me but it was no use. Uncharacteristically, I lost control and balled like a baby. I think the bouquinistes were a little uncomfortable with my outburst but they looked the other way and continued their blathering about the war and about the Emperor's capture. This was, said one of them, the end of the Empire and the beginning of the new Republic.

Only a few days later we had the Third Republic and the Government of the National Defense. And the officials—you know their names: Jules Favre, Louis Jules Trochu, Jules Ferry, Jules Simon, Léon Gambetta. These and many who had opposed the Emperor and his war were now in charge. But now the enemy was in Champagne and approaching Paris. A siege had begun. Bazaine, declining to continue to fight, surrendered with some 173,000 troops becoming prisoners of war. This, and his suggestion to Bismarck that he should lead the new government of France-under-Germany would lead to his conviction as a traitor.

Within a few weeks the city was surrounded. Yet news began to trickle in regarding the captivity of the Emperor. We heard of his, some would say, traitorous proposal to Bismarck that after the surrender of Paris he, Louis Napoleon, could be reinstalled as a puppet emperor. Bismarck wisely rejected the idea. The Empress Eugénie refused to believe Louis wasn't in fact dead; he would not capitulate, she maintained, but if so, he should kill himself in dishonor. Angry crowds approached the palace after the news reached Paris that the Emperor had surrendered. Eugénie fled to England.

How was I to get news of Jean-Léon, of Teo and of Jeffrey Flaherty? There was some talk of using hot air balloons to deliver and receive messages. Could one leap into the basket of one of those things and fly from Paris over the enemy lines to…where? Napoleon III and his aides, it was said, were being held in a castle in Wilhelmshöhe, Germany. It seemed an impossible situation. Even Phoebe's suggestion to join the Red Cross as a way of crossing the border with immunity seemed flawed and too dangerous to consider. But then again…

*　*　*

Metz, September 19, 1870

The Graoully Dragon was stirring in his watery grave. Legend had it that the terrifying beast—"gäulich" in German, hench "le graoully" in French—had lived in the old snake-infested Roman amphitheater from which it would periodically take wing over the city snorting fire and carrying off maidens. Early in the first century AD, Saint Clement was sent to Metz to spread the gospel and, if possible, rid the city of the flying monster. By wrapping his shawl around the dragon's neck, St. Clement was able to drag the Graoully into the River Seille and drown him. Now images of le Graoully were abundant in Metz, including a frightening statue of him in the crypt of the Metz Cathedral.

Across from the Cathedral, on the other side of the cobble-stoned square called the Place d'Armes, sat a long, neoclassical building with a facade of arched windows that served as the town hall: the Hôtel de Ville de Metz. Inside, a grand staircase led to a ballroom hung with crystal chandeliers where the incongruous installation of several desks had turned the otherwise elegant venue into a work area for the quartermaster staff of the Army of the Rhine. There was pandemonium among these enlisted men whose duty it was to procure food for Marshall Baizaine's troops, now surrounded by the Prussian Army. Canned rations were so low that the cavalry's horses were beginning to be sacrificed for their meat value.

The siege of the city was a bit of a stand off. Prussian big guns were unable to take out the French artillery. The ancient ramparts and the French rifles held off attempted invasions. The French, however, were trapped and being starved into submission. They would not be able to hold out much longer. What was needed were reinforcements, food, and medical supplies—but Napoleon III's Army of Châlons had surrendered at Sedan—they could not look for help from that quarter. How, with the city surrounded as it was, could they even get word to the outside world of their plight?

In the ad hoc work room at the Hôtel de Ville, the Maréchal des logis, Sergent Mathis Sauvageau, was studying a map of Metz and its vicinity. Suddenly he noticed an odd notation along the bank of the Moselle River. This indicated the site of the ruins of a bridge that had carried an old roman aqueduct from Jouy-les-Aches, a few miles south of Metz, to Ars-sur-Moselle on the other side of the river. Of course! Metz had originally been called Divodurum when it had been a major Roman town. L'aqueduc Rain de Gorze a Metz, the Metz aqueduct, supplied water to Divodurum and ran in underground tunnels for 22 kilometers between Metz and Gorze.

Sauvageau traced his finger along the map between the river crossings at Jouy-les-Aches and Metz. It must have come into the city about here, he thought, and terminated about here where there had been an old cistern. Nothing left of it, though…unless…. Just millimeters from where his finger had stopped on the map was an octagonal shape that indicated the site of the Chapelles des Templiers, the Chapel of the Knights Templar, at the end of what was now Rue de la Citadel. There were stories about the Templars hiding religious artifacts in tunnels under their temples. Why, the Holy Grail might even be buried here in Metz! And what if there were an entrance there to the old aqueduct? It was worth a look.

Sergent Mathis Sauvageau sent a runner to the pavilion at the north end of the Place d'Armes which was used now as a guard station. The runner returned with two soldiers who were promptly assigned the duty of exploring the Templar chapel and looking for an entrance to the underground aqueduct.

"Find it," he told them, "and return here for further instructions."

Thus it was that Teo Presume and Jeffrey Flaherty set off to the location of the small chapel where in the twelfth century the Knights Templar had established a Commandery and constructed a number of buildings. The chapel was the only structure not destroyed at the time the order was abolished. It was now used for storage, a shame since the Romanesque architecture with its thick octagonal walls was unique to the region of Lorraine. The Gothic vaults and faded murals of the chapel were faint echoes of a religious zeal that gained power and wealth, and ultimately, charges of heresy for the order. And the burning at the stake of the last Templar Grand Master, Jacques de Molay.

On the lintel above the entry was a carved patted cross, the cross pattée, symbol and emblem of the Knights Templar. It was weather worn and crumbling. Jeffery pushed open the heavy door and the two explorers went inside. A high ribbed vault above the nave led to a small apse whose straight walls, high ribbed vault, and semicircular form echoed the octagonal shape of the building. Here might have been an altar but now wooden boxes were piled haphazardly in the recess. Everywhere the walls between the vault ribbings were covered with frescos: the saints, scenes from the New Testament, the Last Supper, geometric designs of intertwined cross forms. High narrow arched windows sent shafts of golden light into the chapel as if Heaven herself was shining down on the soldiers.

"These Knights," Teo questioned, "weren't they racist and brutal?"

"They fought and murdered Muslims to capture the Holy Land for Christians and yes, they had no affinity for people of different religious beliefs or nationality or race. God told them to eliminate the unbelievers. They acted quite unchristian like to obtain their goals and became extremely rich. That led to their downfall."

"Good riddance to them."

"And good luck to us to find a secret passage."

The chapel was small for the height of its ceilings and the effect was eerie as if they were inside a great decorated bottle. None of the walls had doorways, hidden or otherwise. They were about to give up the search when Teo noticed an anomaly on the floor. A large slab of stone butted up to the outside wall of the square shaped choir in an odd manner; it seemed to be leaning against a low railing that ran along the edge of the wall like a border. It appeared to have been moved to make room for a very large crate. And they could see a patch of darkness under the slab which might indicate an empty space beneath.

"You see that, M. Flaherty?" asked Teo, pointing to the slab.

"By now you should be calling me 'Jeffery' don't you think? Yes, I see that. Let's see if we can lift it or slide it over."

In a short time they had maneuvered the heavy stone from its resting place enough that a body could squeeze down through the opening. There was a chamber below and in the dim light they could just make out a boxy shape that must have been a stone sarcophagus. They had found a sepulcher in which some long dead knight was interred. There were letters and symbols carved on the stone coffin but it was too dark to read them. They did, however, recognize the shape of a shield on which was carved the cross pattée.

"A Templar Knight's tomb. An important one to be buried under the chapel," said Jeffery.

"Now what?" Teo wanted to know.

"We make some light."

Jeffery had found a torch set into a metal holder on the wall. It was obviously as ancient as the tomb, but when he set a match to it, it burst into flame illuminating the chamber. There, just behind the stone sarcophagus, was an opening in the wall, low and narrow and smelling of damp and stale air. Jeffery thrust the torch into the opening and saw a passage leading slightly downward. The curved walls and ceiling of the passage were of quarry stone and covered with mold—much older than the chapel or the sepulcher. They ventured into it.

When they finally returned to the Hôtel de Ville to report to Sergent Sauvageau, they were able to say with certainty that the passage they had found was indeed part of the old Roman aqueduct. It was low and confining but passable if you stooped from time to time. How far it went they could not say but there was the hint of outside air and a subtle draft which meant that it came to the surface at some point. Sergent Sauvageau was delighted.

"Since you are familiar with the aqueduct now," he said, "you are elected to follow it to its termination, which I assume will be the ruined bridge at Jouy-les-Aches. You will cross the river and continue, using the aqueduct if there are enemy troops present, and, avoiding capture or assassination, you will find any French division which may be in the area and relate to them our severe need of reinforcements and provisions. Any questions? Good. You may start immediately."

"You know," said Jeffery as he and Teo went back to the guard station to gather supplies and arms for their excursion out of the beleaguered city, "we might make it all the way to Paris before we find any French troops."

"That would be all right with me," said Teo. "I could go for some of that good Paris food…so much better than eating horse!"

Had they only known how ironic that statement was.

$$*\quad*\quad*$$

Wilhelmshöhe Castle in Westphalia

High on a plateau above the city of Kassel, where brothers Jacob and Wilhelm Grimm had been born and had written many of their early fairy tales, stood the rambling Schloss Wilhelmshöhe, a neoclassical palace which once had been the residence of another Napoleon, Jérôme Napoleon, who reigned as the king of the French puppet state of Westphalia between 1807 and 1816. Now, under Prussian rule, the castle had been offered to Jérôme's nephew, Louis Napoleon, recently captured and forced to capitulate, as a temporary prison befitting his royal rank.

With him were his advisors including Jean-Léon Richelieu. They were housed now in the south Weissenstein Wing which connected to the central block of the palace, the Corps de Logis, by a long curving hall. The north block, the Kirch Wing, mirrored the Weissenstein, and together, the three blocks presented an imposing structure with a semicircular plaza leading to the central portico that mimicked the Pantheon in Rome. The hallway, which the prisoners were free to roam, was hung with old masters, including Lucas Cranach the Elder, Rubens, Frans Hals, and Albrecht Dürer. What a jail house, thought Jean-Léon!

Prisoners? Bismarck had told Louis Napoleon that he still recognized the former Emperor as the only legitimate ruler of France, in spite of the coup against him by the official New Republic that had just taken place in Paris. Prisoner? No...he was a visiting monarch with all the privileges of his station...except the ability to leave the grounds of the palace. Food and wine of the finest nature were being provided, overseen by captured French soldiers, a token imperial guard, albeit with out weapons. And Bismarck sat with the man who was sick and aching from ulcers and other maladies, and he talked with him, assuring him he would be reinstalled as Emperor if only...

"Does Marshall Bazaine recognize the new government, or will the troops at Metz acknowledge and follow arrangements which might be entered into by you?" Bismarck asked. "Perhaps if Marshall Bazaine were to find it suited his purpose to stand fast with the Emperor, and the Emperor were willing to make peace on Prussian terms, well then, Prussia would assist him to regain his throne with the aid of Bazaine and his 140,000 French troops."

Jean-Léon Richelieu, hearing this discourse between Bismarck and the Emperor, was mortified. What men will do to stay in power! And the lies they were willing to believe. And the Emperor was nodding his head in affirmation!

"Send one of your aides to Metz," said Bismarck, "with an escort, of course, to explain to Marshall Bazaine the new arrangements. If he surrenders he can march on Paris to restore the monarchy as Lieutenant-Général de l'Empire. You will be reunited with the Empress. Your son will inherit his birthright. There will be an end to bloodshed and starvation. All we want is our provinces in Alsace and the Lorraine."

And so the next morning, Jean-Léon Richelieu accompanied by two of Otto Bismarck's personal body guards, set out for Metz with a document written in the Emperor's own hand relaying the proposal to Bazaine which, Jean-Léon was sure, would appeal to Bazaine and which, he was doubly sure, was a proposal of the highest treason imaginable —treason against the French people!

Byron Grush

22

The Siege of Paris

Prussia marched on Paris. From the north came Crown Prince Albert's Prussian Army of the Meuse. From the south came Crown Prince Frederick Wilhelm's Third Army. The railway to Orléans was cut and Versailles was invaded and occupied. Kaiser Wilhelm I now used the palace as his headquarters. By September 19 Paris was completed encircled and cut off from the rest of France. Minister President of Prussia, Otto von Bismarck, wanted to shell the city to force a quick surrender but Field Marshall General von Blumenthal who was directing the siege refused. Civilians would be killed which violated the rules of engagement. Besides, he maintained, a quick surrender would leave France with its army intact and they would soon be able to renew the battle. Destroy the army, he demanded.

Paris had fortifications in place that she had anticipated needing for many years. In 1840 a 33 foot high wall was erected that surrounded the city, a modern enhancement to the old Enceinte. There were 15 forts along the wall and now many of the troops who had escaped the battle of Sedan had filtered back to Paris. The Grand Mobile and the newly organized Parisian Garde Sedentaire contributed to the man power. The levée en masse included the Francs-tireurs, civilian guerilla fighters. French General Trouchu had nearly 400,000 soldiers at the ready. But they were tired, ill equipped, and discouraged. Food supplies were estimated to last for only about three months.

Meanwhile back in Metz, Jean-Léon Richelieu had just handed the Emperor's dispatch to Marshall Bazaine. After reading it thoroughly and grimacing, Bazaine responded:

"The old bastard never misses a trick, does he?"

"If you don't mind me saying so," said Jean-Léon, "I think it is a trap. We've dealt with Bismarck before, as you know. He is disingenuous if not deceitful. My advice is to ignore it and continue to fight."

"We have run out of rations and are in the process of devouring our cavalry: 20,000 horses…but they won't last long. At some point we will have to surrender. This might give us some leverage."

"Don't forget about Gambetta's Third Republic. The people are with him. This could be seen as an act of treason."

"I don't think I have to worry about that. The Legionnaires are on my side. If we bring peace to France by any means it will not be seen as treasonous."

"If you say so."

"Go back to Wilhelmshöhe Castle and give the Emperor the missive I shall now compose. We can be deceitful to the enemy as well as he to us. Let Bismarck think he has won. And then…we bring down the hammer!"

With over 280 miles to travel between Metz and Kassel, the German body guards escorting Jean-Léon elected to camp overnight in the Saarland forest. There would be no French soldiers to offer succor for the Emperor's advisor. It was, Jean-Léon knew, the first duty of any prisoner of war to escape. Therefore, once the horses had been hobbled and the campfire lit, he began planning. The guards had brought a ration of beer with them to ease the boredom of the trip. They generously offered Jean-Léon a cup. With his uneasy knowledge of the German language he was still able to enquire of his captors what spirited drinking songs they might know. The bottle was passed and the voices were raised in a rousing tinklieder as the stars began to appear one by one in the night sky.

Ja lustig, lustig ihr lieben Brüder,
so leget all' eure Sorgen nieder,
und trinkt dafür ein gut Glass Wein.

Auf die Gesundheit aller Brüder,
die da reisen auf und nieder,
dies soll unsre Freude sein.

Denn unser Handwerk das ist verdorben,
die letzten Saufbrüder sind gestorben,
es lebet keiner mehr als ich und du.

Let's have fun, my dear brothers,
Time to lay down all your worries
Drink instead a good glass of wine.

To the health of all our brothers,
Who travel round, up and down the country,
This will be our joy today.

For our craft it has been run down,
The best drinkers have all passed away.
There's no one here left but you and me.

Soon the words came slurred and beer sloshed wildly from the tin cups. Jean-Léon bided his time. When the snoring of the guards drowned out the neighing of the horses he quietly stole away from the campsite. He led all three horses down into a shallow basin well beyond the camp and tied their reigns to a long rope he found in one of the saddlebags. Reaching into his vest pocket he pulled out the missive Bazaine had written to the Emperor. This he tore into small pieces and scattered in the brush. Mounting the lead horse, he led his purloined cavalcade out of the woods. Now, he thought, which way is France?

Émilie-Claire cursed in a combination of the worst French and English words she knew. She was stopped along the road, only four hours out of Paris, where the front wheel of her wagon had come loose and was lying on the ground before her. From the trees along the side of the road a cheeky starling was chirping insults at her. She responded with a rude gesture. The wagon had been borrowed from a merchant at Les Halles who had used it to haul vegetables and it was draped with a large flag with a white field and a bright red cross. Émilie-Claire was determined to make the journey to Kassel, deep into Germany, and to rescue her beloved husband, Jean-Léon, disguised as a Red Cross nurse.

"Merde! Son of a bitch! Connard salope! Ve te faire foutre! Damn it to hell! Nique ta mere!"

In the thick bushes bordering the forest two errant soldiers listened to the harangue. "If I didn't know better," said one, "I'd say that voice was familiar."

"I'm going to take a look," said the other.

Émilie-Claire saw a motion in the brush out of the corner of her eye. Enemy soldiers? She turned and saw…no, it couldn't be…but it was! There, peeking around a mulberry bush was her ward, Teo Presume. Teo called to his companion to come out and soon Jeffrey Flaherty, Teo and Émilie-Claire were reunited on the road she had taken from Paris. Embraces and the kissing of cheeks were in order.

While they struggled with the broken wheel they brought each other up to date. Jeffrey described his and Teo's flight from Metz through the old Roman aqueduct, sometimes crawling through muddy dampness, sometimes needing only to stoop. The smells, the sharp rocks underfoot, the rats…. Then crossing the river, hiding from German troops in the forest, sleeping in a barn, always in fear of discovery. It had been a long and dangerous journey while they searched in vain for a French division to come to the rescue of the troops at Metz. They had decided to return to Paris.

Émilie-Claire told of the plight of the Parisians whose lovely city was surrounded by Prussian and German soldiers. Of the hunger and the depression and the isolation. The cost of food that had been so plentiful. The arming of mere children. The constant fear that the Prussians would breech the walls and come tumbling through the streets wreaking havoc. "At least they haven't shelled us…yet!"

"All the more reason for us to go back," said Jeffrey.

"You'll never get past the Germans. And no one would open the gate for you for fear that you were spies or saboteurs."

"Well, there is one way that I can think of."

"No, Jeffrey. I must go to Jean-Léon. I cannot take you back to Paris."

"Just put us in the wagon as if we are wounded and the Germans will let you through their lines. They must need more capable men in

Paris now. We can be of use. If Jean-Léon is not dead he is certainly being held prisoner. It is best to wait until the war is over. He'll be returned." Jeffrey didn't add, "One way or the other."

When the wagon reached the German lines just outside of Paris it was searched and the rifles Teo and Jeffrey had carried were confiscated. Apparently the groans and wailing coming from the two soldiers were sufficient to convince the Germans that they were, indeed, wounded. "Don't come back this way again," the German sentry admonished Émilie-Claire. "We aren't allowing the passage of ambulances anymore."

Well, no good deed remains unpunished, thought Émilie-Claire. Now she would be unable to travel to Jean-Léon's side. She would not know of his fate, nor he of hers. Now they had Paris to worry about and defend. Now all Parisians were united against a common enemy—for the time being.

Paris was cut off from the rest of France. Attempts at getting messages in and out were doomed to failure: runners were captured; dogs carrying messages were intercepted; canisters floated down the Seine were destroyed. It seemed nothing would work. But then the photographer, Félix Nadar, suggested using hot air balloons. He had, with his own balloon the Neptune, created an air force of one which he called "No. 1 Compagnie des Aérostatiers." Used for tethered observation, the balloon was somewhat ineffective—they already knew where the enemy was; why not send the balloons out and away, he suggested. Use them for communication. More balloons were produced in the now idle clothing factories. Now messages could be sent aloft and carrier pigeons could be shipped to outlying districts to return with communiqués.

On October 7, French War Minister, Léon Gambetta, left Paris in a balloon for Tours where he meant to set up a provisional government. German sharp shooters managed to wound him when his balloon dipped low above enemy territory. He recovered and made it successfully to Tours. But perhaps it was too little, too late. What was left of the grand French army? Where would the retaliation come from?

Paris was starving. In a desperate effort to feed the population during the siege, the animals in the Paris Zoo were being sacrificed. Even Castor and Pollux, the adorable elephants that had entertained children and adults alike, met the fate of other exotic animals and household pets and strays. Characteristically French, however, these bizarre foodstuffs were usually served with the appropriate sauce. Menus in restaurants might include:

- *Consommé de cheval au millet. (Millet horse consommé)*
- *Brochettes de foie de chien à la maître d'hôtel. (Dog liver skewers)*
- *Emincé de rable de chat. Sauce mayonnaise. (Sliced cat with raspberries)*
- *Epaules et filets de chien braisés. Sauce aux tomates. (Braised dog shoulders)*
- *Civet de chat aux champignons. (Mushroom cat stew)*
- *Côtelettes de chien aux petits pois. (Dog chops with peas)*
- *Salamis de rats. Sauce Robert. (Salami of rats)*
- *Gigots de chien flanqués de ratons. Sauce poivrade. (Dog legs flanked by raccoons)*
- *Begonias au jus. (Flowers)*
- *Plum-pudding au rhum et à la Moelle de Cheval. (Plum-pudding with rum and marrow of horse)*
- *Loup de loup à la sauce au chevreuil (wolf haunch in deer sauce)*
- *Terrine d'antilope (antilope terrine)*
- *Ragoût de kangourou (kangaroo stew)*
- *Tête d'âne en peluche (stuffed donkey's head)*
- *Consommé d'éléphant (elephant consommé)*

Bon appétit. At least there were ample reserves of wine—red, white or sparkling.

Meanwhle, on October 27, Bazaine surrendered at Metz without a fight. On October 30, the French National Guard was defeated at Le Bourget. Other Prussian victories in the suburbs were lowering the French morale. Learning that the Government of National Defense had elected to negotiate with Prussia, a revolt took place in Paris on October 31 in which Parisian workers and some members of the National Guard led by Louis Auguste Blanqui seized the Hôtel de Ville and set up their own revolutionary government. Blanqui was an old school revolutionary who had been condemned to death for his activities during the reign of Louis Philippe but had been released from prison when the Revolution of 1848 took place. He was imprisoned again a year later for his opposition to the Republic and in 1865, escaped and left the country. In 1869 there was a general amnesty and Blanqui was free to return. He again organized demonstrations, some of them violent. He would be arrested again.

November 28, the Battle of Beaune-la-Rolande

In the scope of the Franco-Prussian War it was not a very significant battle. Except to Frédéric Bazille. Bazille was a member of the Gleyre atelier along with Pierre-Auguste Renoir, Oscar-Claude Monet, Alfred Sisley, and Jeffery Flaherty. He was the one with the independent income who helped the others buy supplies and pay the rent. He was a promising young artist with an excellent future—except he had joined the 3rd Zouave Regiment, that fierce regiment with ties to Africa and Afganistan. He wanted to see action…he was seeing it. The regiment was now attached to General Charles Crouzat's Twentieth Corps just outside of Paris.

Three Prussian brigades were stationed at Beaune-la-Rolande, a small commune in the Loiret Department in north-central France. General Crouzat had decided to attack the Prussian corps there in order to relieve some of the pressure on the beleaguered city of Paris. All together he had a force of 60,000 with 140 big guns. The Prussians had only 9,000 men and 70 guns. However, it was yet another French fiasco, possibly one of the worst.

The town was protected only by a walled churchyard and another six foot high wall on the south. Crouzat opened fire with his artillery but the Prussians withdrew away from the village. The French found the roads barricaded and stopped at the outskirts. When the fighting began again in earnest, the Zouave Regiment fought brilliantly; however, all of General Crouzat's officers were either killed or wounded and this slowed the attack. A second attack saw the Prussians "waiting until they saw the whites of their eyes" before firing. This was a way to counter the longer range of the French rifles. They successfully repelled the French once again. It was the third attack by Crouzat that determined the outcome and broke the spirit of the French troops.

Frédéric Bazille's commanding officer was lying mortally wounded on the field before him. The Zouaves were milling around, unsure as to what action to take. The Prussians had regrouped and, along with their artillery, had begun a counter attack at the east side of the town where Crouzat's forces were deployed. It was getting dark yet Crouzat ordered a third attack, straight through the center of town, intending to wipe out the enemy by shear brute force. Bazille rallied the Zouaves in his regiment and led them forward.

In spite of the superiority of French fire power and greater numbers, the Prussians were virtually untouchable. Securely fortified within the town, they were returning barrage after barrage of small caliper bullets that ripped through the French lines like angry bees. Crouzat's fighters were losing their enthusiasm for the battle. It seemed pointless to die for a tiny hamlet, especially one where a handful of Prussians could so easily withstand their underwhelming and pathetic onslaught. Many emptied their rifles at the enemy and turned and ran, ignoring orders.

Still Bazille persisted, leading his men valiantly toward the concentration of Prussian troops. From a low slinking position they would suddenly stand and discharge several rounds then drop again. The colorful uniforms of the Zouares flashed through the smoke and dust of battle, possibly instilling fear in the hearts of the enemy…or, more likely, presenting colorful targets. Like his comrades, Bazille stood and aimed his Chassepot rifle at the helmeted heads peeking over the wall by the church. Another barrage rang out from inside the town. Frédéric Bazille, only 28 years of age, was struck twice and fell bleeding to the ground. Before he could be dragged away from the chaos on the field of battle, he was dead.

What fine paintings might he have produced had he lived? What would he have contributed to that revolution in art which would come to be called impressionism? Who would mourn for the loss of excellence in the face of such terror? 700 Zouares lay dead or wounded. 8,000 Frenchmen were dead or wounded or were taken prisoner. Prussian soldiers killed amounted to 817 and 37 officers. In spite of superior numbers, the French had lost the day.

23

The Capitulation

Paris, January 1870

"I surrender."

"What?"

"I surrender to you all my heart and all my soul."

"Jeffrey! Don't be…ne sois pas un âne! It is still possible that Jean-Léon will return." Émilie-Claire turned away, her face reddening. "I can't…I can't deal with this right now."

They were walking in the park along the Champs-Élysées, bundled up against the cold, when they heard the artillery shells exploding. They sounded too close for comfort. On January 6, Bismarck had finally been given the go-ahead to shell the city. He had begun with the forts on the outskirts but soon had the heavy Krupp cannons directing fire into the city itself. So far, little damage and few casualties had resulted. But it was just a matter of time before the impending devastation would convince the Government of the National Defense to reconsider their own strong stand against capitulation.

There were still French armies outside of Paris, and attempts at breakouts had occurred, but so many Prussian forces surrounded the city that little could be done to move them. On January 19 troops led by General Trochu, some 90,000 strong, attacked the German lines between Bougival and St. Cloud but were driven back with severe losses. Resistance at Belfort was admirable but after a siege of 103 days the citadel fell. The gallantry of its people would one day be immortalized by a huge sandstone monument, the Lion of Belfort.

At the Palace of Versailles on January 18, a gathering of German and Prussian royalty and military commanders met to proclaim the unified Germany for which Bismarck had hoped for so long. In the Hall of Mirrors, the pride of King Louis XIV of France, between the mirrored arches and the arcaded widows, beside the marble pilasters with their gilded bronze capitals, Wilhelm I, stood next to Crown Prince Frederick on a dais as he was given the title of Kaiser, Emperor of Germany. Otto von Bismarck, soon to be made Chancellor of Germany, stood watching proudly as his monarch made history for the German people. He sneered at the irony that the ceremony was taking place in the former palace of the now humiliated and vanquished French Empire.

Émilie-Claire and Jeffery had reached the Place de la Concorde and crossed over into the Tuileries Garden; it was a familiar route for a walk and the doing of things mundane seemed more important than ever these days. The shelling had stopped for the moment. Émilie-Claire looked deeply into Jeffrey's eyes.

"I admire you greatly, Jeffrey. You know that," she said. "But I just can't think about romance right now. Please understand."

"I'd better get back to my unit," Jeffrey said, dismayed and discouraged by Émilie-Claire's rejection. "The National Guards already think me suspicious for leaving Metz in the middle of the fray. They accused Teo and me of deserting. They can shoot deserters, you know. But many of them are in sympathy with the workers…the 'Reds,' some call them, who think the government is going to surrender the city to the Prussians. There is a meeting…"

There were serious stirrings of revolution. Louis Auguste Blanqui through his journal *La Patrie en Danger* was able to spread his ideas. The publications of Karl Marx had reached Paris and helped to plant the seeds of revolution. Already on the streets a poster had gone up condemning the government:

To the people of Paris

The Delegates of the Twenty Districts of Paris.
Has the government which on September 4th took
on the task of national defense carried out its
mission? No!
We are 500,000 combatants yet 200,000
Prussians hold us back! Whose responsibility is it
if not that of those who govern us? Their only
thought was to negotiate instead of forging
cannons and making weapons.
They refused mass conscription.
They let Bonapartists alone and jailed
Republicans.
Can the Grand People of 89, who destroyed the
Bastilles and turned over thrones, wait in inert
despair, for the cold and hunger to turn its heart to
ice while the enemy is counting its every beat, its
last drop of blood? No!
The population of Paris will never accept this
shame and misery. They know that there is still
time, that decisive measures will allow for workers
to live and for everyone to join the battle.

GENERAL REQUISITION – FREE RATIONS –
MASSIVE ATTACK

The politics, strategy and administration of
September 4th, in continuity with the Empire,
have been judged.

MAKE WAY FOR THE PEOPLE!
MAKE WAY FOR THE COMMUNE!

The Delegates of the Twenty Districts of Paris

On January 22 elements of the National Guard and the proletariat under the influence of the Blanquists held a demonstration demanding the overthrow of the government of the National Defense and the establishment, in its place, of a Commune. The Breton Mobile guard, which had been defending the Hôtel de Ville, was ordered by the Government of the National Defense to "shoot to kill" the demonstrators. A massacre took place—the workers had been unarmed. Neither Jeffrey Flaherty nor Teo Presume had been among the Guard on that tragic day. But the action infuriated them and drew both closer in spirit to the movement than they had been before.

The Deputy to the National Assembly, Jules Favre was sent the next day to Versailles to meet with Bismarck to seek a general armistice. Although he was not empowered to negotiate a treaty, he offered to cede one of the forts to the Germans which had impeded their conquest of Paris. "We are starving," he implored Bismarck. Would he agree not to enter Paris and to allow free elections? Would he allow the Guard to remain armed in order to suppress the Paris Commune? Finally, Bismarck agreed to cease the bombardment of Paris and to an armistice for a period of three weeks provided all the forts were turned over to the German army.

German army rations began being shipped into Paris by train. On January 25 President Jules Trochu, having sworn never to surrender, resigned. Jules Favre now assumed the role of President of the Government of National Defense. Two days later in Versailles, he signed the surrender. He broke down and cried on his daughter's shoulder during the carriage ride back to Paris.

Émilie-Claire had moved into a small loft apartment on the Rue Ramponeau in Belleville, just down the hill from the Parc de Belleville. The narrow, cobblestone street appealed to her sensibilities and the neighborhood bustled with working class Parisians who seemed to speak their own version of French. Her windows did not have a view of the park, but she could lean out over the wrought iron balcony and see the tops of some of the trees, now barren of leaf and dusted with snow. On her wall she had hung the sketch Jeffrey had done of her and a small watercolor Manet had given her, a study, he said, for one of his Spanish canvases.

She studied Jeffrey's portrait; how idealized he had drawn her! In the mirror her eyes looked sunken with the dark circles of worry. The bright eyes that gazed back at her from the drawing must belong to some other woman. How she wished she was that woman!

Jeffrey. What to do about Jeffrey. It was true they had some history. Their love-making was memorable. He was brilliant and devoted and handsome—and young. And impulsive and insistent and exciting—and desirable. But as she had told him recently, there was still a chance that Jean-Léon was alive and would return. And if not she could be true to his memory. As hard as that might be.

She was cooking a chicken. The scrawny thing had cost her the outrageous sum of twenty francs. Well, she still had her money and she wasn't about to eat German army food or zoo animals. She had found a source at Les Halles for herbs, again expensive, but necessary. A little rosemary and sage and the ugly little thing might yet prove to be tasty.

Knocks on her door. Jeffrey stood on the threshold. She let him in, sat him down at the table. Some carrots were boiling on the stove. A bottle of wine needed opening. A candle lit, although it was not yet twilight time. Not romance. Just friends. The errant soldier and his one-time lover partaking of a meal that many Parisians could not afford. But that was about to change. The war was over. Or was it?

"Because of the terms of the surrender," Jeffrey was telling her over glasses of a reasonably delicate Bordeaux, "the National Guard has been permitted to keep their weapons although the regular troops have been disarmed. The Paris Commune is now certain to survive to oppose the remaining powers of the government. The Germans will allow free elections for France, but Trochu is determined to rid Paris of the Communards, so we shall see."

"You know so much of this struggle for the hearts and minds of a defeated France, Jeffery. Are you involved with these 'Reds' when you shouldn't be?"

"The Central Committee is moving all the cannon and mitrailleuses that the army abandoned to places in Montmarte and La Villette, and of course, here in Belleville. There will probably be barricades like in the old days of the revolution. We will not be fighting the Germans, however."

"And Teo? Is he becoming a 'Red' as well?"

"He also believes as we do that the regeneration of the Republic of France is impossible without the overthrow of the politics and social policies of the Second Empire that are retained by those of Bonaparte III's old rivals who are now in power."

"Oh, Jeffey! You sound like you are quoting the party line. When did you start to think like a communist?"

"It was the workers who were sent to die on the battlefields. It is the workers who must now rise up against injustice."

Émilie-Claire looked at Jeffrey in wonder. How he had changed in the short time the war had raged! Perhaps there was some truth in what he was saying. But the outcome of such a stand against the hurt and healing government…if it was not successful it would be suicidal. The new order that had been born out of frustration could be shattered like fragile window glass in a storm; the shards of idealism washed away by the tide of retaliation. And now the chicken was burning.

'I'm leaving him!" Phoebe told Émilie-Claire who had come to the Château des Ternes for a visit.

"But why? I thought of you as the perfect couple. And the children…"

The two were walking in the gardens of the old château where weeds had taken over and smothered the perennials. The gardener, like the footman and the cook's husband, had gone to serve in the army. Left to care for themselves, the Gardinier family had faltered at domestic chores and the estate was beginning to take on a patina of decay.

"But that's just it. François has been terrible to Geoffroy Pierre. He has as much as told him to leave the house! François just can't cope with how Germanic Geoffroy seems to him."

"Well, his formative years were in Germany."

"Yes, and when the Germans bridged the Seine here in Neully, Geoffroy acted…Oh, Em, he cheered them on! You can see why François was angered. But still, Geoffroy *is* his son. How can he reject the boy like that?"

Émilie-Claire kicked at a rock that sat in the middle of the overgrown path they were following. A frightened toad hopped away from under it.

"It's tragic what this stupid senseless war has done to people," Émilie-Claire said. "Oh, the divisiveness! And for what? The

Germans gained a couple of provinces on their border and a huge cash settlement. Not much to show for the number of dead…on either side."

"I heard they wanted 6 million francs."

"How many francs per dead body does that work out to?"

"And François and his friends from the Haussmann days…you know the war put their real estate business on hold…they bought a foundry and turned it into a munitions factory. They weren't just being patriotic. They wanted to make as much money off of the war as possible. Demons! You see, this separation has been coming for some time."

"What will you do?"

"I'll join Jeanne-Alice at the ambulances. There are still many many wounded soldiers to care for."

"And where will you live?"

"Well, I had hoped…"

"Of course you may come to live with me. We started this adventure together and we shall continue it together. I warn you, though, it's a walk up. You don't mind climbing stairs, do you?"

In February national elections were held in France—only very few people knew about them. Adolphe Thiers, a former deputy during the Second Empire and a venerable statesman of 74 years who had argued against the war, was elected chief of the executive power of the French Republic and later would become its first president. The next day German troops marched down the Champs-Élysées in a victory parade. In Versailles a peace treaty was signed by Fauvre, Thiers, and Bismarck. The indemnities to be paid by France to Germany now stood at 5 million francs. German troops would slowly withdraw from France as the money, paid in installments, was received.

Along the Rue Pigalle a surrender of another sort was taking place between Prussian soldiers and les prostituées who worked the district. Even at Le Rat Mort the enemy celebrated ordering huge steins of biére and singing rowdy drinking songs that served to drive out many of the local intellectuals and artists who had claimed the place in the past. Yet many of the defeated French regular army soldiers fraternized with the Prussians and celebrated along with them as if they had always been fast friends.

And in the back rooms of Le Rat meetings were taking place that would set Paris on a dangerous path.

National Guardsmen did not befriend their former enemies the way the army had. Indeed, they were largely opposed to the surrender and to the existing government of the National Defense headed by Thiers and officiated out of Bordeaux instead of Paris. The Guard greatly outnumbered the regular army personnel present in the city but still feared reprisals from Thiers. A new Central Committee was formed by the Guard consisting mostly of radicals aligned with the rising Paris Commune.

A plan was set forth to take control of the cannons abandoned by the army and place these in various parks around the city to defend against a possible attack by Thiers. There were upwards of 400 of these bronze, muzzle-loaders. Thiers also wanted them. As the cannons were basically obsolete, ownership of them was mostly symbolic.

Jeffrey Flaherty and Teo Presume were on the butte Montmartre one dismal afternoon. On top of Montmartre there were 170 of the abandoned cannons. The small group of Guardsmen which had been stationed there, including Jeffrey and Teo, looked down from the steep hill toward the city below. Two brigades of the French Army were climbing up to seize the cannons. During the confrontation that followed, the brigade led by General Claude Lecomte opened fire killing a guardsman. As word spread of the killing, a crowd of people converged upon Montmartre, surrounding the soldiers who were trying to move the cannons. Lecomte tried to retreat but seeing no easy exit ordered the soldiers to fix bayonets and fire on the crowd. The soldiers refused.

Jeffrey and Teo, in the first confrontation they would have with the army regulars, now moved on General Lecomte and his officers. With the help of the mutinous soldiers, they took the general and his staff to the Chateau-Rouge where the National Guard had its headquarters. A crowd followed and hurled insults and rocks at the prisoners. A call came to put them on trial and then execute them along with another captured general, General Jacques Leon Clément-Thomas. They were moved to the Rue des Rosiers by a vigilante committee from the 18th arrondissement. Later that afternoon the angry crowd of guardsmen and army deserters seized the two generals, beat them, then shot them both.

Jeffrey was appalled by the violence although Teo seemed to take it in his stride. It was time, people were saying, to man the barricades. What barricades, Jeffrey wondered? He would soon see them rising in keys positions around the city: on the Rue de Rivoli near the Hôtel de Ville, on the Rue Ramponeau in Belleville, Émilie-Claire's street, in Villette, Ménilmontant, and Montmartre. He would see the army evacuating back to Versailles where Thiers would add to their numbers with prisoners released by the Germans for that express purpose. He would come to understand that the war was now between the Commune and the Army of Versailles—between the people and the government.

Byron Grush

24

Man (and Woman) the Barricades!

At Vendôme, during the Prussian occupation of that city, Coralie Cahen, self-proclaimed nurse of the Société de Secours aux Blessés Militaires, the French Red Cross, had set up an ambulance to care for the wounded—both French and German. French troops had been forced to abandon the town but Coralie remained at her station. When a German officer raised a Prussian flag over her ambulance, she protested.

"This ambulance," she maintained, "is and will remain French!"

"We are now the masters here," replied the officer.

"Maybe in the town but not here! We are covered by the Red Cross and the French flag and you have no right to touch either. I will close down the ambulance unless you take down that flag. I am treating Germans as well as Frenchmen…that will end."

The German officer finally complied with her wishes and thanked her for treating his own soldiers. The Germans saluted her when they left the city. She had gained an advantage over the soldiering aspects of war by her humanitarian efforts. After the armistice she made three trips into Germany to visit prisoner of war forts and managed to rescue from their imprisonment over 300 French soldiers.

Back in Paris, Coralie now had a small staff which included Phoebe, her daughter Jeanne-Alice, Arianne Mercier who had been with Jeanne-Alice at Metz, and an ambulance driver named Louise

Michel. She would meet with them at the Palais de Justice on the Île de la Cité where hospital beds had been set up in the long corridors. There she would assign various tasks to her crew, sometimes sending them out to one of the many locations around Paris where war casualties were being brought.

The makeshift hospital at the Grand Hôtel was overcrowded now that so many wounded were being allowed to return to Paris. The Comédie-Française on the Rue de Richelieu was full of beds and the Odéon had been transformed into a hospital by its major star, Sara Bernhardt. During the siege of Paris the hospital at the Odéon was at risk and forced to close, so Bernhardt rented an apartment on the Rue de Provence and moved her patients there. Other private residences were flying the flag with the white field and bright red cross—sometimes only as a protection against the invaders.

Phoebe went with Louise Michel one morning riding in a horse-drawn wagon they would use to transport the injured survivors of a massacre that had occurred at the Place Vendôme. It wasn't clear exactly what had happened, but 12 people were dead having been fired upon by guardsmen. The crowd of protestors declaring themselves the "Friends of Peace" (organized by the government at Versailles) had fired at the guardsmen who were blocking their entrance into the square; the guardsmen fired back. As their wagon approached the scene of the incident Phoebe could see the bloody results of the confrontation—bodies were everywhere, some still moving in a bizarre writhing dance of death.

"How have we come to this?" Phoebe asked. "Frenchmen killing Frenchmen."

"You see that monument?" Louise responded. She pointed to the towering column that stood in the center of the square. The original column, modeled after the Trajan's Column in Rome, had been erected by Napoleon I to commemorate his victory in the battle of Austerlitz. It had been covered with a spiral of bronze plates made from captured cannons and topped by a sculpture of Napoleon I wearing a laurel leaf and holding a sword in one hand and a victory globe in the other. The statue had been taken down and melted to be recast as a statue of Henry IV but it was then replaced with a more modern version of Napoleon I by Louis Napoleon in a continuation of the celebration of the Empire. Off again and on again, the statue became a symbol to evoke hatred.

"We will pull that grinning despot down," Louise continued. "The Commune is taking control of Paris. It is righting the wrongs of the Bonapartists. Already we are occupying the Hôtel de Ville. Already we have confiscated the gun powder stored in the Pantheon. Already we fly the Red Flag over the Ministry of Justice and the Ministry of War. M. Clemenceau is no longer mayor of Montmarte. The Central Committee makes all the decisions. Blanqui is our honorary president…although he is still in jail in Brittany. We have voted to abolish the death penalty, military conscription, and night work in the bakeries…"

"Wait a second…night work in the bakeries?"

"Bakers were slaves to the leisure class, working all night to provide them bread for the morning. It was wrong."

"You know what you are being called, don't you? The 'Red Virgin of Montmartre.' Are you really that dedicated to your cause?"

"Of course. And I am hardly a virgin."

Émilie-Claire and Phoebe had just settled down for an apéritif one evening when Jeffrey Flaherty came knocking at their door.

"He always knows when dinner is almost ready," said Émilie-Claire.

"Oh, be kind to the poor man, he's been out there with that bunch of ruffians all day. Besides, I want to hear all about what has been happening with the Guard."

No undernourished chicken for the table tonight since foodstuffs had been rolling into Paris again from the surrounding farms and the sea shore. Émilie-Claire had been working all afternoon on her version of bouillabaisse using freshly caught monkfish, mullet, and mussels. Leeks, celery and potatoes had been simmering in a broth of garlic and tomatoes seasoned with herbes de provence and a pinch of saffron. She served the broth separately in large soup plates with bread and rouille and placed the fish on a plate in the center of the table. Portions of the seafood were then transferred into the broth where chunks of the bread lathered with the garlicky mayonnaise floated like little boats.

Afterwards, Émilie-Claire brought out coffees and a bottle of Armagnac for a pousse-café.

"You've missed your calling," said Jeffery. "You might have been a chef de cuisine at La Maison Dorée."

"Way too much responsibility and hard work," Émilie-Claire answered. "There was a time when I didn't cook. I had to learn during the siege and I have to tell you, I took to it with gusto. I now enjoy cooking...when I can get good ingredients, that is. But tell us what you have been doing since we last talked. Has the Commune taken over the entire country yet?"

"Yesterday," Jeffrey began, "we used a dray wagon to transport the guillotine to the Place Voltaire. There we broke it up and piled its bloody planks before the statue of Voltaire where we set fire to it. A small crowd gathered to watch and shake their fists at the monstrous invention. Well, how many of that company had surrounded the guillotine in the past when it preformed its gruesome tasks, I wonder?

"There have been some good things as a result of the rise of the Commune. But some...the separation of church and state, while it might seem like a good idea, has led to the taking of priests and nuns as hostages. They think they can trade them for Blanqui, but that won't happen. And their model for government is flawed. They have no president, no commander in chief, no central leadership, only endless committees and commissions. What is that expression? 'Too many cooks spoil the soup?' Sometimes it seems no one is in charge and chaos reigns supreme."

"What of the artists?" asked Phoebe. "What of your Batignolles Group? How are they faring?"

"Renoir, you know, was nearly arrested. He was sketching along the Seine and the Communards took him for a spy. They were about to throw him into the Seine when someone recognized him. Monet and Camille are in London, I think. Sisley is struggling since his father's business failed. His only means of support now is his paintings. Bazille, as you know, was killed at Beaune-la-Rolande, a tragic loss. Manet left Paris soon after the surrender. He is in Bordeaux painting and ignoring the current uprising.

"Zola is particularly critical of the Commune. He calls them assassins and arsonists who flee from the regular army and take their vengeance upon the monuments and houses of Paris. Victor Hugo calls the Commune a bunch of idiots and the war between them and the National Assembly a supreme folly. Anatole France and Gustave Flaubert concur with Zola.

"Gustave Courbet…well, he isn't really one of us, but an important painter, I guess…he is a member of the Council of the Commune. He organized a Federation of Artists right after the surrender which included André Gill, Honoré Daumier, Jean-Baptiste-Camille Corot, Eugène Pottier, Jules Dalou, and Édouard Manet. Their main concern was the survival of the art collections in the Louvre and the Museum of the Luxembourg Palace. He advocates for the destruction of the Vendôme Column calling it a monument to barbarism. He wants to replace it with a new column made of melted-down German cannons…a column of the People."

"I know about that," said Phoebe. "Louis Michel, the woman ambulance driver I worked with, told me they would pull it down. She is a shocking radical! She has joined the Guard and offered to assassinate Thiers!"

"There are many anarchists in the movement now," said Jeffrey. "It is they who I fear will bring destruction down around our necks."

"Will you continue with the Guard?" asked Phoebe.

"For the time being. There are committees organizing to build barricades. I can be useful at that and no killing is required. We have learned that Thiers in Versailles has petitioned Bismarck to release French prisoners so that he can build up his Army of Versailles. For what purpose? To invade Paris and eradicate the Commune!"

Émilie-Claire studied Jeffrey Flahety's face as it was lit with the blush of his passionate declaration. How different he was now from that boyish and shy student painter she had first met so long ago in front of the Café Tortoni. So unsure of himself then; and now on fire with a cause he really had no stake in, but to which he rallied willingly. He had managed to escape one civil war in his own country, only to find himself in the center of another. If only common sense could keep him safe throughout what was surely to come.

Belleville was swarming with activity. Émilie-Claire walked up the Rue Ramponeau watching men and women piling heavy paving bricks across the avenue to build a barricade. Others were maneuvering cannons into place. They hadn't asked yet for her furniture to top the barricade with bristling broken wood but that would come. The red flags were in place. There were shouts of "Vive Paris! Vive la Commune!"

Émilie-Claire had no way of recognizing some of the women working on the barricade of course, but along with members of Louis Michel's newly organized Comité de Vigilance de Montmartre, the tall figure of Paule Minck moved through the street shouting orders and Victorine Brocher heaved paving stones up on to the barricade. Minck had opened a free school in the Church of Saint Pierre de Montmartre and Brocher ran a cooperative bakery. Both were active in the IWA.

Did Émilie-Claire feel a sense of guilt at not participating in the defense of Paris—the defense, that is, of the Commune of Paris? Perhaps, but she was appalled by the things she had heard about certain woman radicals, the ones they called pétroleuses, who were poised to throw bottles containing petroleum or paraffin into the basements of buildings to start fires. There were also rumors of plans to dump the tons of gunpowder liberated by the Guard into the sewers under Paris with the aim of blowing the city up. Much of this was myth concocted to instill terror, but you never knew.

On the First of April the Commune and the National Guard came together in a meeting in which it was decided they should take an offensive position against the growing threat of the Army of Versailles. Thus five battalions of the Guard crossed the Seine at Neully and attacked Versailles troops who had been skirmishing around the outskirts of Paris. The regulars in the Versailles Army easily repulsed the onslaught. There were only about a dozen casualties from the fighting, but another precedent was set by the commanders on both sides: prisoners caught carrying weapons were now to be shot.

Two days later the Guardsmen tried again. This time a larger force made it all the way to the edge of Versailles where several National Guard forts were now occupied by the regular army. They came under heavy fire and were forced to flee back to Paris in failure. Again prisoners were executed. The leaders of Commune, incensed by the brutal treatment of their fellows did what they could do best: they issued a decree. The decree stated that anyone suspected of complicity with Versailles would be arrested and held as a hostage. Further, in the event that a prisoner of war was executed by Versailles, the Commune would retaliate by executing three of the hostages. Among those taken hostage by the Commune were Abbé

Deguerry, the Curé of the Madeleine church, and Georges Darboy, the Archbishop of Paris.

François Arnaud Gardinier was lonely. Château des Ternes was nearly empty now that Phoebe had left him and his daughter, Jeanne-Alice, was playing nurse in the city. His servants had left, either to join the regular army or the Gard Nationale, or by any other means to leave Paris before the Germans came. His cook remained but did not live in the castle having a family of her own to care for when she was not on duty. Thus, François was alone save for his son, Geoffroy Pierre. Geoffroy had spent almost all of his formative years living in Berlin but, reluctantly, had been brought back to his birth home in Neuilly-sur-Seine. His unhappy homecoming had made him so severely depressed he rarely spoke. When he did, it was in guttural German. François had been threatening to throw him out of the house but when he saw how his ranting against the boy was affecting Phoebe he stopped. Too late to save his marriage, however.

François had his business of course, but there was little emotional reward in buying and importing cheap French wines. Most of the profits from this increased trade went to paying off the debt to Germany, but François knew how to skim just enough for himself to approximate his former standard of living. Now he was feeling more and more isolated. And with the communists taking over the city government even the wine business was at risk.

He stood at a window on the top floor of the castle where not long ago he had watched forces of the Prussian army marching toward Paris. And now another army had bridged the Seine and paraded before him: the Army of Versailles. And now it was his turn to cheer the invaders on just as Geoffroy had cheered on the Germans. Soon the Republic would be restored. Versailles would crush the insurrection and all would be right with the world once again.

On May 16, a bright and sunny Tuesday, the Column Vendôme fell, toppled by the Communes and the National Guard. Louis Michel was there and with her husband and a group of Communards posed for a photograph beside the broken statue of Napoleon I. An embankment of sand bags had surrounded the square, cables had been attached to the column and the tug of war began with the 73 foot column. It landed on the sand bags with a resounding thud and its bronze plates were scattered all along the Rue de la Paix—a fitting tribute to the fall of the Empire, yet not a realistic new paving for the Road to Peace. As a band played "La Marseillaise" and the "Chant du Départ," red flags were draped over the shattered column. Later, the metal was taken to be melted down and cast into coins.

Four days earlier, members of the Commune had gone to the home of Adolphe Thiers on the Place Saint-George in order to confiscate works of art and furniture. Thiers, who was now in Versailles, had refused to negotiate with the Commune in an exchange of hostages for the release of Blanqui. The looting attracted an angry mob which destroyed the house. This destruction was a preamble for the coming attacks by radical Communards and Guardsmen on key government buildings and other symbols of bourgeois power.

By the 21st of May the Army of Versailles had entered Paris. On the 23rd the Tuileries Palace was set on fire by the Communards; it burned for 3 days. The fire spread to the library of the Louvre which was destroyed completely. The art galleries were saved by heroic efforts of the museum curators and the firemen who battled the flames. A precedent had been set: buildings deemed symbolic of Bonapartism would be torched.

Palais Royal, Palais de l'Industrie, Hôtel de Ville, Barracks Napoléon, Ministère des Finances, Theatre of Porte St. Martin, Théâtre du Chatelet, Théâtre Lyrique, Caisse Municipale, Théâtre des Del. Comiques, The Arsenal, Barracks d'Orsay, Palace of Légion d'Honneur—all would go up in flames. The Church of the Madeleine, The Triumphal Arch, Church of Saint Eustache, Hospital of Lariboisière, Prison of La Roquette, Tower of St. Jacques, Place de la Concorde, Column of July, Palace of the Luxembourg, Odéon Theatre, Church of the Pantheon—all would be damaged to some extent. Some by shot and shell, some by the action of radical incendiaries, but the result was the same: the City of Lights was a casualty of civil war.

Barricade à l'angle des boulevard Voltaire et Richard-Lenoir pendant la Commune de Paris de 1871.

Byron Grush

25

La Semaine Sanglante

Yes,—to arms! Let Paris bristle with barricades, and from behind these improvised ramparts let her shout to her enemies the cry of war, its cry of fierce pride of defiance, and of victory; for Paris with her barricades is invincible.
—the Commune and the Committee for Public Safety, May 22, 1871

What you call freedom is what the people call oppression and crime. The people no longer want to feed it with their flesh and blood.
—Louis Auguste Blanqui

I have seen criminals and whores
And spoken with them. Now I inquire
If you believe them made as now they are
To drag their rags in blood and mire
Preordained, an evil race?

You to whom all men are prey
Have made them what they are today.
—Louise Michel

The Bloody Week! On Sunday morning, May 21, 60,000 troops of the Army of Versailles under the command of Marshall MacMahon entered the city of Paris through an unguarded section of the city wall at Point-du-Jour.

Solidarity! All over France there was sympathy for the struggle going on in Paris. The Red Flag flew in many towns and provinces: in Rouen, in Le Havre, in Grenoble, in Nîmes, in Bordeaux, in Périgueux, in Varilhes, in La Charité-sur-Loire, in Cosne et in Saint-Amand, in Voiron, in Tullins, and in Saint-Marcellin. "Long live the Commune!" they shouted. "Down with Versailles!"

Bells rang throughout the city and the call to arms echoed in every neighborhood. Before Haussmann's remake of the Paris, during the previous insurrection, the narrow winding streets and strategically placed barricades had presented an excellent defense against the enemies of the People. But now, the Communards struggled to erect more barricades and found the widened boulevards detrimental to their security. Individual districts which had formed with their own committees and assets were fighting separately, without support from each other. They were outnumbered by the invading Versailles Army nearly 5 to 1.

Louise Michel was stationed at the barricade on Place Blanche along the Boulevard de Clichy at the foot of Montmartre. She was part of a women's battalion that had been hastily organized from within members of the Commune. They had pulled paving bricks from the streets to make the foundation of the barricade and piled sandbags on top of that. There were openings for two of the cannons which had been wheeled down from Montmartre but it was doubtful that anyone knew how to operate them. Louise found herself often in charge, a roll from which she did not shy. She had discovered throughout the struggle that she was a good organizer and a passionate one. Others looked to her for inspiration.

Arianne Mercier had been inspired by Louise Michel and so agreed to help build the barricade. Arianne had in turn convinced Phoebe Stapleton Gardinier to contribute her sweat to the project as well. Thus both Red Cross volunteers were present at the finishing ceremonies as the red flags of the Commune were placed on top of the barricade where sticks of broken furniture bristled and members of the women's battalion were positioning themselves to watch the road. And they were present when a wagon load of rifles arrived to be passed out among the warriors.

"I don't know how to operate a gun," said Phoebe. "And I wouldn't be able to shoot anyone."

"I can shoot," said Arianne. "I went hunting with my father many times when I was a girl. This can't be much different. Just bigger game."

"How can you joke about something like that?" Phoebe asked.

"Well, could you help with loading the guns during the battle?"

"I don't want to be anywhere near a battle. I'm going home."

But she was stopped by Louise Michel who told her to please help unload the wagon of rifles and be quick about it. It was hard to refuse the woman who seemed so able to command. Phoebe fell to the task. Maybe I can learn how to load a gun, she thought to herself. It wouldn't be like killing anyone.

There were barricades now in the Square Saint-Jacques, at Notre-Dame de Lorette, at Trinity, at La Chapelle, at the Bastille, at Buttes Chaumont, and on the Boulevard Saint-Michel as well as other strategic locations. After entering the city at the Point-du-Jour the Versailles Army had taken the fortifications there easily and had begun to advance. They searched houses and arrested members of the National Guard who they promptly took to the cemetery at Longchamp and shot. There were rumors that they had also murdered women and children and old men in the hospitals, but perhaps these were just rumors.

The Versaillais had taken over most of the 15th and 16th arrondissements and now were converging on the 17th in the Batignolles. An advance brigade was positioned at the Place de Clichy, just a stone's throw from the barricade at the Place Blanche where Phoebe was beginning to regret having taken on the job of ammunition loader. The wooden cases of bullets were heavy, heavier than the paving stones she had lifted an hour ago. Her arms ached and her frock was damp with sweat.

The first volley came soon and the women's brigade returned fire from their higher positions, now and then hitting an enemy combatant, but for the most part they were just wasting bullets. The regulars in the Versailles Army were slow to deploy, purposely, as this was intended to unnerve the Communards. They shot at the barricade in order to make the Communards take cover while they maneuvered their cannons up the Boulevard de Clichy.

Phoebe handed a loaded Chassepot rifle up to Arianne Mercier who was hanging by one arm from a piece of cabinet wood at the top of the barricade. Arianne hefted the rifle up and swung around to take aim at the approaching Versaillais. Before she could fire, three bullets ripped through her and she fell, landing near Phoebe, crumpled and twisted into a nonhuman shape. Phoebe rushed to her but the woman's soul had fled from her body.

Angered by seeing her friend so brutally annihilated, Phoebe took up the rifle and climbed the barricade, determined to avenge Arianne. As she reached the top she hesitated and took cover behind the broken door of an old armoire. This had the shattered remnants of a beveled mirror still attached and by peering into this she could see the battlefield below. She still didn't understand exactly how the rifle worked so when she took aim and squeezed the trigger, nothing happened. She yelled out a fine string of French swear words.

In the mirror she could see that the Versailles soldiers were readying a cannon. In her anxiety she believed it to be aimed directly at her. She saw the smoke before she heard the roar of the cannon blast. The cannon ball hit the barricade a few feet below her. The impact threw her back and off the barricade and she landed in a heap on the street below. Dazed, she was certain she had broken ribs and had suffered lacerations that dripped blood. Just before loosing consciousness, Phoebe shuddered at the realization that the Versaillais didn't take prisoners—they only detained them long enough to line them up against a wall and shoot them!

One by one the barricades were falling. Paris police and gendarmes collaborated with the Versaillais and pointed out Communards and their supporters. Hundreds were being executed after short tribunals. Thousands were being sent to Versailles to stand trial and eventual exportation. There were retaliations. On May 23, Jules Bergeret, a former military commander of the Commune, sent a squad of a dozen men to set fire to the Tuileries Palace in order to rid Paris of the last vestiges of royalty. The dome was blown up with explosives. The fire spread to the Louvre.

On the Rue Truffault a woman carrying a tin milk can was stopped by a gendarme. He examined the can to discover that it contained not milk, but petroleum. "She is a pétroleuse!" he exclaimed. The woman made a hasty retreat down an alley, abandoning her fire bomb, but the gendarme emptied his revolver into her.

The barricades on the Rue de Rivoli and the Rue de la Coutellrie were still holding strong; the Hôtel de Ville was in flames and the fire threatened to spread into the neighborhood where the last defenses of that district were weakening. Cries of "Vive la République! Vive la Liberté! Vive l'Humanité!" resounded.

On Montmartre a group of seven insurgents was surrounded and ordered to lay down their arms. One drew a pistol and shot one of the soldiers in the leg. The seven were taken to a hole and dropped down into it, then shot. People on the street seen carrying guns or even having hands blackened by gunpowder were lined up against walls and executed. The sight of blood and brains in the gutters became commonplace.

The Central Committee of the Commune authorized the destruction of private property as well as public buildings such as the Ministry of War. Tickets were pasted on the walls of houses that were to be targeted by pétroleuses. These small, postage stamp-sized documents pictured a bacchante's head and the letters, B.P.B. for "bon pour brûler," (good for burning). Pétroleuses were to be paid ten francs for each house they fired.

At the Théâtre du Châtele, the Versaillais set up a court-martial. Captured guardsmen were brought before it in groups of twenty, judged to be guilty, then marched out to the square and placed before a mitrailleuse machine gun which spit death into them with a ratcheting sound that could be heard for miles. A stable on the Rue Saint-Denis was used to store corpses.

Émilie-Claire Lebeau-Richelieu watched out the window of her apartment as the barricade on the Rue Ramponeau came under attack. Belleville had always been a stronghold for the Communards. Yet there were some, Émilie-Claire knew, like that M. Blanchard on the first floor, who, if and when the barricade fell, would be among the first to hang the tricolor flag from their window. Already there were Guardsmen who wore an arm band showing they had changed sides…what was the expression? Turncoats? Which side would Jean-Léon have been on, she wondered. Probably neither. And both sides would have had reasons to put him up against a wall. It was a blessing he was not here, although his actual fate might even have been worse.

There was a knock on her door. It was Jeanne-Alice, with the looks of anxiety, fear, grief, and worry mingled on her face. Her hair was in disarray. Her frock was blood-stained and dirty. Only the Red Cross arm band was pristine.

"Jeanne-Alice! How did you get past the fighting in the street? Are you hurt? Do you need anything?" Émilie-Claire was concerned by the condition of the girl's dress and her contorted expression.

"They…both sides…are thankfully still acknowledging the Red Cross and passing us through. Although they searched me for bombs and weapons…thoroughly, I might add."

"What news is there? Is Paris destroyed?"

"It is burning here and there and the ashes float through the air and settle on the sweaty faces of the combatants. It isn't just the fighting that is brutal. Each side has taken to mass executions! The Communards have even shot Georges Darboy, the Archbishop of Paris!"

"Phoebe?"

"She was at the barricade at Place Blanche. She was wounded. I was able to get her and some others to the hospital at Saint-Sulpice."

"Thank God!"

"But those taken prisoner may not fare well. Louise Michel was among them."

An explosion shook the building. Émilie-Claire and Jeanne-Alice rushed to the window. Smoke was rising from the barricade; a gapping hole had been blown in the middle of it and troops of the Versailles Army were pouring through.

"Looks like there will be some more work for me," said Jeanne-Alice.

"Wait until I get my Red Cross arm band and I'll come with you," said Émilie-Claire. Maybe now I can do some good, she thought, for someone besides myself.

Père-Lachaise Cemetery, May 27, 1871

It is the last holdout of the Commune. The men and women of the uprising, termed the Fédérés by the Versaillais, are spread out among the tombs of the elite and the wealthy and the famous; the dead providing protective cover for the living. From behind Gothic-themed mausoleums that seem to have sprouted like giant mushrooms of stone on the hillsides and along the cobbled paths the Fédérés peer out at the soldiers who search to destroy them. When the opportunity arises they leap out with brandished knife in hand and slash at the enemy.

The bust of Honoré de Balzac looks sternly down upon the scene from its pedestal on his grave. He has been interred here for twenty years and he thinks he has seen everything. But now Frenchman clashes with Frenchman in an inhuman comedy. If he could, he would shut his eyes in shame for his countrymen. Victor Noir, shot by Prince Pierre Bonaparte is here also; a bronze sculpture of the murdered man is laid out on a slab in a pose that suggests he has just fallen, fully clothed, with his hat lying next to him. The hat is filled with flowers. The area of his crotch, a bit more raised than propriety would normally desire, has been polished by the rubbing of women who believe touching the region of his supposed sexual arousal will guarantee childbirth for them. His tragic repose only echoes the fate of the embattled.

The bones of the ill-fated lovers, Abélard and Héloise, are mingled here in an elaborate tomb topped by a Gothic sepulchral chapel where stone effigies of the couple lie next to one another, their hands clasped in prayer, their bodies dressed as at the end of their days—he in his monk's robes, she in her nun's habit. Their story of intense love and forced separation and the famous correspondence between them has attracted modern romantics who place love letters at the tomb. Now chassepots with bayonets attached poke out from the decorative arches.

The language of the dead is silence—save for the creak of a wind-blown crypt door or the rattle of bare branches against a scarred tomb. Those lurking amongst the monuments also make little noise—except perhaps a breath drawn deep and raspy or a groan of an empty stomach. Soon the gurgle of death throws will join the serene and subtle conversation between quick and still. And now and then is heard a crack of gun shot and a corresponding screech that abruptly cancels the intonation like an exclamation mark.

Even on the most sunny of days the graveyard is draped with shadow. Shadows that are still; shadows that move about. One small shadow darts along a path and stops behind the tomb of Jean-Babtiste Moliére. A great dark sarcophagus sits high on a pedestal;

the bulk of the monument offers cover for the shadow, who is a youth—really just a boy. He hears movement on the other side of the tomb: the cocking of a rifle. Carefully, he peers around the side of the tomb. Luckily he has picked the approach that puts him at the other soldier's back. He draws his knife and plunges it into the soldier. His victim staggers but does not fall. The boy strikes again and again until at last the man is still, a rumpled heap in a pool of blood at the foot of the monument to the great playwright.

Next to Moliére is the tomb of the writer, Jean de La Fontaine, teller of fanciful fables. The shadow flits past this and heads down the avenue toward the chapel. In his search for errant soldiers, isolated and therefore vulnerable, he will pass by the last resting places of Frédéric Chopin, Jacques Louis David, Jean Auguste Dominique Ingres, the banker James Baron de Rothschild, the balloonist Etienne Robertson, the composer Vincenzo Bellini, Eugéne Delacroix, and Théodore Géricault whose sculptural likeness will scowl down at him from his perch where he reclines, palette and brushes in hand.

The shadow boy is sneaking around the side of an old mausoleum, intent on striking another blow for the Commune. A lone soldier is idling beside the statue of a hooded figure, gloomy and ominous in its stark, simple lines. If you looked inside the cowl it wore to see its face of sadness you would see only an empty space, a dark and foreboding eternity of emptiness. The soldier leans against this, oblivious to the approach of the assassin shadow.

Now he looks up, discarding the pipe he had been trying to keep lit, and sees the boy. The boy's stealth has been faulty; he has attracted attention from another group of soldiers who are nearby. The boy suddenly finds himself surrounded. Bayonets point at him. Yet there is no commotion, only the quiet sense of understanding that this is the end for the shadow boy. They do not kill him…yet. They march him to the east side of the cemetery where awaits a wall. A simple wall of moss-covered brick. A wall pockmarked with tiny craters, the effect of projectile upon stone. Projectile slowed in its advance by live flesh.

There is already a pile of bodies which have been dragged to one side to await transportation to an open pit some distance away. The pit contains nearly 800 bodies layered neatly in rows and sprinkled with lye. The boy joins a group of Fédérés who stand with backs against the wall. There are two women and a small child among them. Some of the men thus arrayed cross their arms against their chests, a display of defiance and solidarity. The boy looks at the line of soldiers facing them with rifles pointing. Some among them are younger then himself.

147 men, women and children will have been executed against that wall by the end of the day. It is the end of the Commune. The end of the insurrection. The end of the Bloody Week. But it is not the end of the bloodshed.

Byron Grush

26

Traumatized in Paradise

Excerpt from: *Dame Impétueux, la Mémoire de Émilie-Claire Lebeau-Richelieu*, (English translation, published by Charles W. Karr & Co., Chicago, 1897)

I thought for sure I had lost my dear sweet Phoebe. Jeanne-Alice had taken her to the hospital at the seminary at Saint-Sulpice. At the first opportunity I hurried there to collect her but found that the Versailles troops had captured the seminary and executed the hospital staff, doctors and nurses, including Dr. Faneau who ran the ambulances, and all 80 of the patients! I searched for her through the bodies but did not find her.

There were massacres everywhere. 300 had been caught in La Madeleine Church and were gunned down mercilessly. Women suspected of being pétroleuses were brutally bayoneted in the very streets where they lived and walked innocently to market. We heard that 42 men, 3 women and 4 children taken to the Rue des Rosiers were forced to kneel and were shot in front of that same wall where the generals, General Lecomte and General Thomas, had been executed in March. Eugene Varlin who had been a member of the International and very influential in the Commune was among them. The director of the war effort for the Commune, Charles Delescluze was killed at Place du Château d'Eau; he was their only good strategist.

Of course, the Communards took their cruel revenge as well. The hostages being held at La Roquette prison were taken to the wall on the Rue Haxo and shot by a firing squad while people from that neighborhood looked on and cheered. Civilians suspected of working with Versailles were often shot in their homes. Even after the last barricade fell in Belleville and the Versailles troops patrolled the streets there were sharp-shooters installed on roof tops and balconies; they would pick off the soldiers one by one.

I only ramble on about atrocities to show the mood of the city after the fall of the Commune. Some were saying that the Communards were villains who burned the city out of spite and left us under the thumb of an equally evil set of villains. Some thought the Versaillais were cowards who had given the city to the Germans, then slaughtered their own people for no reason other than their lust for power. You could go to a café and be sitting next to someone with either attitude and never know what to say or do to avoid conflict. No one trusted anyone else.

Against this fated background I set out to find Phoebe. Where to start? I walked from the seminary around to the front of that magnificent church of Saint-Sulpice with its double colonnade of Doric columns and its twin towers that oddly don't match. Above the door the sign from the Revolution was still there: "Le Peuple Francais Reconnoit l'Etre Suprême et l'Immortalité de l'Âme" (The French people recognize the Supreme Being and the immortality of the soul). This was somewhat comforting after having experienced the Commune's rejection of the church for being in league with the Bonapartistes; and they executed the Archbishop.

An elderly woman sat on the steps beneath the colonnade. Her clothes were old and soiled and her face was lined and creased from worry. She worked her hands in the air in front of her as if she were sewing or knitting, but those hands were as empty as the look in her eyes. Cautiously, for I calculated that she might be deranged, I approached and quizzed her about the recent horrible happenings at the seminary. Were any patients saved, I wanted to know. She only moved her head in a slow rotation and I was unsure if this meant "yes" or "no." Then she raised her arm and pointed in the direction of the Luxembourg Palace.

Of course! The former residence of Marie de Médicis had been converted into a prison during the Revolution and more recently into legislative offices. There had been an ambulance there where many wounded men had been housed. A powder magazine positioned in the garden had exploded and damaged part of the roof, and the incendiaries encouraged by the Central Committee of the Commune had attempted to torch the building by drenching it with petroleum, but were stopped by the soldiers (and promptly executed). But it was still functional and was now being used by the new masters of the city for interrogations and tribunals. Might Phoebe have been taken there before the massacre?

It was only a short walk to the Luxembourg. The gardens were still cluttered with cannons and piles of ammunition and patrolled by soldiers of the Versailles Army and members of the National Guard who had come over to Versailles. I entered from the Rue Vaugirand and crossed through the cour d'honneur. The courtyard was filled with tents where I saw two or three soldiers busied with domestic chores such as sewing their garments or polishing their boots. No one stopped or challenged me.

I entered the building at the end of the courtyard and found myself in the cavernous space of the Salle des Conférences. Every surface was rich with gilded architectural elements: arches, freezes mimicking Grecian structures, statues of neo-classical style, and monumental paintings of historical scenes. It was truly the "Second Empire style" preferred by Napoleon III…gaudy and incoherently overdone (the Emperor had added this hall to the Palace). The romantic decadence of the Salle seemed far too opulent for state offices, but then, the French *are* the French.

There was a man seated at a desk who wanted to know where I thought I was going. I explained I was searching for a friend who may have been apprehended mistakenly. He replied that there were no mistakes and if such a person was a friend of mine I should be wary of joining them in their incarceration. It took a bit of smiling and complimenting him on his uniform before he softened and directed me to the council chambers where trials were being held.

There a scene that might have leaped from the pen of Victor Hugo presented itself. The council seats were filled with rag-tag persons of questionable character as well as better mannered men and women such as one might see at the market or strolling in one of the parks on a sunny day; all were apparently waiting to be paraded in front of the panel of judges who sat beneath a half-dozen statues of famous orators and statesmen. Signally or in small groups the detained were questioned, examined for evidence of powder on their hands or clothing, and after the brevity of that inquiry, were sentenced either to deportation or the firing squad. I did not witness anyone being released nor were any represented by a lawyer.

I determined that Phoebe was not among those waiting there, which did not give me much encouragement as she might have been previously processed by this inquisition. I saw that new groups were being led from another room to fill the empty spaces left by those who had been dealt with, whatever fate awaited them. I moved carefully to this doorway and waited until I felt I was unobserved before I entered.

It was the library, lined with what seemed to be thousands of volumes. High on the vaulted ceiling were wonderful paintings by Eugéne Delacroix. But huddled in collections of misery and despair were more prisoners…I say prisoners, because that was surely what this was: a prison! And I had wandered into it with no idea of how I was to get out.

I went from group to group looking in vain for Phoebe. I did not find her there. And then one of the worst moments of my life occurred. I was corralled together with four of the prisoners by guards who had seen me enter the library. Promptly we were escorted into the council chamber and lined up before the judges. The judges, four in number, set incredulous eyes upon me and singled me out for interrogation. It must have been the clothes I wore. Although they were my daily garb, they where more fashionable than what might adorn the average woman. They recognized me as someone of the aristocracy rather than someone of the working masses, and this undoubtedly made my situation more dire. So, even in front of a room of doomed revolutionaries who had taken an ill-fated stand against oppression, I pleaded my case in the most self-serving way.

"My name is Émilie-Claire Lebeau-Richelieu. I am the wife of Jean-Léon Richelieu who is an advisor to the Emperor. Do you think I would stand at the barricades in opposition to the army of France?"

"We have no love here for that deposed person," responded one of the judges. "You say your husband advised him? For that he could be accused of the crime of helping to lead our nation into a war we could not win."

"My husband advised him against the war. He was a true patriot in that way. He has been killed on the battle field, or so I must believe. I no longer support the Emperor."

"And where do you live, now that the Tuileries are a pile of ashes?"

"At 26 Rue Ramponeau."

"That's in Belleville, the hot seat of the Fédérés! And you maintain you had no collusion with the Reds?"

"There were many of us in Belleville who were neutral. As I said before, I am not one to stand upon the barricade and wave the red flag. I did help with the Red Cross after Belleville fell. That is why I am here. I am looking for a friend who also was a Red Cross volunteer who may have been caught up in the…what do you call this? The retaliation?"

I hated these men who would sit in judgment against people who had fought for their rights. Men who were ruthless and arrogant in their persecution of many who were actually innocent of their charges. It was the French Revolution all over again…but this time the guillotine had been burned. Yet I needed to control myself. The comment about "retaliation" was a dangerous one. The four men deliberated, whispering among themselves and nodding or shaking their heads. Finally:

"M. Martel, my esteemed colleague says he recognizes you from certain events of state he attended before the war. We agree, although two of us reluctantly, that your story is believable and that you are innocent of the insurrection. You are free to go."

I nearly swooned with relief. Now all I had to do was to leave the room, chased by the jeers and boos of that body of poor souls who awaited their own judgment. I ventured too near some of the crowd and a woman reached out to tear at my clothes. This was an even worse moment than standing before the judges had been. My sympathies were with these poor individuals, misguided though they may have been. But I was a coward and could not stand up for them.

And I still hadn't learned what fate might have overtaken Phoebe. I could picture her in front of those judges. She would not have pleaded innocence as I had done. Of even if she had her resolve would not have stood long against those belittling judges. I left that horrible court of retribution feeling as if I had betrayed Phoebe after the fact. I practically ran down the grand staircase to get away from the scene of my betrayal.

You may think I am being unduly hard on myself. Consider the contrast between my actions and those of "the Red Virgin of

Montmartre," Louise Michel, at her own trial (I learned of this much later and the learning of it awakened my guilt). *She* stood defiant before the judges, maintaining not her innocence, but her opposition to Versailles. She might be seen as being a Communard but those revolutionaries had nothing to do with the murders or the arsons, she said. She acted alone, she said. And she berated the judges as cowards: "If you let me live," she said, "I shall never stop crying for revenge and I shall avenge my brothers. If you are not cowards, kill me!"

They deported her to New Caledonia.

[Author's note: At this point in her narrative, Mme. Lebeau-Richelieu digresses into a long comparison of fashion styles in France versus those in England and America. She tends to ramble. While this may be interesting to some, it does nothing to further our story. So we will skip ahead to the next instance where she continues her search for Phoebe.]

Two weeks had passed and still I had no word of Phoebe. If she were alive, would she not have gotten in touch with me, even if she was incarcerated? Of course, if she had been placed on a prison ship bound for New Caledonia...

I could not turn to Jeffrey Flaherty for help as I had done in the past because Jeffrey was no longer in Paris. Once he saw the tide turning for the Commune, and knowing he could never go over to the Versaillais, he left for Calais, intending, I supposed, to take the boat train to England where he would be safe. I tried to persuade Teo to go with him, but because of his bad experiences in London, he declined. Would he leave Paris, perhaps for the south? Again he balked.

Finally, Teo slipped out of Paris before he could be arrested. I had promised to join him later...but now later was getting to be later and later and later. I would not go without Phoebe, and, to tell you the truth, I had great hopes that the turmoil would die down and Paris and the rest of France would begin to heal itself.

But watching the wagons traversing the streets with their loads of decaying bodies depressed me so! The smells, the flies, the fear of plague or worse! And it was not over. More trials, more executions, more reprisals. People mourned. People were afraid. Yet there were those who had escaped suspicion and who therefore exercised their God-given rights for leisure and the contemplation of philosophic truths and the indulgence of spirits at their favorite cafés. Zola was one.

I found him at the Café Guerbois, seated at a table near the back, expounding upon his theories of naturalism and environmental influences to a not-so-rapt audience of two: his wife, Gabrielle, and the art collector, Dr. Paul Gachet. I was actually looking for Manet who had not been at his workshop, but I supposed that Zola would have to do as I desperately needed help. He might have some information about Phoebe's possible hereabouts, being that he was a journalist.

Émile Zola had been outspoken in his criticism of the Commune. He had advocated the shooting of "those who burn and who massacre" at first, but now it seemed he sang a somewhat different tune.

"We are getting sick of these executions," he was saying. "They are shooting everyone including innocent people. It may be ages before the nightmares subside and our people can purge themselves of their fears and hatreds of each other."

"Well it's very well and fine to talk," said Dr. Gachet, "but what can one do to help the situation? If you support the Fédérés in any way you put yourself at risk. Extracting the innocent from those condemned is no easily accomplished feat!"

"That is exactly why I am here," I interjected, trying to get Zola's attention. "I think my friend Phoebe Stapleton Gardinier has been taken into custody. She may by now be dead or deported. And she is as innocent as…"

"The driven snow? A new-born babe? A dove, a lamb, a new-laid egg, a cloistered nun, the immaculate conception? Or as Balzac would say, as innocent as angels?"

"I was going to say, as innocent as milk…and as pure and devoted and loving and…"

"And why do you ask me about this Phoebe Gardner?"

"Gardinier. I thought you might know something about where people are kept when they are wounded or disabled in some way. She fell from a barricade and was in shock. Taken to the hospital at Saint-Sulpice just before the massacre, but she wasn't part of the deaths there…I checked."

"You say she fell from a barricade but she was *pure as milk!*"

"It's complicated. Can't you help me? You are a good friend of Manet's and he and I were…"

"Also good friends. Why don't you look in the Pitié-Salpêtrière Hospital on the Île-de France? They may have taken her there if she was incapable of standing trial."

"Isn't that an asylum for hysterical women and prostitutes?"

"Not entirely. Ask Dr. Gachet."

I looked at Dr. Gachet but he avoided my eyes by turning his head and pretending to signal the waiter. It was a horrible thought…and a slim chance, but probably my last resort. I thanked Émile and took my leave of the two men and Gabrielle. (Gabrielle was Zola's ex-mistress and only recently had married him. She had been silent throughout my pleading with Zola…apparently that was a role she was used to portraying.)

London had its Bedlam; Paris had its Pitié-Salpêtrière. The institution began life as an arsenal for storing the saltpeter used in the making of gunpowder. It evolved into a maison d'internment for the poor, the destitute, and women of the streets who received a modicum of medical care, but who nonetheless were deposited there for various reasons that often smacked of the punishment of isolation and alienation for the crime of being "abnormal" or socially unacceptable—or possibly, their husbands were just tired of them. Women could be diagnosed with "hysteria" and sent to Pitié-Salpêtrière for treatment. This included a portion of the day out in the fresh air in the courtyard, albeit chained to a bench. The conditions were patently deplorable.

There were reforms underway, I was told, due to the influence of a Dr. Jean-Martin Charcot who was a pioneer in the study of nervous disorders. The terrible medieval atmosphere of the place was being modernized with laboratories and other facilities so Salpêtrière was becoming a teaching hospital of sorts. Still there were rumors of rats running wild through the halls at night and the screams of the inmates echoing even into the neighboring avenues.

It was a huge place. I didn't know where to begin, so I began at the front desk where a woman sat eating an apple an eyeing me as if I were some new strain of germ. It turned out she could actually be civil after I explained I was looking for a friend who might be being treated here. She tossed the half-eaten apple into a waste basket and took a large ledger from a drawer and paged through it. To my surprise and to the conflicted combination of joy and dread that possessed me at that moment, she found an entry for a Mme. Gardinier.

"Diagnosis hysteria," she said. "Patient of Dr. Charcot. East wing. Bonne journée."

With some difficulty I found my way to the east wing. I passed rooms with locked doors behind from which a dreadful crying or shouting issued. I passed patients…or, more properly, inmates…in the hallways dressed in dirty smocks who cowered in corners or leaned against the walls clawing at their own bodies. The expressions on the faces of these women unnerved me. They were all women…Salpêtrière is only for women: sad women, destitute women, hysterical women, unwanted women.

Near the end of the hallway I was traversing stood a wooden stand holding a placard. It was next to a door, slightly ajar, which led to a room where, through the opening, I could just make out an assembly of men seated on chairs, silently watching with great awe something which was taking place in front of them, unseen by me from that vantage point. The placard read:

A Demonstration
Of the Technique of
Animal Magnetism of
Doctor Mesmer and its Affect
Upon Hysteria
Presented by Dr. Charcot
One O'clock Prompt

I pushed open the door. I had never seen such a collection of facial hair! Mutton chops, long beards, short beards, mustaches that drooped, mustaches that were twirled into points. At the front of the room stood a stout man, presumably Dr. Charcot. He alone of those present sported no beard, mustache or sideburns. He had a broad forehead and swept-back gray hair that gave him a distinguished appearance. With one hand he gestured as he spoke…the term "hypnotism" was central to his lecture. With the other arm he held up a woman who had apparently swooned. She was dressed somewhat indecently in underclothing which partly exposed her breasts. This semi-erotic tableau had the attention of the men, of course. I was shocked. It took me moments to recognize the mesmerized woman: it was Phoebe!

27

Healing in Provence

"But she is my best subject! I can not let her go. I have many demonstrations to give of my technique. Hysterical women make the best subjects for hypnotism."

Dr. Jean-Martin Charcot sat at one end of a long table of ebonized wood with Arabesque designs of inlaid mother of pearl along its edges. Émilie-Claire and François Arnaud Gardinier sat at the other end, their faces reflecting as blurs in the polished black surface. Émilie-Claire had persuaded Gardinier to accompany her to the Pitié-Salpêtrière hospital to rescue Phoebe. He was still her husband, although they had separated, so his influence would be paramount to obtaining her release.

"What if she won't come back to me?" François had protested when Émilie-Claire had approached him with her request.

"You would leave her in that awful place to punish her for rejecting you? How inhuman!"

She had shamed him into cooperating and now the two of them faced the prominent doctor who seemed to desire to keep Phoebe for his own purposes. Could she also shame the good doctor?

"Phoebe does not strike me as a hysterical woman," she said to him. "I've known her for many years and she has always been steadfast and calm."

"She was brought here in a state of delirium. No doubt a trauma stemming from her experience on the barricades."

"She looked quite calm and relaxed when I saw her yesterday."

"That is the effect of the hypnotism."

"So she is cured then? There is no reason not to release her into her husband's custody. He can observe her better than you and your staff can. If there is any relapse he can…"

"I can see that you are adamant. Be aware that outside of this hospital she is at risk from the police who believe her to have been a Communard. She could be picked up again."

"They will not come near her at Château des Ternes," said François Gardinier. "I have the means to hire medical help if it is needed. I insist you release my wife at once."

"And if I refuse?"

"I have friends in high places…they know where my loyalties lie. They can be very helpful to your program here…or just the opposite."

It was two full days before Phoebe was released to her husband's custody. It was only one short day after that before Phoebe arrived once again on Émilie-Claire's doorstep. Phoebe was distraught. She trembled and Émilie-Claire cradled her in her arms as one would a small child.

"I can't be with that monster." Phoebe cried. "I hate the man. I hate this town. Take me away!"

Émilie-Claire knew that distance was the answer. Distance could cure. Distance could save. "We'll go south," she said. "To Aix-en-Provence or maybe Marseille…the ocean air and all that."

The following morning the two women, with bags bulging and a picnic basket stuffed with cold game hen, assorted cheeses, and a bottle of decent Bordeaux, stepped up into a carriage bound for the Gare Lyon where they would board the train for Marseille. During the trip south they made the acquaintance of a matronly lady, a Mme. Paget, who extolled the virtues of a certain town, much smaller and more peaceful, where lived a distant cousin she was on her way to visit. At Avignon they changed trains for Arles.

Camden Place, at Chislehurst in Kent, July 10, 1871

Louis Napoleon had been released from Wilhelmshohe Castle in March. Because of the revolt taking place in Paris he could not return there, nor to Versailles where his presence would certainly have caused an uproar. He left for Camden Place in England to join the

Empress Eugène and their son, Prince Napoléon Eugène Louis Jean Joseph Bonaparte, known as the Prince Imperial. The British viewed the Royal family with more regard than did the French at this period. Even Queen Victoria visited Camden Place which now had become the centre of the French Royal Court (in exile).

Under a towering oak near the entrance to the big house the carriages of a visiting entourage were parked. Waiting in the shade under the watchful eyes of drivers and footmen, the horses munched on oats from feed bags and flicked their tails at flies. While inside Camden Place, in the splendidly furnished country house that resembled a classic French Château, festivities were underway honoring the visit of Princess Beatrice, the youngest child of Queen Victoria and Prince Albert.

Previously, there had been talk of a marriage between Beatrice and the Prince Imperial. Now that the Royal family was in exile, that possibility was dubious, but Beatrice remained attracted to the Prince. The visit had been made upon her request and the Queen, who was opposed to seeing her youngest daughter leave the nest, had only reluctantly agreed.

It was unseasonably hot, even for Kent. The party migrated outside to the back terrace where tables had been set up under huge umbrellas which had been imported from India and had tassels that hung from their edges quietly waiting for a breeze. Silver bowls holding iced bottles of champagne were surrounded by crystal goblets. The British guests sat around the tables speaking in their best French, a circumstance which their hosts politely endured. The Prince and the Princess strolled together through the gardens.

A lone figure stood unseen in the thick shrubbery a short distance from the terrace. His hand held a loaded pistol. Patiently he waited for sight of the Emperor. He had come a long way. He was obsessed with this man who had caused the downfall of his adopted country and who yet lounged in luxury and had the praise of the elite and the powerful. Perhaps Louis Napoleon was not alone in blame for the destruction of the lives and the liberties and the happiness of the innocent. But it was useful to focus hatred against him. It afforded the opportunity for action. And hatred without action only led to depression. And depression killed from the inside.

Jeffrey Flaherty could kill this object of his obsessive anger and rid himself of these terrible feelings of helplessness and dread. Jeffrey

Flaherty could raise the pistol and aim once the former ruler showed his face. Jeffrey Flaherty could pull the trigger and make a statement to the world that evil could be destroyed if the meek would only act. And if by acting he would become just as evil?

Sweat rolled down his face. His hand shook from having gripped the pistol tightly for so long. He watched and waited and then, from the doorway into the house came the man, dressed in his royal way with medals and sash and a ceremonial sword hung at his waist. On his face a forced smile failed to disguise the physical pain of the stone in his bladder. Here came the man who had ruled France for twenty years. Here came the man who had survived numerous assassination attempts. Here came the man who had waged war with Russia, with Italy, with Mexico, with China, and with Prussia.

Jeffrey slowly raised the pistol and sighted down the barrel. This was the moment. Now was the time. Suddenly a large bird (could it have been an owl?) took flight from a nearby tree. Louis Napoleon turned his head and followed it with his eyes, providing Jeffrey with a perfect profile. He aimed at the man's temple. But now he saw Napoleon III no longer as a symbol but as a man. He was about to kill a man. He lowered the pistol and it dropped from his fingers to the ground. Jeffrey walked away, through the trees and bushes, past the waiting carriages, and up the road toward the town of Chislehurst. He had made his decision: he wasn't a killer.

Excerpt from Émilie-Claire's Daily Journals

August 3, 1871—Arles

   What a delightful small town…especially after the turmoil and dust and dirt and death of Paris! Death…well, there is the presence of death here too, but in the form of the old Roman ruins they call the Alyscamps Necropolis. Outside of town some roads are lined with the tombs of the ancient Romans, overgrown with vegetation, and often occupied by rodents. No one has been buried here since Renaissance times. It is the very picture of romantic morbidity.

   Phoebe and I have been here a week now and we prefer our walks to be through the Jardin d'Eté, a delightful park with fountains and tree-lined paths— not as grandiose as those of Paris, of course, but relaxing and full of color and life. Children play here and there are dogs. Dogs! No longer are there those gentle companions of mankind in Paris; they have all been eaten!

Luncheon at the Dead Rat

There is a Roman coliseum just down the Rue Porte de Laure from the park. A ruin, but maintained by the Arles townspeople as an arena for their bullfights which they hold every weekend. As you pass by it during one of these festivals you can hear the shouts of the crowd seated upon three tiers of old stone and see the colorful scarves of the women being waved above their heads. I have not felt it would be prudent to attend a bullfight with or without Phoebe. We have seen too much blood in recent times.

There are many cafés and restaurants on the Rue Voltaire where the buildings have retained their charm without the modernization we have seen in Paris. One of our favorite restaurants is on the corner of the Rue Amédée Pichot and the Rue Léon Blum. They offer a surprisingly good cuisine. It is the Restaurant Carrel, owned by Albert Carrel and his wife, Cathérine Carrel-Garcin. We had fish there with a garlicky rouille sauce and a salade niçoise with eggs, anchovies and those gorgeous big green olives. Cathérine was a great host and offered to rent us a room above the restaurant but we had already found lodgings at the Hôtel de l'Amphithéâtre on the Rue Diderot. It is so called because it is within spitting distance of the coliseum and another old first century Roman amphitheater, the Theatre Antique d'Arles where are held plays and concerts...and the occasional bullfight.

While I am on the subject of cafés I should mention the Café de la Gare at the Place Lamartine run by Joseph-Michel Ginoux and his wife Marie. The café society here is so different from that of Paris. This one is open all night and becomes the refuse of "night prowlers" and you might say low life of all kinds. Yet visit it by day (as we have) and you find the proprietors to be friendly and accommodating and, well, very entertaining. The café interior has bright red walls and a green ceiling which seem to vibrate in the gas light. The central furnishing is a large table for the game of billiards, or pool I think it is called. Outside there is a long yellow awning which shades tables during the day's harsh sunlight. It is lit up at night and illuminates the whole narrow street with a gay glow.

Oh, I am beginning to sound like a travel brochure! "Be sure to stop at the...etc." Well, we have explored this charming hamlet from end to end and found it to be serene and seeped in history and peopled with a tolerant population who will stop to chat with strangers like us. Some ask, upon learning we have recently come from Paris, what is the situation now. We say little. We are here to escape the memories.

Today we ventured onto the bridge called the Pont de Trinquetaille which is made of iron and spans the Rhône River. As we stood, looking out across the river at the azure horizon, I tried to ascertain the state of Phoebe's recovery by skirting around the edges of certain topics we have avoided until now. I knew her history up to the incident on the barricade and from her rescue at the hospital, but the time in between was a blank. I wasn't sure she hadn't repressed her recollection of that transition because any mention of it brought a look of confusion to her face.

Below us on the river small boats scurried to and fro. Fishermen, I supposed, or maybe they were transporting goods up the river. They wore colorful clothes and some of them sang with an accent I couldn't decipher. There are so many colors here…houses painted orange or yellow with red roofs, lime trees of pale green, gardens of chrysanthemums in yellow and red and gold.

I probed Phoebe for her thoughts. What did she remember of her time at Saint-Sulpice? No reaction. Then her vacuous expression took on form as her brows knitted and the ends of her mouth turned down. She was remembering something. Then she seemed to brighten.

"He came for me."

"He? Who was he?"

"The doctor. I was frightened. I didn't know where I was or why I was there, except it was sort of a hospital and my head ached something terrible. He talked to me in the most gentle voice and I…I calmed. I seemed to sleep but I was awake, wasn't I? He took me out of there. Then I was at the other place."

"The Pitié-Salpêtrière hospital."

"I don't know. I guess so. And he put me in front of many men in a big room and I was afraid again. But he could talk to me in that gentle voice and I was asleep/awake again."

"Did anyone touch you or do anything to you that you didn't want them to do?"

"No. But it was strange. I had dreams…awake dreams. And I remembered things from long ago. My first husband. My father. Those times seemed so very real, but they couldn't have been, could they?"

"You were being hypnotized. That made you relive those memories. Were they good memories?"

At this point Phoebe froze up again and stared off into the distance. I had made some progress, but there was more work to do. Gentle work…as gentle as the doctor's voice.

Tomorrow I want to travel into the country to see the olive groves and the fields of wild sunflowers. The golden fields of grain and the canal that flows past the road. There is a little bridge over the canal that makes you feel you are in Japan or China or some other exotic place. Phoebe is healing, although slowly. The warm sun and that brilliant blue sky are the best medicine there could possibly be for her. And for me.

Rouen, some weeks earlier

As much of Paris lay bleeding, Teo Presume had slipped away by night. There were still Prussian soldiers in the north of the city and gangs of Versaillais patrolled the streets, looking for Communards. He left the way the army had entered: across the Seine at Point-du-Jour. From here he had walked, following the meandering river, through the towns of Aubergenville, Mantes-la-Jolie, and Giverny, stopping at these for food or shelter. No stranger to a walking tour, he kept to the smaller roads and avoided people. At Vernon he found a barge that was heading up the Seine and he convinced the captain, a Greek named Zacharias Dimitriou, of his experience as a cabin boy crossing the Atlantic (which was partly true). Dimitriou took him on, not as cabin boy, but as a deckhand.

One week later, after what for anyone not indentured to labor with heavy ropes and scrub buckets would have been a pleasure cruise, they sailed under the medieval stone Mathilde Bridge at Rouen from which, in 1431, the ashes of Joan of Arc had been dumped into the river. After navigating along grass-cover banks beyond which fields of apple trees rose gently toward chalk cliffs hung with ancient yew and the occasional castle, past small villages of half-timbered houses with thatched roofs, steering among small boats—bateax à rames filled with cheeses or the cages of chickens and ducks, the barge came to dock at the Grand Port Maritime de Rouen. Tomorrow, said Captain Dimitriou, they would continue on to Le Havre at the edge of the English Channel, change cargo, and then return to Paris. Teo considered his situation and his aching muscles and decided to jump ship.

Victor Hugo called it "La Ville de cent Clochers" (the city of 100 bell towers). It had once been under the sway of the English; William the Conqueror held court there; Richard the Lionheart was crowned Duke of Normandy in Rouen; Joan of Arc was tried by French clergymen in the English ruled city and burned at the stake there at the Place du Vieux-Marché. More recently, it had been occupied by Prussian soldiers. The proletarians of Rouen had stood in solidarity with the Communards in Paris. Now the Prussians were mostly gone and the city had settled down to its usual leisurely pace.

Teo explored the old section. He was fascinated by the cathedral with its mismatched towers and carillon, the ruins of the Rouen Castle where Joan of Arc was threatened with torture but would not yield, and the abundance of half-timbered houses lining the narrow streets providing a display of oddly asymmetrical grids of wood filled with white or colored clay or plaster. He looked for lodging. Luckily, he still had most of the money that Émilie-Claire had given him. He found a small apartment in a building on the Rue du Gros Horloge, near the archway where the famous old astronomical clock was mounted. In the mornings that followed he would be awakened by the bells in the nearby bell tower that were driven by the clock.

One morning he had wandered past the Cathédrale Notre-Dame de Rouen down the Rue Martinville. He stopped to look at the ossuary, the Aître de St Maclou, with its macabre decorations of bones and skulls. Plague victims were deposited there in 1348 when the cemetery had been filled to capacity. On the steps sat an old man—at least he seemed old and decrepit to Teo. His clothes were a shambles, tattered and torn. He wore boots many sizes too big. He had a long unkempt beard. He wore a black eye patch over one eye. He might be a pirate, thought Teo. Teo started to move away from the man when something made him hesitate. A strange sense of familiarity had struck him. Something about the eye patch.

The man looked up at Teo. There was no look of recognition or even of curiosity on the man's face. But Teo saw that beneath the beard, beneath the dirt and soiled clothing, there was a man he knew quite well. A man who had married his guardian, Émilie-Claire. A man who had been as a father to him for too short a time. A man they had thought to be dead. There on the steps of the ossuary, under a sculpted image of the Danse Macabre, looking derelict and despondent and as dusty as the façade of the ossuary, sat Jean-Léon Richelieu.

28

The Return of Jean-Léon Richelieu

It was late September of 1870. The Emperor's trusted advisor, Jean-Léon Richelieu, was to have been escorted by German body guards from Metz to Kassel, with a deceitful message for the Emperor from Marshall Bazaine. The Emperor was being held at Wilhelmshöhe Castle and because of a promise made to him by Bismarck that he could remain in his royal capacity, he was urging Bazaine to surrender to the Germans. Bazaine's return message would convince the Emperor to agree to Bismarck's devious plot; Richelieu knew that the message should never be delivered. It was with some devious skill and much luck that Richelieu managed to get the guards drunk one evening as they camped along the way.

Once the guards were snoring soundly, he quietly stole away from the campsite. He led all three horses down into a shallow basin well beyond the camp and tied their reigns to a long rope he found in one of the saddlebags. Reaching into his vest pocket he pulled out the missive Bazaine had written to the Emperor. This he tore into small pieces and scattered in the brush. Mounting the lead horse, he led his purloined cavalcade out of the woods. Now, he thought, which way is France?

He had stolen food and weapons from the guards but had left them with a cask of strong ale which was only half empty. He expected this to give him a good head start in his escape. It wasn't until he reached a small river, which he suspected was the Moselle, that he began to understand that he had been traveling in the wrong direction. The Moselle emptied into the Rhine at the ancient hamlet of Koblenz only a mile or so distant. He released the extra horses and removed from his clothing anything that might identify him as a Frenchman. The saddle and harness of the horse were German-made so there was a chance he could mingle with the townspeople. He needed directions and he needed a plan.

The old city was fortified, triangular in shape, bounded on two sides by the two rivers, and defended on the third side by a circle of forts perched upon the hill tops. Richelieu rode into the town without a problem and quickly located a stable along the riverfront near the Florinsmrkt. Here he left the horse for feeding and a good brushing. A few doors down was the Koblenz Altes Gasthaus, an inn and restaurant. Richelieu clearly needed food and a good night's rest in a comfortable bed.

After enjoying an order of Kowelenzer Spiessbraten (roast pork belly in spicy beer sauce) and a bit of Halver Hann (gouda with onions) on rye bread, all washed down with a frosted mug of Kösch, he retired for the evening. Early the next morning he ate a quick breakfast of sausages and eggs. He paid his bill from a purse he had lifted from one of the German guards (good—it was local currency) and augmented his portable food supply with some homemade sour kidneys and a small tub of black pudding. He wrapped these in paper and headed for the stable.

Here was where his troubles began. His German was adequate although some of the local dialect confused him. But it was his accent that gave him away. The proprietor took him for a spy and was in the process of calling the polizei when Richelieu decided to run. He might have attempted to convince the stable owner he wasn't a spy, but the man was in a rant about the verdammt französisch. He ran. He thought he could hear the heavy pounding of following footsteps—or was it just his heart?

He had lost his food and his money somewhere along the way. He could not risk going back to search for them. Presently he came to the river. Larger than the one he had crossed to enter Koblenz, this must be the Rhine. A boat! Actually, a barge loaded with wood. Places to hide presented themselves. He leaped onto the barge and hid between two piles of logs. Panting, he shut his eyes and tried to rest.

He must have dozed off for when the barge suddenly banged against a piling he woke with a start. It was docking. He wasn't in the same city for he could see the twin spires of a cathedral rising above the skyline. Men scrambled all over the barge and were beginning to off load the cargo. Richelieu jumped to the shore. There were shouts—he had been seen! But apparently, no one cared to stop their work to chase after him. Off he went into the city center where he could only hope he might blend in with the population.

He walked past the cathedral. Prussians were all Protestants, weren't they? This was a church that reminded him so much of France that he thought for a moment he might be home…but no, the Rhine didn't flow through France. In a store window he saw a reference to the Stadt von Köln—of course! Cologne. It used to be part of France, hadn't it? Did they still practice the Napoleonic code? What did he remember about Cologne's history? The Prussians had arrested and imprisoned the archbishop because of conflicts about marriages between Catholics and Protestants. The people of Cologne tended to be anti-Prussian. Maybe he would have better luck here than he had in Koblenz. He turned around and entered the cathedral.

He stood gazing up at the exquisite stained-glass windows when a priest came up and spoke to him.

"Beautiful, aren't they?" the priest asked, but in a dialect that was difficult for Richelieu to fully understand. He had gotten the gist of it, however, and answered in his best classical German:

"I'm in awe of them," he said. "How old is this church?"

"You are French, are you not?" said the priest. "We speak Kölsch here. It is a variation of the German spoken in the north. I will speak more slowly and deliberately. What can I tell you of our beautiful church? It dates back to 1320 and it is still under construction. The windows are from the 14th century. If you will follow me I will show you the high altar of which we are most proud."

On the high altar was a golden shrine. It contained, the priest told him, the relics of the Magi. It was a superb example of medieval gold working from Milan and it had been crafted in the 12th century. The priest then led Richelieu to the Lady Chapel where the altar featured a triptych of the Adoration of the Magi.

"1440," explained the priest. "Painted by Stefan Lochner, one of our greatest painters. And now, tell me why you are here in Cologne. Our countries are at war, certainly. You do not seem to be a soldier."

Richelieu studied the face of this priest, looking for any sign of deceit, but saw only kindness. Honesty, as it was said, was the best policy, and the man didn't seem to represent a threat. So:

"I was advisor to the Emperor and captured with him at Sedan. I was being used to send messages between the Emperor and the commander of the French troops at Metz in an effort by your Otto von Bismarck to trick him into surrendering. I couldn't be a party to the deception so I escaped and destroyed the message. Thus I am running from both sides and I plead your understanding and succor."

"So you're not a spy, you're a deserter. Well, you don't need to worry. While you are here you are under the protection of the Church and the Holy Father. As long as you stay here, that is."

"Shall I sleep in the bell tower like Quasimodo then?"

"I do not understand the reference, and no, you may not sleep in the bell tower. You can stay in the monks' quarters until you have a plan. Perhaps you will decide to return to your Emperor and ask his forgiveness. That would be the proper thing to do. I would not wish to see you executed by Bismarck's hoodlums. And...I did not tell you that if you are ever asked."

"Thank you Father. And now would you hear my confession?"

"I think I already have."

Across the Rhine from Cologne, nestled within that city's crescent shape, lay the town of Deutz. The abbey there began as a Benedictine monastery created in an old castle by the archbishop, the future Saint Heribert, in 1002. It had been burned and rebuilt four times. It had been dissolved as a monastery during the Napoleonic era of secularization but had survived as a parish church later known as Alt St. Heribert. It had fared better than most monasteries of that period; the Church of Saint Pantaleon, high on a hill above Cologne, had been used by the Prussians as a horse stable and a Protestant garrison. Fewer than nine monasteries remained after secularization. But monastic life was now returning to Germany and Central Europe.

The Deutz Abbey housed fewer monks than in its heyday, but it was self-sufficient and dedicated to daily prayer, religious study, and industrious labor, orchestrated by the ringing of bells. Bells summoned the monks to prayer at midnight and again when the sun rose. Bells commanded prayers every third hour during the day. Bells announced the single meal of the day, meatless and conducted in absolute silence. Bells, bells, bells.

Eventually Richelieu became accustomed to the routine. He had stayed at the abbey for many weeks now. News had come to Cologne and Deutz of the siege of Paris. It seemed a good time to stay put and wait. The monks mostly ignored him; their devotions took precedent over social matters. One of the monks, Brother Dieter, had taken Richelieu under his wing and helped him to understand the succession of bells and their meanings. Another monk, Brother Gunther, had not been so helpful. It was becoming clear that Brother Gunther resented the presence of the Frenchman and would take subtle actions to disrupt Richelieu's day. Brother Gunther would send Richelieu on an errand to the market or some other place out of earshot of the bells, just as meal time approached.

Brother Dieter, observing this behavior on the part of the other monk, confronted Brother Gunther. Brother Gunther complained to the Abbot about Brother Dieter, making up false claims about the monk's transgressions. Jean-Léon Richelieu had experienced political infighting before, having served in his own country's government where it was commonplace, yet he had never before been the cause of such a conflict. It greatly disturbed him. It was time to move on and to hope that by removing his influence the community here might return to its peaceful existence.

He went to Brother Dieter and told him he was leaving the abbey. He had no resources, no money, no way to travel west. Brother Dieter gave him a bag in which he had placed some food and a pair of warm stockings. There was no money with which to purchase a train ticket, so Brother Dieter told him a story that a newcomer to the town had once divulged to him which concerned the man's travel by train hidden in a freight car. It hadn't exactly been a confession since Brother Dieter wasn't actually a priest, and although it involved breaking the law…well, it was man's law, not God's. And so Richelieu learned how to wait until the train was just beginning to pull out from the yard, how to run along side and leap into the open freight car, and how to hide from the railroad police.

In this way Richelieu was able to enter the neighboring country of Belgium by train. He was forced to disembark from the freight car when the train stopped in the yard at Liège, not far from the Belgium border with the Netherlands. The yard police chased him off the premises. Now he was stranded again, this time in the city that claimed to be the birthplace of Charlemagne.

"No, Monsieur, there is no mail going into nor out of Paris. There is a war on, you know," said the Liège postmaster.

"So I've been told," said Richelieu. "What about to Metz?"

"Metz has fallen. They surrendered finally. A very wise choice. Where have you been?"

"Actually, in a monastery. Near Cologne."

"Ah, you are a monk? You are obviously not Belgian. French, I would say. Not a good thing to be right now. But if you are a monk…"

"No, I was just passing through. I was a sort of a guest."

"Not a deserter or a spy, I hope. I myself am not political. I have no family in the army. Personally, I think it is a waste of resources. We are an independent state. We owe no allegiance to any King, Kaiser or Chancellor or anyone else. So are we enemies?"

"Oh, I hope not. I've never killed anyone. I talked against the war. I wasn't listened to. Now all I want is to get home to my wife and family. At least to get word to them that I am alive."

"If they are in Paris, you will have a long wait, I fear."

The postmaster was a small man whose lack of height was only exaggerated as he stood behind the high counter. He had the tiniest mustache Richelieu had ever seen; highly waxed and turned up at the ends into a pair of thin crescents that looked like question marks. He was being quite friendly, considering that Richelieu could be a spy or a deserter. So Richelieu asked:

"Where can a job be had around here? For a foreigner?"

"I'd try the docks. Many a foreigner gets work on the boats. Low pay if at all. Might get you into France, though."

"Oh? The river goes west?"

"The river comes from the west, somewhere in France. It flows to the sea. But boats go both up and down it. You try the docks, Monsieur. And good luck to you."

Another journey by boat, thought Richelieu. Not as comfortable as the freight car. Comfortable? Irony, he thought to himself, is the spicy seasoning of existence. He found the dock area along the Meuse River near the center of town. Another medieval city complete with hill top castle and Gothic cathedral. Boats and barges of every sort were lined up along the quay. Flat-bottomed barges heaped high with cargo, oared dories and dinghies rigged with sail, fishing smacks with ochre sails, a paddle steamer billowing black smoke, but nothing ocean-going—no tall ships, no tartans or schooners with masts rigged and shrouded, no brigs or galleons, no frigates or clippers: this was the river, not the sea.

Richelieu had his eyes on a French lougre—a small ship that the Dutch called a logger and the English called a lugger. It had four-cornered sails fore and aft set on its three masts and a lug topsail. It might, he thought, be used as a packet, transporting passengers as well as cargo and mail. Cramped quarters no doubt, but speedy and reliable for the frequent traveler. Extra crew might be needed to see to the comfort of the passengers—comfort: there was that word again.

The weather was getting colder and colder. The thought of a trip on water in November wasn't appealing. The river came up from the south and originated in France. A little warmer in the south of France, perhaps. But Paris was his goal in spite of the invading Prussian army and the impossible miles and miles between him and Émilie-Claire. He waved to a man on the boat who was working on the rigging. He shouted to get the man's attention. Finally the man looked at him. "No more passengers," he yelled back. "All full up."

"No, you don't understand," said Richelieu. "I'm asking for a position as crew member. Have you an opening?"

The man laughed. "Even if I did, you don't look very sea worthy, my friend. And that missing eye! Certainly a handicap. You don't look as if you could lug these sails up even a foot. Go away."

"I need to get to Paris."

"We don't go to Paris. Nobody goes to Paris. Get yourself a horse and stop bothering me."

A horse. Where was he going to get a horse? And a warm coat? Dejected, he wandered back into the town proper. It seemed a working class place, no fancy restaurants and theaters, no broad avenues and ornate architecture—except for the Palais des Prince-Evêques, the Palace of the Prince-Bishops, a stately and rambling building displaying decorative and structural styles mimicking Italian Renaissance, German Gothic, and French Rococo, all at the same time. Richelieu walked slowly along the Place Saint-Lambert, past the Palace, past the site where St. Lambert's Cathedral once stood waiting to be demolished by the régime of the French Revolution, and up the Place du Marché casting about for some idea, some plan.

Was there a stable somewhere? Perhaps he could steal a horse. Right now he needed to steal some food. And a warmer coat. To the south he could see the spire of another cathedral. The clergy were always helpful to needy strangers. He headed in that direction. A scattering of narrow streets and clustered buildings created a labyrinth through which he jigged and jagged, always keeping the spire in sight. The closer he got, the more it seemed to retreat into the distance. He began to realize just how hungry he was. He was weak and becoming delirious. He staggered and fell against the stoop of a house. Blackness took him.

When he woke he was lying on a soft but lumpy mattress—filled with straw or something that poked at him. His boots were on the floor beside the low bed. His clothes were draped over a wooden chair. He was dressed in what appeared to be a woman's night gown and covered with a thin sheet. The room was dark, lit by a single candle which sent flickering shadows dancing. There was a picture hung on one wall of a pastoral scene—sheep in a meadow. He was alone. He tried to rise but fell back again onto the bed.

The second time he woke he knew better than to try to sit up. His head seemed to be revolving on his neck—to keep up with the spinning of the room. He closed his good eye and found that to help somewhat. His throat was so dry that he could barely force a sound from it. He was hot; he was cold. He alternately trembled or lay still as death. Again he lapsed into unconsciousness.

Her hands felt cool on his forehead. She smelled like lilacs…or was that another delusion? She was saying something in a soft voice that soothed. He blinked open his eyes. It was no delusion. It might be an angel come to take him into eternity. But he felt so bad, so racked with aches and pains—he was too miserable to be dead. He concentrated on her words; they began to form into images—letter forms floating in the air—letters made with that gothic German script that was so hard to read. One by one the letters dropped to the floor and shattered. And he was asleep again, drifting in an inky sea that lapped and sucked at him. He sank.

"You are awake. Are you feeling any better?" Someone's voice. The lilac woman. He risked raising his eyelid. He tried to answer. The croak that emerged was an attempt at the word, "water." She must have understood for soon a beaker of cool water was held to his lips.

"Sip it slowly," she said. "Don't try to talk just yet. You have been ill…very, very ill. I couldn't afford a doctor but I've seen things like this before. Oh, don't worry…it's not the plague."

"How long?" he managed to get out.

"Three weeks since I found you on my steps. I hope you don't mind the bed clothes…I have no husband nor father nor brother here to borrow from. You look quite pretty in my night gown." She laughed. "My name is Ursula Van Aarle. I'm originally from the Netherlands, of which this country is now no longer part. I washed your clothes and saw the labels, so I know you are French. I won't hold that against you."

I am French? Who am I? Where am I? Such thoughts frightened him for he truly did not understand what had happened to him. His name? Why was that so hard to remember? This woman…was she someone he was supposed to know? He let out a low moan and fell back into unconsciousness. It would take time to recover from his illness. He had all the time in the world.

Byron Grush

29

The Kindness of Strangers

Ursula Van Aarle lived in a small third floor apartment in an 18th century building on the Rue de Pont. The building was typical of the Mosane Renaissance style of many of the older buildings in Liége and reflected the adaptation of stone to the half-timbered building techniques of the region. Windows facing the narrow cobble-stoned street were hung with delicate sheer curtains; Ursula's one extravagance in decorating. Mostly her furnishings were hand-offs or cheap flea market finds. The hand-knotted wool rug on the floor was an heirloom she had inherited from a deceased aunt; it was a bit thread-worn.

She worked in a bookstore on the Rue de Bex, a few blocks walk from her apartment. The owner, Nikolaj Alders, had known her father from the old days and had taken her on as an apprentice in spite of bad economic times. She had been only 16 when she arrived in Liége as an orphan from the town of Breda in the Netherlands. Alders had taken pity on the girl and given her a job. Now she was a young woman of 23 and Nikolaj let her run the shop on her own— he was aging ungracefully and ailing from acute rheumatism, and besides, she was much better at selling books than he.

She loved the old man, the way he shuffled through the shop, his rumpled shirts, the way his spectacles were perched on his forehead where he never could find them. Nikolaj doted on the girl; his only niggling complaint about her was the man she let stay in her apartment. She had lied and said the Frenchman was a cousin. Nikolaj didn't believe her. He didn't begrudge her to have a lover— but this man was too old for her.

He wasn't her lover. Jean-Léon was her responsibility. She had certainly saved his life when she had found him on her doorstep, sick and delirious, and had brought him in and nursed him. Was there an old adage about saving a life and becoming obligated therefore to protect the person you had robbed of his eternal serenity? Or did he whom you had saved then owe you a life debt? In which case you were pledged to allow his benefaction. And if he lacked the resources to repay your kindness, well, that just meant that your job was not yet finished. And Jean-Léon, although physically recovered, still had not fully regained his mental faculties. He was still confused about his history and identity.

As winter melted into spring she began bringing Jean-Léon to the book store to help her with the unpacking and shelving of new arrivals. Dutch, German, and French were spoken in various degrees by the residents of Liége, with Belgium Dutch and Belgium French having a vocabulary and dialect unique to the region. Jean-Léon's first attempts to wait on customers were abject failures. Ursula would stand next to him during a sale and translate when necessary, until he learned at least the most common phrases: "I'm looking for…," "Do you have a copy of…," "How much does this cost?"

One day in early March, Jean-Léon happened to wait on a woman looking for a German edition of Karl Marx's "Das Capital," which had recently been published in that language. She was chatty. German troops had just paraded down the Champs-Élysées in Paris, she told him, and there was talk of the rise of a Commune. She had relatives living in the City of Lights and she wished to learn more about this movement of the proletarians against the bourgeoisie. How would it affect her relatives?

Karl Marx…where had he heard that name before? A vague memory of…a château, an emperor, a sparkling and dynamic city…. Germans marching in Paris? How could that have happened? He lived in a fog of forgetfulness; a brume obscured his awareness even of current affairs. He went to find the book in the dusty shelves near the back of the store. Ah, there it was. When he returned the woman had left and taken with her a copy of Gustave Flaubet's *Madame*

Bovary, in French, which she hadn't paid for. Jean-Léon had wanted to ask her about Paris.

Later that evening he quizzed Ursula on the matter. Why hadn't she told him bout the Germans being in Paris?

"I didn't want to upset you," she told him.

"It might have helped me remember."

"Has it?"

"No, not completely, but bits and pieces are coming back. Paris is the key. I know it must be. But it is all still so indistinct, so blank."

He drifted; reality was receding into a gloom. He tried to force himself back. A name came to him through the haze: Thiers. And another: Trochu. And: Bazaine. Little flashes like sheet lightning over a darkened sky or the explosions of swamp gas in a bog. Then the gloom set in again, solidified.

"I have a strong feeling that I must go to Paris," he told Ursula.

"You can't go just yet. You are not well enough."

"I am too well to just remain inactive. I have to do something."

She would not help him. He went to visit Nikolaj Alders who lived in an apartment above his book store. He knew the old man disliked him, but there was a chance…. He asked for his help to leave Liége and travel to Paris, a circumstance he believed the old man would relish. Alders willingly gave him some money that he had been saving and had kept in an old tobacco humidor by his bedside. Jean-Léon thanked him sincerely. "It's a bargain," the old man answered.

He bought a horse and saddle from a man who had a stall on the Place Saint-Lambert where he was selling vegetables. He had stopped to buy some food and as an afterthought asked if the horse might be for sale. After some negotiation they struck a deal and Jean-Léon was now outfitted with a fine mare to take him back to Paris. No more traveling by water. No more cramped freight cars. No more walking. The river, however, was still to be his highway to France; he would follow its course as it came up from the west.

The river Meuse was a serpentine waterway lush with wetlands and filled with fauna and flora unique to the basin. Jean-Léon saw spotted corn crakes on the wing calling "crex, crex" to their mates, tiny whinchats hopping after bugs, snipes nesting in the beech trees along the river's bank. Once, a large dark shape burst from the underbrush. Its bristly coat and enormous snout identified it as a wild boar. The mare reared up at the sight of it. Another time he caught a glimpse of the black and white face of a badger which quickly ducked behind a fallen log.

When he camped for the night he lit a fire and kept it going to keep the wild boars away. He had been told he might encounter lynx in the wilderness surrounding the river basin. Even wild horses. After the handful of decadent cities he had been living in this was a delightful wonderland of nature. It soothed and energized. It entertained the senses. There was a road that followed the general course of the river, so he was never struggling through brush and brambles. The river's sweet scents wafted to him on the wind; the sound of frogs and crickets lulled him to sleep at night.

The Meuse met a tributary, the Sambre, at the town of Namur. From that point the Meuse dipped southward, angling slightly toward France. The Sambre came from the west, the general direction Jean-Léon wanted to head. He decided to follow the Sambre. Some said the river was the site of the Belgic conferedation's battle with Julius Caesar in 57 BC. Some said not. Although much smaller than the Meuse, the Sambre was highly navigable between Namur and Charleroi. The area between was known for its many coal mines. Jean-Léon elected to stay the night in Namur.

The next morning, after having slept in a real bed and eaten a hearty meal of carbonade famande, the Belgium version of beef bourguignon made with beer instead of wine, Jean-Léon replenished his traveling food supply and headed out along the Sambre toward home. Behind him the cathedral of Saint Aubain rose majestically above the house tops. His horse was slow but steadfast. By early evening he had reached Charleroi. Poets (and sometime lovers) Paul Verlaine and Arthur Rimbaud had lived there briefly and both had written poems about the town. Verlaine wrote mostly about the industrial smell of the place:

> *So what does it smell?*
> *Train stations thunder,*
> *The eyes are astonished,*
> *Where Charleroi?*

Sinister perfumes!
What is it ?
What was rustling
Like sistrums?

Brutal sites!
Oh ! your breath,
Human sweat,
Cries of metals!

Arthur Rimbaud wrote about a restaurant called the Caberet-Vert where he ordered slices of bread and butter, along with lightly chilled ham and gazed at "la fille aux Tétons énormes, aux yeux vifs (a girl with big nipples and bright eyes)". Rimbaud was a lad of 16 when he stayed in Charleroi in October of 1870. He stood at the train station watching the arrival of wounded French soldiers who would be treated there by Belgians who felt a touch of solidarity with the French. He applied to the Charleroi newspaper for a job as a writer which he didn't get, and so a few days later he left for Brussels. He was still many years from fame and infamy.

Jean-Léon crossed the Sambre on an iron-arched swing bridge and entered the city. Ahead, up the Rue de la Station, was the railway depot. A faster and more direct way to reach Paris! He would have to wait until the following morning for a train. Less than a block away from the station was the café and inn called the Caberet-Vert, the Green House: the same establishment where the year before Arthur Rimbaud had dined and ogled the waitress. Although not elegant by any means, it would do for a meal and a good night's rest. He would sell the horse tomorrow and ride in style in a comfortable train car for a change. Then he would recline on velvet cushions and watch the landscape fly by. He would order oysters in the dining car. He might smoke a cigar—although he couldn't remember if he smoked.

True to its name, the Caberet-Vert was painted a bright green. Inside the café the walls and most of the furniture were also painted green. The clientele was primarily working class and the waitresses did in fact wear low cut blouses that emphasized their abundant breasts. The menu offered bouillon, beef, and vegetables for 50 centimes and café et cognac for 30 centimes.

The next morning he sold the horse to a man at the green market a few blocks from the inn. He realized less than half of what he had paid for the mare, but it would be enough for the fare and would leave him a few extra francs. Just about 190 miles by rail to Paris. The conductor looked askance at Jean-Léon as he climbed up the steps with his baggage, a well used saddlebag. He found a seat in the second class car and settled down to enjoy the trip.

Pulling away from the station the train passed the tumbled remains of ancient ramparts which the city was systematically demolishing. Rows of factories with tall smoke stacks lined the railway, streaming dirt-colored smoke into the air—Verlaine's "sinister perfumes." Yet a glistening could be seen on the spire of the cathedral as it receded into the distance—Rimbaud's happy "backward ray of sun." The train followed the meandering Sambre, crossing it at intervals. Small towns flashed past separated by groves of beech and elm, oak and birch.

About 75 miles from Charleroi the train pulled into the Gare de Saint Quentin and stopped for passengers to embark or disembark. Jean-Léon walked to the rear car where there was an observation platform. He needed the fresh air but was reluctant to leave the train, should it pull away while he was absent. The Gare de Saint Quentin was adjacent to a canal extending the River Somme through the town's industrial district. There wasn't much to see so Jean-Léon was pleased when another man came out onto the observation platform and struck up a conversation. The smallest of small talk ensued: the weather, destinations, etcetera.

"Headed for Paris?" the man asked. "What do you do there?"

"That is a very good question. I can't tell you because...because I haven't decided as yet."

Something about the man unsettled Jean-Léon. Perhaps it was his bowler, a headpiece worn mostly by Englishmen...only this man was decidedly French—his accent indicated the south. Perhaps it was the nervous twitch that presented upon the man's lower eyelid. Jean-Léon's caution might have induced him to say a polite goodbye and return to his seat, but he stayed. There was a lunge as the train again started its journey; black smoke and soot tumbled over the roofs of the cars. As the train gained momentum, the bowler-wearing man took from his vest pocket a small hand gun. This he pointed at Jean-Léon's midsection and uttered a phrase he must have gotten from too much reading of the novels of Alexandre Dumas: "Your money or your life!"

Reluctantly, Jean-Léon handed over his purse. Meager though his finances were, it was a piece of bad fortune to lose the money. Just then the train picked up speed and the man pushed Jean-Léon over the low railing. He fell to the tracks and rolled, cracking his head on a rail. He was unaware of how long he might have been unconscious when strong arms pulled him off the tracks and laid him on the cinder-strewn embankment.

He was a man without a name, without memories, without purpose. He walked aimlessly knowing only that he must go forward. Whoever it was that had dragged him from the rails had deposited him on the steps of the nearby Chappelle de la Charité. Someone there had cleaned his wounded forehead. Water, food, sleep on a straw-filled mattress in a back room of the church, and a morning's awakening to confusion and despair. Now he walked. He followed the River Somme as it wound through endless farmland. Tiny communities were dotted along the waterway—he stopped at some to beg for food and water. Always there seemed to be a kind stranger who would help. At Brie, at Clery-sur-Somme, at Bray-sur-Somme he lingered for a while, hoping someone might recognize him.

Finally the river led him into the city of Amiens. There was a great cathedral there, Gothic in age and beauty, crusted with sculptures of saints and biblical figures that stared down at him as he stood in the square, considering whether to enter. There was something intimidating about the ostentatious edifice. Jean-Léon turned away from it and nearly collided with a man who had been standing behind him. The man was almost a doppelganger for Jean-Léon in his dirty and unkempt clothing. Except for the lack of an eye-patch, the rumpled slouch hat the man wore tipped back on his head, and the canvas bag slung over his shoulder filed with what looked like apples, Jean-Léon might have been looking at his own image in a mirror.

"Bonjour," said the man. "Would you like an apple?"

"I have no money," Jean-Léon answered.

"It makes no difference. I couldn't sell them all at the market this morning. They will just become rotten. They're very tasty."

"Merci. I would like one. Who are you and where am I?"

"My name is Michel Travert, entrepreneur extraordinaire. You are in the town of Amiens and that little rock pile behind you is the Notre-Dame Cathedral. How is it you don't know where you are?"

"I have had an injury to my head. I've lost all recollection of my identity and origin. I've been wandering."

"That is most unfortunate. Would you like a macaroon? I've one left." The man pulled the meringue confection from his pocket and held it out. "I've been attempting to exploit the market here in Amiens but I found the competition quite fierce for fruits or anything else I can scrounge up. I'm going to return to my own town tomorrow. I'd not be averse to having a companion on the trek."

"I think I would like that. One place is the same as another to me right now. I could help you selling apples?"

"Well, of course you could. We may need to acquire some goods along the way. You can help pick…or act as a watchman. Often there are objections to my procuring of product. It is settled! Tomorrow we head for Rouen. Tonight we find a nice dry alley."

Rouen, two weeks later

Teo Presume had come to Rouen after escaping the bloodshed in Paris that threatened his own safety. It was the city in which Joan of Arc had been imprisoned, tried and burned at the stake. It was a city which had been occupied by Prussian troops none too recently. It was a city where Teo might at last find peace and contentment. It was a city to explore.

One morning he wandered past the Cathédrale Notre-Dame de Rouen and down the Rue Martinville. He stopped to look at the ossuary, the Aître de St Maclou, with its macabre decorations of bones and skulls. On the steps sat an old man—at least he seemed old and decrepit to Teo. His clothes were a shambles, tattered and torn. He wore boots many sizes too big. He had a long unkempt beard. He wore a black eye patch over one eye. He might be a pirate, thought Teo. Teo started to move away from the man when something made him hesitate. A strange sense of familiarity had struck him. Something about the eye patch.

30

Au Revoir Mon Amour

Excerpt from: *Dame Impétueux, la Mémoire de Émilie-Claire Lebeau-Richelieu*, (English translation, published by Charles W. Karr & Co., Chicago, 1897)

When I got the letter about Jean-Léon from Teo, bless his heart, I determined to travel to Rouen immediately. There were circumstances which prevented my immediate departure; for example, the bank was giving me some trouble about withdrawals. Apparently the new regime in Paris was seeped in suspicion and had ordered that accounts be frozen until such time as the patriotism of the depositor could be established. I had some money, but probably only enough for a one-way ticket. I decided to send Teo the money and instruct him to bring Jean-Léon to us in Arles. This would be a fine place for him to recuperate. There was a good hospital here and not far away, at Saint-Rémy-de-Provence, there was the Saint-Paul-de-Mausole, which was an Augustine monastery and now was used as an asylum…if it should come to that.

I suppose it was risky sending funds through the mails…you never knew if your package would arrive safely, but I did the only thing that made sense and wrapped a wad of bills in paper and addressed it to Teo in Rouen. I included a note giving him directions to bring Jean-Léon to Arles. He would have to go to Avignon and then transfer, being very careful as the train passed through Paris. I waited. And waited. And began to despair that the money had gone astray or that something untoward had befallen the two men.

We had moved from the Hôtel de l'Amphithéâtre to a house on the Rue Simon Bolivar, a very narrow alley where fragments of the old stone walls from the original ramparts had been incorporated into some of the buildings. There was an extra room there which I fixed up for Jean-Léon; he would not share my bed right away, or so I assumed.

Two weeks later they arrived. I can't describe for you the mixture of elation and trepidation that gripped me upon seeing my long lost husband for the first time and then realizing that he didn't recognize me. A bittersweet reunion, sanguine but forlorn—his appearance sallow like a pale fruit going to rot on a windowsill. My tears could not have been interpreted completely as joyful for my anxiety was close to panic. He was in a permanent state of disorientation…what the British call being at sixes and sevens.

"He'll be okay after a while," said Teo, attempting to calm me. "He just needs to adjust to his new environment."

"And new people?" I asked. I knew then that we would need to seek professional help, and soon. The Hôtel-Dieu-Saint-Espirit was on the Rue Dulau. It was operated as a charitable hospital. I went alone to investigate whether the doctors there ever treated mental cases. Mental cases! I was horrified at the thought that Jean-Léon might sink into an uncommunicative state and need to be institutionalized permanently.

There was a lovely garden on the grounds. The hospital had two large wings that enclosed a courtyard of oleander and primroses and a variety of other flowers. There was a small fish pond in the center. I entered and walked through a long hallway which was being used as a ward, past beds where people lay coughing and nurses in white uniforms attended them. I knew the facility had been greatly expanded because of the cholera epidemic of the 30's, and I hoped these were not patients left over from that most contagious episode of recent medical history.

I was able to talk to a doctor, a M. Félix, and I described Jean-Léon's case as best I could. They had no expertise in mental afflictions he said. I should consult a Doctor Théophile Peyron at the asylum at Saint-Rémy, he said. I had anticipated this but hoped the local doctors could at least look at him. Diseases of the body, he said. Not diseases of the mind. Is not the mind part of the body? Some of these doctors are fools! I was furious.

Just south of Saint-Rémy-de-Provence, about 12 miles from Arles, was the Saint-Paul-de-Mausole, a former monastery and now an asylum for those suffering from mental afflictions. It was surrounded by cornfields, vineyards, and olive groves, which seemed an idyllic setting for the housing of a religious order, but a bit remote for a medical facility. It was close to the old Roman ruins at Glanum and was itself an imposing edifice complete with Romanesque bell tower and arched walkways. But unlike the garden- and tree-lined hospital at Arles, it gave one a feeling not of comfort, but of detachment.

I walked along the side of the old Romanesque cloister and thought I heard the angelus ringing. There were sounds, but they were not made by bells, rather by raised human voices. I also heard banging sounds as if someone were striking metal against metal. Curious. I entered and asked to see Doctor Théophile Peyron.

He was a small man, late 30s or early 40s, his thin face weighted down by a pair of heavy black-rimmed spectacles. He seemed dour, not particularly entranced with his work at the asylum, and as dull as its long, arched hallways (these were made of slabs of quarry stone, tomb cold and filled with the hallow echoes of the howls and cries of the inmates). He had a stiff, military demeanor, and entertained my inquiry with some irritation, or so it seemed. Later I understood that this was simply his way of distancing himself from clients. Apparently patients can become attached emotionally to their doctors and this can interfere with their recovery. How anyone could become attached to this man, however, was a challenge to the imagination.

He would see Jean-Léon, he said; however, I should realize that because of the war there were many instances of what was termed "neurasthenia," a weakness of the nerves caused by the noise of bombardment and the stress of battle, and this circumstance, although regrettable, was not so dire as to require institutionalizing. I pointed out Jean-Léon's loss of memory. Perhaps, he said, this was due to some trauma to the head…a physical ailment. Wonderful, I thought. The hospital won't take him because of his mental condition and the asylum might not take him because of his physical condition. I could have screamed.

Byron Grush

I am detailing these first impressions because I have to wonder if the somewhat cavalier attitudes of these so called professionals might have had a bearing on the ultimate outcome. Yes, if this were a novel, I could be writing "and we all lived happily ever after." But it is not...and we did not.

The following morning Teo and Phoebe helped me get Jean-Léon into a carriage we rented from Joseph-Michel and Marie Ginoux who ran the Café de la Gare. Phoebe went with me to take my poor husband to see the doctor at the asylum. Dr. Peyron was very genial this time and spent a good deal of time examining Jean-Léon. This entailed trying to get his attention long enough to ask him questions. Phoebe asked the good doctor about the possibilities of using hypnotism, a technique with which she was all too familiar. Dr. Peyron discounted this idea claiming it was legerdemain and not appropriate for cases of neurasthenia...which was his diagnosis. At any rate, he said he would allow Jean-Léon to have a room at Saint-Paul-de-Mausole where he could be treated by a healthy diet and moderate daily exercise. In addition to this he would be given hydrotherapy in the asylum's bath rooms—warm baths to relax or sometimes cold baths to shock. I was unsure of all this but I consented (and agreed to the fee that was to be charged—which I could pay once my money was released from the Paris bank—which condition I did not share with the doctor).

Two months passed and autumn was creeping up on us. If I were to keep to the accurate chronology of my memoire I would now write about those sometimes happy days we spent in Arles while Jean-Léon was in the asylum, but as I have begun the story of Jean-Léon, as painful it is to tell, I must continue while I still have the presence of mind to do so.

Jean-Léon was mostly uncommunicative when we brought him home. I had, of course, visited him several times a week while he was being treated. I saw little improvement until just a week before we brought him home when he looked into my eyes and a light seemed to shine across his face...he had recognized me! But just as suddenly, the light faded and a dark scowl took its place. "I must go to Paris," he said.

He repeated this assertion again once we reached Arles. "Why do you wish to go to Paris?" I asked. He was unresponsive, simply staring off into space in his usual manner. I wondered...should I take him back to Paris? Would that trigger his memory? Or make things worse? I hesitated to find out.

He took to strolling out alone, usually to Le Jardin d'Été which was next to the Théâtre Antique d'Arles. He seemed drawn to the park's gay colors and meandering walkways. We would go looking for him when he did not come back within a reasonable amount of time. We found him once at the end of the Rue Voltaire staring at the two ruined tower guard houses that form the Porte de la Cavalerie to the ancient ramparts of the old city. Or he would wander in the opposite direction toward the Place du Forum where there was often a lively street market with stalls of old books.

The footbridge across the Rhône, Le Pont de Trinquetaille, was another of his favorite places. A long stone stairway led from the Quai de la Roquette up to the iron structure. We would find him about midway across the bridge, looking out at the Rhône, perhaps studying its ebb and flow toward the sea, its rolling shadows and its boiling highlights with their greenish tinge…like the color of absinthe when the sugar has dripped into it and swirled. He would have that glazed look as if he had imbibed a great volume of the Green Fairy, but Jean-Léon didn't drink.

I was making a fabulous meal for that night: gratin d'aubergine with olive oil, chopped onion and tomato, and daube provençal. The beef had been marinating for a whole day in a very good Côtes du Rhône, some fresh thyme and rosemary. Marie Ginoux prefers rabbit but I find there is too much work involved stripping the meat from the bones. I braised the beef in the early afternoon because the stew would need to simmer for at least five hours. Of course I added chopped onions and carrots and the reserved marinade, and I like to add niçoise olives, although some cooks do not. It finishes with a dusting of a little orange zest.

I was just thinking about a nice green salad with which to end the meal when Teo came bounding into the kitchen. Jean-Léon was missing again and Teo had gone to find him; his search of the usual haunts had proved fruitless. "He'll be back when he gets hungry," I said, but I wasn't convinced. I decided that the stew could take care of itself. "We should all go and look," I said. So it was that Teo, Phoebe, and I started off in different directions.

I wondered if he had crossed over the bridge to the other side of the river. He had not done so before, but there was always a first time for everything. I crossed and I wandered aimlessly, approaching people on the street to ask if they had seen a man with a black eye patch. Another maze of narrow streets and alleys challenged me. There was also a dock where barges were moored, and I worried that he might have boarded one thinking that the river led to Paris. I asked questions of the sailors. That is when I learned the worst.

Someone had been seen jumping from the bridge several hours earlier, a sailor told me. There had been an attempt at rescue but the man or woman...he wasn't sure which...had disappeared quite completely. The authorities had been notified and were now searching downstream with boats and grappling hooks. Grappling hooks! I shuddered. I hurried along the quay but no small boat was in sight.

I had just found him and now he was gone again. I was too worried to cry or to become hysterical...there would be plenty of time for that later. I walked back onto the bridge and stood looking out over the water. There was light brown effluence emerging from pipes along the river wall and merging with the smooth, green-gray surface of the river. Clumps of refuse floated slowly in little circular patterns before being taken by the main current in the center of the stream. Sea birds swooped down and snatched small fish that wriggled in their beaks as they flapped away to feast. The river was at its normal business of collecting, receiving, and spewing forth the artifacts of civilization. Now it contained a great prize: the former advisor to the Emperor, the kindest, most gentle of men, my only love, my Jean-Léon.

I suppose rivers are unconcerned about the affairs of humans. They find their way from spring to sea with little help save the occasional dredging or canalling. They must distain the dam, the lock, the spilled coal and leaked oil of the traffic that uses them. They must thrill to the abundance of fish, otter, and turtle. They carry sustenance to the land as if they are the veins and arteries of the living earth. And humans dump things into them with no appreciation of their beauty.

As I stood there becoming mesmerized by the flow below me I gained a sense of what Jean-Léon must have felt. It was compelling, entrancing, beckoning. Become one with me, it deemed to chant in a song made of tiny ripples and the breaking of wavelets against the embankment. The rest of the world left my field of vision—the city and its slate-roofed buildings were gone, the bridge itself dissolved under my feet—there was nothing but the river and its constant motion. I understood briefly how easy it would be to merge with that unreality, how comforting.

I shook myself awake…for I seemed to have been in a dream. I ran to find Teo and Phoebe. Later at home—the stew had burned—we tried to formulate a plan. There was a chance, of course, that Jean-Léon had simply wandered off out of town up some obscure road. There was chance the person seen jumping from the bridge had been some jilted lover or despondent street walker. Businessmen who had lost their fortunes were known to take their own lives. Suicide was a common cure for life's dire disappointments. We would go to the authorities tomorrow and learn what we could.

We asked everywhere, even going downriver all the way to Port-Saint-Louis-du-Rhône where the Rhône enters the Mediterranean. No bodies had washed up; no one had seen a man with one eye. He had vanished. If it had not been for Phoebe…she has been my rock…I might have followed him into the brackish waters of that cruel river. But I persist in living. There will never be another man in my life. But I had Phoebe and Teo (although Teo moved on after some months during which he complained that the town was too dull). Dull is exactly what I needed. Dulling the pain was my goal.

[Editor's note]

Jean-Léon Richelieu's fate was never learned. Most likely he did perish in the river that day. Émilie-Claire and Phoebe stayed together and eventually moved to Nice on the Mediterranean where they opened a restaurant on the Rue de France which they called Le Brasserie Américain (although they served strictly Mediterranean fare: ratatouille, the inevitable bouillabaisse, and dishes featuring fresh sea food such as squid, monk fish, and eel, followed by salade niçoise with olives and anchovies, and also some entrees borrowed from nearby Italy such as risotto with mussels, prawns, and asparagus, and Émilie-Claire's signature daube provençal, which by popular demand, she now made with rabbit).

Paris healed gradually. The first president was Adolphe Thiers, followed by Patrice de MacMahon and then Jules Grévy in 1879. His health failing, Napoleon III underwent two operations to remove his bladder stone performed by the eminent Sir Henry Thompson. On January 9, 1873, the emperor died; his funeral was held at the Church of Saint Mary in Chislehurst. His son, the Prince Imperial would be killed while serving in the British Army in Zululand in 1879.

In 1872 Edgar Degas traveled to New Orleans in the United States where his mother had been born. He completed 22 painting while living there. The same year Édouard Manet sold 24 canvases in a single sale to the art dealer, Paul Durand-Ruel. This sustained him for some time, allowing him to move into a large studio space in Paris on the Rue de Saint-Pétersbourg. There he painted *The Repose (Portrait of Berthe Morisot)*. His health began deteriorating around 1880 and in 1883 his left leg was amputated; he died ten days later—Oscar-Claude Monet, Antonin Proust, and Émile Zola were among his pall bearers. His last work was called *A Bar at the Folies-Bergère* and was shown at the 1872 Salon. The Impressionists heralded him as one of their own although he never acknowledge being an Impressionist.

Monet, Pierre-Auguste Renoir, Camille Pissarro, and Alfred Sisley organized the Société Anonyme des Artistes Peintres, Sculpteurs et Graveurs (Anonymous Society of Painters, Sculptors, and Engravers) in 1872 in order to exhibit independently. Monet exhibited *Impression, Sunrise,* a view of the landscape at the port of Le Havre. The art critic, Louis Leroy, wrote a criticism of what he called "L'Exposition des Impressionnistes," thereby coining the term "Impressionism." This was intended as a derogative comment, but the trem was eagerly adopted by the artists. Monet eventually moved to Giverny where he painted his most famous works.

Jeffrey Dolan Flaherty never realized success as a painter and returned to the United States just in time for the Panic of 1873 which led to the Long Depression. Still infused with proletarian ideals, he sought out workers' unions, a difficult task at the time. There were two major organizations, the National Labor Union and Uriah Smith Stephens' Knights of Labor, the later being a secret organization meant to infiltrate businesses to organize. He opted for joining the National Labor Union and worked for many years trying to improve working conditions for its members. In 1886 he found himself in Chicago where the May Day strikes were occurring. At the McCormick Harvester Company police and strikers clashed and a striker was killed. The next day there was a demonstration against police brutality at Chicago's Haymarket Square. A bomb was thrown, policemen were killed and many people were injured. Jeffrey was arrested along with several of the anarchists.

History tells us that the trial was conducted in "an atmosphere of extreme prejudice." The judge, one Joseph Gary, exhibited hostility toward the defendants. The jury pool was allegedly rigged and it was a forgone conclusion that the verdict would be guilty. Seven of the eight defendants were sentenced to death and one to 15 years in prison. After numerous unsuccessful appeals, the governor, Richard James Ogleysby, finally commuted two of the sentences to life imprisonment. One man, Louis Lingg, the night before his execution, took his own life in the bizarre manner of holding a blasting cap between his teeth. Four of the defendants were hung the next day; they sang the Marseillaise as they waited on the gallows.

Jeffrey died in prison having contracted pneumonia two years later.

Byron Grush

An Afterword

The description of the river as being the color of absinthe can be attributed to Vincent Van Gogh who lived in Arles in 1888 and painted the Trinquetaille iron bridge there. In a letter to his brother, Theo, he wrote: "where the sky and the river are the colour of absinthe—the quays a lilac tone, the people leaning on the parapet almost black, the iron bridge an intense blue—with a bright orange note in the blue background and an intense Veronese green note."

Nearly all of the restaurants and cafés in the novel were real and the menus presented are as accurate as possible. The menu described in the chapter on the Three Emperor's Dinner is on display at La Tour d'Argent restaurant in Paris. Modern chefs have attempted to recreate the dinner with varying success. The eating of the animals from the zoo, including the two elephants, is well documented.

Most of the historical incidents in the novel took place in the chronological order given. However, the great flood of Chattanooga that Jeffrey Flaherty describes happened in 1867, when Flaherty was in France. The area was plagued by flooding before that, but this was "the big one" that would prompt the city to raise its street levels.

Emile-Adolphe Vidocq was the son of the first wife of François Eugène Vidocq, the world's first private detective, although the son probably didn't follow in his sleuth father's footsteps. The first Vidocq was the model for many fictional detectives and his story may be found in *Memoirs of Vidocq, principal agent of the French police until 1827*, written by himself.

Trilby by George du Maurier, published in 1894, is a novel about two English artists and a Scottish artist, who settle in Paris in the 1850s. It represents the Bohemian life of the city as rich and boisterous and, besides giving us the notable character of Svengali, offers us a view of the artists' studio, which may be based on the atelier of Charles Gleyre. Murier studied art with Gleyre in Paris in the late 1850s and was familiar with the studio.

Emile Zola's series of Rougon-Macquart novels, *L'Histoire naturelle et sociale d'une famille sous le Second Empire (The natural and social history of a family under the Second Empire)* tell the story of a French family between the years 1851 and 1871. *La Curée* is the 2nd novel in this 20-volume series. It is concerned in part with Baron Haussmann's renovation of Paris and is a stunning portrait of the corruption in real estate speculation of the period. Zola was a principle figure in the Batignolles Group which included painters Monet, Degas, Renoir, Sisley, Cezanne, Pissarro, and Bazille. He was outspoken about the rise of the Commune, harshly criticizing it and then mellowing once the atrocities against the Communards began.

The author, Charles Dickens was a frequent visitor to Paris and has given us a vivid description of the Paris morgue. His novel concerning the emerging era of industrialization in England, *Our Mutual Friend*, 1864 to 1865, has been called "a social problem novel," delineating the crisis of urban populations. The similarities and the differences between London and Paris in the nineteenth century are illuminating, and Dickens and Zola are a good source for the flavor and detail of the people and the times.

The train accident at Staplehurst took place more or less as described in our novel, although Teo and the Detective were not present. Dickens was traveling with his mistress and her mother and did help the injured in a heroic manner. His own account of the accident was probably not embellished much more than was necessary to tell an exciting tale.

General William Booth founded what was to become the Salvation Army under circumstances both risky and dire in Whitechapel. He was ostracized by the Methodist hierarchy and harassed by the police. He had four children who took up his mission and spread it internationally in the following years. An account of the general was written by George Scott Railton, entitled *The Authoritative Life of General William Booth* in 1912.

Another resident of London at that time was Karl Marx. His pamphlet, *The Civil War in France*, 1871, was the official statement of the General Council of the International on the struggle of the Communards in the Paris Commune. Marx wrote:

Working men's Paris, with its Commune, will be forever celebrated as the glorious harbinger of a new society. Its martyrs are enshrined in the great heart of the working class. Its exterminators, history has already nailed to that eternal pillory from which all of the prayers of their priest will not avail to redeem them.

Another contemporary account of the Commune was written by John Leighton in 1871: *Paris under the Commune, or, the Seventy-three Days of the Second Siege with numerous illustrations, sketches Taken on the Spot, and Portraits (from the original photographs).* It is as wordy as its title, going into great detail and expressing a point of view somewhat different from that of Marx:

Socialism, or the Red Republic, is all one; for it would tear down the tricolour and set up the red flag. It would make penny pieces out of the Column Vendôme. It would knock down the statue of Napoleon and raise up that of Marat in its stead. It would suppress the Académie, the École Polytechnique, and the Legion of Honour. To the grand device Liberty, Equality, and Fraternity, it would add "Ou la mort."

Military strategists are often drawn to the many battles of the Franco-Prussian war, putting forth various theories as to why the French consistently lost in spite of superior weaponry, and sometimes superior numbers. They point to the disorganization and poor leadership of the French and the innovative tactics and decentralization of command by the Germans. I think the French heart was just not into it. French veteran soldiers had been fighting in the Crimea, in Algeria, in Mexico, and in China. These troops were tired, lacked discipline, and tended toward heavy drinking. The new recruits were held back in favor of the experienced ones. The French tactics were outdated in comparison with the Prussians. The Prussian army was fresh from a victory over Austria. They were composed of conscripted troops and were better educated and better trained. As the Prussian Prime Minister, Friedrich Freiherr von Schrötte, said, "Prussia was not a country with an army, but an army with a country."

The Second Empire was a prelude to La Belle Époque in France and the glories that were to come: the finishing of the Palais Garnier Opera House, the construction of the Basilica of Sacré-Cœur, the Eiffel Tower, and the Paris Métro; not to mention the Moulin Rouge, the Chat Noir, Le Cabaret de l'Enfer, Les Deux Magots, Café de Flore, Hôtel Ritz, Maxim's, Le Cordon Bleu cooking school, and the Théâtre du Grand-Guignol—in short, all the things we associate with Le Vie Parisienne. They were the phoenix rising from the ashes of the Siege and the Commune. And of course, Haussmann's urinals were still there on the street corners.

About the Author

Byron Grush was born and raised in Naperville, Illinois, just southwest of Chicago. He is a third generation native of that town. Grush studied art and design at the University of Illinois and filmmaking at the School of the Art Institute of Chicago. At the Art Institute he was a student of Gregory Markopoulos, one of the originators of the New America Cinema movement in the 1960s.

Grush then taught at The School of the Art Institute of Chicago, creating a course in film animation in the mid-seventies. He later became an Associate Professor at the College of Art at Northern Illinois University in Dekalb, Illinois, where he taught in the Electronic Media area. He is the author of a book on hand-drawn animation techniques entitled *The Shoestring Animator*. Becoming interested in genealogy, he wrote a trilogy of historical novels based upon what he had learned about his early ancestors.

He and his wife moved to New Mexico in the late 1990s, and opened an art gallery featuring Outsider and Visionary Art in Santa Fe. They returned to the Midwest to retire in the small town of Delavan, Wisconsin, a place that reminds them of their roots. Grush writes, paints and studies Tai Chi.

Picture credits

Cover images: from postcard, "551. Montmartre – Sur la place Pigalle (le Rat-Mort et l'Abbaye de Thélemé)", G. C. A., Paris;
Affiche La Commune de Paris 1871, Grand Panorama 26 rue de Bondy, before 1883, Gallica digital library of the Bibliothèque nationale de France, Author: Alessandro Castellani

At the Café, *Au café* (Café Guerbois), Édouard Manet (1832–1883), 1869, National Gallery of Art, Washington, D.C.

Français : Barricade à l'angle des boulevard Voltaire et Richard-Lenoir pendant la Commune de Paris de 1871, Cliché pris à l'occasion de l'exposition "La Commune 1871, Paris capitale insurgée" à l'Hôtel de ville de Paris le 5 avril 2011, author: Bruno Braquehais (1823-1875)

Discussing the War in a Paris Café - a scene from the brief interim between the Battle of Sedan and the Siege of Paris during the Franco-Prussian War, Illustrated London News, 17 September 1870, author: Fred Barnard (1846-1896)

Staplehurst Rail Crash, engraving in the Illustrated London News, 1865

Other fiction by Byron Grush

All The Way By Water

Once Upon a Gold Rush

Road of Stars

Dance Beneath A Diamond Sky

Violet at The Breakers: a novella

The New Unwritten Law: a novella

The Scrapple Eater: a novella

1954 or Just press the I Believe Button

Romeo's Revenge and Other Wisconsin Stories

Byron Grush

www.ingramcontent.com/pod-product-compliance
Lightning Source LLC
Chambersburg PA
CBHW071253170626
46809CB00001B/193